"[Caine] can deal out amazing plot twists as though she was dealing cards."
—#1 *New York Times* bestselling author Charlaine Harris

Praise for the
Morganville Vampires Novels

Bitter Blood

"Brilliant storyteller Caine . . . builds a truly chilling air of desperation into the book."
—*RT Book Reviews*

"Every time I think Rachel Caine can't top herself, she does."
—Fiction Vixen Book Reviews

Black Dawn

"[Caine's] imagination easily tops the average, keeping the book constantly interesting. Her suspense scenes, the heart of this series, crackle with vitality. . . . This series continues to provide terrific action and great entertainment."
—*Kirkus Reviews*

"Morganville, Texas, is my favorite town that I never want to visit. . . . [A] spectacular series."
—Fiction Vixen Book Reviews

"I cannot stress [enough] how well written *Black Dawn* is! It is certainly one of the best books in the series."
—LoveVampires

Last Breath

"Absorbing suspense dominates this chick-lit vampire story . . . a gripping, original take on vampires."
—*Kirkus Reviews*

"Caine's signature rapid-fire pace, plot twists, and excellent character development deliver another stellar installment."
—Monsters and Critics

Bite Club

"It's always a blast visiting Morganville. . . . The element of surprise is rare in paranormal YA books these days and yet that's what this series consistently delivers."
—All Things Urban Fantasy

"The vampires in *Bite Club* are badder than ever. . . . *Bite Club* is an action-packed, no-punches-pulled installment."
—Fiction Vixen Book Reviews

"Another mesmerizing addition to a very inventive paranormal series . . . a delightfully creepy and exciting episode of Morganville life (or death)."
—Night Owl Reviews

continued . . .

"Filled with delicious twists that the audience will appreciatively sink their teeth into."   —Genre Go Round Reviews

Feast of Fools

"Thrilling . . . a fast-moving series where there's always a surprise just around every dark corner."   —Darque Reviews

"Fantastic. . . . The excitement and suspense in *Feast of Fools* is thrilling and I was fascinated reading about the town of Morganville."
                                                                —Fresh Fiction

Midnight Alley

"A fast-paced, page-turning read packed with wonderful characters and surprising plot twists. Rachel Caine is an engaging writer."
                                                                    —Flamingnet

"Weaves a web of dangerous temptation, dark deceit, and loving friend-ships. The nonstop vampire action and delightfully sweet relationships will captivate readers and leave them craving more." —Darque Reviews

The Dead Girls' Dance

"If you love to read about characters with whom you can get deeply in-volved, Rachel Caine is so far a one hundred percent sure bet to satisfy that need."   —The Eternal Night

"Throw in a mix of vamps and ghosts and it can't get any better than *Dead Girls' Dance*."   —Dark Angel Reviews

Glass Houses

"Rachel Caine brings her brilliant ability to blend witty dialogue, en-gaging characters, and an intriguing plot." —Romance Reviews Today

"A solid paranormal mystery and action plotline that will entertain adults as well as teenagers. The story line has several twists and turns that will keep readers of any age turning the pages."   —LoveVampires

ALSO BY RACHEL CAINE
The Morganville Vampires Novels

Glass Houses

The Dead Girls' Dance

Midnight Alley

Feast of Fools

Lord of Misrule

Carpe Corpus

Fade Out

Kiss of Death

Ghost Town

Bite Club

Last Breath

Black Dawn

Bitter Blood

Fall of Night

Daylighters

Prince of Shadows

THE
MORGANVILLE
VAMPIRES

Daylighters

Rachel Caine

NAL NEW AMERICAN LIBRARY

New American Library
Published by the Penguin Group
Penguin Group (USA) LLC, 375 Hudson Street,
New York, New York 10014

USA | Canada | UK | Ireland | Australia | New Zealand | India | South Africa | China
penguin.com
A Penguin Random House Company

Published by New American Library, a division of Penguin Group (USA) LLC. Previously published in a
New American Library hardcover edition.

First New American Library Trade Paperback Printing, April 2014

REGISTERED TRADEMARK—MARCA REGISTRADA

New American Library Trade Paperback ISBN: 978-0-451-41428-1

The Library of Congress has cataloged the hardcover edition of this title as follows:

Caine, Rachel.
  Daylighters: the Morganville vampires/Rachel Caine.
    pages cm.—(The Morganville Vampires Novels)
  ISBN 978-0-451-41427-4 (hardback)
  I. Vampires—Fiction. I. Title.
  PS3603.O557D39 2013
  813'.6—dc23   2013025604

Printed in the United States of America
10 9 8 7 6 5 4 3 2 1

Set in Centaur MT

This one's for you, dear reader. You've been such enthusiastic residents of Morganville that I can't imagine dedicating this book to anyone else.

Thanks for taking this long, strange journey with me . . . and I hope you never want to leave our little town. Here, have a resident card. Lines for the blood bank form to the right. . . .

ACKNOWLEDGMENTS

Without Ter Matthies, this whole series would never have existed. Thank you, Ter. Love and respect, and I will always remember your light.

Also: Heidi Berthiaume, Jemina Venter, Sarah Weiss, Janet Cadsawan, NiNi Burkart, Lucienne Diver, and Anne Sowards—all of whom deserve my utmost love and respect.

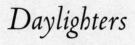

Daylighters

INTRODUCTION

Morganville, Texas, isn't like any other dusty small town. It's got secrets. It's a company town . . . and the company is *vampires*. If you stay, you work for them, signing special agreements for Protection and paying a tax in earnings or blood for the privilege of not being, y'know, eaten.

It's worked for a couple of centuries under the iron-in-velvet touch of the Founder, Amelie . . . but the past few years have been turmoil, trouble, and rebellion. Claire Danvers left to get away from it all, embarking on a special study program at MIT. But even if you can take the girl out of Morganville, you can't take Morganville out of the girl—and she ran headlong into a menacing new enemy who knew way too much about vampires. The Daylight Foundation.

Now Claire's returning home with her housemates (Eve, Michael, and Shane) and her allies (her bipolar mad scientist boss, Myrnin; Amelie's ex-second-in-command, Oliver; Claire's new vampire friend, Jesse) and Dr. Anderson, a captive scientist who was once a Morganville native, now turned traitor.

But home sure isn't the way they left it. . . .

ONE

Claire stared at the creaking billboard that marked the town limits of Morganville, Texas, and thought, *I ought to be crying.* Her best friend, Eve, already was, in helpless, furious sobs. Claire held on to her and did all the sympathetic things right—murmured that it would be okay, patted her on the back, hugged her.

But although she said all the right things, she felt . . . empty. Dry as the sand that blew through the desert outside the police cruiser's windows. They were sitting in the backseat, behind steel mesh, and the doors wouldn't open from the inside. The cruiser was made like a taxi, but it most definitely wasn't one since it took you only where you *didn't* want to go. Namely, to jail.

And across from where their cruiser was parked, four limp vampire bodies were being loaded into two of the town's ambulances—strapped tightly to gurneys, in case the wood still buried in their hearts to keep them temporarily dead didn't work. Claire identified the slack faces as they were rolled by: Oliver, once town Founder Amelie's second-in-command, now disgraced and in exile. Jesse, the vamp who Claire knew the least well, a beautiful woman who looked ridiculously young and fragile now, robbed (temporarily, hopefully) of her vampire life. Then Myrnin, Claire's bipolar vampire boss and friend, his dark hair an untamed mess around his still, white face.

Finally, and most horribly, Michael Glass, Claire's friend and the love of Eve's life. His skin had turned the color of pure white marble, and his blue eyes were open and dull. He looked deadest of them all.

"It's fine," Claire whispered, making sure to keep Eve's face turned away as Michael's body was rolled past. "Vampires can shake this off. It's no problem for them as long as the arrows come out soon; they're not leaving them in the sun or anything. Just breathe, okay? Breathe." It wasn't so much what she was saying as the fact that her voice was steady and calm, a lifeline in a tossing ocean of chaos.

Eve took a deep breath, and her sobbing slowed and hitched to a stop. She sat back as the ambulance doors slammed shut and one after the other the big vehicles pulled away onto the two-lane blacktop heading toward downtown Morganville—if Morganville had anything that could be described as a downtown. She wiped her eyes on the back of her hand, smearing what little eye makeup she had left. The glitter of her ruby wedding ring caught the light, and for a moment Claire's wall of numbness shuddered and threatened to collapse to reveal the pain and fear she'd hidden behind it. "Did you see Michael?" Eve asked. She caught her breath on another sob, and her reddened eyes held Claire's. "Did he look okay?"

Claire couldn't say that, because the sight of his icy skin and blank eyes had thoroughly unnerved her. "He'll be fine. You know he's tougher than this," she said. Which was a totally true thing, and beyond any argument.

"I know—God, why did this *happen*? What do they want from us?"

Eve said it as a rhetorical wail, but it was the question that churned in Claire's mind over and over. *Why?* They'd been heading back to Morganville to warn Amelie about several things, not the least of which was the deadly growth of an anti-vampire organization called the Daylight Foundation—and the fact that one of Amelie's most trusted agents, Dr. Irene Anderson (once of Morganville), had joined the other side.

But they'd been met by the local police instead of Amelie's people, and things had gone downhill from there. The cops had first separated out the humans—Claire, Eve, and Claire's boyfriend, Shane, plus the prisoner, Dr. Anderson. Then, without any warning, they'd taken down their vampire friends, who had just been wheeled into the ambulances and driven off to fates unknown.

Claire twisted in the seat to look into the car behind them. The cops hadn't had an easy time getting Shane into the other cruiser; they'd ended up handcuffing him and threatening a Tasering. He sat stiffly in the backseat, staring holes into the distance as if it were in for a beating. Next to him, Dr. Anderson slumped against the window as though she didn't care whose prisoner she was anymore.

Claire knew why they'd separated her from Shane, and she

knew that Eve needed her right now, but she wanted desperately to be with him and to ask all the questions burning in her mind. *Why would Hannah Moses do this?* After all, Police Chief Moses was their ally, their good and trusted friend. But she'd shown no hesitation, no remorse. The only way to interpret what had just happened was that Hannah had freely and willingly joined the Daylight Foundation.

Nothing was making any sense, and Claire *needed* it to make sense so badly. *Humans have taken control of Morganville,* Hannah had told her, as their friends—their mutual friends—lay still on the ground. *Vampires are being quarantined for their own protection.*

It couldn't be true. It just . . . couldn't. And yet it so obviously was.

"Where are they taking him?" Eve was staring after the flashing lights of the departing ambulances. "She said something about quarantine. What does that mean? Do you think they're taking them to the hospital? Do they think they have some kind of disease?"

"I don't know," Claire said. She felt helpless, and she knew if she let herself feel anything, she'd be just as angry as Shane looked sitting in that other cruiser. He seemed ready to chew through the steel mesh. But if she got angry, she would also have to let in everything else, all the other emotions that bubbled and threatened inside her. And if she did that, she would collapse, like Eve was doing.

Better not to feel anything right now. Better to stay strong.

The driver's-side door opened, and Hannah Moses got behind the wheel of the police car. She settled in and buckled her safety belt in one smooth motion. A deputy got in on the other side—new, Claire thought. Someone she didn't know.

But she did recognize the pin he wore on the collar of his uniform—a rising sun, in gold.

Symbol of the Daylight Foundation.

Eve lunged forward and grabbed the mesh, threading her fingertips into it as Hannah started the engine of the cruiser. "What the hell are you *doing*, Hannah?" she demanded, and rattled the mesh, hard. "Where are you taking Michael?"

"He's safe," Hannah said. "Nothing will happen to him. Trust me, Eve."

"Yeah, you know what? Bite me. I *don't* trust you. You just stabbed us all in the back, you horrible bi—"

Claire grabbed Eve and dragged her away, changing the word to a protesting yelp. "Stop," she whispered fiercely in her best friend's ear. "You're not going to accomplish anything by making her angry at us. Just wait. Be quiet and wait."

"Easy for you to say," Eve hissed. "Shane's coming with us at least. Michael—we don't even know where they're taking him!"

She had a point. Claire really hated to admit it, but there was absolutely nothing they could accomplish locked in a police cruiser. And antagonizing the lady who held the keys to their handcuffs probably wasn't the best strategy.

"We're not giving up," she told Eve. "We're just . . . biding our time."

"And what do you think they're going to do to him while we're biding, exactly?" Eve asked, yanking at the mesh again. "Yo, Hannah! How does it feel to stab your friends in the back? Hope you didn't get blood all over your neatly pressed uniform!"

The deputy turned around and gave her a cold, hard stare. "Sit quietly," he said. "If you don't, I'll shock you until you do."

"With what, your breath? Ever heard of flossing, Deputy Dimwit?"

"Eve," Hannah said. It was a warning, a flat and naked one,

and it was reinforced by the deputy—whose breath, in all fairness, did kind of reek—taking out a Taser.

Although Eve was still simmering with rage, she let go and sat back, folding her arms over her chest. Then she kicked his seat. Didn't do any good, because the seat was reinforced with a steel plate, but she probably felt better for doing it.

"Hey," Claire said, and reached her hand out toward Eve. Eve hesitated, then took it and gripped hard. "It'll be okay. He'll be okay."

Eve didn't say anything. She was probably thinking, *You don't know that*, and she would have been right. Claire *didn't* know that. She felt cold and helpless and vulnerable, and she didn't know how any of this could really be okay ... but for now, in the moments between opportunities, all she could do was pretend.

She expected they'd be taken straight to the jail, or at least to the courthouse, but instead the two police cruisers turned off and headed for the outskirts of Morganville. Claire recognized the area, and she didn't like it at all. Nothing good happened out here on the fringes of town; it was full of abandoned buildings and abandoned people.

"Hey," she said, leaning forward but careful not to touch the mesh. "Excuse me, but where exactly are you taking us?"

"Don't worry. You're not in any danger," Hannah said. "I have someone who wants to meet you. We're almost there."

When Claire had left Morganville, a lot of rebuilding had been under way around town, but not in this area. Nobody had thought it much worth saving, she suspected. It had been home mostly to tumbledown old shacks, rotting warehouses, and long-dead factories.

Now gangs of men moved with purpose, most in orange vests,

and bulldozers noisily leveled uneven ground and piled up the shattered remains of brick, wood, and rusted steel. Other teams were putting up the frames of buildings in areas that had already been cleared. Beyond, it was obvious that a lot more construction was under way, some of it already painted and finished. She could imagine what Shane was muttering in the other car: *Great, I leave town and suddenly there are good jobs.* He liked construction, and there was a lot of men and women out there, dressed in work shirts and jeans, hammering, hauling, bulldozing, and creating.

It was a whole new Morganville. It looked . . . cheerful. Hopeful.

"What brought this on?" Claire asked. "All these new houses?"

"They're for the new members," Hannah said. Her voice was calm and level, and it didn't give away anything at all. Her deputy, the one wearing the Daylight Foundation's rising sun pin on his collar, glanced back at Claire. "By joining the Daylight Foundation, they can receive free new housing if they want it. It's attracted a lot of enthusiasm and support. Half of these people working out here are volunteers." She slowed the cruiser and made a left turn. "There's something to be said for leaving the past behind and building a new future, don't you think? Especially in a town whose history is as dark as Morganville's."

Claire didn't want to agree, because she still felt there was a lot she didn't know and didn't fully understand, but what Hannah had just said made sense—or it would, if she trusted the Daylight Foundation even a little bit.

Speaking of the Daylighters . . . they'd renovated one of the old warehouses and built themselves a brand-new headquarters.

It was a large building just ahead, fresh and gleaming with paint and shining metal, with a big rotating sign on top of the roof. It shone soft gold in the sunlight as it turned—the same

symbol that was on the Daylight Foundation pin the deputy wore.
A simple image, something that should have looked hopeful. Sunrise, a new day, all that.

Claire didn't believe it. What she did believe was that the building, for all the cheerful way it had been painted, looked like it would be easy to defend if it came to a fight. The windows were all high, narrow, and didn't look like they opened at all. Thick walls, too. In fact, if you ignored everything but the construction, it could just as easily have been a prison.

Hannah pulled up in the generous parking lot—a newly paved one, still fresh and black, with bright white stripes marking off spaces. There were about fifty cars already present, but they filled less than a third of the available slots. *You could put half the cars in Morganville in here,* Claire thought, *and have room left over for massive bus parking.* Two police cruisers were already in place, plus Hannah's and the one pulling up in the next slot that carried Shane and Dr. Anderson. She thought she might have recognized a few other vehicles, but nothing jumped out at her with any certainty.

There were, she realized, no vampire-dark-tinted cars in the lot at all. Not a single one.

Hannah turned the engine off, but neither she nor the deputy got out immediately; instead, Hannah twisted to look at Claire and Eve through the mesh. "Here's how this is going to go," she said. "You're going to behave yourselves, get out, and walk with us into the building, and you're going to act like civilized young ladies while we introduce you to the man in charge."

"Or what? You'll put a note in my permanent record?" Eve scoffed.

"Or you'll end up handcuffed, maybe Tasered, and the end result will be exactly the same, only with a lot less smiling," Hannah said. "So I'd really rather skip all the unpleasantness and make this as painless as possible for you."

"Oh, sure, you're only thinking about us," Claire said. "I understand completely."

Hannah gave her a long, troubled look, as if she understood that Claire's apparent surrender was more worrisome than Eve's open aggression. "I'm trying to help you kids," she said. "Don't make me regret it."

"I'm not a kid, and you *ambushed my husband*," Eve said. "I'm going to go out on a limb here and say that there are plenty of things you're going to regret. Probably very briefly, though, if that makes you feel better."

Hannah exchanged a shrug with her deputy. "Well," she said, "I tried. If you want to make it difficult for yourselves, that's certainly your right, I suppose."

The two of them got out, and Hannah opened Claire's door, grabbed her by the arm, and shoved her against the cruiser with firm strength.

Then she zip-tied her hands behind her. "Sorry," she said. "But I can read the tea leaves. The two of you aren't going to go quietly."

Shane was making trouble, too, trouble enough that Claire heard the deputy in charge of him at the other car cursing as he tried to manhandle her boyfriend into submission. Hannah let out an impatient, frustrated growl and spun Claire around to face her. "Calm him down," she said. "Do it now."

Claire lifted her chin. "Why?"

"Because if you don't, he's going to get hurt."

Claire looked past her. Shane must have thrown an elbow before they'd gotten him under control, because the deputy had a bloody nose. Now Shane was dodging and kicking, trying to get past the man's defenses again. Probably just to get to her, because there was no way he'd be getting out of the handcuffs he was wearing.

"Shane," she said. "Don't."

Hannah, moving slowly and calmly, unsnapped the strap on her holster and drew her gun, which she held at her side. She stared straight at Shane. "She's right," she said. "Don't make me raise this weapon, Shane."

"Screw you," he said in a ragged pant and gave Hannah a defiant grin.

She raised the gun, all right.

She pointed it at Claire.

Shane froze in place, his grin fading fast. "You're bluffing."

"Probably seems that way," Hannah said. "But you know me well enough to know I don't point a weapon unless I'm ready to shoot to kill. I like you, Shane. I like your girl, here. But you're testing me, and I really don't think that's a good idea."

He stayed still. The deputy got hold of him and wrenched his bound hands up high enough to make Shane stand on tiptoe, his face twisted in pain. He put a hand on Shane's shoulder. "Walk, punk," the man growled.

Shane walked.

Claire did, too. Eve had fallen into a watchful silence, but even so, Hannah had her zip-tied as well. That was almost certainly a wise move. People underestimated Eve a lot, because of her funny sarcasm and cute-as-a-button face, but they did it at their peril.

They left Dr. Anderson handcuffed and silent in the car behind them, and Claire wondered about that.

Someone had put in a fresh sidewalk to the door of the warehouse, and there were newly planted bushes and sprigs of trees around it. Even so, walking up to it felt like walking up the steps to one of those old-time gallows; she didn't know what was going to happen to them once they were inside. The thick glass doors had the rising sun symbol on them, and the words THE DAYLIGHT FOUNDATION beneath it.

And, in gold lettering, ALL ARE WELCOME IN THE LIGHT. That sounded nice . . . unless you'd met their followers under less well-lit circumstances. Say, in a lab where they were ripping vampires apart.

Hannah opened one of the double doors, and a breath of chilled air raised goose bumps on Claire's bare arms. She had expected cavelike darkness, but as her eyes adjusted from the bright outdoor sun, she realized that it was nearly as bright *inside*, thanks to a giant skylight over the central atrium in which they stood. Bathed in the glow was a wooden desk with the Daylighters symbol on the front of it, and a well-dressed older woman who smiled kindly at them.

"Mrs. Hodgson?" Claire blurted. She knew the woman; she was a neighbor on Lot Street, where their old Victorian house was located. A nice lady, always puttering in her garden with her flowers and waving to them pleasantly. She'd brought over cookies for Christmas a couple of times. Snickerdoodles.

"Claire? Eve? And oh, my, Shane, too." Mrs. Hodgson looked politely distressed at the sight of their restraints. "Now, don't you worry at all. There's absolutely nothing to be afraid of here. You're in the light now. You're safe." She got up from the desk, revealing that she was wearing a fitted suit that was straight out of the 1960s, complete with a strand of shiny pearls, and came around to clip badges on their shirts. "I'll just take care of putting your IDs on. Can't let you in here without identification, can we? There, now. That wasn't so bad, was it?"

"Thanks, Doreen," Hannah said. "Let him know we're here, won't you?"

"Absolutely. Can I get y'all anything? Some water, maybe?"

"Beer," Shane said. "Shiner Bock if you've got it."

"Oh, now, you stop that," Mrs. Hodgson said. "You're far too young to drink, you scamp."

This wasn't a situation where any of them were inclined to be smiling, but Shane did, a little, and shook his head. He mouthed the word *scamp* to Claire, his eyebrows raised.

She raised hers back.

"Just some water might be nice," Hannah said. "Thank you kindly."

She led Claire over to a padded chair nearby and pressed her into it; Eve got seated next to her. The deputy kept Shane standing.

The anteroom was pretty plain, dominated mostly by the desk manned by Mrs. Hodgson, but there were some photos on the walls—Claire squinted against the glare from the skylight and made out the shapes of several people in one of the pictures, standing in front of this very building—but in the early stages of renovation, it looked like. She could make out that one was Hannah, and one was the new Morganville mayor, Flora Ramos. Apart from that, the others were a mystery—except that she noticed a pattern, and a recurring face. A short man, slight build, nothing really remarkable about his features.

Doreen Hodgson came back bearing water bottles, and following behind her was the same man, in the flesh.

He wasn't very imposing in real life, either—shorter than Shane by at least four inches. He wore a plain black suit and a white shirt; the only spots of color on him were his very blue eyes—almost the same startling shade as Michael's—and a red silk tie and pocket square. His face had a vaguely Eastern European shape to it, but that was really all that Claire could tell about him.

That, and the fact that his Daylight Foundation pin gleamed like real gold.

He nodded to Hannah and said, "You can let them go now. I'm sure that we're all going to be civilized. Besides, they can hardly drink their water if their hands are tied. It's important to start this conversation with trust."

Hannah nodded to her deputy, and as he unfastened Shane's handcuffs, she pulled out a utility knife and sliced through the zip-tie cuffs on Claire's wrists, and then Eve's. Doreen hurried to put bottles of water into their newly freed hands—cold, sweating bottles that reminded Claire how long it had been since she'd had anything to drink.

"Thanks," she said, and put the bottle down on the chair where she'd been sitting. "Not thirsty." It was a lie, but she didn't know enough yet to trust anything about this situation—not even a sealed water bottle.

The man's pale eyebrows raised just a touch. "It's a name brand," he said. "I can promise you that it hasn't been tampered with." He extended his hand toward her. "I'm Rhys Fallon. And you must be Claire Danvers."

"Are you in charge here?" Claire asked him, without shaking the hand he was holding out. He lowered it to his side, not visibly offended.

"I suppose you could say that," he said. "Although I like to think that it's more a collaboration, not a dictatorship."

"If you're in charge, you can take us to our friends, right now," she said.

"Your friends . . . ?"

"Michael," Eve said. "Oliver, Myrnin, Jesse. You know. The ones you had shot and carried off."

"Ah." Rhys clasped his hands behind his back and, for the first time, studied Eve. He spent a strangely long time at it, and there was something about his body language that altered, just a little. "Eve Rosser, is it not?"

"Eve *Glass*," she said, and raised her chin to make the point more forcefully. He didn't seem to notice.

"I'm delighted to meet someone who is so . . . legendary in Morganville. The descriptions I've heard don't do you justice." He smiled at her, and that was a little too much wattage to direct at a married woman—an angry married woman at that. "Well, I am very sorry, and I wish I could grant your request, but it isn't possible just now. Michael and your other friends are being well looked after, and after they're completely recovered, they'll be placed into protective custody. You'll be able to visit later, perhaps."

"I want to see my husband, and there's no later and there's no *perhaps*. I want to see him right the hell now. I don't care who you think you are, you can't—"

"Yes, I can," he said, and Claire was struck by the fact that he stated it without emphasis. It wasn't a bluff; it wasn't a boast. It was just . . . fact. It even had a tinge of regret to it. "I'm sorry, Miss Rosser—"

"*Mrs. Glass!*" Eve's face was flushed now, and her fists clenched.

"—but you must accept that things are different here than when you left town. I believe for the better, but you may not agree quite yet. I hope you will, in the end. I sincerely do." He cleared his throat and glanced away for the first time, at Hannah Moses. "We'll have to discuss the . . . legitimacy of your marriage at a later time."

"*What?*" Eve almost went for his throat, right there, but Hannah restrained her with a cautionary hand on her shoulder. "What are you talking about? We were married! In the church!"

"As I said, a conversation for a later time, perhaps. I am sorry to upset you."

He might have been sorry, but he had definitely upset her, bigtime. Eve's cheeks had gone from flushed to pale now, and she looked shaky. She hadn't expected that, at all . . . not that.

Claire said, "I want to see Amelie."

That got his immediate undivided attention. His eyes were very blue, and in fact not at all warm. Not cold, either. Just . . . expressionless. "I'm sorry, perhaps you didn't understand," he said. "It simply isn't possible. And it will not be anywhere in the near future. If you want to talk to the person in charge of Morganville, it is no longer a vampire. It is Mayor Flora Ramos, the duly elected representative, which is as it should be. Or don't you agree that humans should govern themselves? Your reputation was . . . somewhat different. I thought that you had stood up for the free will and rights of humans in this town."

"Depends on the human," Claire said. "As far as I know, Hitler had a heartbeat, and I wouldn't vote him to be in charge."

That earned her a slow, warm smile. "You think Mayor Ramos is Adolf Hitler?"

"You're drawing false connections, and I don't know who *you* are. But I'm betting that Mayor Ramos answers to you."

"That's an interesting inference, and I think you might be surprised about how much free will the mayor has. Shane? You're unaccountably silent." He suddenly turned and looked at her boyfriend, who stared back without any shift in his guarded expression and said nothing. "Are you going to let your girlfriend do all the work?"

"Yeah," Shane said. "Why? Is it bugging you, *Rhys*? What kind of name is that, anyway?"

"Irish. I meant no disrespect, I simply thought you'd be more—" Rhys just shrugged. "Well. Forceful."

Shane just smiled his sweetest, nicest smile, but his eyes were hard. And dangerous.

"He is," Claire said. "So am I. So's Eve. You'd better start answering our questions, right now."

"You know, I appreciate your passion, but you betray your very young age when you speak that way to me, because I am not *your* prisoner, Claire. You would do well to note that fact very carefully."

There was menace in his tone now, something subtle but all the more serious for it. Fallon held Claire's stare for a long moment, and then, without looking away, said, "Ah, Irene. How fare you, my friend?"

Claire turned just as the glass door closed behind Dr. Irene Anderson, who stood there blocking their way out. Once, Dr. Anderson had been Claire's professor at MIT; once, Claire had trusted her, even liked her. Now she just loathed the sight of her— especially free, armed, and with a pale gleam of hatred in her slightly deranged eyes.

Dr. Anderson racked the shotgun she held, just for emphasis. "I'm fine, Rhys, thank you," she said. "Which is more than I can say for all our compatriots back in Cambridge. They killed them. They killed them all."

"Even Dr. Davis?"

"He's dead. They're all *dead*." She aimed the shotgun at Claire, Shane, and Eve. "Hannah, step aside. We can't leave these collaborators alive."

"Irene!" Fallon's voice was an unmistakable whipcrack of command, and she flinched and looked at him, startled. "No one is doing anything so reckless here. Put that down, *now.*"

"But—"

"Did you hear what I said? What is wrong with you, woman? You'd take a shotgun to three people hardly older than children?"

"Trust me, they're adults," she said. "And they didn't hesitate to kill *us* when they had the chance. You're making a mistake, Rhys, a big one. You can't deal mercifully with these . . . vampire lovers. I've told you before, the world is better off if you just end all this once and for all. No half measures. Do *not* underestimate them."

That was kind of a compliment, Claire supposed, but it was also terrifying when combined with the loaded shotgun and the half-crazy look on her face. Dr. Anderson would very much *like* to kill them. And apparently, the only thing that was really standing in her way was Fallon, and as far as Claire could tell, he was thinking about his options.

Hannah had quietly removed her handgun from its holster and was holding it at her side. Now she said, "Irene, please put the shotgun down."

That startled Dr. Anderson, and her eyes widened when she took in the fact that Hannah had her own weapon ready. "You'd shoot *me*?"

"I'm here to keep the peace," Hannah said. "You seem to be threatening it. So I'm asking you nicely, please put that down and let's all be civil."

Fallon seemed to make his decision. He took three steps forward and put himself squarely in the line of fire—a position where Irene couldn't miss him if she happened to shoot. "This isn't like

you, my dear," he said. "Now let me have that thing before someone gets hurt."

Irene hesitated, but she lowered the shotgun from firing position and handed it over to him. Fallon broke it open and held it
comfortably in the crook of his arm, as if he was long acquainted
with proper gun safety procedures. "Thank you," he said. "Mrs.
Hodgson, could you please show Dr. Anderson to her quarters? I
believe she could use a comfortable rest and a meal, and perhaps
some calming medication. Thank you so much."

It was all very warm and kindly, but Claire still felt chilled as
she watched their nice old neighbor lady take Dr. Anderson by the
arm and lead her off through the far door, patting her and mur-
muring in a calm, grandmotherly sort of way. If the last scorching
glance Dr. Anderson sent back toward them was any indication, it
wasn't working.

"I'd apologize for that, but it appears to me that there might be
some justification for how much she dislikes the three of you," Fallon said. "Would you like to tell me your side of it? Or shall I just
take her at her word? If I do that, you may very well be on your way
to jail, charged with murder."

"We didn't murder anyone," Claire said quickly, as Eve took in
a hot breath, ready to start yelling. "We were abducted. We were
held prisoner, at gunpoint. We fought our way free, and yes, people died, but we didn't have a choice."

"They tortured Michael," Eve said. "They were going to kill us
all when they were done with us. They were using Myrnin, Oliver,
and Jesse as lab rats, too."

"But you *did* kill them," Fallon said.

"Ever heard of self-defense?" Shane asked. He sounded as calm
and measured as Eve was angry. "It was a bad scene, and trust me,

whether they were friends of yours or not, they were not good people. They kidnapped Claire's roommate, who didn't have diddly to do with anything, and nearly got her killed in the process. They *did* kill another guy who was just in the wrong place at the wrong time. A human guy."

Fallon considered that for a moment, then looked at Hannah, who shrugged. "We've only got their word versus Anderson's," she said. "Irene may be a friend of yours, but I know these kids, and they generally try to do the right thing. I'm inclined to believe them."

"Sweet. Does that mean I get to hold the shotgun?" Shane asked.

"Perhaps some other time," Fallon said. "In any case, whatever crimes were committed, they were not committed here, and thus would be outside of Chief Moses's jurisdiction. But please don't misunderstand; I take the deaths of my people seriously, and it counts against you. Your earnest cooperation is required to avoid any further unpleasantness. Because if there happens to be any trouble here in Morganville, it will not be so easily overlooked, do you understand? These are not the old rules, the Founder's rules. These are rules of law, and justice, and they will be enforced regardless of who you are or who you know."

Fine words, Claire thought. She wondered if that was what had gotten Hannah on board his train. "I see that your rule of law and justice doesn't extend to vampires," she said. "Seeing as how you're willing to have them shot on sight."

"Non-fatally, you might have noticed." Fallon's voice was mild, but firm. "Everyone will get a fair chance in Morganville. That is why the mayor has joined us, and the police chief"—said with a polite nod toward Hannah—"and most of the other prominent citizens and families. You see, once Amelie's threat to those in Morganville was removed, no one hesitated to speak their minds about how radically the situation needed to change."

There was only one part of that Claire paid attention to—*once Amelie's threat to those in Morganville was removed?* Well, she should have already guessed that; if Amelie was still in charge, she'd have wasted no time in shutting all this Daylight Foundation stuff down—no matter what the cost in lives. What worried Claire was that Amelie was old and clever and ruthless, but somehow she hadn't seen this coming.

What had happened to her? Where was she now?

"Where are you keeping her?" That was Shane asking, as if he'd read Claire's mind; it was also unusual for him to be concerned about the fate of vampires, but then, Amelie had been mostly on their side lately. "Or did you just cut to the chase and kill her already?"

"Of course not," Fallon said. "I'm not here to kill. I'm here to protect the human population of Morganville, and to make sure that they gain the control over their lives that they deserve—that is my first priority. But the vampires are residents of this town as well, and we are working for their long-term good, too."

"So Amelie's not dead, then," Shane said. "You know that as long as she's still alive, you're never going to have control of this town, right? It's hers; she built it. She sees herself as a queen, and she's not the type to just walk away."

Claire felt as if the temperature in this warm, sunlit room had dipped by twenty degrees. Was Shane really somehow warning Fallon to *kill* the Founder of Morganville? Shane's father had been radically anti-vampire; he'd convinced Shane to hate them, too, at least for a while. But she thought he was over that. Mostly.

Fallon, however, watched Shane with steady eyes, and shook his head. "Like Amelie herself, you overestimate how fond people in this town are of her and her kind. Now that they are free of the fear, of the threats and reprisals, they've simply turned their backs on her and forgotten she ever existed. No one will listen to her, or rally to her cause, even if she should decide to make this some sort of a fight. They don't fear her enough."

"Why are we even talking about Amelie?" Eve asked in a low, harsh voice. "They've got *Michael*. And he's who we ought to be worried about!"

Shane didn't answer her. His gaze had fixed on Fallon's, and Claire felt a deep surge of unease. Something was off about him. This wasn't the usual, challenging way Shane confronted someone who had—at the very least—done his friends harm. She couldn't exactly pinpoint how it was different, but . . . it was. Definitely. "Shane," she said, and put her hand on his arm. *"Shane."* That got to him, and the blankness in him faded away. When he looked at her, he was normal again. Well, normal for Shane, anyway.

He cleared his throat and said, "Yeah, about that, we're going to need our friend Michael back. Intact."

"Or?" Fallon asked. It wasn't confrontational, really, just an interested question.

"Look, you clearly do not know who you're screwing with," Eve said, and she was *definitely* confrontational, a whole lot. "I want my husband back, Osama bin Crazy, right the hell now! And don't give me any shit about how you don't want to call him my husband, because he is, and he always will be!" She was so angry now that tears welled up in her eyes, but with a huge effort of will, she refused to give in to the sobs.

Fallon took the red silk handkerchief from his breast pocket and pressed it into Eve's hand. He even patted her fingers gently as they closed around the fabric. "I'm so very sorry to upset you," he said. "Believe me, that isn't my intention. I came to Morganville to bring a peace that has never existed here, and not just a fear-enforced peace on the streets, but real peace in the hearts of those who live here. I'm certain that Michael would not want you to feel such distress on his behalf."

"Don't you dare talk about what Michael would want! You don't even know him!"

And Fallon, without a flicker of resentment, suddenly smiled at Eve—a sweet, disarming sort of smile. "Of course you're right," he said. "I don't know him, but I have a very real kinship to him. You see, as I understand it, Michael was attacked by a vampire and, well, killed. Isn't that true?"

Eve, taken aback, couldn't quite get her words together, so Claire said, "He wasn't *killed*, exactly."

"Oh, no, I assure you he was. Yet that extraordinary house of yours saved him, didn't it? Gave him a pale half-life of an existence as some kind of ghost? He had very little choice in becoming a vampire at all, and I do understand that. I had very little choice in what happened to me, either, and that is why I established the Daylight Foundation—not to destroy vampires, but to rehabilitate them. To *save* them. You've seen the motto on the door: ALL ARE WELCOME IN THE LIGHT. And I most sincerely mean that. I think that if you asked him, really asked, he would tell you that he has no real desire to be a vampire. Only the monsters enjoy that existence."

Eve sucked in a steadying breath and said, "Michael's still Michael, no matter what his diet is, and I want to be with him. Don't tell me it isn't safe. He won't hurt me!"

"I see. I think you honestly believe that. Well, I really must let Michael tell you himself, mustn't I? Perhaps it is best if you see him, then. Hannah will take you for a short visit, and we'll hear no more about it after."

He had a certain draw to him, Claire thought. She could see how he could convince people to follow him ... even Hannah, who definitely was not born gullible. He had a fire in him, and strength, and courage. It was right there, for anyone who looked hard enough.

God, she thought, suddenly and coldly alarmed. *Even I'm falling for it a little.* That wasn't normal. Not for her. Maybe when she'd first arrived in Morganville she might have bought into that kind of charisma, but she'd grown since then. She'd learned how to distrust a nice face and a winning smile.

It was odd, but something about him reminded her of vampires, and the charm they could deploy in the cause of gaining what they wanted. What unsettled her was that Fallon quite clearly wasn't a vampire—she could see the pulse beating in his throat, his color was good, and there was none of that strange sense of *other* that she almost always got from the fanged gang.

She was so caught up in her own reactions that she almost missed what Fallon said, and it took a few seconds to penetrate that he had, in fact, just agreed.

He was going to let them see Michael, which should have been, by any measure, a victory.

Why did it feel so much like a trap?

TWO

Once upon a time—well before Claire had come to Morganville, and probably before she'd entered puberty—there had been a mall in town. It hadn't been a huge one, not like the sprawling temples of shopping that you could find in the bigger cities like Dallas or Houston, or even Midland. It also had never had any of the major chain stores in it, mainly because (as Eve had speculated, probably correctly) Amelie didn't want to have regular traffic in and out of town or to encourage visitors. And as humble as a Sears store might be, it would have still been better than anything else within a hundred miles, and it would have made people—people who weren't in the know—come to Morganville.

So the mall had housed only local stores, and it had struggled along for a few years in the mid-1980s until the last business had failed and bailed, leaving behind one of the largest empty structures in Morganville—which said a lot, considering how many empty structures there were around town. The old tire factory, and the even older hospital, for example, were fairly gigantic. But the biggest difference to Claire was that she had never been forced to run for her life in the old mall. It had always seemed more of a sad place than an actively evil one.

As the police cruiser pulled up to one of the parking spaces in the cracked, deserted lot, she thought that was about to change.

"Right," Hannah said, and turned around in the front seat to look at them. The three of them had been crammed together in the backseat this time, which actually was comforting; Claire loved the warmth and solidity of Shane sitting in the middle, even if it pushed her uncomfortably into the hard plastic of the door. "Rules, people. We've got them, and you'll obey them. First rule is, you do exactly what my officers tell you, without hesitation or question. If they tell you to get down on the floor, you eat dirt. If they tell you to stop, you become a statue. Are we understood?"

"What the hell happened to you?" Shane asked her. "Because I'm pretty sure you used to be cool, Captain Obvious."

"So did you," Hannah shot back. "So be cool now, or end up back in handcuffs. Fallon said you'd get to see Michael, and I'm going to make that happen, but you *be cool.*"

No one had a comeback for that. Eve looked tense, her dark eyes huge, as if she was afraid to do anything to screw up the chance to see the man she loved—but also, Claire thought, as if she was ready to gnaw through steel bars to get to him, if necessary. At moments like these, Eve looked exactly like what she was: strong and determined.

Fallon would almost certainly see that as a threat, that kind of devotion.

"Watch her back," Claire whispered to Shane, and got a nod as Hannah exited the police cruiser and opened Eve's door.

"I'm watching yours first," Shane whispered back, then scooted over toward the exit. Claire followed, blinking at the harsh desert daylight again; the tint on the cruiser's windows wasn't vampire-dark, but it had lulled her into a false sense of being in a kinder, gentler place until the dry, dusty reality hit her full on.

The mall was on two floors, and it was built of bricks the color of dried mud. No windows. It was shaped like a rectangle—no fancy architectural touches here. The rusted steel letters still clung to the side of the building, or at least most of them did: BITTER CREEK MALL. Only a few letters had fallen away, or been ripped off, so the sign actually read BIT ER EEK MA L. Which seemed weirdly appropriate somehow.

Two uniformed police officers stood at parade rest outside the double doors that led into the mall, and Claire recognized one of them. He'd arrested Shane once—though that wasn't exactly a small club of people.

Hannah gave them both brisk nods, and like the most intimidating doormen ever, the cops opened the entrance and stood aside to let them go in.

It smelled abandoned.

That was the first thing Claire noticed—the musty reek of old carpet, dust, mold—the aroma of a place that humans had long ago rejected. A faint undertone of rot, too.

And quiet. So very, very quiet. The sound of their footsteps echoed around an open atrium floored with cracked, dirty ceramic tiles in a brightly colored style that must have been hot back in the dark ages when the place was built, but just looked dated and clumsy now. A dry three-tiered fountain sat lifeless in the corner. The light coming in was dim at best; the skylights, Claire found as she looked up, were filthy, and the plastic had aged to a dull, opaque yellow. It gave all of them a sickly pallor.

"Cozy," Shane said. "Going for the homeless heroin addict market with this place, are you?"

"We worked with what we had," Hannah said. She sounded just a touch defensive. "We're getting it cleaned and made more livable, but they don't seem to care all that much about the decor."

They being the vampires, Claire realized, because despite the hush, they were most definitely not alone. Silent figures loomed in the shadows like abandoned mannequins. Even when the figures moved, it was more like ghosts walking—silent and eerie. So many vampires. But none of them came out into the open tiled square of the atrium.

Eve took in a sudden sharp breath. "Jesus!" she gasped, and Claire knew she'd spotted them, too. There was something deeply unsettling about the way they were being watched. Like prey.

Like enemies.

"Stay where you are," Hannah said, as Eve took a step out toward them. "They know the rules; they stay out of the atrium unless we specifically call their names."

"Or what?" Shane asked tightly. He didn't like this any more than Claire did. "What kind of punishments have you been dishing out?"

Hannah didn't answer that—didn't want to, Claire thought. But she had her hand on what Claire had originally thought was some kind of radio on her belt—a black box with buttons along the top and a flickering green light.

Maybe it wasn't a radio after all.

"Michael Glass," Hannah said. She didn't raise her voice, but then, in a mall full of vampires, she really didn't need to do that. "We're here for Michael Glass. Michael, step forward, please."

He didn't. Amelie did.

It was as if somehow the shadows parted around her, but Claire knew that wasn't the case; Amelie had simply moved forward without seeming to move at all, and suddenly she was standing at the edge of the tiles, her pointed-toe pumps lined up very precisely with the boundary. The Founder of Morganville was dressed in impeccable white, impossibly clean and pure in the dirty, yellowed glow. Her pale silvery eyes seemed almost colorless, and from experience Claire knew that meant Amelie was at her most dangerous.

"What do you want with Michael?" she asked. Her hands were folded in front of her, a calm, resting position, and her body language was watchful.

"Eve wants to see him, to be sure he's all right."

That made Amelie smile, just a little. It was a shivery kind of expression, and she lowered her chin just enough to make it seem terrifying. "Yes, I'm sure all of you are simply brimming with concern for our well-being."

"He's my husband!" Eve said sharply. "Look, I just had to fight to get this far. Don't be a jerkface, Amelie."

That broke Amelie's concentration, and she looked a little puzzled as she worked out the word. "Jerkface?" she said slowly, as if testing the syllables. "Ah. You think I am the one at fault? You have quite a lot to learn, Eve. But if you wish to see Michael, I will send him out—as soon as Chief Moses assures me that he will remain unharmed and will be returned in the same state."

"Returned to *you*? What about to me?"

"It's clear you don't understand the slightest thing about what is happening in Morganville," Amelie said. "So I will forgive you for not comprehending how much danger you put Michael in by separating him from my protection." She nodded slightly, and on the other side of the atrium, Oliver stepped up. He was holding Michael by the arm. Michael broke free, and for just a heartbeat Claire saw him clearly in the dim light: a shock of golden hair wild around his face, clear blue eyes fixed on Eve. Of all of them, he looked the least like a vampire, except for the pallor of his skin. He looked like a Renaissance angel come to life, if angels wore jeans and witty T-shirts.

He was wearing something black around his throat, and for a second Claire thought it was one of Eve's chokers, the dog-collar type, though that would be a strange thing for him to put on. She could barely see it, and then he was a blur, heading at vamp speed across the tiles.

Hannah pressed a button on the box on her belt, and Michael stopped. No, not just *stopped*—he broke stride, stumbled, and fell to his knees, shaking. "Slowly," Hannah said. "Don't make me take it up to the next level, Michael. Move *slowly*."

"Yes," Amelie said from the shadows. "Pray do as she says, Michael."

Eve, after a white-hot glare at Hannah, threw herself out into the open space and down next to Michael. "What did you do to him?" she demanded. "He's hurt! Michael, baby, are you okay? Michael!"

"He's fine," Hannah said, and took her finger off the button. "No permanent damage, I promise. But I have to make sure everybody obeys the rules. It's the only way this works."

The vampires hadn't moved, but there was a new feeling in the air, Claire thought. A kind of tension that was reinforced by what sounded almost like a low whisper of sound.

A growl.

"I'm fine," Michael said. He sounded shaky, but he wrapped his arms around Eve and held on tight. "God, there you are. All in one piece. I was so worried."

"Me? I'm not the one who got an arrow to the chest, bucko."

"I didn't know what happened to you." He raised his hands to cup her face, and brushed her black hair back. It was growing longer again, and she hadn't braided it, so it fell in a sleek curtain. "I was so scared they'd—they'd done something to you. Not hurt?"

"Just my feelings," Eve said. "Seeing as how our old friend there stuck a knife between our collective shoulder blades." She followed her statement up with a rude gesture, to which Hannah didn't bother to react. "Honey—" She reached out toward the collar around his neck. He captured her hands in his and held on when she tried to pull away. "Honey, what is that thing around your neck?"

"Shock collar," Shane said. "Isn't it, Hannah? Like you'd put on a dog. You've got them on all of them."

"We have to maintain order," Hannah replied. "It's the least violent way we could come up with to do it. They need to stay inside this building for their own protection, and we need to have order for the safety of my officers."

Amelie had the same collar on, Claire realized. So did Oliver, standing with his graying hair loose and wild around his shoulders.

And where was Myrnin? Her heart skipped a beat and then sped up. She didn't see him anywhere. Surely he'd be here if he was able to, which meant that he *wasn't* able to make an appearance. That something had gone wrong with him.

Michael had steadied by now, and he kissed Eve's hands and then leaned forward to press his lips to hers—a soft, gentle sort of kiss that made her let out a cry when it was over, and bury her face in the crook of his neck. He held on to her, but his blue eyes remained fixed on Hannah. Hard to read his expression. Claire had never seen him look quite that closed off. "Eve can't stay here," he said. "You can't let her stay here with me, you know that. Not even if she wants to."

"I wouldn't," Hannah said. "I know how dangerous it would be, even if she refuses to admit it."

"Are you crazy?" Eve said. Her voice was muffled against his shoulder, but Claire still heard it clearly. "No, I'm not going *any-where*, and I'm not letting you stay trapped in here without me. They don't get to put you in some kind of—vampire petting zoo. You're coming home where you belong. With us. With *me*."

"He can't," Amelie said. "If he leaves this place, he will be killed. Not by us, of course. By those who are our . . . *protectors*." The irony of that wasn't lost on her, Claire thought, noticing the twist of her lips. The taste of it must have been bitter.

"Is that true?" Shane turned to look at Hannah, but she continued to do a middle-distance stare. "Hey. Talking to you, lady!"

"I heard you," she said. "He's right that it isn't safe for vampires outside of this enclave."

"*Enclave?*" Claire heard the outrage in her own voice, even though she tried to hold it back. "I don't care what kind of cool name you want to give it to make yourself feel better. It's a *prison camp*."

"They're here for their own protection."

"Bullshit!" she spat back, and Shane put his hand on her shoulder. It surprised her enough to stop her from uttering the rest of what she'd been about to say, which probably wouldn't have been quite so nice.

"Claire," he said, "let's take a breath. Maybe—maybe this isn't a bad thing."

"What?"

"Maybe we need to just think a little more," he said. "I mean, having vampires obeying the rules . . . what's so wrong with that? They damn sure don't obey any unless they're scared of something. Not even the rules they make themselves. Right, Amelie?"

"You're being foolish," Amelie said. "And disloyal to your friend."

"Hey, lady, I've been bending over backward for years around here not to judge you bloodsuckers, no matter what kind of horrible things you did. Give me a break. And you know what? For a change, give me a little respect, too. Because I deserve that. We all do. All us poor, stupid *humans.*" Shane wasn't entirely wrong, Claire had to admit, though he also wasn't usually this blunt about it. But then, the vampires usually wouldn't have let him say these things without reprisal. "Maybe we should all show a little good judgment and agree that vamps aren't the safest thing in the world to have lurking around in your neighborhood—"

"Thanks for being on my side, bro," Michael said.

"I'm not saying this is the right way to do it. But maybe it's the right idea, keeping vamps and humans apart." Shane shivered a little, as if he were cold, but Claire realized that his face was flushed and he was sweating. It wasn't too hot in here—probably air-conditioned for the comfort of the guards. He really didn't look good, Claire thought, and she took his hand. It felt hot—feverish.

Was he sick? She could feel the tremors going through him, over and over.

"Shane? What's wrong? You're burning up!" Claire put the back of her hand against his forehead—or tried to. He knocked her arm away. It shocked her, and it surprised him, too. She saw the instant regret in his eyes, but when he tried to talk, he gagged. "Shane?"

"I need to get out," he said. "Can't stay here—" He couldn't get the rest out, just kept gagging. His face looked gray and damp.

"Take him outside and let him have some fresh air," Hannah said. "I'll stay here with Eve. Nothing will harm her."

Claire didn't want to go; she didn't want Eve to feel alone and abandoned. But something was clearly very wrong with Shane, and getting worse with every breath he took. She didn't debate it any further. She just grabbed his arm and pulled him toward the light streaming in through the thick glass doors. When she tried the metal handle, it didn't move. Locked. She knocked urgently on the glass, and the policeman outside finally opened it—but blocked her way. "Just a minute," he said. "Where's Chief Moses?"

"It's okay, Bud," Hannah called from behind him. "Let them out."

He didn't seem inclined, but he did step back, and Claire pulled Shane over the threshold and down the sidewalk, out into the bright, harsh sunlight and the dry desert air. He practically folded up once they reached the curb, and sat down hard there, his head in his hands. The tremors, though, were lessening, and as she stroked his hair she thought he was getting better. "Shane?" she asked. "Shane, what the hell was that?"

"I don't know," he said, and gulped air. "God. I don't know. It felt like I was burning up from the inside out. Maybe—maybe you'd better go back in, for Eve. I can't, Claire. I just can't."

"Why not?"

He was definitely, inexplicably better out here, away from the mall and the vamps. And as he looked up, she saw the strange light in his eyes. It looked almost like fear.

"Because I want to kill them," he said. "The vampires. I want to kill them all. It's like what I've felt my whole life, but turned up to eleven. And if I go back in there, I don't think I can control it."

She stared at him, shocked, and he lifted his shoulders in a very small shrug. He still looked unnaturally flushed, and sweat pasted thin strings of hair to his forehead.

"I don't know," he said. "I don't know why. Please, don't ask me to explain it, okay? Because I just can't."

But somehow she thought he could. She'd seen how he'd acted from time to time around Michael and the other vampires on the trip back. There was something wrong with him. *Really* wrong, in ways that scared them both, but Shane was trying to conceal and ignore it all.

It wasn't the time to dig into it, though, and she shoved down her desire to interrogate him until this made some kind of sense, however twisted; he was right—she needed to go back. For Eve. For Michael.

For Myrnin, because if anyone knew where he was, Michael would.

She kissed Shane, and then she scrambled up and went back to the doors. The deputy—Bud?—didn't harass her about it this time; he just silently unlocked them and let her back in, and she walked over to stand beside the spot where Eve and Michael were still kneeling near the fountain. They didn't seem inclined to let go of each other, but Eve looked up and raised her eyebrows, silently asking the question.

"I don't know," Claire said. "But he feels better out there. It was almost like claustrophobia or something."

"Weird," Eve said. "Because that boy never hesitated to crawl into small spaces, and this isn't exactly restrictive. It's a *mall.*"

"Maybe it's the high ratio of vampires," Michael said, and managed a smile, though it was thin. "I mean, if I wasn't already on Team Fang, I might be a little intimidated."

"Shane? Intimidated? Better be glad he's out there and not in here making you eat those words," Eve said. She shook her head. "No, something's not right with him. It's just wrong, the way he reacted. Wrong and weird and wrong, also. Claire, keep an eye on him, okay?"

"I will," she said, and hesitated for a long few seconds before she glanced at Michael. "Um—I have to ask, because I don't see them, but about Myrnin, and Jesse—?"

"They're fine," Michael said. "Well, you know. It's Myrnin, so *fine* probably isn't so accurate, but she's keeping him calm in one of the rooms that way." He nodded toward the darkness, the northeast corner where some dark, shuttered spaces lurked. "He's having a hard time accepting . . . the situation." He tapped the collar with one fingertip and gave Hannah a quick glance. "You know how he gets when he feels trapped."

Oh, she knew, and she felt heartsick at the idea of how Myrnin, of all people, would have reacted to wearing a shock collar. Hannah would probably have had to replace the batteries in her control unit several times over, because one thing about Myrnin, he was stubborn, and he just did *not* give up. Jesse was probably holding him back with all of her strength to keep him from charging out here—and no doubt not for the first, or the last, time.

She refrained from asking anything more, mainly because she

was acutely aware of Hannah standing there, and she really didn't trust Hannah at all now. She was loyal to Fallon, obviously, or she wouldn't be holding the button for the shock collars. It wouldn't be wise to say too much in Hannah's hearing, since everything would end up reported back to the Daylight Foundation.

But she did turn to Hannah and ask her a question that seemed perfectly obvious. "You can't keep a bunch of vampires in here like this forever," she said. "No matter what kind of little training devices you put on them. What are you planning to do with them?"

Hannah never once looked at her directly. She was watching Amelie, Claire realized—watching for any sign of trouble from the vampire queen. But Amelie didn't seem to be inclined, yet, to give any orders to her people. "We plan to help them," she said. "That's all. We plan to help them get better."

"Yeah," Eve said. "You're *helping*, all right. What is this, Vampire Reeducation Camp? Are you planning on helping them learn to live without blood? Vegan vampires?"

The silence that greeted this was so deep that it made Claire's already tense muscles ache and tighten. There was something in Hannah's carefully controlled expression that made her feel sick and scared. "It's probably time to go now before this gets any messier," Hannah said. "Wrap it up, kids."

Eve raised her head from Michael's shoulder. There were tears in her eyes, but she wasn't crying. She was too angry to cry. "I'm not leaving him."

"Eve, she's right. You can't stay," he said in a gentle voice. He brushed his hand across her sleek black hair, let it drift through his fingers, and touched her lips just as softly. "You have to go, Eve. You wouldn't be safe here."

"Why not? Aren't they feeding you?"

"They're feeding us. I'll be fine," he said, and kissed her. "Eve, I'll be fine. Just go, okay? Claire, take her. Please."

Claire didn't want to, but she could see that he was serious; when she hesitated, he fixed her with a calm, steady stare until she moved forward and put her hand under Eve's arm to get her to her feet.

"No," Eve said. "No, I'm not going, Claire. I can't—we can't just *leave him here* . . ."

"Maybe not, but we also can't get him out," Claire said. The words tasted horrible in her mouth, like ashes and iron, and she had to swallow hard to continue. "Not yet. But we will, Eve. I swear to you, this isn't over."

Hannah said, "It is for now. Michael, you move back to the line. Go on."

He got up and walked back to where Oliver was waiting at the edge of the tiles—exactly opposite from where Amelie was standing in her glowing white suit. Oliver put a hand on Michael's shoulder. Maybe he meant to just hold him back, but it looked to Claire like . . . comfort? Odd, if so. Oliver wasn't much on empathy. Then again, the look on Michael's face—that lost, hollow, helpless look—would have moved anybody.

Except Hannah, apparently, who marched them straight to the door. As she opened it, though, Amelie said, without moving from where she stood, "Thank you for allowing Eve to see him, Chief Moses. I will not forget your kindness." It sounded unmistakably chilling, and Hannah's shoulders stiffened for a second, then deliberately relaxed.

"I'm sure you won't," Hannah said. "Anybody moves, everybody gets shocked down to the ground. Clear?"

"Yes," Amelie said. "You have made yourself very clear indeed."

None of the vamps moved. It was like looking at a room full of pale, silent statues, but the hate in their eyes was like nothing Claire had ever seen before. No wonder Michael hadn't wanted Eve to stay. That kind of trapped fury didn't bother with fine distinctions, and there would be some in that mall who didn't care whom they killed . . . as long as they got to vent that rage on a human.

Just as the door closed, Claire heard Amelie say, soft as a whisper, "Don't worry. We will see you very soon."

The sunlight felt as cold as winter.

Shane was pacing near the cruiser, looking pale and agitated, and he was rubbing his arm as if it hurt him. He stopped and looked at them as Claire walked toward him. "What the hell happened?" He didn't wait for an answer, though; he grabbed Eve's other arm and helped to hold her up. "Dammit, Eve—"

"I want to go back," Eve said. She sounded odd and shaky. "They're going to kill all of them, I know they are, they're going to do something terrible to Michael. I have to go *back*." She tried to pull away, but Shane and Claire held on to her. Hannah opened the back door of the cruiser. She still wasn't looking at them— looking anywhere *but* at them, in fact. Her face could have been carved from stone. "Please, don't do this, Shane, please let me go—"

"You can't even come close to getting in there again and you know it," Shane said. "Eve. You *can't*, and Michael doesn't want you pulling something crazy like that. Come on."

He put her into the car and walked around to block her from sliding out the other door; Claire took the space on one side of Eve as he crowded in on the other. She wasn't fighting them, but she wasn't helping, either. *At least she's not angry,* Claire thought, but she wasn't sure that was an improvement. No tears, no yelling. Just this . . . silence.

And then there was Shane, still acting twitchy on Eve's left, frowning and rubbing his forearm and snapping, as Hannah took the driver's seat, "Can we just get the hell out of here already?"

That made Hannah give him a long glance in the mirror, but she started the engine. Shane's tense body language seemed to ease up a little as the car pulled away from the blank, brooding exterior of the mall. Bitter Creek was a good name for it, Claire thought. Definitely not a happy kind of place.

It worried her that she hadn't seen Myrnin at all.

THREE

Hannah took them home to the Glass House.

It looked different. And it wasn't just the time Claire had spent away from it that had made it that way. Someone had painted it. Done a good job, too—the exterior was a neat, sparkling white, instead of the faded, peeling mess that had been there before. The trim was a crisp dark blue. It looked almost respectable. The lawn was even neatly mowed.

"What the *hell?*" She blurted it out before she meant to, and sent Shane a disbelieving look. He sent it right back, amplified. So, he hadn't been on the work crew, then.

Neither had Eve, apparently, because she gulped, sat up straighter, and said, "Um, what is *that?*"

"The town funded a renewal program for all the remaining

Founder Houses," Hannah said. "To preserve our history. Don't tell me you're not pleased. It looks a hell of a lot better than the tumbledown mess it was before."

It did. The railings were straight, the warped boards had been replaced on the porch, and the windows actually sparkled. At the top of the peaked roof, a new weather vane in the shape of a sunrise (ugh) creaked and turned in the direction of the breeze, and as Hannah opened her car door, Claire heard the thin, whispering sound of wind chimes. Someone had mounted a set of them at the edge of the porch, along with a large potted plant that looked new and healthy.

The place was spiffy and pretty and not *theirs*.

"Tell me you didn't touch anything inside the house," Eve said. "Because I swear I'll cut somebody. We liked the house the way we left it! That is our home!" What she didn't say, but Claire thought she almost heard, was *It's Michael's home.* And her heart ached for him, and for Eve.

"Nobody went inside the house," Hannah assured them. "This was an exterior renovation project. I thought you'd be pleased."

"You could have asked first," Eve said, but after the initial shock, some of her dislike was fading. And yeah, the house *did* look fantastic—restored to all its old Victorian glory, neat and sound. Claire realized it only underscored how little they'd taken care of the place . . . but then, they'd had other priorities, like staying alive. And none of them was much on chores.

"Let's just get inside," Shane said. "Hey, Hannah? Tell the Daylighters not to do us any more favors. I don't want to owe them."

Hannah didn't comment on that. She just opened the back door of the cruiser, and Shane piled out, followed by Eve, and last of all, Claire.

Walking up the steps was a whole different experience. The paint was still new enough to make her dizzy, and its smell mingled with the aroma of fresh-cut grass and new plants in the warm desert air. "Guess we'll have to start watering the damn lawn now," Shane said, and fumbled for his keys. "So much easier to take care of when it was a wreck. Watch the paint on the door. I'm pretty sure it's still wet."

As Claire followed them over the threshold, she felt a shiver of power crawl over her . . . the house, waking up from a sleep, coming alive, welcoming them home. It felt like a fresh blast of cool air, and also, weirdly, like hands stroking her hair. She shut and double-locked the door—ingrained habit, in Morganville—and leaned against the wood to breathe in deeply.

Inside, it still smelled familiar. Old wood, dust, paper—not a clean smell, but a good one. The interior walls needed painting just as much as those outside had; they were smudged, scratched, and dented from hard use. None of the four of them was much on surface cleaning, and as Claire glanced into the side parlor, she saw that the oval coffee table—replaced relatively recently, after half their furniture had gotten smashed in a fight—had a blurring of dust over its surface. The old Victorian sofa looked as saggy and tired as ever.

Shane and Eve had already wandered off down the hall, Shane heading for the more modern, overstuffed couch in the living room and Eve's clunky boots echoing on the stairs that led up to their rooms. Claire went a few steps in, and just . . . stopped. She closed her eyes and felt a peculiar, warm kind of peace sink in.

Home.

She felt almost as if the house itself were saying it to her: *This is where you belong.* She remembered leaving here for her brief journey to MIT in the predawn darkness, carrying her bags down and trying not to wake up any of the others to let them know she was leaving. She remembered the feelings of excitement, of worry, of longing, of fear, of anguish . . . and of devastation.

It felt healing to be back.

It felt right.

"Claire?"

She opened her eyes. Shane was standing at the end of the hall, and his dark eyes were full of concern. She smiled at him and saw the tension ease. "I'm home," she said, and came into his arms. They closed around her, strong and warm. "I'm home, Shane. We're *home*."

"Yeah," he said, and let out a long, slow breath. "Home. But it's not exactly what we left behind, is it?"

"The house, or Morganville?"

"Either one."

"Seems the same in here."

"Not quite," he said. "Not without Michael."

He was right about that.

Eve didn't want to eat, but Shane found enough stuff in the kitchen to pull together a meal of spaghetti and meat sauce, although the meat sauce tasted suspiciously like it had a chili-type origin. Canned chili, at that. Eve forked it mechanically into her mouth, chewed and swallowed, which was about as much as Claire thought they could reasonably expect from her just now. She looked hollow-eyed and exhausted and just . . . empty.

Shane tried to ask her things that normally would have gotten a snappy Eve-style comeback, but she either ignored them or responded with shrugs, until he finally put down his fork and said, "So, Eve, what's your plan, then? Sit there and look sad and depressed until someone just feels so bad about your bruised little fee-fees that they give Michael back?"

"Screw you," she said. It sounded mechanical, but then a fire came on behind her eyes and started blazing hotter and hotter. "Seriously, man, *screw you.* How dare you?"

"How dare *you?*" he replied. "Because the Eve I know wouldn't just sit there and become the poster child for therapy. 'Ask your doctor today for Depressia, the drug that makes you not freaking care about anything.'"

"You think I don't care?" She stood up suddenly, fists clenched, and honestly, Claire thought Eve might lunge right across the table at him. Color was high and hot in Eve's cheeks, and she shook with fury. "How can you even think that, you jackhole? You're the one who walked out in the first place! And maybe if you'd helped me back there—"

"If I'd stayed in that mall, I would've started shit that would've got us all killed, and you know it," Shane said flatly, and Eve pulled in a sharp breath to retort, then let it out, slowly, without a reply. She stared at him for a long moment.

"What the hell is wrong with you?" she asked.

"I don't know," he said.

But he was lying, and Claire could see it; she could see that Eve did, too, and the two of them shared quick, confirming glances. His attention was fixed on Eve, and Claire quickly reached over, grabbed his arm, and pulled up the sleeve of his jeans jacket. It was the arm he'd kept rubbing earlier.

On it, she saw a vivid red scar in the shape of a bite. Healed, but inflamed, as if it was infected. "What is that?"

He yanked free of her, frowned, and pulled his sleeve back down to hide it. "Nothing."

"It's where the weird dog bit him," Eve said. "I remember. It was when you left that night. It wasn't normal, was it? Some kind of weirdo vamp dog."

"It wasn't a vampire dog."

"How do you know?"

"Because I just know. Because if it was some dog the vamps sent out to bite people, then I wouldn't want to kill *vamps*, would I?" Shane blurted out. He looked pale, suddenly, and a little shaky, and when he picked up his fork it rattled against the plate, so he dropped it again. "Look, it was all I could do to not go after them on the way back here from Cambridge. I couldn't even stand to be around Mikey in the van for long without wanting—wanting to go at him. Hurt him. But that was nothing to how it feels back here. And in the mall . . . it was too much. It was like I had to attack. Needed to rip them apart. And no, I don't know what it is, and yeah, I'm fucking afraid, okay? I'm *terrified*."

That left a ringing silence in the room. Eve opened her mouth again, closed it, and slowly sat down in her chair. Claire felt frozen in place, unable to think what to say. Her throat felt thick and tight, and she swallowed to clear it, then stretched out a hand toward him.

He flinched, but it was just a small move, not a real withdrawal. She rested her fingers gently on his shoulder, then stroked his hair. He felt hot, the way he had back at the mall. Feverish. "Shane, you're sick," she said. "Something happened to you. And we need to find out what it is and how to help you."

"Sick or not, at least I'm not the one locked in a cage with a shock collar around my neck," he said. "Eve's right. We can't leave him like that. I'll be okay."

"You're not," Eve said, and gave a bitter, brittle laugh. "Okay, none of us are okay. We need to do a lot of things, but first of all, Shane, we need to find out what's happening with you. I may be depressed, but at least I'm not Mr. McMurdery Wolfenstein." She paused for a second, and then shook her head. "Okay, I was about to say we should see if Myrnin knows what it could be, but . . . no. Can't go to any vampires, I suppose. Emergency room?"

"They won't know anything," Shane said. "But I know someone who does. Hannah. She was there when I was bitten. She said there were more dogs, more bites. She'd know something, anyway."

"I don't trust Hannah."

"No kidding. I don't, either, but it's not like we have a ton of options, Eve. I don't want to go save Michael and end up—doing something I'd regret. Which right now seems really likely. I nearly lost it back there. And I might do it again, and I swear to God I don't want to." His face tightened, and his eyes darkened until they looked almost black. "So if Hannah knows something about what's happening to me, then she's going to tell me."

That was ominous, and Claire's sense of disquiet grew stronger. "Shane, don't—"

He was already up from the table, with his plate and fork in his hand. It wasn't like him not to finish a meal, but there was still a small twisty mountain of spaghetti left when he carried it into the kitchen.

Eve pushed her food around some more and said, "Claire, we're in trouble. You know that, right?"

"Yes," Claire said. "Eat your spaghetti."

Eve obediently lifted a forkful to her mouth, chewed, and swallowed, then said, "You know I love you, but trust me, one thing your fancy Boston trip didn't teach that boy? How to make decent spaghetti sauce."

Eve's critiquing the food was, for some odd reason, funny, and Claire's breath hiccuped into a laugh that just kept going. And Eve started laughing, too. Shane slammed back through the kitchen doors and glared at them, which only made them keep helplessly, hopelessly giggling at the look on his face. "Sorry," Claire gasped.

"It's not funny."

"I know! But—the food—was—"

"Pretty bad." Shane's body language relaxed, just a little. "Yeah, I forgot the art of combining crappy ingredients into an awesome whole while I was off in Fancytown, didn't I?"

"Fancytown? You saw where I lived!" Her giggles finally dribbled away, but at least she was left with a happier afterglow than before. Eve managed another bite, for solidarity, probably.

"Good point." He sat down and leaned his elbows on the empty spot where his plate had been. "You guys need to keep a leash on me, okay? I don't think I can trust myself right now."

"An *actual* leash? Because I have one," Eve said. "It has spikes on the collar and everything."

"Been there," he said. "Remember?" And with a shock Claire did remember; it seemed like a long time ago now, but a wicked awful female vampire had once led him around on a leash at a party, and the memory of it still turned her stomach. And his. And Eve's, apparently, because she dropped her fork onto the plate, shoved the whole thing away, and rested her forehead on her palms.

"Sorry," she sighed. "Mine's more for recreational purposes anyway. I don't think it would do much to hold you back."

"Recreational—okay, freak, I don't even want to know that," Shane said. "Let's pretend that never happened. What I meant was, I'm counting on the two of you to check me if I'm heading for the cliff."

"Roger that," Eve said. "I'll T-bone your ass right off that course."

"Try not to break anything while you're at it."

"Like a nail?" She inspected her black-painted nails, which were looking a little ragged—not a lot of manicure time recently. "I see your point." Then she folded her hands and looked at him, with all the banter put aside. "What are we doing, then? Going to see Hannah, or not?"

"Going," Claire said. "But, Shane, you're not doing the talking. I am. Clear?"

"Clear," he said and nodded. "One request."

"What?"

"Can we stop for a burger? Because, seriously, I am starving."

Everything in Morganville, even the burger places, either had been given a face-lift or was in the process of getting one, and as Eve piloted her big black vintage hearse around the town, they spent a lot of time slowing down, gawking, and shaking their heads. "Wish I'd invested in the hardware store now," Shane said. "I'd be rolling in money just from paint sales." He was right about that. Almost every building had a gleaming new coat already or had people on ladders applying one. The few buildings that didn't had bright, fluttering orange stickers applied to them—either a sign that their paint jobs were on the way or that they were being fined for not having one.

"It's worse than that," Eve said, and pointed straight ahead. "Check out Dog King."

The Dog King was a relic from the 1950s, complete with vintage sign—a little drive-through hot dog and burger joint that had, at its best, looked sketchy, except for its totally awesome sign of a dachshund wearing a crown, a hot dog bun, and a cocky grin. Its leaning shack had been torn down and rebuilt as a shiny new store that was painted a very questionable teal blue. At least the sign hadn't been touched.

"Right, Dog King it is," Eve said, and turned into the newly paved driveway. It was still an order-at-the-window kind of place, so that hadn't changed, and she got a bag of mini-dogs and burgers and fries, sodas all around, and tossed the results at Shane and Claire to sort out as she piloted the beast of a car. Sharp turns were a thing the hearse wasn't great at doing, but she managed not to scrape any of the oh-so-new paint on the building, or the fence.

Claire was past noticing after that, because the hot dog she grabbed was melting in her mouth with deliciousness that totally erased the not-so-great chili spaghetti experiment. Two mini-dogs for Claire later, and two burgers that Shane practically inhaled, Eve was parking the car in front of the (not surprisingly) newly refurbished Morganville City Hall, where Chief Moses had her office. They sat in the parking lot and munched through the rest of the food, watching the foot traffic come and go.

"You seeing what I'm seeing?" Eve asked finally, as she crumpled up the last of the wrappers and three-pointed it into the bag that Shane held up for a basket.

"Morganville has never looked this good," he said. "It's like that old movie about the robot wives or the pod people or something. Seriously, look at the grass. It's actually green. And *even*."

"No, moron, I mean the pins. Lots of pins on cops." Eve pointed to an imaginary collar. "Daylight Foundation pins. If it gets any more popular, they'll put it on the freaking flag."

"Great," Shane said. "Everybody got pinned. We live in a giant evil frat house now."

The massive Gothic front of the building looked old, but it had been rebuilt fairly recently; the aging of the stone was done with sandblasting. Still, it looked broody and impressive, looming over them as they walked up to the big, heavy doors. Two cops lingering by the entrance gave the three of them cool, blank looks that were, well, pretty normal, actually. The police in town had never been friendly, especially toward Shane and Eve. One shrugged, though, and opened the door for them as they approached.

Both, Claire noticed, wore pins.

Inside, it was business as usual in Morganville—clerks bustling around, phones ringing, people standing in line for permits or tickets or whatever. But there was a difference, somehow; it was intangible, but there. Claire couldn't quite put her finger on *how* it felt wrong, or at least strange, but it had something to do with the overly friendly smiles, the happy tones of their voices.

"Someone's been spiking the Cheery Kool-Aid," Eve said.

"Think you mean *cherry*, slick."

"I meant *cheery*, dumbass. Try to keep up," Eve said, and gave Shane a shove on his shoulder. "Enough sightseeing. This is your show. Get it on the road."

He trudged up the steps leading to the second floor, went down the hall, and opened the door that led to Hannah Moses's office. Not the office she had once, briefly, occupied as mayor; this one had a harassed-looking female cop sitting behind a desk working a multi-button phone. She shot them an irritated glance as the three of them stepped in. She hit the HOLD button and said, "Chief Moses isn't seeing anyone today. She's in meetings."

"Can you tell her it's Shane Collins?"

"I don't care who you are. She's *busy.*"

Shane leaned both hands on the officer's desk. "Tell her it's about my dog bite. I think I might be rabid."

There was something in his face that convinced the woman. She frowned, stared him down for a few seconds, then hit another button on her phone and said, "Yes, I need you in the office, please. Thank you."

"Excellent," Shane said. "We'll be right over here." He walked to a small line of guest chairs. Claire took one, with Eve beside her, while Shane flipped through an assortment of ragged magazines . . . and then the door opened.

It wasn't Chief Moses. It was, instead, the biggest, most muscle-bound policeman Claire had ever seen. Broader and taller than Shane.

His gaze fixed immediately on the officer behind the desk. "You got some kind of trouble here?" he asked. She merely pointed over her shoulder at Shane and kept talking to whatever constituent was on the phone at the moment.

"Crap," Eve said. "Um . . . guys?"

It was too late. The officer was lumbering over, and Shane was standing up, fast, dropping his magazine to the floor. "I think there's some misunderstanding," he said. "Because I didn't ask for Officer Friendly. I asked for—"

That was as far as he got before the cop grabbed his shoulder, spun him around, and pressed him flat against the wall, rattling the bland artwork hanging there. "Shut up," he said, and reached for handcuffs.

"You mean, I have a right to be silent? How about my right to an attorney, do I have that? Ouch. Look, you haven't done this before, have you? Let me help you out—"

"Shut up, smart-ass. You're creating a disturbance."

"I just want to see Chief Moses!"

"Chief Moses is busy. You get to see me instead."

"Should we be doing something?" Eve asked Claire, who was still sitting frozen in her chair. "Because I'm kinda used to Shane being arrested, but this seems wrong. And weren't you going to ask the questions?"

Claire snapped herself out of the feeling of unreality that had settled over her, and stood up. Officer Friendly's (the name really did fit him) eyes flicked over to scan her, then dismissed her.

She tried anyway. "Sir, we know Hannah Moses. She wouldn't want you to do this. We only need to ask her some questions. Important questions."

The lady on the phone, who had just finished her call and finally replaced the receiver, rolled her eyes. "Yeah. About a dog bite."

Oddly enough, that stopped Officer Friendly for a couple of seconds, and then he grabbed Shane by the shoulder, turned him around to face him, and said, "You got bit by a dog?" It was said with both concern and eagerness, such a weird combination that Claire couldn't quite wrap her head around it. Neither could Shane, by his expression. "When?"

Shane managed to shrug, despite the handcuffs and the grip on his shoulder. "A while back."

The cop turned Claire's boyfriend back around, skinned up one of Shane's sleeves, got nothing, and tried the other. He stared at the ruddy scar for a second, then took out his keys and unlocked the handcuffs. "Sorry, kid," he said. "I'll get the chief. Have a seat."

Just like that, he left. All of them—even the officer/receptionist—looked silently confused, and it lasted for a full minute until the frosted-glass door opened again to admit Hannah Moses.

"Sorry," the lady behind the desk said, "but this young man was very insistent—"

Hannah ignored her. She walked to Shane, grabbed his arm—the correct one—and looked at the scar. "Dammit," she said. "Come with me, all of you."

She led them into her office, where she slammed and locked the door behind them.

"I just—," Shane began, but then she held up one finger to stop him, went behind her desk, and opened a drawer. She flipped some kind of switch, then nodded. "What is that, spy crap?" Shane asked.

"Spy crap," she affirmed, and sat down in the wheeled office chair. "I knew you'd been bitten, but in the press of everything else, it slipped my mind. I'm sorry. What kind of aftereffects are you feeling?"

"Hang on a minute. Who the hell is trying to listen in on *you*? All the vamps are back there not shopping at the mall," Eve said. "Unless . . . you don't trust your shiny new boss. I think he *is* your new boss, right? Fallon the Fanatic?"

Hannah didn't answer that. She just fixed Shane with that steady look and waited until he said, "The bite's feeling pretty weird, actually. Not so bad when I left Morganville, but it flared up on the road, and got worse when I came home. It started small, sort of like an ache in my arm, but then I started feeling this . . . urge."

"An urge to hunt vampires. Fight them. Kill them," Hannah said. "Which is why you left the mall so suddenly. You couldn't control it anymore."

"Yeah," he said. "It felt like something was taking me over, and I didn't like it. Still don't. Look, I'm not saying I'm some vampire groupie or anything, but I don't *hate* hate them, not like I used to do. Not like my dad did." It was unusual, Claire thought, for Shane to look like this—helpless. Lost. "I just don't know what I'm *doing*. I only know I don't want to."

"Hannah . . ." Claire sank down in one of the visitor chairs and leaned forward, staring at the chief. "Please tell us what's going on. Please. We need to know."

Hannah looked away, as if she was composing herself for a moment, and then she nodded. "The Daylight Foundation has been conducting research for a long time," she said. "It's an old organization, very old, though they've only recently come out of hiding. They conducted cutting-edge genetics experiments; some worked, some didn't. Some ended up creating things they found useful."

"Like the devil dogs," Shane said. "Like the one that bit me that night."

"The dogs were part of Fallon's advance team," Hannah said. "He'd seen an opening, with Oliver's exile from Morganville. He thought there was enough unrest, given what had just happened, to depose Amelie from her position. And he was right, damn him. He was dead right."

"But—I thought you were—" Eve pointed to the Daylighters pin on Hannah's collar.

For answer, Hannah unbuttoned the crisply starched sleeve of her uniform shirt and rolled it up, revealing a jagged bite mark that looked every bit as inflamed and angry as the one Shane had been hiding. "Some of us don't have a choice," she said. "Either I'm his hunting dog or I'm his dog handler. He keeps the instincts in check with a medication he gives me. Without that, I'm just another one of the pack." She nodded at Shane as she refastened her sleeve buttons. "Like you, kid."

"Wait a second, I'm not part of any—"

"No?" Hannah cocked her head at him. "Only because Fallon hasn't bothered to make use of you yet. He hasn't needed to. But he will, Shane. He certainly did me, and others."

"How many others?" Eve asked. "And what do you mean, exactly, about him *making use* of them? Because if there's anything I hate more than vamp mind control, it's mind control by somebody who isn't a vamp."

Hannah's dark eyes flashed toward her, suddenly hot with anger that had, Claire realized, been simmering under the surface the whole time. "You've got no idea," she said. "I just got my life back from one vampire's mind games, and now to have this son of a bitch doing this. . . . You think I don't hate it? Don't want to rip his head off? Fact is, I can't. I can't even raise a hand to him. It's part of the—the programming." The woman was generally so controlled that it took Claire aback, seeing her lose it even that small amount. There was a tremendous tide of rage under that surface of calm. Rage and frustration.

"How many?" Shane asked. "In the pack?"

"Six," Hannah said. "Including you and me. I don't know if we were just unlucky, or if somehow those dogs of his were programmed to target specific individuals. I'd like to think he picked us because . . . because we're the ones most capable of fighting him, as humans."

Shane swallowed hard. "Yeah, I'll do my best to take it as a compliment," he said. "But how do I handle this? What do I do?"

"Stay away from vampires," she said. "Which ought to be pretty easy to do, now that they're in the enclave—and yes, I hate using that word. But if you feel a surge of what you felt back there, you'll know he's activated you for a hunt. Once that happens . . . once that happens, you won't be yourself."

"What do you mean, 'won't be himself'?" Claire asked, but Hannah just shook her head and changed the subject.

"Eve, I'm keeping an eye on Michael, I promise you that. I am trying to make sure they all stay safe. Right now, the best way to do that is to keep them confined and compliant."

"Are you still Captain Obvious?" Eve asked. "Which side are you on? Because I don't get you, Hannah. I really don't."

"Captain Obvious won," Hannah said. "That's the problem— none of us really thought about what we'd do if we managed to defeat the vampires and take control. We never thought about what we would do with them—what kind of future they'd have. So in a certain sense, I no longer get myself anymore." She seemed sad about it, and angry, and there was a moment of silence before she continued. "Now, all of you, please go home. Shane, there's nothing that can be done about what you're feeling, but if you find yourself struggling, just—stay as far from any vampires as you can. That will help."

Shane leaned on her desktop and looked her straight in the eye this time. "Why does he need a pack of people pre-programmed to hunt down vampires, Hannah?"

"For strays," she said. "Not all the vampires are going to stay in the mall. Eventually, they'll get out, and he will need to track them down. That's where you—where *we*—come in."

That was the end of the meeting. She crossed to the door, opened it, and there didn't seem to be any choice but to leave, with Officer Friendly scowling at them from the outer office. The receptionist ignored them with stubborn intensity as she answered more calls ... and then they were out in the hall, and Shane was restlessly rubbing his arm and looking more disturbed than ever.

"Did that help?" Claire asked him. He shook his head.

Eve said, "At least we know he's not the only crazy one in town. Come on, Dog Soldier. Let's go."

They spent about an hour cruising Morganville, noting the changes. A lot of it was cosmetic—buildings painted, roads repaired. But there were also new places going up all over town, and it was Shane who pointed out the Daylighters symbol that was cropping up on nearly all the business signs or store windows. As if they were proudly saying, *No vampires allowed.*

But oddest of all were the people. So many Morganville natives out and about, walking, chatting, taking their kids to the small municipal park. Shopping. It looked so damn normal that it gave Claire the creeps, because their body language was completely different now. It wasn't the Morganville she'd gotten so used to seeing; that much was certain. Where before, people had walked with a kind of guarded, reflexive awareness of what was around them, these folks were almost giddy about *not* looking paranoid. Oblivious. Safe.

It was an improvement, she knew that; people felt happy and safe—their smiles just radiated it. *But then why do I feel so bad?* Claire was afraid that maybe she just didn't want change, even change for the better. But that wasn't it; she'd rolled with a lot of changes in Morganville thus far.

This was something deeper, and more disturbing.

They just want the vampires gone. They don't care how it happens. So all those happy smiles, they were the smiles of the winners of a very long, slow, quiet war. The dead weren't around to bother their consciences. Whatever Fallon did, he would do offstage, in the dark, and they'd never have to confront any of it.

Claire knew it wasn't maybe rational to want to save the vampires; after all, they'd been the bogeymen under Morganville's bed for generations, and they'd been responsible for so many bad things. But *individual* vampires had been responsible. Wasn't blaming an entire group for the acts of a few wrong?

Does that make me the villain now? She wondered that with a chill, left out from the smiles, the warmth, the camaraderie. The all-human, all-new Morganville. *Am I the one who's going to be responsible for ruining everything for these people?*

She found herself holding Shane's hand as they drove around. His skin still felt hot, and she wondered if maybe Hannah was wrong—if his bite could be infected, not just . . . engineered that way. Maybe he just needed antibiotics. They ended up facing supernatural weirdness so often, it was easy to forget that plain old bacteria could screw up a person just as much.

When she proposed that they stop in at the hospital, though, he rejected that out of hand. "Not worth it," he said. "I'm okay, Claire. Really." He wasn't. But she didn't push him, because she knew it wouldn't help.

Eve pulled the hearse up the drive and around to the back of the house, into their small, rickety shed/garage, which was not really big enough for it. Michael had remote-parked his vampmobile—

provided by Morganville free of charge to all the vampires, in the until recently days—since Eve's hearse had heavy vampire tinting on the back windows where he could shelter when he needed to. None of the rest of them could drive Michael's car, anyway, because of the thick black windshield and windows, so for now, best they left it where it was, parked underground beneath Founder's Square.

But not seeing Michael's car here, wedged in beside Eve's . . . it just seemed significant. And it made Claire shiver to think it might never be parked here again.

Coming in through the kitchen reminded her that they hadn't properly cleaned up from the Great Spaghetti Disaster, but she didn't care just now, and clearly, neither did Shane or Eve, who ignored the destruction on their way through. She followed. They both went upstairs. At the top, Eve opened the door of the room she now shared with Michael, looked in, and was still for a moment before she said, "I'm going to get online and see what I can find out." Then she went in and quietly shut the door behind her.

Shane stood for a few seconds, his head down, and then said, "I need a shower. See you in a few, okay?"

"Okay," Claire said. She wished he would have said something else, something more significant, but she also understood the need to be alone. Eve was walling herself off so she could both work through how she was feeling and do something productive. Shane . . . well, obviously, he needed to think, too.

And all of them needed showers, that was true. Self-evidently, aromatically true.

She went to her bedroom and sat down on the bed. The familiar creak of the springs made her feel at home, but most of her stuff was still stuck back in Cambridge. She would need to figure that out eventually, she supposed. Need to think how to get her clothes back, and her books, and all the photos she'd taken with her.

She hadn't taken everything, at least; there were still a few pairs of underwear, a bra that had seen better days, a couple of pairs of jeans, and some older shirts. She assembled an outfit from the slim choices, then dug a pair of sheets out of the linen closet in the hall and put them on the bed—more for something to do than any intent to sleep.

When all that was done, she stretched out on the bed and listened to the sound of the shower running. When it stopped, she gathered up her things and waited at the door. Shane appeared there after a few minutes, wrapped in a towel that showed a blindingly gorgeous span of chest and shoulders, and rode low enough on his hips to make her helplessly fill in the rest of the information in a rush of memory. She pulled in a sharp, needy breath as he pushed his damp hair back from his face and gave her a smile. "What?" he asked.

"I—my turn." She felt the color in her cheeks, and knew it was ridiculous, but she couldn't help it. This . . . *this* felt like coming home, this sweet tension that suddenly pulled between them, a gravity that it was so easy to obey. Despite everything, all the insanity and fear and general weirdness of Morganville, they had *this*, and it was torturously beautiful.

He cleared his throat and moved out of the way for her—but not far enough that they didn't brush against each other as they passed. "See you when you get out?" He made it a question.

"Maybe." She raised her eyebrows, and saw the answering spark in his eyes.

"You're killing me."

"You deserve it, don't you?"

That got her a pants-melting smile. "Most likely."

She shut the door on him and leaned against it, suddenly and wonderfully short of breath, and it took her a moment before she could push away, put down her clothes, and start stripping for the shower.

It was still warm and steamy when she got in, and she used Eve's herb-scented shampoo and body wash, then—with all appropriate mental prayers for forgiveness—borrowed Eve's razor, too, because the state of her legs and underarms was especially bad. The water began to run cold by the time she was done, so she rinsed her hair and scrubbed soap off quickly, then ducked, shivering, out into the cooler air.

After drying herself off, she combed her wet hair back and contemplated the pile of sad clothing she'd brought in with her.

Then she wrapped the towel around her body and carried the stack back into her bedroom instead of putting it on.

It didn't really surprise her to find Shane there, sitting on the edge of the bed and still in his own towel. But it did feel good. Really, really good. She put her things on the bare top of the dresser and pretended not to notice him as she put the clothes away again.

"Really?" he said. "That's what you're going with in this situation? Ignore me?"

"Absolutely," she said. "At least until I do this."

She walked over and shut the door, and locked it, just in case . . . Well, just in case. Then she turned, leaned against it, and looked at him.

"Oh," he said.

"So," Claire said.

"Uh-huh."

"You're sitting on my bed."

"Yes."

"Wearing a towel."

"Apparently so."

"And . . . nothing else."

"Why, do you have on long underwear under yours?"

"No."

"Prove it."

"You first." She took a step closer and folded her arms.

"Why me?"

"You started it." Another step forward. She didn't consciously plan it, but it seemed like the world had tilted itself toward him. The floor was sloping. Not at all her fault, really, that she was moving in his direction. She could feel the air changing around her. Growing warmer.

"I think you actually started it, stalking me outside the bathroom door," Shane said. He had that look in his half-closed eyes, that unmistakable, intent expression that made her skin feel too tight on her body, made all the heat snapping in the air between them draw in and down and glow golden inside her. "So you first, then."

"I'll make you a deal," she said. One more step forward, one she didn't consciously even take. Her knees were brushing his now, and it wasn't possible for the brushing of *knees* to be sexy, was it, except it was, it was, and her heart was thundering inside her chest now, flooding her body with tingles and pulses like starlight. "I'll help you take that off if you help me with mine."

He pretended to consider it, but he wasn't fooling her, not at all, not even a little. This was a game, one that was lazy on the surface and full of tension underneath. What was it Eve had said to her once? *Restraint is the sexiest.* At the time, Claire had thought she meant it in the ropes-and-handcuffs sense, but now she was starting to realize that it meant something else entirely.

It meant enjoying the anticipation.

Shane reached out and put his hands on the outside of her legs, just above the knee. Just about where the towel ended. Then he slowly slid them up to about mid-thigh, and she could feel the warm ghosts left by his palms. The rest of her shivered in response, and she bit her lip.

His eyes widened, and his smile took on a wicked slant. The room seemed so quiet, except for the soft rasp of their breathing, the whisper of the towels moving.

She reached out and tugged on the fabric around him, and at the same moment he closed his hands on the hem of her covering and pulled.

And then she was falling, falling, falling into his arms, into a bright and burning fire that only blazed hotter as their bare, damp skin met . . . and then their lips, in an explosion of need and want and desire.

And for a while, anyway, in the breathless brush of his skin on hers, in the deep and perfect whispers, she forgot about Morganville.

She forgot about everything.

Claire woke from a sleep so deep and contented that it was like floating on clouds. She became aware of the world around her gradually—the sunlight striping over her bare leg, and the rustle of leaves on the old post oak tree outside her bedroom window. She felt warm and heavy and perfectly *home*.

She turned her head, and saw Shane was still sleeping beside her, and she rolled toward him. He murmured something and put his arms around her, but it was more reflex than conscious action, at least until she kissed him. Then the mumbling became a low sound in the back of his throat, almost a purr, and his hand ran slowly down her spine, fingers brushing over each and every bump.

"Well," he said, when there was space enough between them for words, "that's a pretty nice start to a day. God, is it morning? How much morning?"

"Um . . . eight thirty of morning."

"Breakfast?" He sounded hopeful. The whole world sounded hopeful, at least for the moment, and she laughed and kissed him again and sat up. The clothes she'd gathered to put on last night were in the drawer, so she got them out and put them on, glancing behind her as she zipped her jeans to see him noting the *lack* of his clothes on the floor. After a sigh, he picked up the towel, wrapped and tucked it, and kissed her on the way to the door. "Back in a minute."

The locked door ruined his suave exit for a few seconds, but he managed, and Claire sat down on the bed to pull on her shoes. The good feeling was still there, bubbling and humming, but real life started bearing down, too. . . . And the shadows, though driven out by the morning sun, were slowly taking hold.

She ran a brush through her hair, which needed it badly, and dashed into the bathroom to scrub her face, brush her teeth, and take care of normal bathroom business. By the time she was done, Shane was in the hall, waiting, dressed in comfortably loose jeans and a Transformers tee about two washes away from dissolving into rags. "Eve's downstairs," he said, and there was something unhappy in his voice. "You'd better talk to her."

That . . . didn't sound so good, and Claire hurried down the steps even before he'd shut the bathroom door.

She found Eve in the kitchen, standing at the sink, gulping down the last of a gigantic cup of coffee from a black mug with red skulls on it. Eve had gone full Goth today: black cargo pants; heavy, thick-soled boots; a tight dark red shirt with bright red crossbones over the heart, like a pirate's badge. A thick choker of chain links, shining with silver plate. Equally thick silver bracelets on both wrists. She'd put reddish streaks in her black hair and twisted it back into a bun, into which she'd thrust silver chopsticks—although they were rather pointier than normal chopsticks. Her makeup was more like a mask—rice-powder pale, with vivid red eye shadow and plenty of liner.

She had a heavy backpack leaning next to her feet.

"So let me guess. . . . You're going jogging?" Claire said, and opened the cabinets to pull out her own coffee mug. It was one Shane had found for her, with strange little aliens on it. She edged past Eve to take the coffeepot from the burner, and poured. Then she held the remainder out silently, and Eve just as silently extended her cup. It filled her cup only a quarter of the way. Claire put her cup aside and tackled the coffeemaker, trying to seem as normal and domestic as possible. "You look awesomely Gothic today."

Eve nodded.

"Going somewhere?"

"I'm going to the mall," she said. "And I'm going to get Michael out."

Claire filled the water reservoir, replaced the filter, and spooned in more ground coffee. "I see you've totally thought out your plan, which obviously involves getting the support of your best friends before tearing out to get yourself killed."

Eve gave her a scorching look, made all the more effective by the war paint. "I'm not taking any more crap from the Daylighters.

We tried talking it out. Talking got me five minutes of face time with *my own husband*, who doesn't deserve any of this. I'm done with the subtle approach. This time I'm not taking no for an answer— and don't try to talk me out of it, Claire, because you don't know how this feels. We just got Michael out of a cage back in Cambridge, and now he's—he's just in a bigger cage, held by the same people who want to hurt him. I can't stand it, and I *won't* stand it."

The passion in her voice, and the determination, was scary. Claire swallowed hard and tried to concentrate on what she was doing with her hands—*swing the door shut with the coffee, put the pot back in place, press the brew control*—and it did help slow her down and keep her voice rational as she replied, "I didn't say you had to, did I? I just said you should involve us."

"So you can talk me out of it?"

"So I can make sure you don't *die*, Eve. Because Michael doesn't deserve having to deal with that, does he? He doesn't deserve to see you hurt, or killed, because of him. You know he'd tell you the same thing: be smart, and be careful. Pick the battle you can win." She held Eve's stare, hard as it was. "Tell me if I'm wrong."

She knew she wasn't, and so did Eve, who changed course. "Look, I'm not some fragile flower everybody has to shelter all the time. I may not be as much of a total-destruction mayhem machine as Shane, but I can wreak havoc when I want." She paused for a second, distracted. "Why is it you can only wreak *havoc*, anyway? Why not, I don't know, *world peace?*"

"Good question."

Eve shook a finger at her. "Don't you try to throw me off, CB. My point is, I'm strong even if I'm on my own."

"I know. But you have to admit, we're all much stronger if we stick together." Claire risked a quick grin. "Besides, why should you have all the fun?"

"If by fun you mean total war, you might have a point. It is a little selfish not to share. Because I intend to unleash hell if anybody even thinks of telling me that Michael can't walk out of there," Eve said.

She drained the quarter cup of coffee, and Claire noticed she was drinking it black. That, for Eve, was kind of a danger sign; her coffee preferences varied by her mood, and black was her hard-core extreme. Claire added cream and sugar to her own, stirred, and blew on it to cool it before tasting. Anything to kill a little more time.

"What about the rest of them?" Claire asked. "Amelie. Myrnin. Even Oliver. Do they deserve to be trapped in there with shock collars on their necks? God, you saw the place. That's not a prison, it's—it's a holding pen."

Eve stopped, eyes widening. "Holding pen for what?"

"God. I don't even want to guess. The Daylighters want vampires dead, right? Abominations against nature, and all that. They've never made any secret of it, never mind what Fallon says about it. He's the face guy, the one who makes everybody feel better about herding people into *enclaves*."

"They've got plenty of support, too," Eve pointed out. "I think that now that the vamps have been shuffled offstage, nobody's going to think much about what happens to them, as long as they don't have to watch it happen. Even then, I'm not sure that most of them wouldn't simply justify the hell out of it."

Claire shivered. Eve was right about that. Human nature was all about shifting blame . . . and responsibility. How else could you explain concentration camps and genocide and all the awful things people did to each other every day? They just carried on with life and pretended that the evil didn't exist, as long as it was happening out of their direct view.

Morganville's human population wasn't any different. Didn't really matter if something was right, as long as it was of material benefit and it happened to someone they hated.

"You think they'll kill them?" Claire asked.

"Don't you?" Eve took a larger gulp of her coffee. "Screw that. I'm not going to be a bystander, wringing my hands. I'm doing something. Right now. You guys can jump in, or stay out. Either way."

"Hang on, didn't I say we were coming?" Claire said. "You know Shane would never avoid a good fight, and I'm not going to turn my back on this, either. But let's be smart about it, okay? That means thinking through it. Calmly."

"I'm so done with calm," Eve said. She dumped the rest of her coffee in the sink, put the cup down with a clatter, and hauled the backpack up to rest on her shoulder. "Diplomacy is your crack, Claire. It isn't mine. I'm more of a straight-ahead kind of girl, and right now, I'm going right into their faces. With my *fist*."

Claire sighed. She chugged the rest of her coffee, even though it was too hot and too bitter, and rinsed the cups. The spaghetti dinner remains were still crusted up on plates, and she dumped those all in and ran hot water with a spray of soap. Just in case they didn't die and might need something to eat off of later.

"Let me get my stuff," she said. "Don't go without me."

"Five minutes," Eve said. "Then I'm out."

"Promise."

Claire took the stairs two at a time, and ran into Shane sitting at the top; he'd clearly been listening. They exchanged a look, and he grabbed her hand. "I want to help," he said. "I do, you know that. But if I go back there . . . Shit, Claire, I don't know what would happen. No, actually, the problem is that I do know exactly what would happen, and it wouldn't help either one of you."

She bent and kissed him, very lightly. "Then stay here," she said. "But I have to go with her and try to stop her from doing something crazy. You know I do."

"Can't we just knock her over the head and dump her in a closet until she cools off?" His jaw was tight, his dark eyes fierce, but he wasn't angry with her. It was all directed inward, at his own problems. "I feel crap useless right now, you know? And sick of being somebody else's butt-puppet."

"Seriously? Butt-puppet?"

"Seems appropriate."

"Then fix it," she said. "Shane, I know you. You're smart. Think how you can use this, not let it use you."

He laughed a little, and it sounded raw, but real. "You're way too good for me, you know that?"

She put his hand against her cheek and smiled. "I know. Got to go gear up—" She realized, too late, that all her gear was *gone*. Even her backpack was missing now, because it had been towed away by the cops with the vans. "Um . . . right. I assume you've got some good stuff tucked away?"

"Me?" Shane stood up in one smooth, fluid movement, and for a moment she felt that gravitational shift again, pulling her in. "You know me. I'm a Boy Scout. Always prepared."

"Show me your goodies, then," Claire said, and caught herself in a laugh. "By which I mean—"

"I know what you mean," he said, and leaned in very close to whisper in her ear. "Though if you've got a few minutes—"

She shivered, tempted in some utterly instinct-driven part of her, but she shook her head. "Later," she said, just as softly. "Why are we whispering?"

"Because it turns you on?"

"Oh, and it doesn't you? Because that's a little obvious."

He cleared his throat and stepped back, held his hands palm out in surrender, and said, in a normal tone of voice, "Okay, then, armory it is. Buzz killer."

She smacked him on the arm, which of course did absolutely nothing except hurt her own palm, and followed him down the hallway to his room.

"Wow," she said as he swung the door open. "I thought you moved out when you followed me."

"I did," he said. "This is what I didn't take with me."

What he hadn't taken was pretty much a complete room, right down to the twisted sheets still on the bed. Clothes in the closet. Much-abused cross-trainers and heavy work boots piled in the corner. Shane went to a chest in the corner and pulled open the first drawer.

"Have at it," he said. "See, want, take."

Shane was a slob in his room—seriously—but in the way he kept and stored his weapons, he was meticulous. The top drawer held silver things—chains, jewelry, weapons. Claire took a silver-coated dagger, chains for her throat and wrists, and skipped the rest. He closed that drawer and went down one, revealing a selection of guns that, even given that they lived in Texas, was probably excessive. She shook her head. He raised his eyebrows, but went down another drawer.

Crossbow. She liked that. It was one of the small, light ones, easy to aim and with surprising power, and she grabbed the bolts that went with it.

"Can I interest you in an honest-to-God army flak jacket?" he asked, and kicked the bottom drawer. "Guaranteed effective, but it'd probably be way too big for you. Plus, it's not exactly easy to get up if you go down. Sort of the overturned-turtle problem. Matching helmet, though, so at least you look cool while you're flopping around helplessly getting murdered."

She shook her head. He stepped forward, took her head between his big, warm hands, and tilted her chin up so that their eyes met. "You need to figure out how to stop her from doing this, you know?"

"I know," she said. "I'd just rather be fully armed while I do it. In case."

He kissed her, very gently. "I've got your back. Way back, obviously. Just—don't ask me to go too close to the vamps right now, okay? Including Michael. I don't want to hurt him." He meant that, she knew it—for all that had happened between them, all the strangeness, he and Michael were at heart brothers and best friends, and always would be.

Without Shane, Claire knew that stopping Eve—not to mention protecting her—would be severely challenging; Eve was a madwoman when she was determined about something, and she was never more determined about anything than about Michael.

They were going to need help. Without Hannah on their side, and with the vampires out of reach, Claire tried to imagine who might be willing and able to jump . . . and failed, at least until she felt a small shiver of air press by her and was reminded of something.

"Shane," she said, "have you seen Miranda since we got back?"

The Glass House was complicated. It wasn't *just* a house, and hadn't been for a long time. It had a certain power to it, a certain sentience that Claire couldn't explain, except that it must have come from what Myrnin did to the town to make it safe for the vampires. The thirteen original Founder Houses had all been linked—a kind of active transportation and defensive network that Claire couldn't define, still, as anything but magical. Few of those remained now, but the Glass House was the first, and still the strongest. It had the capability of doing crazy stuff, but the most striking was that it could choose to save people who died within its walls. Michael, at first. Then Claire, briefly. And most recently, teen psychic Miranda, who had sacrificed herself so that Claire could live.

But Miranda, already psychic before her death, had powers that the rest of them didn't have; her abilities allowed her to go outside of the walls of the house, and sustain herself in real human form out there, too. But she still lived here—was trapped here, in a very real sense, because she couldn't stay away indefinitely.

Shane was shaking his head. "No. Haven't seen the kid, which is weird. Should have thought about her earlier, but she just kind of keeps to herself."

"I think she might be useful," Claire said. "And besides, she's probably lonely, don't you think?"

"Lonely isn't the worst problem someone in Morganville can have. But check the third floor. She made that her space up there after you left."

The third floor didn't exist. Shane was referring to a secret room in the attic—one with a hidden door off the main second-floor hall. A room Claire hadn't been in for some time . . . but it made sense that Miranda would find it cozy. After all, she could, when she wanted, ghost in and out without making any sound at all—and it was a cool, if creepy, place. Just the thing for a teen who was more than a little creepy herself at the best of times.

"Be right back," she said, and went to the area of the wall outside his room where the secret door was concealed. She knew how to open it, and after a couple of false starts, she got the paneling to move. It creaked, of course. That was almost certainly required. "Miranda? Mir, are you there?"

A light shone at the top of the steep, narrow steps leading up. As the door swung shut behind her, Claire ascended, and as she got to the top she came out into a room she hardly recognized. The Victorian furniture was still in place, and all the stained-glass heavy lamps, but the walls had been covered over with posters—movies, bands, games (and most of it Claire wouldn't be ashamed to have on her own walls). The old rugs had been rolled up and put away, and the floor was a shining, polished brown now. There was a brand-new table on the far side of the room, with a flat-screen TV hooked up to a game console. And an antique chest that Claire thought must have been dragged out of storage in the attic; it was open, and clothes spilled out of it, mostly dark in color and old in style.

Miranda was on the couch, hands folded on her stomach as she stared up at the ceiling. She was a small, thin girl, dressed in black that echoed Eve's clothing choices. And to be honest, she looked more dead than alive.

Claire frowned and stopped where she was. "Miranda? Are you okay?"

"Go away," Miranda said.

That wasn't normal. "You're not okay."

Miranda cracked one eye to stare at her. "I'm *bored*. Do you know what's going on?"

"Um . . . I'm not sure. There are a lot of things that could fit that definition."

"Here! In *Morganville!*" Miranda sat up and swung her legs down to glare full force. "They rounded up the vampires and put them in a prison. Did you know? Where have you been? Everybody took off and left me and I didn't know what to do! I didn't even know if I was supposed to do anything at all!"

"I'm sorry," Claire said. She sat down next to Miranda and put her arm around the girl; Mir felt solid, warm, alive, and well. She wasn't, of course, but she could seem eerily real within the Glass House. "I'm sorry. We didn't mean to abandon you. It's just—things happened."

"They happened here, too. It's like people just—went crazy, you know? First the vampires just . . . I don't know, it was like they just surrendered, and then Morganville changed. It wasn't safe out there anymore for me. These people, these Daylight people, they—they scare me." Miranda shivered harder, and Claire rubbed her arm in a futile attempt to make her feel better. "I'm scared to leave the house. It all feels so wrong out there. It's so *quiet*."

"Well, we're back," Claire said. "And trust me, it's not going to be quiet much longer. Have you been up here the whole time?"

"Mostly," Miranda said. "The Daylighters tried to come inside while you were gone. I kept them out, and then Father Joe from the church came to warn me. He told me to stay off the streets. They were hunting down anything that wasn't strictly, completely human—that's where the vampires went. I can vanish, but he was worried they might still be able to get to me." She shook her head. "Claire, when they were in the house—I heard one of them say that if they wanted to really cleanse the town, they needed to destroy all the Founder Houses. There was an argument, but it sounded like he was winning when they left. Do you think they'd do that? Try to destroy us?"

If the Daylighters really wanted to get rid of all of the nonhuman, supernatural elements of Morganville, then they were going to *have* to go after the Founder Houses. Claire was a little surprised she hadn't already thought about it. The house could defend against most intruders, but it couldn't defend itself against fire, or wrecking crews. And that made her feel frantic, deep down inside. *No, you won't,* she thought fiercely. *You won't destroy our home.*

"When did Father Joe come to see you?"

"I don't know. It's hard to tell." Miranda, it was true, didn't pay much attention to days and nights, and certainly not if she'd been hiding out here in Amelie's safe room with no windows or clocks. "A few days, maybe?"

"When did they come into the house to search it?" Claire asked. "Please, *think!*"

"Yesterday," Miranda said. "Yesterday early. I felt the sun coming up." As ghosts did. Their lives were tied to sunrises and sunsets.

"Why didn't you come down and tell us?"

Miranda looked away, and her voice got very small. "Because you left me," she said. "You all left me here. *Alone.*"

It was hard to remember sometimes how young she was, until she said something like that. "You were sulking."

"No, I wasn't!"

"Mir."

Her shoulders rose and fell, just a little. "Maybe."

"Miranda, if the Daylighters decide to tear the house down . . ."

"I go with it," Miranda said, and met Claire's eyes again. "You think I don't know that? But the vampires aren't here to help you do anything now. How are you going to stop them?"

"I don't know yet, but we will," Claire said. She heard the strength in her voice, and it surprised her. "*We* will, and that means you, too. No more sulking. We're going to need your help."

Miranda nodded. "Just tell me what I can do."

"We're having a house meeting downstairs, right now. And I guess we have to tell Eve her suicide mission's off, if she wants to have a house to come back to later."

"She's not going to be happy," Miranda observed.

Man, was she right about that.

FOUR

Eve was, to put it mildly, pissed off, to the point that Claire thought for a second she was going to slug someone—probably Claire herself—and charge out the door. But she was also a Glass House resident, and she knew what Miranda was saying. She knew the danger.

"You're not just making this up to keep me here?" she demanded, still standing at the back door with her backpack on her shoulder. Miranda shifted and looked scared, but Claire put a hand on her shoulder to keep her steady. "Oh, relax, kid, I'm not going to bite. She's really serious? They might try to tear down our house?" That last was directed at Claire, and at Shane, standing on the other side of the room. Shane, arms folded, just shrugged.

"Can we afford to think she isn't?" he asked. "Look, Claire was all ready to go. Crossbow packed and everything. But you know this is more important. This house—" He fell silent for a second, looking down at his feet. "This house is our home. And we have a responsibility to keep it safe, for Michael. If they're coming back here, then we have to make sure they get a fight when they do. You know that's true, Eve. We fight for each other, and we fight for this house. Against vampires, humans, anybody and everybody. That's how it's always been."

Eve let out a long, slow breath, closed her eyes, and nodded. Her shoulders sagged, and she let the backpack slip off to clunk heavily on the floor. "Michael would never forgive me if I dragged you all off to rescue him and we came back to a smoking hole in the ground," she said. "But that doesn't mean I have to like it."

"You wouldn't be Eve if you did," Shane assured her. "C'mon, a little perimeter defense planning will cheer you right up, I promise. I'll even let you hold the flamethrower."

Claire turned to Miranda and said, "Do you think you're strong enough now to go out again?"

Miranda nodded eagerly—so eagerly she was almost bouncing in place. "What do you want me to do?"

"I need you to do a little spy work for us," Claire said. "Since you're so good at being invisible. The Daylight Foundation seems to be behind all of this urban renewal we've got, so they'd be the ones to make a plan for demolition, too, wouldn't they?"

"I guess."

"Go to their headquarters and see if there's something you can find that tells us when they plan to tear down the house."

That made Miranda take a step back. "I can't."

"You just said—"

"I *can't!*" Miranda shouted over her, and then her voice dropped almost to a whisper. "I've tried, okay? I can't get close to it. It hurts, and I start—I start unraveling. It's like—it's like there's no air in there. I can't go in."

She was shaking, just thinking about it, and Claire put her arm around the girl. Her skin felt cold under Claire's palm, and she grabbed the afghan from the back of the couch to drape over Miranda's shoulders. *I'm trying to warm up a ghost.* It did seem silly once she thought about it, but still, the kid was cold, and distressed.

"So, obviously, Miranda's not going to be able to do our sleuthing for us," Eve said. "Um, question. Aren't we overreacting? Didn't they just finish repainting our house? Why would they decide to tear it down after all that work?"

Miranda raised her hand slowly. "I know that one," she said. "The people who were here, the ones who did all the painting and stuff . . . they were from the city council. The new mayor lady was with them. It was the Daylighters who got upset because I threw them out of the house when they tried to get inside. And it's the Daylighters who want to tear the house down. Not the mayor. I think she likes the house."

"So—we see the mayor," Eve said. "Get her to stop Fallon."

"Do you really think she can?" Shane asked. "I like Ramos, but this is Fallon we're talking about. He wrangled the frickin' *vampires.* The Daylighters were killing people in Boston; they won't mess around here, either. If the mayor goes up against the Daylighters, she won't live through her term."

That was depressingly true, Claire thought. "We need to find out if they have real plans to tear down our house," she said. "For Miranda's sake, if nothing else—she can't run. She can't survive if the Glass House goes away." That was a nightmare they all felt in their bones. They'd seen it happen to Michael when the house had caught on fire. He would have burned with it.

"I can go to City Hall," Miranda offered. "Jenna could take me there. I could see if they've got anything on file. Maybe there's a permit? They seem to like permits and things. They even had one to fix up the outside of the house." By Jenna, she meant Jenna Clark—a newcomer to Morganville, once host of the reality show *After Death*. A genuine psychic, one who'd stirred the lingering ghosts of Morganville into solid activity with her arrival . . . and had ended up showing Miranda how to survive outside of the Glass House's restrictions.

"Jenna didn't leave town?" Claire felt oddly surprised by that; she'd thought that Jenna would have moved on after realizing the danger that Morganville constantly represented. She didn't *have* to stay. "Why would she do that?"

"She kind of started dating this guy," Miranda said. "Rad, the mechanic. And I think she liked it here. She bought a house and everything."

"Then could you please go to Jenna and see if she'll take you to City Hall? But be careful. Don't get caught, whatever you do." Miranda, after all, could turn invisible . . . but Jenna couldn't. The plan had the added safety of Jenna driving, so there would be a quick escape handy in case something went wrong. And from Claire's experience with Morganville, things did go wrong. Frequently.

Miranda nodded. She'd gone, in those few moments, from a scared girl to a bravely confident young woman. It made Claire sad that she would never see Miranda truly grow up, that the girl was stuck at the age she was now, unable to move either forward into death or backward into human form. But at least she was conscious and—at least mostly—alive, even if her life came with strings and restrictions. And for the first time in her life, Miranda seemed . . . happy. Stressed, at the moment, but happy to be wanted, worthwhile, and part of the Glass House gang.

Putting her at risk should have been a harder decision, and Claire felt guilty about it, but she also knew it had to be done. Claire had been in danger regularly, from the first day she set foot inside these walls; it was part of what it meant to live here. Part of being with people who cared enough to take risks.

"Can you get to Jenna's on your own?" Claire asked.

"I think so."

"Okay, then go. We're going to start making sure the house is safe while you're gone."

"Good," Miranda said, "because I love the house. I love you guys, too." She looked directly at Claire when she said it, and Claire hugged her, hard. The girl felt cool and bony, but very real.

"Be safe," she said. "Come back soon. I'll call Jenna to let her know you're on your way."

Eve hugged the girl, too. Shane didn't, but Miranda was shy around him, and always had been. She just nodded, and he nodded back in that laconic tough-guy way, and then she was just . . . gone. Dissolved into the air.

Unsettling, no matter how many times they'd seen it happen.

Claire picked up the house phone—it still worked, even though she didn't imagine any of them had bothered with bills for a while now—and dialed Jenna's cell, which they'd scrawled on the wall next to the phone in grease marker. It was a messy version of a contact list, but it worked in a pinch. She filled the other woman in when she picked up, and Jenna seemed happy to help out.

She hung up the phone and turned to the other two. "Well?" she asked. "What now?"

"Land mines in the flower beds?" Shane asked. "Also, we could replace that picket fence with razor wire. Maybe electrified."

"Be serious."

"Why do you think I'm not?"

Claire rolled her eyes and looked at Eve. "How about you?"

"What's the easiest way to bring down a house like this?" Eve asked. It was a surprisingly practical question—and a chilling one when Claire thought more about it.

"Fire," she said. It had been tried before. The Glass House was old wood, and however alive it had become, however self-aware, it couldn't control how flammable it was. Not for long, anyway. The old wooden structure, the bones of it, was its weakest link. "If they don't want to have a whole construction crew out here to demo the place, they'll just set it on fire. Arson."

Eve nodded. "We can spray fire retardant on the house. Don't know where we'd get it, though."

"Rad has some," Shane said, in a much more serious tone than before. When they looked at him, he shrugged. "Dude likes to set himself on fire. He's training to be a stuntman since he gave up his mixed martial arts dreams."

"I knew that guy was insane," Eve said. "Okay, then, we hijack Rad's stash. What else do we need?"

"Fire extinguishers," Claire said. "That should help with the whole arson risk. I'm not sure how we defend against a bulldozer, though, if they decide to knock the whole house down." She held up a finger as Shane opened his mouth. "Do *not* say flamethrowers, or anything to do with dynamite." He closed it without speaking.

"We need to know what exactly they're planning to do," Eve said, and took in a deep breath. "I'll go to the Daylight Foundation."

"How do you plan on finding anything out there? With the power of your awesomeness?" Shane asked. "I'm not making light of your awesomeness. But it lacks the stopping power of, say, a .357."

"Not all of us need weapons," Eve said. "Some of us have charm."

It was the way she said it that made Claire's skin go tight and prickly, and she leveled a stare at her best friend. "No," she said. "You're not even."

"Not even what?"

"Going to run off with some crazy plan to—what? Make Fallon tell you what he's going to do with the Glass House?"

"Why not? He thinks I'm a hysterical little girl. He treats me like I'm a china doll," Eve said. She'd taken one of the sharpened chopsticks out of her hair and was restlessly scraping the wood of the table with it. Half of her sloppy hairdo came down. "You think I can't charm it out of him, and make him let Michael go at the same time?"

"I think you'll get yourself killed," Shane said quietly. "Or worse."

"What's worse?"

"Don't know," he said. "But these guys are the worst kind of bastards—the smooth kind. The ones who seem like they're nice and polite and kind and doing it all for the right reasons. The ones who make you feel like the villain for not going along with it. And I don't know what Fallon's really capable of doing. Do you?"

He was right, and it was sobering. Eve frowned, but she didn't argue. She just yanked the other chopstick out, twisted her hair back into shape, and stabbed the sticks through it again to hold it up. Mostly. The frown stayed, and from the flinty look in her eyes, the subject was closed. She wouldn't debate it, but she also wasn't going to change her mind.

Claire sighed. "Much as I love listening to you two snipe at each other all day, we have actual problems to solve. I'm going to get fire extinguishers, and when I get back, Shane, you can go get the fire retardant stuff from Rad. Eve—" She hesitated, then shook her head. "Whatever you plan to do, I know we can't stop you. But be careful. We're one 911 text away, and don't you hesitate to yell for help if it starts looking the least bit weird."

"I know," Eve said. She lifted the backpack to her shoulder. "I will."

Shane couldn't resist the dig. "I thought you said not all of us needed weapons."

"I don't *need* them," Eve said. "But I'm not crazy, either. Banzai, bitches."

She slammed the door behind her, and Claire sucked in a deep breath as she locked eyes with Shane.

"Guess there's no chance of going back to bed," he said. "Because being in bed this morning? That was *really* nice." It sounded plaintive. She absolutely agreed with that.

She went to him and kissed him—and it felt sweet and warm-verging-on-hot, and even a little desperate. "Later," she promised him. "I'll go get the fire extinguishers. It shouldn't take too long, so please try not to get into any trouble until I get back."

"There are times when I wish you were slightly less practical, do you know that?"

"God," she sighed. "Me, too."

Splitting off from Shane and Eve felt weird. Eve had taken the hearse, which left Claire suddenly worried about how she was going to haul a buttload of fire extinguishers back from Morganville's local knockoff version of a Home Depot. But then Shane, at the last minute, dashed off and came back with a set of car keys and a note. "Here," he said. "Go see Rad. He's got my time-share car at his lot. Tell him I'll be by later for the other stuff, so he can get it all together."

"You're sure he'll actually give me your car?"

"Don't let him bullshit you into thinking I owe him money. I don't. The agreement is I get the car when I want it, and he drives it when I don't. It's how I worked off all the extra stuff he put into it. But be careful. It's a whole lot of car, little lady."

"Funny," she said, in a tone that indicated it was not, and kissed him quickly on her way out the door.

She jogged part of the way, just to enjoy the exercise, and the strange fact that people were out on their lawns, waving hello, smiling and cheerful. Morganville had always been exciting, but she couldn't say it had always been *friendly*, and this made an unexpectedly nice change. When she stopped, out of breath, she ended up talking to the postal worker delivering mail, and a couple of passing strangers.

Just like a normal town. Which was so not normal.

I'm going to ruin it, she thought, and that horrible feeling swept through her again, that awful knowledge that even if what she was doing felt right, it might be very wrong. But she couldn't just . . . do nothing.

Maybe there was no right side, but she knew one thing: letting the Daylighters win had to be the worse of two bad choices.

It didn't take long to arrive at Rad's motorcycle shop, which also doubled as a mechanic's shop. The bikes he sold were generally tricked out and customized, though he had a few consumer base models for variety, and in the back he had a line of cars in various stages of disrepair, and a few that he kept under dust covers.

One of those, Claire knew, was Shane's. His time-share, as he liked to call it. She recognized the shape under the canvas cover.

Rad was sitting behind his battered desk in the office, feet up, sunglasses on. He was a massive guy, tattooed and bare-armed to show them off, and with the glasses blocking out his eyes he looked the exact opposite of all the friendly faces she'd seen coming here. Old Morganville in the flesh. He gave her a nod, put his boots on the floor, and said, "Hey, Claire. Long time no see around here."

"Not that long."

"Seems that way." He shrugged. "Lot's changed since you left town, and that's a fact."

"Not around your lot so much."

"I see what you did there, with the wordplay," he said and crossed his arms. "I never liked the damn vampires, and I'm glad to see 'em gone. I never made any secret of that. The new administration seems like it's got it going on." He was, she felt, trying to find out where she stood. She didn't have the inclination to debate it, or the time.

"I just came to pick up Shane's car," she said. "He gave me the keys."

"He still—"

"He also said to tell you he doesn't owe you anything, so don't try it."

She handed over the note, and he read it; his teeth showed briefly, and they were surprisingly straight and clean. "Yeah, okay, can't blame a guy for trying to make a buck. Got about a half a tank left, so it's good to go. I'll take the cover off for you."

"Shane'll be by later," she said. "He, ah, needs to borrow fire retardant from you. Well, not borrow so much as maybe use it all up. But we'll pay you back."

"Oh, that sounds just great. Can't wait to have that conversation. You know, every time I have anything to do with you guys, I end up in a fight somewhere down the line, and I'm really trying to cut down. Anger management and all that crap. Hey, I got a girlfriend now and she doesn't like it when I get into trouble."

"Does she like it when you set yourself on fire?"

He considered that. "Fair point. I guess I could give up the foam. What do you want it for?"

"I'd . . . rather not tell you. I promise, we're not looking for a fight," Claire said. "But people may be coming for us, and we have to fight back, don't we?"

"Sure," Rad agreed. "No crime in that. Some of my best fights were self-defense." He flexed his muscles a little bit, but it wasn't as if he was trying to show off, more like he was just remembering the good times. Claire supposed Rad would have a top ten list of his best fights. She'd actually be surprised if Shane didn't, too, and if some of them didn't match up with Rad's list, only on opposite sides. "Okay, I'll hold my grudges against Shane, not you. You're too pretty, anyway. Let's get you the car."

He led her out to the back, which was a dry, cracked dirt lot with occasional struggling weeds poking up through the hard ground; the weeds looked as dry as the dirt they were breaking through. Most had burrs, so Claire was careful to avoid them as she helped Rad untie the canvas and fold it back in sharp, dust-raising snaps until it was a neat square that he tucked under his arm.

He stepped back to admire the car. "Love this damn beast," he said. "Your boyfriend has damn good taste in wheels."

It was a muscle car of some kind, all matte black, with murdered-out wheels and some shiny chrome here and there, just for emphasis. It did look powerful, and intimidating. Claire slid behind the wheel into the shiny leather seat and had to immediately rack it forward four notches so her feet could meet the pedals.

Pedals, not just plural, but triple. Gas, brake, and clutch. She'd had lessons in driving a stick shift, but that had been ... a while ago. And she'd had her dad coaching her patiently through the process. Plus, that had been a nice, tame small car, not Shane's Detroit-built monster.

She took a deep breath and went through the steps, just as she remembered them. She fumbled the shift from reverse to first, and winced at the grinding of gears; she saw Rad shake his head sadly from where he stood leaning against the wall. That stiffened her resolve, and she accelerated out fast, hitting second gear before she'd reached the end of the lot. She shifted hard enough to scratch rubber.

It felt good. So did seeing the surprised look on Rad's face. She gave him a quick, jaunty little wave out the window, which was risky but worth it, and she was in third before she hit the end of the block, roaring through a green light and heading for Macom Hardware.

The parking lot was full, which was a very odd sight; she couldn't remember ever seeing a business with that many customers in town, and yet there they were, whole families out in the daytime, pushing carts into the store, chatting on their cells, living a ... normal life. She found a spot and shut off the low, growling engine, but she couldn't quite bring herself to get out of the car just yet. She felt displaced, and sad. If she, Shane, and Eve succeeded in freeing the vampires, these same smiling, happy people would go back to being exactly what they were before—scared and anxious, afraid to leave their homes for anything but necessity, afraid to let their kids run and play. Afraid for a good reason.

How could she really want to bring that *back*?

But what other choice did she have?

It took her a good minute to get herself together, grab her wallet, and walk into the store. She got a shopping cart from the small remaining selection—of course it was the one with the wobbly left wheel—and headed for the back corner of the store, where she remembered seeing fire extinguishers. It wasn't easy; Macom's wasn't built for heavy customer flow, and it was a little like playing one of those traffic games, where one block had to move for another to pass. Fifteen minutes and several apologies later, Claire finally spotted the red cylinders in the corner, and parked her cart as much out of the way as possible while she loaded them into it. There were six on display, and she took all of them. Next to them was a box of strange-looking oval things, but it had the words FIRE SUPPRESSION GRENADES on it, and that was something she thought Shane would love.

It wasn't much of a line of defense, but it was pretty much all she could see, given the limited selection available, though on an impulse she grabbed boxes of preloaded rock salt rounds for their shotgun. Not that she *wouldn't* shoot someone trying to burn their house down, but she'd rather not shoot them into the hospital, or the graveyard. These might be people she knew, people she cared about, and she couldn't be their enemy.

Even if she was, at least for now, their villain.

Twenty minutes more to maneuver to the register and check out, and then another five to load everything in the car. Five more minutes of powering the Beast (that was what she decided to call Shane's car) down the surprisingly busy streets toward the Glass House.

When she got there, Shane was sitting on the front porch in

the sun-faded rocking chair that Eve had put out there, half as a joke because none of them were porch-sitting people—and he had a shotgun.

Two uniformed police officers were standing on the steps. The tall blond woman had her hand on her gun, but she hadn't drawn it; her male partner, also tall, but skeletally thin, hadn't bothered with his sidearm. He was leaning on the railing and trying to look casual.

In that, Claire supposed he was trying to match Shane, who had broken open the barrel of the shotgun, taken out the rounds, and was cleaning it. She smelled the gun oil as she parked the Beast in the driveway, and instead of unloading the car, she grabbed the box of rock salt shells and walked up the path. The female officer immediately pivoted to watch her with cool, analytical eyes and a blank expression, but she moved aside to let Claire come up the steps.

"Thanks for letting me borrow the car," she said, and leaned over to kiss Shane on the cheek as if the cops weren't there. "I brought you a present."

"Varmint rounds. Cool. Plenty of varmints around these days." He opened the box, took some out, and began slotting them into the breech of the shotgun. Then he flipped it shut and racked a round, while staring at the cops. Well. That escalated fast.

"I'm sorry, I guess I didn't get the memo—are we having problems here?" Claire smiled as winningly as she could at the male policeman. His name was Charlie, she remembered—Charlie Kentworth. "Officer Kentworth, how are you? Is there something wrong?"

"We just wanted to come in for a minute, but Mr. Collins here didn't seem too keen on the idea," Charlie said. "I thought we could have a nice civilized chat, but seems like I interrupted his weekly shotgun cleaning."

"Well, you know, a man's got to have routines," Shane said. "Cheer up, Charlie, at least it's only rock salt. It'll only damage your dignity. Might not even break the skin." The smiles they exchanged were pure challenge, and Claire resisted the urge to roll her eyes. It definitely wasn't the time.

"Sorry, why did you want to come in? Not that we don't love visitors, Officer Kentworth. Just that I only got back in town yesterday, and I'm still getting settled in." She switched gears and looked at the woman with him. "I don't think we've met before." She offered her hand, but the police officer didn't move to take it.

"Officer Halling," the woman said.

"That's your first name?" Shane asked. "Officer?"

"It is as far as you're concerned." The woman hadn't taken her hand off the butt of her gun, and as she shifted position, Claire's eyes were drawn to the flash of gold on her collar: the Daylight Foundation pin. "We've had a report that you keep illegal weapons in your home. We'd like your permission to conduct a search of the premises."

"I thought that they issued warrants for things like that," Shane said, and ran the oiled cloth he held over the shotgun as if he didn't have a care in the world—and as if he didn't, in fact, have things inside the house that would get him arrested. "I mean, they did when the bloodsuckers ran things around here. I'd think we'd have a little more due process with humans in charge, right?"

"Are you saying you won't let us inside?" Officer Halling said. Her eyes were a peculiarly cold shade of storm blue, and although there was nothing to show it in her body language Claire had a premonition that she was really, really angry. There was no way to guess why. Maybe she was just an angry person, generally.

"That's what I'm saying," Shane said. "Michael Glass owns this house, and since he's been put in your fancy new *enclave*, I guess I have to do what I think he'd want, which is say no. Claire?"

She nodded. "Come back with a warrant," she said. "That's not too much to ask, is it?"

"No," Halling said. "It's not. We'll be back soon."

"Well, you know where to find us," Shane said, with a wildly sweet smile, as he put the shotgun casually on his shoulder. "Laters."

"Sorry about the trouble," Kentworth said, and Claire got the sense he was embarrassed by his partner's antagonistic edge. "You two . . . I know it sounds like a cliché, but please don't leave town."

"Why would we? We're Morganville residents. We live here," Claire said.

Halling made a noise in the back of her throat that wasn't *quite* a growl, and led the way back to the police cruiser. Shane sat in the rocker, looking for all the world as if he might fall asleep, he was so relaxed—at least until the cruiser turned the far corner.

Then he came up out of the rocker like someone had set it on fire. "You got the extinguishers?" he asked, setting the shotgun aside.

"In the car. What was all that about?"

"I have no idea, but I'm getting the strong idea that we're just not wanted around here anymore, Claire. And I don't know why, because we're just so *charming*."

"Well, you are," she said, and kissed him lightly. "Come on, help me get it all inside."

He carried an armload of the extinguishers, while she snagged the last couple and the box. They dumped the lot in the front parlor, raising a faint cloud of dust from the old cushions of the couch, and Claire waved it away, coughing.

"What—" Shane's attention was riveted on the box she'd put down, and before she could even begin to answer, he was ripping into it, looking as thrilled as if it were magically Christmas. "Do you know what these are? Do you?"

"Some kind of weird grenades," she said. "Don't get too excited. I don't think they explode or anything."

"These are *excellent*. You arm them and throw them into the fire. If it isn't too big, it'll explode into a powder that puts the fire right out." He grabbed her and kissed her. "You brought me *grenades*. You are officially the best girlfriend ever."

"I'm the most worried girlfriend ever," she said. "Because this is getting a little too crazy. The cops? Really? And you decided to clean the shotgun to, what, intimidate them?"

"C'mon, this is rural Texas. Shotguns are as normal as garden gnomes. Besides, that gun oil really stinks up the house."

"So do your shoes, but I don't see you leaving them outside."

"Did Eve text you that joke? Because it sounded like her."

"She's been tutoring me," Claire said, and stood back from him a little, because being so close to him made it harder to be logical. He had that effect on her. "Do we need to put anything in the pantry room?" The pantry room was a hidden room just off the kitchen, behind shelves of ancient canned goods. It was basically just a dirt room, windowless, that had almost certainly been used for visiting vampires from time to time, or for even less savory things, but it was safe enough for storage.

"Now that you mention it, I have a bag full of stuff that might do well in there," he agreed. "You know, my sparkly unicorn collection. They'd probably jail me on general principles for that."

"I'm serious!"

"Me, too. I would never joke about sparkly unicorns." He held up a hand to stop her from getting irritated. "Okay, yes, I will hide all the stuff that needs hiding. Give me fifteen minutes, and then I'll head out to grab the stuff from Rad. Though, damn, *grenades*. Not sure we need much more than that. They might even make good offensive weapons."

"But they only blow out powder, right?"

"If I throw it at somebody and yell 'Grenade!' I'm willing to bet they'd duck anyway. At the very least, it would be hilarious."

"Until they shot you."

"Well. Yeah. That might not be as funny."

One more kiss, and Shane was off. It took him less than fifteen minutes to gather things into a giant duffel bag, which he dragged downstairs and into the kitchen. She heard him stashing it in the dirt pantry room, and went to double-check that he hadn't left any telltale traces on the floor, but he'd swept up neatly, and if she hadn't known about the secret room she'd never have guessed it was there.

Another minute and Shane was gone to get the fire retardant stuff from Rad. He sternly told her to lock up behind him—as if she ever forgot, in Morganville. The Beast roared off down the street, and a profound silence settled over the Glass House. It was rare that she was alone in the place; there was almost always someone else to talk to, or at least to be aware of in another room. But it seemed calm, quiet and peaceful.

"We'll take care of you," Claire said to the house, her face tilted up to the ceiling. She patted the wall. "Don't worry. We won't let anything happen to you."

The air around her immediately warmed, as if she'd stepped

into a patch of bright sunlight. It was the Glass House's equivalent of a hug, and she smiled and picked up the first two fire extinguishers to carry them upstairs. She stationed one in Michael and Eve's room and one in her own—opposite ends of the hall, and they could cover most anything from there. The rest were distributed downstairs, where she thought any kind of arson would probably start. Their enemies had once tried to burn the place down with well-placed Molotov cocktails, and now she made sure that no window was more than a few steps from a fire extinguisher.

Then she set the grenades out, scattering them around to be sure they were all within easy reach.

She was setting out the last few when she heard the crisp sound of a knock—loud, authoritative, nothing tentative about it. Definitely not Shane, and she wasn't expecting any visitors.

Claire slipped one of the extinguisher grenades in her jacket pocket and went downstairs to check the peephole in the door.

Officer Kentworth was back. Officer Halling was with him, and so was a plainclothes man that Claire recognized as Detective Simonds. From everything she'd heard about him, he was a nice enough guy—and a good investigator. She wasn't sure whether that last part was a good thing just now.

She opened the door and held on to it, blocking the entrance. "Officers?"

"Miss Danvers," Detective Simonds said, and gave her a pleasant smile. "Mind if we come in?"

"No offense, sir, but I'd rather wait until my friends are back if you don't mind."

"No offense taken, but I'm sorry to say that was just a courtesy question." He slipped a piece of paper out of his jacket pocket and handed it to her. "This is a warrant from a judge allowing us to search this house for illegal weapons."

Well, it wasn't unexpected, but it still felt bad. Claire swallowed hard, but she stepped back and opened the door wider for them. As the three cops walked in, she felt the temperature in the hallway start to chill down. So much for the warm hugs. The house was picking up on her uneasiness, and it had never liked uninvited guests.

"Kentworth, check upstairs," Simonds said. "Halling, this floor and the basement. Miss Danvers, how about you make me a cup of coffee in the kitchen and we sit and talk a minute."

"Sure," she said. Her heart was pounding, and she hoped that she didn't look as guilty as she felt. "Follow me."

She led him through the living room and through the kitchen door, and wished she'd grabbed a hoodie to put on over what she was wearing because the house felt positively icy now. She could almost see her breath. Simonds, wearing a light jacket suitable for the hot sun of Morganville, was shivering. "Damn," he said. "You sure like to keep it chilly in here. Your electric bills must be insane."

"Not really," she said. "I think the house is just really well insulated." She turned on the coffeemaker and did all the little things necessary to make it go. They waited in silence while it wheezed and steamed and filled the carafe, and then she filled two mugs, put milk and sugar on the table, and dosed her own mug in silence.

Simonds sipped his black coffee, made a polite lie about how good it was, and added a splash of milk. He stirred for an inordinately long time, and he kept watching her. Not actively intimidating, like Halling, but very, very observant. "Let's cut to the chase,

Claire—may I call you Claire?" She nodded silently. "Morganville got a makeover while you were gone, no doubt about that. I know there are a lot of things different about it, and you're probably not feeling too good about them right now. But I promise you, it's all for the best. You believe me?"

"Not really," she said, and took a careful sip from her own mug. "I don't trust Mr. Fallon, and I don't trust the Daylight Foundation, either."

"Why not?" he asked. Interesting that he wasn't wearing a pin, she thought, but he might have taken it off just to lull her into a false sense of security. "I honestly want to know, Claire. I'm not just shining you on."

"Because I've seen what they're capable of doing," she said. "The problem with fighting monsters is that you can become a monster by convincing yourself anything goes. Evil for evil. I've seen it, sir. I've seen them murder people for their own beliefs. And I won't be a part of that."

He looked thoughtful, and grave, and they sat in silence for a moment before he shook his head. "I can't speak to that," he said. "But I can tell you that from the moment the Daylight Foundation arrived in Morganville, they had a plan, and they did nothing but help those in need. You say they're willing to kill, but they didn't even kill the vampires—in fact, Mr. Fallon went out of his way to ensure that they were treated well. Maybe you've seen bad things they've done, but I've seen things too—good things. I can walk down these streets in peace. That has to count for something."

"It does," she admitted. "But there are a few hundred vampires trapped in that mall on the edge of town, and they can't stay there forever. What do you think the Daylighters intend to do with them long term?"

"Fallon says he's going to make sure they're safe, and I believe him," Simonds said. "Look, I worked with some vampires, and they were good people—okay, blood drinkers, but they never hurt anybody. In fact, the ones I worked with sometimes put their lives on the line to save regular people. I know vampires aren't just monsters; they can be good or bad, just like us. But fact is, they're not *natural*, and a good percentage of them don't have any kind of conscience. You can't argue with that."

She couldn't. She knew a lot of the vamps were dangerous; some were outright awful and needed to be locked up forever. Some were self-interested to a sociopathic degree, and many of them wouldn't see much wrong with killing someone who was in their way. Vampires didn't become vampires by being squeamish . . . or selfless.

But that didn't mean they deserved death. And she suspected— no, really, she *knew*—that ultimately that was the answer Fallon had. Death. Ridding the world of vampires forever—and everything supernatural, like the Founder Houses. Like Miranda.

"You want some more coffee?" Claire asked. He'd drained his cup quickly. Simonds nodded, his expression still and unreadable. He had a nice face, long and thin, with a smooth dark chocolate skin tone and warm brown eyes, and under other circumstances he might have been a friend.

But not now.

She filled his mug again, and realized that she'd been avoiding looking at the kitchen pantry. That was probably the kind of giveaway he was watching for, she thought, so she put the coffeepot back on the burner, walked to the pantry, opened it, and got out another bag of coffee beans. She put it up in the cabinet above the coffeemaker.

"How old is this house?" he asked her. She could hear rummaging upstairs now—Kentworth, going through her bedroom. Claire felt an angry flush in her cheeks, and sat down hard in her chair to clutch her coffee mug. She didn't like the idea of someone pawing through her things, meager as they might be. And ridiculously, she hated the idea of him seeing the still-messy bed where she and Shane had spent the night. That felt really intrusive and creepy. "This is one of the Founder Houses, right?"

"One of the original thirteen," she said. "I think only a few of them are still left now."

"Beautiful place," he said. "All original construction?"

She immediately felt as if a trap was looming, and covered her pause with a sip of coffee. "No idea," she said with a smile. "I haven't been here that long, you know." She knew that people tended to underestimate her—she was small, and young, and could look very innocent when she wanted to . . . and Simonds didn't know her very well.

But she could tell that he wasn't buying it, and as he opened his mouth to ask her something else, probably something a lot more intrusive, he was interrupted by Halling's sharp voice on the other side of the kitchen door. "Detective! Better come see this!"

He got to his feet fast, the friendly surface of him immediately gone; what was left was all serious business. He pointed at her. "Stay here," he said, and shoved through the door to join Officer Halling. There was muffled conversation. Claire tried to listen, but she couldn't quite make anything out . . . and then she heard his footsteps coming back and she retreated fast, to stand next to the kitchen table.

Simonds shoved the door open and gestured for her to join him. She didn't like the grim look on his face—not at all.

Halling had found something in the basement. As Simonds led the way down the narrow steps into the chilly concrete room where they kept the washer and dryer and the dust-shrouded shelves of storage from generations back, Claire's mind raced. What could they have forgotten? Shane and Eve were both known to stash things and forget them; what if Shane had overlooked a cache of weapons he'd meant to hide? That wouldn't be good.

And then she spotted what Halling had found. It wasn't weapons.

There was a dead body on the floor of their basement.

It was one of the mall cops that had let them in to see Michael. There was a knife sticking out of his chest, a silver-coated one— and it looked familiar. They had lots of those around the house; Shane silver-plated everything for use as anti-vamp weapons.

Claire stopped on the steps and grabbed for the handrail; she felt light-headed, and suddenly needed to sit down and just *breathe*. It seemed impossible. It *was* impossible. How in the hell had this man gotten here, gotten in, been killed? She hadn't done it, and she knew Shane and Eve hadn't. Couldn't have.

"He wasn't killed here. There's not enough blood," Halling said, crouching down next to the corpse. The man's eyes were open and covered with a gray film, and he looked unreal, like a department store dummy. "He'd been dead a few hours, at most."

"Find out how long he's been missing," Simonds said. "And make sure the other guards on the vampires at the mall are still safe. Go!"

Halling headed for the stairs, and Claire scrambled out of the way as the officer's long legs pushed past. She felt sick and weightless, as if she were falling into an endless black hole. What the hell was going on?

She took out her phone as Simonds moved to inspect the body, and quietly texted Shane not to come home. He sent back a question mark. She replied with an exclamation point, and then quickly put the phone away before Simonds caught sight of it.

"Do you know this man?" he asked her. She shook her head.

"I've seen him," she said. "I saw him at the mall, where they were keeping the vampires. But I don't *know* him."

"Any explanation for why he'd be dead in your basement, Miss Danvers?"

She could only shake her head again. She didn't have any idea what else to say. Simonds sighed, stood up, and took out his cell phone to make a call. He requested additional units, and a forensic kit—Morganville wasn't big enough to have an actual forensic *team*—and then looked up at her. He seemed sorry, she thought. But not very.

"Stand up," he told her. "Come down to the floor."

She did stand up, but in that moment she realized that if she let him arrest her, she'd have no chance at all to clear herself. Fallon might well have arranged this—a plot to put them all behind bars and get them out of his way.

She couldn't take that chance.

"I'm sorry," she said. She reached in her pocket and brought out the round shape in her pocket. She yanked the pull ring and tossed the thing down the stairs toward where he stood. "Grenade!"

Shane was right. Nobody waited to see what happened when they heard that word.

She dashed up the steps, and hit the door at the top just as there was a muffled *whump* below. She looked down to see a cloud of thick white powder spreading over everything, as if she'd thrown a giant bag of flour. Simonds, who'd taken cover at the far end of the basement in a crouch behind an old freezer, coughed and fanned the air as the stuff settled on him.

He was okay.

"Danvers!" he yelled, and drew his pistol from under his coat as he swiped at his face to clear his eyes. "Stop where you are!"

She was committed now, and she ran.

The house slammed and locked the basement door for her; she headed toward the front door, but heard footsteps ahead—one of the other cops. It didn't really matter which anymore; either one would probably shoot her as a fleeing suspect.

She crashed through the kitchen door, heading straight for the back entrance; it flew open ahead of her, and she felt a giant shove at her back as if the house itself was *pushing* her out.

She felt the bullet pass by her before she actually heard the shot. It was a tiny shock wave beside her waist, close enough that it left her feeling scorched.

The door slammed behind her and locked tight before the officer—whichever one it was—could draw a bead for a second shot.

She tumbled down the steps and rolled to her feet, then ran for the back fence. She knew it was wobbly at the corner, and she shoved it out, then squeezed through into the narrow, dirty alley. A lady watering plants in another yard gaped at her, and asked her something in a sharp, urgent voice, but Claire didn't pause.

She just ran.

She made it as far as the end of the alley before a police cruiser blocked her off with a burst of flashing lights and a sharp blare of siren. Claire skidded to a halt, backpedaled, and turned to flee the other way, but it was cut off, too.

A dusty Detective Simonds was squeezing through the hole in

the fence, and he had his gun aimed right at her. "Stop," he said. "Claire, don't make this ugly. You've got nowhere to go."

He was right. It could only go wrong now.

She put her hands up.

"Walk to the fence. Lean against it, hands above your head."

She thought she was going to be sick, but she did it, and he at least warned her before he put his hands on her and began patting her down for any weapons. She answered his questions about concealed weapons and sharp objects without really noting what she said; her mind was racing in a blinding blur, and she thought she was probably just a couple of breaths away from passing out. He read her some rights, and she numbly agreed that she understood.

Then he took her wrists down from the prickly wooden fence and clicked on handcuffs, and she caught her breath on a sob.

But I didn't do anything.

Shane would have warned her that for people who lived in the Glass House, that hardly ever mattered.

FIVE

It took half an hour for her head to clear, and by that time she'd been taken in the back of a squad car from the house to City Hall. The jail was one floor down in the basement of the Gothic castle structure, where they booked her with calm efficiency. She didn't talk. She didn't really think she could, honestly. There was no one else in the cells with her, but Simonds posted a uniformed guard outside her bars anyway—as a precaution, he said, though he wasn't specific about what he was expecting.

"I didn't do anything," she finally told him, as he got ready to leave her. "Detective, I *didn't*. None of us even knew that man was down there!"

"I'll take your statement later," he told her. It wasn't unkind, just calm and brisk and a little disinterested, as if he'd already written her off as a lost cause. "Tell me where your boyfriend and Eve have gone, and we can talk about how I can help you out."

"I don't know where they are." She didn't, actually. The police had taken her cell, and she hoped Shane had heeded her text, run for cover, and turned off his phone. She desperately hoped he'd thought to warn Eve, too. Miranda could conceal herself easily, but Eve stood out like a sore thumb, and so did Shane in his muscle car. Both knew Morganville well, so they'd have places to go to ground. But still—she worried.

Simonds said, "I hope you think hard about telling me where they are, because if we can't find them, you're on the hook by yourself, Claire. I don't want to see that happen any more than you do. Fact is, you saw the victim alive, and just a few hours later he was stabbed, moved, and dumped in your own basement. Seems pretty straightforward. Maybe you thought you could smuggle Eve's husband out of the mall and something went wrong. . . . Look, it's perfectly okay to want to save your friend. Maybe you thought he was in real danger. Maybe Mr. Thackery—that's his name, by the way, the dead man in your basement—maybe he tried to stop you. Could have been self-defense, I know that."

She shut up, because his calm, friendly tone frightened her. He was good at drawing things out of people, even things that they didn't mean; she knew too many things that implicated her already, and one wrong statement could bring Shane and Eve into it, too. Better to be silent until she could figure out what the *hell* was going on.

He took her silence well enough, brought her some bottled water, promised some food, and left. The policewoman stationed outside the door—not Halling, thankfully, because Claire honestly couldn't stand the sight of her—had a Daylighter symbol on her collar, but she didn't seem inclined to chat or judge. She dragged a chair over and sat down to read a magazine instead.

Claire drank her water without tasting it, then stretched out on the narrow, hard bunk. After a few moments, she wrapped the blanket around her shivering body and finally closed her eyes. Just to think.

She woke up in the dark.

Her breath stopped in her throat, because it was *too* dark, even if she'd slept through sunset. All the lights were off in the hall beyond her cell, and she heard something metallic scrape just before the cell door swung open with a horror-movie creak. Claire fought her way free of the rough blanket and stood up, ready to fight. But she didn't need to.

She had a visitor.

It was Myrnin.

He was dressed in clean clothes that were at least two sizes too large for him, and probably scavenged from a clothesline or an unattended Laundromat dryer. Even picking from someone else's clothes, he'd managed to make it a peculiarly Myrnin ensemble of a tie-dyed T-shirt under a bright orange hoodie and khaki cargo shorts. Evidently nobody had been washing shoes, because he was wearing a pair of plastic flip-flops that he must have found in the trash; they looked like they'd seen better days in the previous decade, and they were also too large for his feet. On the plus side, he was at least wearing shoes.

"Well," he said, and gave her a slow, delighted smile. "This is something I didn't expect. You, behind bars. What a turnaround."

"How did you get out?" Her eyes widened, because he was still wearing the shock collar around his neck, like a particularly ugly statement necklace. "Didn't they stun you?"

"Oh, yes, many times," he said. "Some of us don't really mind that sort of thing as much. If they'd been equipped with your devious little invention, then that would have been a different story altogether." The weapon he was talking about had the ability to destroy a vampire's ability to fight back, and she hated the thought that she was responsible for creating it. She was, and she had to own it, but that didn't mean she had to like it. "I presume Fallon is still having our traitorous friend Dr. Anderson construct new models, so they haven't had a chance to fully outfit their guards quite yet. Lucky for me."

"Are you—are you the only one who—"

"Got out?" Myrnin finished. He leaned against the bars as if they had all the time in the world. She remembered the cop stationed outside the door, and in the faint emergency lighting she made out the shape of the woman crumpled on the floor next to her overturned chair. "I fear so. Oliver has made several brave attempts, but he doesn't really have the skill at ignoring pain that I do. I think it's bothering him a delightful amount. He did cover for my escape, though, for which I suppose I have to be grateful."

She couldn't really keep track of what he was saying, because she was now worried about the policewoman. He'd moved so fast and decisively, and the woman wasn't moving. "Did you—is she—?"

"Oh, bother, don't make that face, Claire. No, I didn't kill the wretched woman, I only knocked her out. I know how you feel about such things. Though she does smell delicious."

"No biting," she warned him.

"As always, I am at your command." He said it in a way that made it very clear he wasn't, not at all. "Come on, then, unless you enjoy being put on trial for a murder you did not commit."

"How do you know about the murder?"

There was a tiny shift of his balance, but his expression didn't change. "I've spoken to Shane. He witnessed you being taken away by our overenthusiastic detective. Lucky for your young man, he decided that discretion was the better part of valor."

"Is he okay?"

"Well, I'm fairly sure our definitions of that word vary considerably, dear Claire, but he seemed to be breathing and ambulatory, though understandably angry."

She couldn't seem to take her eyes off of the ugly, blocky shock collar around his neck. "Does it hurt?"

"This?" He touched the shock collar, eyebrows raised. "I'm out of range. It does chafe a bit, if that doesn't make me seem pathetic."

"Do you want me to—take it off?"

"Don't be ridiculous, I'll need it later, and if you break the seal it will sound a very noisy alert and activate an explosive that would remove both my head and your hands, which I think we can both agree would be undesirable."

"Wait, what? *Explosives?*"

"Don't worry, they won't go off unless they're triggered by someone trying to remove it without the appropriate tools. Besides, I must go back tonight before they miss me, which means the collar must be intact. Oh, and my head. They'd notice."

"But—"

"We are in the middle of a prison break! Come on, now, don't dally. Do you have any baggage?"

"It's a prison, Myrnin, not a hotel."

"Well, modern prisons are so much nicer these days, one never knows," he said, and marched out of the cell and down the corridor, stepping over the fallen policewoman with his oversized flip-flops dangling precariously. "Come on, then."

She hesitated for a second, because as bad as her situation was, she wasn't sure that going with Myrnin wouldn't end up worse . . . but there wasn't much choice, really.

She stepped outside the cell, and became a fugitive.

Myrnin led her to the stairs, bypassing the elevator. As they jogged up, he said, "I've cut the power to the building, by the way. Oh, come now, move along—your somewhat strange little friend is anxiously waiting."

"My—wait, who?"

He shrugged. "The ghost girl. She seems to find me quite alarming, and she was hardly able to manifest herself at all to explain to me where to find you. I think she's afraid I'll try to bite her. I believe she may have, you know, mental issues." He made an unmistakable circle at his temple, and Claire just stared at him in dumb amazement. *That isn't just pot, meet kettle,* she thought. *That's the whole chef's rack.* "Oh, and I also knocked out several people on several different floors, including Mayor Ramos and her assistant. I thought that might nicely confuse the issues while we make our clever escape."

"About that. Exactly what is the plan for our clever escape?"

"Front door," he said cheerfully.

Of course.

There wasn't any chance of talking him out of it, sadly, and she had no choice but to follow close behind him as he shoved open the fire exit door at the top of the stairs, with a fine disregard for whether there might be an ambush waiting beyond. There wasn't. There were, however, two armed police officers standing outside the front doors, but Myrnin hit them with the force of a neon-colored hurricane and left them unconscious in his wake. "See?" he said as he marched on in his flip-flops. "Successful plan. And I'm being extreme humane. You really can't fault me."

A car was idling at the curb, and through the open passenger-side window, she saw Miranda's pale, anxious face; the girl was gesturing frantically. Next to her, painted an eerie shade of green from the dashboard light's glow, Claire glimpsed Jenna—the psychic who'd become Miranda's foster mother, in a way, and from whom Miranda pulled the power to stay alive and together outside the boundaries of the Glass House. She looked tense and very worried.

As she should have been.

Sirens howled, and behind them, the lights suddenly flared on inside City Hall. Their grace period was officially over—and they were too far from the safety of Jenna's car.

Jenna made a split-second decision and hit the gas, hard. Miranda let out a cry of protest, but it was too late; a few seconds later, Jenna's car was taking a right turn out of the City Hall parking lot and speeding away.

"Well," Myrnin said, "that wasn't in my plan. I suppose it's time to run."

He yanked her into a full-tilt race.

It was getting dark, and between gasps for air Claire managed to say, "That hoodie kind of glows in the dark. You might want to take it off!"

"My skin is even more reflective," he said. "And I quite like the color, don't you? So festive."

"Where are we *going?*"

"Clearly not that way," Myrnin said, and made an instant course correction when he spotted a police cruiser's lights heading toward them. He grabbed Claire's arm and dragged her over the lawn to the shadows of some evergreen trees. "Hush." He didn't take the chance she might not agree; he grabbed her and slapped a hand over her mouth. Her protest—faint as she'd meant it to be—disappeared entirely. He was holding her way too tightly against him to break free.

A searchlight from the police car slid over the trees, but they were well concealed by the thicket of branches. Myrnin waited until the danger had passed, then let her loose, and towed her back out onto the open lawn. "Where are we *going?*" she asked him in an urgent whisper. "Because I am not feeling good about this! We're both fugitives now, you know!"

"Duly noted. Save your breath now—we have to run. Do keep up."

She didn't think she could. Myrnin did hold back a little from genuine vampire speed, but even so, she felt as if she was running faster than was safe in the dim, failing light. Streetlights flickered on as they made it to the shops across the street from City Hall. They ducked into an alley as more police cars moved past and swept the bricks with searchlights. Myrnin didn't seem bothered by the nasty puddles soaking his feet, but Claire tried to avoid the worst of it. It definitely wasn't clean water. She wasn't sure it *was* water. "Where are we going?"

He hadn't answered that question the first time, but as he watched the street outside, he said, "Your friend Jenna seems to have offered us some form of safe haven. Pity we missed the ride. I mistrust her, but both Steve and Shane—"

"*Eve!* Honestly, Myrnin, how long have you known her?"

"It's a very odd name, you know. Efa, now, that's a proper sort of name. Or even Aoife," he said. "Fine. Eve and Shane assure me it is the best we can do at the moment. I believe their alternative was that we'd end up dead in a ditch, which doesn't sound attractive."

"Probably wasn't meant to. Are we clear?"

"Apparently." Myrnin snatched her hand and dragged her into another flat-out run. This one wasn't as hard, simply because they were on sidewalks, though when he veered sharply down an alley, that was frankly terrifying, and she decided she'd better just commit to trusting him not to smash her face-first into hidden obstacles.

There were a few worrying moments where she brushed past things that would have definitely been painful, but overall, they emerged into the street on the other side unscathed.

And there were people out on the streets. Myrnin skidded to a stop and backed her up into the shadows. "Damn," he said. "I had forgotten that the residents here had lost all their well-taught caution. What is the world coming to?"

"Safety?"

He let out a disbelieving, humorless laugh. "Don't be ridiculous. They are full of the flush of victory just now, and brotherly love, but human nature inevitably asserts itself. Criminals will take advantage of all this newfound trust to commit crimes, righteous men will stumble and fail their ideals, all manner of chaos will come; men have ever been their own nightmares. It's how the world works, and while vampires certainly don't help matters, they're hardly the root of evil. There is no safety, Claire, and there never can be—it's only an illusion. But that is as it should be, don't you think?"

She didn't have an answer for that. She watched the people strolling on the streets, enjoying a failing sunset. Trusting each other's better natures. Some of them might be genuinely good people who would never hurt anyone, but some of them weren't. And it chilled her to realize what Myrnin was telling her—that with or without vampires, Morganville would always be dangerous. Just dangerous in an entirely different way. A less obvious way.

A lull came as true dark fell and the last remnants of orange slipped away. Myrnin, without a sound, grabbed her hand and urged her into another run down the sidewalk. He didn't pause when the sidewalk came to a sudden end but darted into a deserted lot, then through to another sidewalk, a sharp left turn, then a right, and she was lost, entirely lost, and everything was moving too fast for her to get her bearings. Her heart was beating so fast she thought she'd collapse, and air burned hot and thick in her lungs. She didn't even have time to consider the pain in her legs and feet until, suddenly, it was over. He had stopped so quickly that the momentum sent her crashing hard into him. He hardly even wavered.

For a moment, they were pressed together, and she knew he could hear her too-fast heartbeat drumming in his ears, smell her sweat and blood, and she saw his pupils slowly expand to drink all that sensation in . . . and for a moment, she saw the hunger. It was dark and desperate, and she wondered just how far she could trust him.

But then Myrnin gently pushed her back as she struggled for balance, held her until she found it, and said, "I do believe we've arrived."

The house was like many others around it—small, faced with clapboard, built into a square. It had a little character because of the dark blue trim on the windows and front door, and a little pride in its new Daylighters-approved paint job, but all in all it was

Morganville through and through—a little lopsided, a bit run-down, a shade odd. Myrnin led her up the cracked sidewalk to the front porch, and before he could reach for the iron door knocker, the door opened.

Jenna stood there—tall, blond, with piercing pale eyes. She just *looked* the part of a psychic, somehow, even to the faraway expression on her face . . . but there was nothing psychic or dreamy about the consternation, as she saw Myrnin.

There was just worry, and calculation.

He waited a second, then made an abrupt flapping motion with his hands. "Well?" he demanded. "I'm a vampire, you silly woman. Ask me in! We're wanted felons, you know!"

She didn't seem convinced that was a good idea, but she stepped back and said, "Please come in, both of you." He rushed in, bringing Claire with him, and Jenna swung the door shut behind them.

Claire had just begun to catch her breath when suddenly Miranda appeared out of thin air, rushing at her, and her solid body crashed against Claire's as she wrapped her arms around her. "You made it!" she said. "I didn't know if you could. I'm so sorry we left you there. I'm so sorry, but I was scared to leave Jenna for long . . ."

"It's okay," Claire said. She was still gasping for air, and she felt sweaty and horrible, but there was something good about seeing Miranda. The girl backed away, and Jenna put her arm around her; that, too, was good, the motherly vibe from the psychic for the ghost girl. Jenna had, from the beginning, felt protective of Miranda, and it looked as if that relationship had gotten closer—something Miranda desperately needed, because she'd been basically abandoned by her own family. Something good had happened in Morganville for a change, after all: two sad people had found each other, and made each other better.

Shane was standing in the doorway, patiently waiting for her to notice him. She knew that expression—or lack of one—on his face. It was specific to situations where Myrnin was involved, and Shane was trying very hard not to let his jealousy show. He had nothing to be jealous *about*, and he knew it, but seeing her clutching Myrnin's hand probably hadn't been his most favorite moment ever.

That, and Shane's anti-vampire instincts were probably churning, being so close to one of them now.

"Hey," Shane said, and raised his chin. His most neutral greeting. She came to him and hugged him, then kissed him. That broke through the wall he'd put up between them, and his arms went around her to hold her tight. "I didn't know what else to do. I couldn't let them keep you there. You're not exactly built for jail."

"Well, you have to admit, it was probably my turn to get handcuffed and thrown in the hole," she said. Her smile didn't have much strength, though, and faded quickly. "The man in the basement—he was killed with one of our knives, Shane." She managed not to *quite* make it a question.

He got the message anyway, though, and responded with a frown. "Well, it wasn't me. Wasn't Eve, I guarantee you. She'd at least have moved the body someplace else. She's no dummy."

"Where is Eve, exactly?"

"Out," Jenna said. She sounded very blunt, and very disapproving. "I warned her, but she said she couldn't stay. She went back to try to see Fallon."

"I thought she went to see him when she left our house!"

"They wouldn't let her in. She came back to find me, and we both saw you get taken to jail. Not sure which one of us held the other back, actually, but maybe your good sense is starting to rub off on us. We didn't jump in and get ourselves arrested, at least," Shane said. Claire swung around to stare at him, wide-eyed; so many questions ran through her mind that she couldn't pick a single one out of the blur.

"But—" Claire couldn't express how much she didn't like the idea of Eve—angry and frustrated even more than she had been—heading at Fallon like a guided missile. It was pretty obvious, though, that there wasn't much either one of them could do about it at this point.

"Look, it makes sense. It's pretty clear he's running the show here; if she can get in to see him—and I really don't see anybody stopping her—then nobody's going to storm Fallon's office to march her out in cuffs. And if she can really intimidate him into letting her see Michael, maybe she can give him a chance to get away, or bust Amelie out. She's the only one who's got a shot at being our inside man. Woman. Whatever. Let's face it—none of us is exactly in a mastermind position right now."

"Does she know even about the dead guy?"

"Oh, she knows," Jenna said. "Eve thinks the guard was killed at the prison and moved to your house, and she thinks she might be able to find out who did it, and why. I think her exact phrase was, *I'm going to Nancy Drew this crap.*"

"Bet she didn't say *crap*," Shane said.

"I'm paraphrasing."

Eve's plan was dangerous, and Claire immediately felt a rush of adrenaline, thinking of her trapped alone without anybody to trust. Michael, sure, but Michael couldn't help—not unless something changed drastically.

Myrnin had been uncharacteristically quiet since they'd arrived, and she glanced over to see him frowning down at his flip-flops. He probably missed his vampire bunny slippers.

"Do the guards at the mall know you're out?" she asked Myrnin. He didn't look up.

"That's very doubtful," he said. "I did kill the guard who spotted me, after all."

They all stopped what they were doing, and there was a second or two of silence.

Shane's head suddenly snapped around, and he turned his whole body after it, facing Myrnin.

And took a step toward him. He said, in a voice tight with fury, "Would that be the dead guard in our damn *basement?*"

"Well, of course, how many dead guards could there be? Why, did you kill one, too? Wasteful."

Shane snarled. It came from somewhere deep in his chest, a wet animal sound that Claire had never heard before, and hoped she'd never hear again. He took another step toward Myrnin, and Myrnin's eyes flared an immediate, alarmed crimson. "Claire," he called sharply. "Mind your young man. Do you really want me to have to kill him?"

It was the offhanded way he said it that terrified Claire. She forgot sometimes, despite her best efforts, that Myrnin was only mostly sane, and only mostly human.

And she wasn't sure what Shane was right now, either.

Jenna and Miranda instinctively got out of the way, and even though every instinct in her body screamed at her to do the same, Claire stepped in the middle, faced Shane, and met his eyes squarely. They didn't look right. Not right at all. The color—the blankness—it was all wrong.

He lunged forward, staring past her at Myrnin, and she could have sworn she saw a poisonous spark of yellow in his eyes.

She didn't move. She lifted both hands, palms out, and he ran into them, jolting her hard and driving her back a step—but it shifted his focus away from Myrnin and onto her.

And the alien look in his eyes flickered, and died away, leaving just Shane. Angry, yes, amped up well beyond where he ought to be, but whatever had been set in motion, she'd stopped it.

For now, anyway.

Shane held up both hands, backed up a step, and then spun around and stalked away, breathing hard. "Why are you protecting him?" He didn't quite yell it at Claire, and she knew it cost him to hold it down to just an angry accusation.

"Good question," she said, and turned to Myrnin. "You killed a man," she said. "And you brought him *to our house?*"

"In all fairness, I was looking for you," he said, "but you weren't yet home. I had to do *something* with him. Normally I would have taken him to the graveyard—by the by, it's a great place to dispose of an excess corpse, one just digs up an old grave and—"

There were parts of him that she just would never reach, and knew she should never, ever try, for both their sakes.

Shane turned around, and Claire instinctively grabbed hold of his arm, because she still sensed the suppressed violence in him. He was under enough control not to lunge at Myrnin—which would end badly anyway—but she also knew sometimes he just couldn't quite control those impulses, and she didn't want to see anyone hurt. "You dumped a dead man in our house, and what? Just forgot about it?"

"I was busy, and how in the world would I have known you'd be stupid enough to allow the constables to roam freely through—"

"They had a warrant, and we are not your temporary storage for murdered bodies!" Claire said, and realized that she was a little too upset about things, too. Almost as much as Shane, and without the excuse of the dog bite's infection. "You *killed him.* Where did you get a knife? *Our* knife?"

Myrnin shrugged, clearly not taking any of it too seriously. "You're quite careless with those things," he said. "I believe I originally got it from you. The guard in question had confiscated it from me when I was arrested, and I decided that I wanted it back. But I let him keep it in the end." He grinned, and his vampire teeth looked long and terrifyingly sharp. "Oh, don't frown at me so, Claire. He had it coming, you may be assured of that. He was a brutal thug of a man. I was defending a lady's honor, in fact."

"Jesse's, maybe?" Claire asked. Because Jesse—the red-headed bartender that both he and Claire had made fast friends with—was not just a vampire but one that Myrnin had surprising affection for. "What happened?"

Myrnin didn't answer, not directly. "Enough of this. Time is wasting. The Lady Grey will ensure that no one notices my absence for now, but I'll need to be back in time for their nightly audit of their prisoners. Before then, I have things to obtain. I've stripped the building of all materials that might be of use, but I shall need some things that simply aren't available in that place."

"Materials for what?" Claire asked.

"Never you mind," he said. "But these followers of Fallon's madness have started a war, and I intend to finish it." Myrnin's eyes seemed to flare red for a second, alarmingly bright, and she remembered the hunger she'd sensed in him before, and the frightening sharpness of his teeth. He didn't seem to be himself just now, and she realized, with a creeping sense of alarm, that they almost certainly wouldn't have bothered with his usual medications at the prison—and in this state, he might not be willing to take them on his own.

There were a few things scarier than a bipolar vampire off his meds, but to be honest, not that many.

"Myrnin," she said, and drew his instant attention. Unsettlingly. "You can't go out there again. It's too dangerous for you." *Too dangerous for innocent people wandering around thinking it's safe.*

"If you're implying it would be better for you to go in my place, it's certainly far too dangerous for you, Claire, seeing as you are a half-convicted murderess." He said it with entirely too much relish. "And before *you* offer your boy's services—he's in no better shape, is he? No, it's best I go alone, and quickly. I've been in this town for too many of your short lifetimes to be caught by the likes of Fallon and his Daylighters when I have some warning of their intentions."

Jenna exchanged a quick look with Miranda, and said, "I'll drive you. Where are you going?"

"To my lab, of course."

"I don't know where that is."

Myrnin sighed. "I *can* drive, you know."

Claire flinched and made a quick throat-cutting gesture behind his back to Jenna. Myrnin on his best days was not a good driver. Her eyes widened, but Jenna caught herself, smiled, and said, "I'm sure you can, but it's much safer if you're out of sight, don't you think?"

"Ah, perhaps so," he said. "Let's crack on, then. The night won't last forever."

Jenna pointed at Miranda. "You're staying here," she said. "I know you want to go, but stay with these two. Promise me." Miranda nodded soberly. Claire grabbed Jenna before they headed out and whispered quick instructions on where to find Myrnin's medications.

Shane let out a slow breath as the door shut and locked behind them. "I'm sorry," he said. He sounded exhausted, and he sank down into a crouch against the wall and cradled his head in both hands. "God, I'm sorry. What the hell was that?"

"I think—I think it was just the stress, and him being so close," Claire said. "You're okay now." She said it with confidence, but in truth, she really wasn't as sure as she pretended, and after a few seconds of silence, she bent her head and half whispered, "Please, tell me you're okay."

"He killed someone, and he doesn't seem to care much," Shane said. "I don't think I'm your biggest problem right now."

"What do you think he's planning to do?"

"Whatever it is, I guarantee you that it's not going to be safe for anybody near him."

"I wish Jenna hadn't gone," Miranda said. She looked paler now, and a little translucent. Without the Glass House sustaining her, it was hard for her to stay visible and solid, and with her connection to Jenna fading through distance, she probably couldn't manifest a body much longer. "What about the house? Who's going to protect it now? We're all *here!*"

"Eve's not," Claire said.

"Eve's with the Daylighters. She can't help the house from there."

Miranda was right, and Claire felt a surge of anxiety when she thought about the house all alone, vulnerable, and still under threat—maybe more now than before, since everyone knew they were on the run.

It was the perfect time to strike.

"We need to go," she told Shane. "We need to get there in case they try something."

Miranda was thin as glass now, her eyes huge and dark in that ghostly face. "You need to go now," she said, and it seemed as if her voice, like the body she inhabited, was growing hollow and faint. *"Now! Go now!"*

And then Claire felt it, too . . . a sense of something shivering inside her, a vibration almost like an earthquake, not physical but emotional, mental, psychic.

The house was crying out.

SIX

Claire ran for the front door.

"No!" Shane got in her way fast and pushed her back. "No, you know they're looking for us. You can't—"

"You heard her!" She didn't try to make an end run around him—he was way too good on defense. She simply reversed course and went the other way. She didn't know Jenna's house, but it was square and small, and it made sense that there would be a back door on one of those compass points. She bet on the back, since Morganville architects were more cookie cutter than cutting edge; she spotted the door, set in the right corner of the kitchen, as she plunged into that small room. Jenna kept her kitchen spotless and pretty, and Claire had a moment of pure envy, but just a flicker, because the panic inside her was starting to take over.

She threw open the back door, hit the back porch, launched herself off it at a run, and dashed around the house. She heard Shane calling after her, but he clearly didn't want to make a public fuss, so it was just the one mention of her name, and then she heard the door thump shut and footsteps on the path behind her.

There was no way she could outrun him, but she wasn't intending to . . . only to try to lead him most of the way, so that he'd see it was a better idea to go on than turn back.

She'd made it to the brightly lit parking lot of Morganville's one and only apartment complex (ten whole units, built in an old-fashioned L shape) when he stretched out one long arm and dragged her to an unwilling halt. Then he grabbed her other arm. "*Claire.* This is crazy. We can't be out here. You know that!"

"You're the one making us get noticed," she said. "I was just a girl out for a jog. Now I'm getting accosted by an angry boyfriend."

"I'm not—" He took a deep breath and let go. "Okay. Just walk back with me. Calmly. We can do this. Let's just—"

"No," she said, and turned on her heel to head toward the Glass House, still several blocks away.

"What is *wrong* with you?"

He couldn't feel it. Maybe that was because he was famously blunted to psychic things; maybe he was just blocking it out. But he honestly had no idea that the house was screaming for help, and she couldn't say no to its need. That house had saved her life at least once. She owed it.

But she came to a sudden and frozen halt as she heard Monica Morrell's smoky, lazy voice say, "Stop right there or I'll blow your head off, Preschool. This means you, too, Shane. Don't get stupid. Well, you know. Stupider."

Monica was Morganville's crown princess of mean—a pretty

girl who'd grown up rich, powerful, and entitled to whatever she wanted, and she'd wanted it all. She'd grown up a little in the past couple of years, but that had just taken her from actively evil to passively unpleasant, in Claire's opinion. They'd never been friends, the three of them, but they'd had moments of not-quite-hatred.

This, however, wasn't one of them.

Claire realized that they'd managed to somehow stage their parking lot argument standing right beside Monica's shiny red car—the only one like it in Morganville, instantly recognizable if she'd been paying the slightest bit of attention. And, of course, it was parked in front of Monica's apartment. Monica herself was leaning against the open door's frame, tall and sleek and party-ready in a peach-colored minidress that fluttered in the wind and threatened to go into R-rated areas at any second.

What mostly concerned Claire wasn't the dress, but the gun. It was, in Texas terms, a lady's weapon—a small black automatic that most men would probably dismiss as a purse gun—and Monica had it aimed right at Claire's chest. At this distance, it wasn't too likely she'd miss. Purse gun or not, it'd definitely do damage.

Claire slowly put her hands up. Shane said, "Jesus, Monica—"

"Hands up, Collins," she said, and gave them both an impartially happy smile. "I heard a rumor that you butchered some poor sucker in your house. But unfortunately it wasn't a *blood*sucker, or everybody would have just shrugged and gotten over it. Too bad for you, I mean. I suppose I really ought to make a citizen's arrest and put you back in jail. You know, public safety and shit. Plus I think there might be a reward. Totally bonus bucks."

"You're enjoying this way too much," Claire said.

"Damn right I am, and I have every right to *love* seeing the two of you wearing orange jumpsuits. It is just so your color, Shane."

"Bite me, Bitch Queen."

Monica blew him an air kiss. "Don't think I wouldn't leave a mark." There was an evil, bright light in her pretty eyes. She'd always had some kind of perverse sadomasochistic crush on Shane, and the fact that Shane had shoved her away repeatedly had set her off in ways he'd never expected. Most people still assumed that Monica had been behind the fire that consumed Shane's family home and killed his little sister, Alyssa. Claire had never been so sure, and she knew that Shane had mostly given up that conviction, too. Monica wasn't above trolling in the wake of a tragedy, but she hadn't started the fire.

It didn't make her a better person, though.

"I'm only going to say this once," Shane said, "and I can't believe I'm saying it at all, so never ever repeat it, but we need your help. Please."

Monica blinked. That was obviously not what she'd expected—or, truthfully, what Claire had expected, either. Monica was an effortless button-pusher, and Shane was usually way too easy to manipulate ... but not this time. "Excuse me?" she asked, and cocked her head to one side. "Are you actually pretending that we're friends?"

"Monica, I am pretty sure you have no idea how to have a friend who isn't an empty-souled suck-up, but you're not a fool. You know you've built up way too much bad karma around here, and it's all coming back on you. The vamps are out, humans are in, and you've acted like the Queen of All Bitches for half your life. You'd better start counting up your allies. I'm pretty sure you won't get past your middle finger."

That got a long, measured look—much more thoughtful and adult than anything Claire could say she'd ever seen in Monica before. Maybe even the eternally self-involved could sometimes grow up, at least enough to recognize their own danger. "I'm listening," Monica said.

"Could we do this inside?" Claire asked. She'd caught a glimpse in the distance of a Morganville police cruiser, searchlights flaring.

Monica debated a full fifteen seconds before she stepped back and lowered the gun. "Yeah," she said. "But don't expect me to go all Southern belle on you and offer an iced tea and cookies. I am not your grandma. And don't touch my stuff."

Neither of them hesitated. They moved fast, and were inside and locking the door behind them before she got the last words out. The relief was immense, and Claire turned to put her back against the door.

"Wow," Shane said. "This is—" He ran out of words. Claire fully understood why.

It was the girliest room Claire had ever seen. Pale carpet, pink satin couch, pale yellow armchair, also silk. Fairy lights strung around the light fixtures. A bookcase filled not with books but with pictures of Monica, in blinged-out pink frames. A giant custom Andy Warhol–style print, only Marilyn Monroe had been replaced with Monica's face. There was a sharp, high-pitched volley of barking, and Claire looked down to see a tiny little teacup Chihuahua with a frilly pink collar and mean bulging eyes yapping at them from under the yellow chair.

"Channing, hush," Monica said, and picked up the little thing. It shivered constantly, studying Shane and Claire with frenzied intensity. It stopped barking, but kept growling, in a pitch that wouldn't have intimidated a butterfly. "This is Channing. Channing, this is Asshat and Nerd Girlfriend."

"I think that's my new band name," Shane said. "Asshat and Nerd Girlfriend. It's got a ring to it. Did you name your dog after *Channing Tatum*?"

"He has qualities," Monica said, and put the Chihuahua down. It immediately attacked Shane's shoelaces. He watched it with a puzzled frown, as if he couldn't decide whether to laugh or . . . really laugh. It really was ridiculous. His shoe was bigger than the whole dog. "Sit. Don't touch *anything*."

Claire perched on the pink sofa; Shane evidently decided that the color might be catching, so he took the yellow armchair, which was marginally more manly, and tried to shake Channing off. That resulted in enthusiastic leg humping. Claire covered her mouth to stop a totally inappropriate burst of giggles, while Monica ignored the drama and poured herself a stiff drink from a bourbon bottle. She didn't offer to share, not that Claire would have accepted. "So talk," Monica said, and downed half the drink in one gulp. "Because I can totally still shoot you as home-invasion robbers. Nobody would doubt it, because you're all jailbreakers and killers and all."

"We need to get home," Claire said. As surreal as this whole scene was, from the pastel apartment (was that a *pink teapot* on the stove?) to Channing having doggy hate-sex with Shane's leg, the anxiety that had twisted up her guts was sinking deeper. The house needed them. *Now.* And they were wasting time. "The Daylighters want the Founder Houses destroyed. They're trying to dismantle everything Amelie's built, you know that. Myrnin always said the Founder Houses were the heart of Morganville. If they manage to destroy them . . ."

"We'll have fewer ugly Victorian eyesores to deal with?" Monica asked, and drank the rest of her bourbon. "Okay, anything those idiots with a sunrise fetish want, I'm against, that's obvious. Even if it means associating with . . . well." She gestured at the two of them, somehow getting across distaste, disgust, and resignation all with one twist of her mouth. She poured out another generous slug of alcohol. "Everybody's all warm and fuzzy about how evil is defeated and the sun's out again, and it's morning in America or whatever, and I don't know about you, but I don't believe these jerks give a crap about making anybody's lives better. They just want people on their side. All this new construction and paint and architectural Botox . . . it's just smoke. It's the vamps they want. And it's the vamps they've got."

It was a surprisingly accurate observation, coming from Monica, and even Shane forgot about Channing for long enough to stare.

Channing evidently lost interest, since Shane wasn't being horrified anymore. The dog sniffed the carpet, then trotted off to munch miniature crumbs of food from a tiny pink bowl that was decorated with a jeweled crown.

"What do you want from me?" Monica asked them. "Because you know I'm not going to get myself arrested or anything. Not for the two of you, for God's sake. That would just be epically pathetic."

"First of all, we need a ride," Shane said. "To our house. Can you manage that, Princess Picky?"

She shot him the finger and finished her bourbon, and Claire winced. That was two shots of bourbon that she'd witnessed, and from the way Monica was moving—not quite wobbling on her high heels, but definitely *fluid*—there was no way she was sober. "I'll drive," she said.

"Oh *hell* you will not," Monica said, and snatched up the keys—on a pink jeweled ring, of course—from the coffee table. Which was white, with pink curlicues. "Nobody drives my car but me."

"Maybe you ought to not try to drive with the gun in the other hand," Shane said. Monica looked down at her right fingers, still curled around the purse gun, and seemed faintly surprised. She shrugged and put it down next to the bourbon. Claire had a sudden, sadly hilarious vision of Monica in thirty years—bloated, saggy, drunk, and armed, sitting in this still-pink apartment.

While Monica was drunkenly focused on putting the gun down, Claire plucked the keys from her fingers. Shane was up and moving at the same time, and as Monica fumbled to pick up the weapon again, he slid it out of her reach. She tried to punch him, but he ducked and weaved gracefully, avoiding her as easily as breathing. "You're not driving," Claire said. "But thanks for the car, and you can come with us, because I don't want you calling the cops on us for grand theft auto."

Monica pouted. It was pretty obvious turning them in had immediately bounced to the top of her to-do list. "Give me back my gun."

"Obviously that's a no," Shane said.

"It's an *heirloom!*" He gave her a look. "Fine," she said. "But this isn't over."

"It never is, with you," he said. "Just don't make trouble and we'll all get along fine."

Claire sincerely doubted that, but she opened Monica's apartment door and checked outside. There was no sign of the police cruiser; it had moved on to new territory. "Hurry," she said, and led the way. Shane kept Monica ahead of him, with one hand gripping her upper arm tightly—half to keep her steady on those heels and half to ensure she wasn't going to bolt and raise hell. But she kept quiet and got into the passenger seat as Claire took the driver's side. "What?" she demanded, when Shane stood there in the doorway, frowning at her. "Seriously? You are not getting shotgun in my car, loser."

"At least I can get a choke hold on you easier from back here," he said as he got in the back. "Silver linings."

"Touch me and die. And don't scratch it," Monica said, and leveled a stiff index finger at Claire. Behind it, her eyes were bright with bourbon and malice. "I'll cut you twice for every dent."

After having driven Shane's beast of a car, this was a piece of cake, really—automatic transmission, smooth steering, posh leather interior. Claire had been ready to hate Monica's car, but it felt . . . well, it felt great. Maybe being rich wasn't so bad, if you could avoid being a bitch along with it.

She made Monica scream a little by steering way too close to a rusty trash can, but she missed it by inches and swung out of the parking lot onto the main road. It was risky, riding around in this open car (Monica, of course, had a convertible), but they didn't have time to put the top up, and anyone who knew Monica would know she never put it up anyway unless it was raining.

Which it so rarely did, in Morganville.

In fact, the night was clear and cool and full of stars—so many stars glittering overhead in the cold black sky that it seemed oddly unreal. The moon was only half full, but it still shed a fiercely focused light, giving edges sharp corners and shadows their own density. It tingled on Claire's exposed skin like that menthol rub her mom had always put on her when she'd coughed. The difference was that Morganville smelled not medicinal but dusty, with a curious note of raw lumber.

It smelled to her like sunburns felt, and she had a strange moment of thinking that the sunlight the Daylighters worshipped so hard would dry them into parched husks, to be blown away by the constant desert winds.

It wasn't a long drive to the Glass House, but anxiety continued to beat in her chest like an animal trying to claw free. She expected to see Eve's hearse pulled up in front, or on the side, but instead she saw a couple of beat-up pickups lining the street in front of the house—never a good sign. She whipped the wheel hard and sent Monica's convertible squealing in a sharp right, up the house's gravel driveway. Monica yelped at the sound of the rocks thrown by the tires hitting the undercarriage with glassy pings. "Hey!" she said, and glared as Claire hit the brakes hard, bringing them to a sliding stop. "Where did you learn to drive, freak?"

"Myrnin's school of demolition driving," Shane said, which wasn't true, but it was funny, and Claire didn't correct him. "Right, thanks for the ride, let's not do it again, thanks for not making me kill you."

He dived out of the backseat, moving fast and keeping to the shadows. Claire wondered why, but then she saw the figures moving at the back of the house.

"Get out," Monica ordered, and forced the issue by practically climbing into Claire's lap before she could move. "Out out out, stupid!" She jammed the car into reverse just as Claire scrambled out, and Claire only just got the door slammed before Monica hit the gas and sent the car rocketing backward down the drive. It left some scrapes on the street as she bottomed out, and the flare of sparks was pretty noticeable, but Claire supposed that whole "don't dent it" theory was out the window while Monica was driving.

"What the hell is going on here?" Shane asked, as the sound of Monica's convertible faded. "Because I guess you were right that it's something."

"I don't know," she said. "But the house was reaching out to me, *really* distressed. I can't believe you don't feel it."

"It doesn't like me. Never did. I think it always thought I was trouble for Michael, and you know what, that house is a pretty damn good judge of character because I totally was when I got here, wasn't I? So, back door or front?"

"I saw whoever it is around back," she said. "Front makes more sense."

"No point in being subtle," Shane agreed, and gave her a brief, crazy smile before he ran for the front door. She caught up with him as he slowed down and braced for a door-busting kick. She managed to stop him, put a finger to her lips, and then took the key from her pocket. She quietly unlocked the door and eased inside.

Shane was disappointed that he couldn't make a grand entrance, of course, but he slipped in after her and shut and relocked the door. Nothing looked wrong in the front hallway, and she took a couple of steps forward to peer into the front parlor. Nothing there, either. The extinguishers were still exactly where she'd left them, and she didn't see anything that indicated there had been an intruder.

But she felt it, knotted and tangled in her guts. The house was angry and violated and afraid, and it needed her.

She just didn't know *why*. Or what it expected her to do.

"Claire," Shane whispered, and made a series of hand gestures she was surprised she actually understood: he was telling her to go down the hall, up the stairs, and check the hidden room. He was right, too; it was, in many ways, the heart of the house, and if something was going on, it was probably happening there.

She pointed at him and raised her eyebrows in question. He pointed off to the kitchen, then made another of those utterly mysterious gestures that somehow made perfect sense to her, as if they were sharing some invisible playbook. He was going to retrieve the hidden weapons from the pantry.

She gave him a thumbs-up and headed down the hall.

The living room didn't look disturbed, either. It was silent, completely silent, and she felt her skin shiver into goose bumps at just how eerie it seemed . . . as if the whole house was holding its breath.

The stairs always creaked if you were careless, but she knew how to get around it. She balanced her weight carefully on the balls of her feet as she stayed on the left side, close to the wall. There was only one slight moan of wood near the top, and she froze, listening for any change—but she heard nothing. The hallway with their bedrooms on it stretched out in front of her, and she was nearly in the middle, heading for the hidden door, when the creature stepped out of the bathroom, right into her path.

Her brain reported *creature* because it couldn't think of anything to match what she was looking at—upright, bipedal like a man, but wrong, proportioned in strange ways. The arms were too long, the face too sharp and all the wrong shape, as if bones were broken under the skin. An oddly muscled back hunched forward under the straining white tee it wore.

She'd never figured that a monster in her house would be wearing blue jeans and cross-trainer Nikes, either.

The worst of it, though, the absolute worst, were the eyes— gleaming acid-yellow eyes, with slitted pupils—and the hands, because they sprouted claws that looked big and terrifying enough to make Wolverine feel inadequate.

Then it opened its mouth and snarled, and all the rest of it faded into insignificance beside the rows of gleaming, razor-sharp teeth.

Claire stumbled back and turned to run, but there was another one coming out of Michael and Eve's bedroom, blocking her escape. This one seemed smaller, but still twice her size, and it somehow also looked female—probably because it was wearing a dress, a bright summery yellow dress, and why would a monster wear a *dress*, anyway? It made no sense . . .

And as she watched, it twisted, and twisted, and changed, and she felt her stomach rebelling as the creature snarled and ripped at the clothes. It pinned her with brilliant, alien, *insane* eyes that were straight out of hell.

What was it Shane had said?

Hellhounds.

They were still changing, but they were looking more like dogs all the time.

Her brain was babbling because it was unable to find a single thing useful to say about this situation. She was caught between two things that looked like they'd escaped from the monster vaults, and they were coming closer, trapping her between them.

And then they were sniffing her.

She threw her hands over her head and hunched down into a ball—instinct, not strategy—and the next thing she realized was that they were all over her, taking in great, noisy breaths through their noses. That was alarming and gross and somehow terrifying all over again, because it seemed so *wrong*. She could smell them now—a kind of sickening mix of animal musk and the kind of body spray that was supposed to make the opposite sex crawl all over you. It was a vile combination, and she found herself gagging a little, but silently, because she couldn't manage so much as even a scream. Some instinct had locked her voice down tight. *Stay quiet, stay small, close your eyes, and make it all go away.*

And, surprisingly, it did. The loud snuffling stopped, and when she dared to glance up, she saw that the two things had dismissed her and were moving off down the hallway, using all four legs now. The hallway was littered with shredded, cast-off clothes. They stopped, snuffling the walls, and then glided into Shane's room like ghosts.

Claire let out a sudden, explosive breath, shot to her feet, and fought a very strong impulse that wanted her to run for the stairs and get the hell out of this house, away from these things, before it was too late.

Instead, she ran forward, her vision fixed on the place on the wood she needed to press to open the hidden door.

She hit it and raced inside as the panel sighed open, pulling it shut with a hard slam just as she saw the first gleam of yellow eyes from the shadows of Shane's bedroom turning her way. She raced up the stairs, her heart pounding hard, and stopped only when she'd reached the top and entered Amelie's hidden lair—Miranda's bedroom.

No Miranda, but there was someone lying on the sofa.

It was Amelie, and she was dressed in red, a dull crimson that seemed completely wrong for her, and her skin was alabaster white, and all Claire could think at first was *why is she wearing that color?* before she realized that it wasn't a color at all.

It was blood, soaking her shredded white dress.

Amelie's eyes opened, carnelian-red to match her dress of blood, and she said, "You need to flee, Claire. You can't help me. If you go now, they will ignore you. You're not the prey they're tracking."

"What happened?" Claire asked, and came closer. Amelie's frail white hand rose, trembled, and gestured for her to stop, and Claire obeyed, because when a vampire who'd lost that much blood said to stay away it was probably a good idea to listen. "What are those—things?" But she knew. She remembered Hannah, and the bite on Shane's arm, and it felt like gravity reversed under her feet.

"They are not things," Amelie said. "They are humans, modified to track vampires, to harry us until we are too weak to fight or run. They are Fallon's loyal dogs, with no will of their own. But they will not harm you if you go now." She sounded alert, but horribly weak. Claire swallowed hard and edged closer. "Did you not hear me? Leave, Claire. They will not kill me. They'll save that honor for their master."

"I can't. I can't just leave!"

"I made a terrible mistake," Amelie whispered. She closed her eyes again, and her hand dropped back to her chest. "I thought—I thought I could reason with him. He was one of mine, once. One of us. I never believed he could turn against us so thoroughly. My folly, Claire, only mine. I brought this on us. If I had killed him when I had the chance . . ."

"How do I stop them?" Claire asked, and grabbed Amelie's hand now, squeezing it to get her attention. Amelie's eyes flickered open again, but stared straight up, avoiding hers. "Amelie! You can't just give up—you have to tell me what I can *do!*"

"You can do only one thing," Amelie said, and suddenly Claire wasn't holding Amelie's hand . . . Amelie was holding hers, in an unbreakable grip. "You can help Myrnin. Do nothing for me, do you understand? Let them have me. They won't kill me, as I said.

But you *must* stand aside or they will tear through you to reach me." Her head turned, just a little, as if she was listening. Claire heard nothing, but she felt something inside—a kind of shifting, a pain that went beyond any physical senses. The house was hurting.

And the hidden door was being shredded under the attack of six-inch claws.

"I want to help you," Claire said. "Please."

"There's no escape from this room. Myrnin's portals are broken, and the only way out now is through the creatures below. You can't help me. All you can do is escape, and I *want* you to escape, Claire. I want you to go. Gather your friends and those you love. Leave the Glass House, and never come back. Leave Morganville. Go. My cause is lost, and it's a cause you could never understand in any case." Amelie attempted a smile. It didn't look right. "Never forget that I'm the monster."

"I can't just leave you here to die, Amelie. You're not—" She swallowed hard. "You're not the monster."

Amelie studied her directly for a few seconds, and the power and hunger and strength of the woman behind that stare left Claire feeling light-headed. It was like looking into history somehow . . . history hundreds of years deep. "You're so young," Amelie said. "And so stubborn. It's served you well, but it will not serve you now. There is one thing you can do for me, then. One last service you can perform."

Claire nodded. She was afraid, but she wasn't afraid of Amelie, really. She was afraid of what would happen when Amelie was gone.

When there was nothing at all to stop Fallon.

"Hold still," Amelie said, and pulled Claire's wrist to her lips.

The pain of her fangs going in was brief, and Claire felt an in-

stant unsteadiness take hold, a kind of unreal, whispering faint-
ness that made it necessary for her to fall to her knees beside the
sofa. She didn't try to pull away; there wasn't any point. Amelie
would drink as much as she wanted, and maybe that would be
everything, and maybe not. But either way, nothing Claire could
do would change the outcome.

Being bitten by Amelie wasn't like being bitten by any of the
others she'd survived before. It was surprisingly easy somehow, as
if Amelie's bite injected some kind of Valium along with it. She
felt peaceful, which was very strange; she ought to have felt horrified, or angry, or anything at all except stupidly relaxed.

It went on for a long moment, and then Amelie let her go with
a soft sigh, and the peace that had been echoing through Claire's
head evaporated like ice in the desert sun and panic kicked in
again, hard and very real. She was weak and drained, and her head
was spinning, and when she tried to get up she couldn't. All she
could do was edge slowly back, scooting with her hands until she'd
put a respectable distance between her and the queen dressed in
blood who lay on the couch.

Amelie sat up. Blood drops ran down her arms like red fringe,
and she looked down at herself with a frown, then stood as a hollow sound came from the door below. It wasn't down, not yet, but
they'd clawed through the wood and reached the metal behind it.
"Wipe my blood from your hands," she told Claire. "They will
smell it on you, and that would be a dangerous thing. When they
come for me, go down the stairs. Get Shane and leave. Promise me
you will do this."

"What's going to happen to you?"

"They will hurt me," Amelie said flatly. "I will fight them, but
they will take me. Don't interfere. You can't save me. I thank you

for the gift of your blood, Claire, and I will honor it. But you must honor me as well now."

It came to Claire in a blinding flash that there was one possibility that Amelie hadn't thought about—a dangerous one. Potentially fatal.

But maybe, just maybe, one that could work.

"If you get out of here, can you hide?" Claire asked her. "Is there someplace you can go?"

"Morley has promised me safety in the town of Blacke, if I can reach the borders of Morganville," Amelie said. "From there, perhaps we can find a way to strike at Fallon. But it's of no use to speculate. I will never leave this attic except in their hands."

This, Claire thought, was going to require two things: precision timing and a whole lot of luck. The house was on her side, though; she could feel it anxiously waiting for any chance to help. And Shane would be armed and dangerous and looking for her, very soon.

She heard the shriek of metal warping and being ripped apart, and waited another few seconds, staring at Amelie. She couldn't hear these creatures, because they moved like ghosts, but in her peripheral vision she saw one of them on the stairs. As it reached the top, she saw the blur of the second one close behind it.

"Sorry," Claire said. "I'm not giving up on you just yet."

She rushed forward, and before Amelie could stop her, she wrapped the Founder of Morganville in a hug.

It was weird and nauseating. The blood from Amelie's dress squelched wetly between them, smearing Claire, and beneath the garment the vampire felt like a cold marble statue, stiffly unyielding. It lasted only a second, and then Amelie's shock cracked, and she shoved Claire backward. "What are you *doing*?" she demanded, but there wasn't time to explain, because the hellhounds were coming.

Claire threw herself sideways, across the couch, knocked over the lamp, and jumped the low railing to land awkwardly on the steps below. She lost her footing and fell, tumbling down the rest of the way, and caught herself just before she would have rolled into a nasty jagged metal mess that used to be the hidden panel's door.

Claire shoved it out of the way, panting with fear and adrenaline, and saw one of the monsters leap down behind her on the stairs. It sniffed the air, and those yellow eyes widened, fixed straight on her, and took on an unholy shimmer as it opened its mouth to snarl.

Then it let out a howl that froze her bones, and Claire didn't wait to see if it was going to give chase.

She just left Amelie behind, and ran.

SEVEN

She was halfway to the stairs when the creature burst out of the door, still giving that eerie, wailing howl, and Claire plunged the rest of the way at a dead run. She couldn't let it catch her. It was following the scent of Amelie's blood on her, and it would treat her like a vampire—it would rip her to shreds, assuming that she would heal.

But she wouldn't, of course. If it caught her, it was all over. Her calculated risk would have failed. She'd thought that if Amelie had only one of these things to deal with, she might be able to fight her way free. That was Claire's theory, anyway. She hoped she hadn't just sacrificed herself for nothing.

"Shane!" Claire yelled as she reached the stairs and began racing down them. She didn't feel the scrapes and bruises and muscle strains she was sure she'd earned with that first tumble down the hidden room's steps. She'd pay for it later, but for now her panic was overriding all the normal responses. Nothing was broken, at least; she could still put her weight equally on both legs. That was all that mattered.

Shane was at the bottom of the stairs, standing there with the heavy duffel bag of weapons, staring up at her. He wasn't moving. He looked . . . odd.

"Shane!" she called again, and looked back over her shoulder. She saw the monster coming into view, all yellow eyes and gleaming claws and the remains of that ridiculous sundress. "Shane, I need a weapon!" She didn't even care what it was, not yet. There wasn't time to be scientific just now.

But Shane *wasn't moving*. No. Now he was, to drop the duffel with a crash to the wood floor.

Something was happening to him. His eyes . . .

He was changing.

No. She'd forgotten in the crush of events, forgotten what the effect could be if he came face-to-face with a vampire . . .

. . . or someone who smelled like one.

He closed his eyes and when they opened, they gleamed acid yellow, with pupils that shrank into vertical slits.

Claws burst bloodily out of his fingertips, like some nightmare version of a superhero, but what he was becoming was something else, something far worse, and the howl that came out of his throat was nothing but rage and animal fury.

Claire screamed back, a full-throated cry of heartbreak and rage and fury and fear, and did the only thing she could—she rushed down, trying to get past him before he was fully changed. They'd gotten *Shane*. What was even worse was that he was close, he was fast, and she had only the tiniest chance of evading him. The only thing in her favor was that the change had just started on him, and he was still confused and in pain.

She had no choice but to try to get by him.

"Please," she whispered. There were tears of sheer terror in her eyes, and heartache, because even now she couldn't help but feel horror at what was happening to him, at the pain he was feeling. "Please, Shane, it's me. It's Claire."

He was changing fast, and there was nothing of Shane left in his eyes, just pure instinct and rage. His clothing hampered his shift, but that wasn't going to last long; his claws were even now ripping at the tough cloth of his jeans to shred them.

Claire took in a deep breath, grabbed the railing with both hands, and vaulted over it, the way she'd seen Shane do a million times. She landed on the bounce of Michael's armchair and launched half a dozen feet into the air, to come to an awkward, stumbling landing still on her feet in front of the darkened TV.

Shane howled behind her, and when she looked back she saw he was almost completely hellhound now, muscles bunching and shifting and driving him to all fours. His body didn't look human anymore.

She saw all that in a rush because then he was on her, leaping the distance to slam into her chest.

She somehow got her hands between them, pressing against skin—no, not skin anymore, *fur*, stiff and harsh against her fingers—and Shane's mouth—*muzzle*—was opening and the teeth, the teeth were sharp and endless, and she knew she was about to die.

And she closed her eyes so she wouldn't see it coming.

He made a sound that resonated inside her—a high-pitched whine of pain and anguish. She felt the raw heat of his breath on her neck and forced herself to open her eyes again and stare right into his.

"It's me," she whispered. "Shane. It's me."

He snarled, but it turned into a whine again, and then his body tensed and she thought, *This is it, it's the end.* She'd risked her life, and this time, finally, she'd lost it on the gamble. She wasn't afraid exactly—shock had already taken over to protect her from that. But she was sad. Sad that it was going to be Shane, of all people. Sad that this would be another thing he'd have to live with after all the losses he'd suffered in his life.

She felt his body move, and it took her a second to realize that he wasn't lunging down toward her, but away.

Away, to collide with the second hellhound leaping for her from the stairs.

They tangled up in a snarling, slashing heap on the floor beside the couch.

She didn't wait to see who won; against all his instincts, all the programming that was running through his veins, Shane had given her a chance, and that was all she could ask. She had to keep moving, no matter what, and draw them away from Amelie if she could.

The house really was on her side, because as she darted through the kitchen door, a spray of water jetted out from the sink as if a pipe had ruptured, and hit her squarely in the face and chest, drenching her and rinsing away most of Amelie's blood. She paused for a second to scrub frantically at her skin, and then as the water cut off, she grabbed for one of Shane's beloved extinguisher grenades. She armed it just as the kitchen door smashed open, and Shane and the other hound broke through. She tossed it straight at them as she opened the back door, and it hit the ground right in front of Shane's feet, then exploded into a choking cloud of white powder that shimmered and billowed in the air.

It made a great distraction, and she took full advantage of it to run, fast, out of the backyard and onto the street.

The pole lights were all on, gleaming golden, and she considered running to a neighbor's house for help—but she didn't know which, if any, of her neighbors could be trusted anymore. (Not that they'd been all that trustworthy in the first place, honestly.) Shane's muscle car must have been stashed somewhere back at Jenna's house, but she hadn't asked him where to find it, and she didn't have time to play hide-and-seek, not tonight. The police were looking for her, and now she had—what *were* they? hellhounds? *werewolves?*—on her trail.

Although they hadn't followed her out here. Not yet. The quick-rinse solution seemed to have done its job, along with the powder bomb; it must have confused them, and maybe destroyed their sense of smell temporarily.

Claire just picked a direction, ultimately, and began to run. She stayed at the edges of the streetlights, watched her back, and kept an eye out for police cruisers, but it seemed quiet enough. Too quiet, maybe.

The quiet shattered in a rising wail of police sirens, and she took a welcome breather hiding behind a hedge as three cars streaked by, red and blue flashers painting the world in primary colors before it sank back into shades of gray. They were headed toward the Glass House, she thought. She doubted Amelie had dialed 911, but maybe one of the neighbors had gotten too alarmed to ignore all the strangeness. Morganville was, after all, a law-abiding town now.

Or maybe someone had just spotted her and recognized her as Morganville's Most Wanted. That wouldn't be nearly as good.

Claire eased out from the bushes again. She was shivering now, since the water she'd been drenched with was slowly drying in the cold desert air, and despite the run she was getting chilled out here, quickly. Normally she'd have run to Myrnin's lab, but going there would only expose her to more danger. Still, she craved the comfort of someplace familiar, even if it was unwise. Or creepy. The known was always better than the unknown.

Stop it, she told herself sternly. *You're a scientist, right? Stop being afraid of the unknown.* That steadied her. Science had helped her think of tainting herself with Amelie's blood to draw off the attackers, and science had helped her remember the extinguisher grenades. The unknown wasn't full of terrors, it was full of undiscovered advantages. Better to run toward something than run from something.

The Glass House was in mortal danger now; if Amelie managed to take advantage of the confusion and get out of there, escape to the little town of Blacke, there was no way Fallon was going to allow the Founder Houses to be left standing. He would destroy Amelie's last refuges, and their home.

Claire knew she couldn't defend it just by staying and fighting for it; that was defensive, and she needed offense now. She needed to get to Fallon.

She needed to stop this—for Shane, for Michael, for the safety of the Glass House. Besides, she wasn't alone if she ran toward the center of the danger . . .

Because Eve was already there.

Claire kept to the shadows on the way to the edge of town. She remembered the way, at least, and if nothing else the constant walking she'd done at MIT over the past few weeks had prepared her for the relatively short distances of hiking Morganville. There was no problem with lurking in the darkness these days, no vampires ready to strike at least. Though she had no idea where Myrnin was now, or if Amelie had actually managed to fight her way free of the Glass House. If she had, then Shane would be . . .

Would be hunting Amelie.

That thought crushed her heart. Shane had always, deep inside, loathed the vampires; he'd willingly signed up to find a way to deliver Morganville from their clutches when he'd been with his dad's crew. But Claire thought that he'd come to accept them, a little—particularly Michael. Having your best friend grow fangs was guaranteed to cause a serious reevaluation of your prejudices.

But it seemed as if the hate had always been thrust upon him, that it wasn't something he'd chosen for himself—and this was no different. She didn't want to see Shane like that, lost to bloodlust and rage and violence. He was better than that.

They were all better than that.

Claire stopped at a small, neglected water fountain in one of the few parks along the way, and washed off again, trying to get any trace of Amelie's blood off of her. She wasn't sure how good Shane's senses would be outside, but she suspected that when Fallon created hunting dogs, he did an expert job of it. And as much as she wanted to be with Shane, she never wanted to see him like that again.

The cold, cutting wind felt much worse once she'd dampened her clothes, and she thought grimly that she was bound to come down sick after this—if she survived.

The worst she endured on the way to the Daylight Foundation, though, was the chill, and an attack of a couple of wandering tumbleweeds that—as tumbleweeds did—blew straight for her even when she tried to avoid them. The tiny burrs on the rounded plants made them hard to pry out of her jeans and left itchy places on her fingers where they pierced skin. The tumbleweeds also had a tendency to come blowing across in packs, so she had to play dodge-the-weeds more frequently than she liked . . . and then she saw the glow of a neon sign ahead as she turned the corner. This part of town was still mostly under construction, though the sites lay silent now, workers all gone home and tools left abandoned for the night. The smells of new wood and dust mingled, and made her suppress a sneeze as she paused at the intersection. To her left, a neon sign two stories in the air glowed orange and bright yellow.

The stylized image of the sunrise, worn by the Daylighters as a pin.

Claire moved carefully, but she saw no one, again. There were a few cars still in the parking lot, and as she got closer she spotted Eve's distinctive black hearse with its elaborate chrome. At first, Claire felt a surge of relief, because it meant that Eve was still here, somewhere, . . . but then she realized that if Fallon had decided to dump her in with the vampires at the mall, he'd hardly have troubled to move her car yet. So the presence of the hearse really didn't mean anything at all, except that Eve had parked it there. It wasn't an indicator of where she was.

Claire needed to get inside to find her, and to find a way to get to Fallon.

Doubts had settled in on the walk, and she was trying to ignore them. Eve had come here with the exact same mission—to stop Fallon. How far had she gotten? *How can I be sure I can do any better?*

She wished that Myrnin hadn't gone off with Jenna. She needed him now, more than ever.

The first step—the only step—was to try to find out what was happening inside the Daylight Foundation. If Eve was still there, she had an ally. If she wasn't, that was one more incentive for Claire to find Fallon and end this, once and for all.

She heard a howl in the distance, long and eerie, and that decided her.

Sometimes the safest place to be was right in the heart of the enemy.

The front door was impossible; there were still lights on in the lobby, and as she positioned herself at the right angle, she could see that a jacketed security guard was sitting behind the desk where the receptionist had been earlier. No sign of Eve, or Fallon, for that matter. Claire went around the building to the side and found windows— all locked. The offices were darkened, though. She wondered about alarms, and went all the way around the perimeter, just in case.

Good thing she did, because she found that one of the windows at the back had been left open. Not much, just a crack, but enough to reassure her that it wasn't alarmed. She found a rusty piece of rebar on the ground nearby and used it to lever the window up. It must have been stuck, which was why it hadn't been closed in the first place, and she was afraid she'd shatter it, but it finally came loose and slid upward.

Even fully open, it wasn't a big opening, and she had to shimmy through carefully. Her hips barely scraped through, and she tumbled head over heels into a dimly lit storage area full of racks of books and bottles. It all looked boringly normal, actually. There was nothing sinister about toilet paper and cleaning sprays, and even the books were all about how to make yourself a better person. This was the public face of the Daylight Foundation. The private face was, of course, that dismal mall and those vampires in their so-called enclave, waiting for——for what?

Extinction.

Claire tried the supply closet door. It opened from the inside—— a safety precaution against getting locked in, she supposed——but when she tried the outer handle it didn't move, so she found a piece of tape and secured the lock so it didn't engage. She and Eve might need a fast way out. Hopefully not, but smart people planned for contingencies along the way.

The hallways were silent, just as normal and boring as the supply closet had been——carpeted, blank, peppered with wooden doors and nameplates. It still smelled of fresh paint. Hannah Moses had her own office, and Claire felt a tingle of alarm when she saw it, but luckily it was after hours; the door was locked, and no lights showed beneath. How did that work, exactly? Did the chief of police have to actually split her time between working for the city and working for Fallon, or was it——at least on paper—— more of a volunteer kind of thing? Hannah didn't have a choice, no more than Shane had, but Claire supposed Fallon would want to make it look aboveboard. At least for now.

She was halfway to the lobby when she heard the sound of voices. At the intersection of another hallway she turned right, following the sound, because one of the voices was Eve's. She recognized the tones easily, but the words were smeared and indistinct.

There was only one door on that hallway, and it was at the end. Fallon's office.

Claire moved closer, trying to hear what they were saying, but she caught only random words. Michael's name was mentioned—— not a surprise——but what worried her was the way Eve was talking.

It sounded . . . relaxed. Calm. Almost drowsy. Had he done something to her? Drugged her?

She was about three steps from the door when she heard Fallon's voice very clearly. He'd moved closer on the other side, and he
said, "I know it seems strange to you, but I do admire you, you
know. I admire your audacity in coming here. I admire the strength
of your conviction that there's something of the young man you
loved left buried inside the monster. Maybe there is, because he's
so very young. I hope so, for your sake."

"You have to let him go," Eve said. "I'll kill you if you don't."
The words were fierce, but not the voice. She sounded almost on
the verge of the giggles. "You drugged me. You drugged my water.
That was mean."

"I didn't want to harm you, Eve," he said. "You're what I'm
fighting for—humanity. You simply can't accept the truth. That's
not your fault, but it is dangerous, both to you and to me. You and
your friend Claire, you're not like the rest. You see vampires as humans with a problem—but that's wrong, very wrong. There's
nothing human left in them."

"Michael's still Michael."

"You're wrong about that. I see that I have no choice but to
prove it to you, Eve. You're a remarkable young lady, you know—
I've never seen anyone stand quite so firm on a relationship with a
vampire before. It makes me sad. It also gives me hope."

There was the sharp, musical sound of a desk phone ringing
then, and Fallon answered it. He didn't say much, but what he did
say sounded razor-edged and angry. "How? Whose incompetence
allowed that to happen? Yes, I'll want to talk to them. Keep them
there. I'm on my way." He slammed the phone down and cursed in

some liquid, fluid language Claire didn't recognize, but she was sure it was cursing; it had that tone.

"What's happening?" Eve asked. It sounded like she was trying to stand up, but not managing the job very well. "Michael? Is Michael safe?"

"Let's go and see him," Fallon said grimly. "I'll have some questions for him, and all the rest."

There was something in those words that warned Claire to get out of the way, and she turned and ran quickly down the corridor to the intersection, whipped to the right, and pressed herself against the wall. She made it with only a second to spare before she heard Fallon's door click open and heard Eve say, in that lazy, almost dreamlike voice, "Where are we going?"

"To visit young Michael, remember?" Fallon said. "And show you that he isn't worthy of your love. Come on, my dear, let's have your arm—there you go. How are you feeling?"

"Dizzy," Eve said. She didn't sound good. "Did I drink? I really should get home now. It's late. Claire's going to worry. She's a worrier, you know. Claire. She thinks too much. Thinks all the time. I wish she'd just let go sometimes and be . . . you know. Just be."

"I'm sure she's fine," Fallon said, and Claire gritted her teeth. What a liar he was—he'd have known exactly what had happened to her at the house, known all about the dead guard, too. He'd know she'd been arrested and taken to the police station. He probably even knew she'd been broken out, and that there were hellhounds on her trail.

The thing was, no matter how many date-rape drugs Fallon gave Eve, she wasn't going to get over loving Michael—which meant that she was going to be in even more danger once he realized that.

Claire heard footsteps and wondered if she ought to move, but there really wasn't any place to hide; the door behind her was locked, and running to the storage closet would be noticed. So she stayed very still, held her breath, and listened as Fallon and Eve made their way past her to the corner and then turned left, toward the lobby. Away from her.

Eve was walking on her own, but only just barely; she seemed unsteady in her combat boots, and was holding on to Fallon for support. He seemed happy with that. Claire's eyes narrowed when she saw that he'd put his other arm around Eve's shoulders, as if he had the right to do that.

No doubt about it, Fallon intended to do something to Michael; he wanted Eve to have her heart crushed, her love destroyed. And Claire couldn't let that happen—but she had no idea how to stop it, either. As Fallon and Eve reached the lobby, she realized that one thing Eve didn't have on her was her purse, a black coffin-shaped thing with silver studs. Eve loved that purse. She'd never leave it behind, unless she'd been drugged enough to forget it.

Claire backed up and ran as quietly as she could down the hall to Fallon's office. He hadn't locked the door—confident of him—and she quickly scanned the room. It was big, which she'd expected; a golden sunrise plaque decorated the wall behind Fallon's large wooden desk. The whole room was done up in golds and oranges and browns, tasteful and soothing.

Eve's black coffin purse lay discarded on the floor next to the visitor's chair across from the desk. Claire picked it up, checked inside, and found Eve's car keys. There was a small container of pepper spray clipped on them, for emergencies. No sign of the giant backpack she'd brought, unfortunately; Claire really could have used an arsenal right now, but Fallon must have confiscated it and locked it away. She slung Eve's purse over her shoulder and went around to the other side of the desk, sat in Fallon's still-warm chair, and began pulling open drawers. Boring stuff. Office supplies. A few folders, but mostly they were concerned with civic planning and nothing to do with vampires.

There was, however, a locked drawer. Locked drawers were always interesting.

Claire opened the office supply drawer and found a long steel letter opener. She slipped it between the cracks at the top of the locked drawer and tried to pry it open; she managed to get it separated a bit, but the letter opener was too springy to really work.

A pair of sharp, long-bladed scissors worked much better as a lever.

The lock broke free with a snap, and the drawer slid smoothly open, revealing a whole collection of neatly ranked files. They all had printed labels, and Claire recognized every single name in there.

Every one was a vampire.

She grabbed Amelie's, Myrnin's, Oliver's, and Michael's and spread them out on the desktop. Amelie's was thicker than the others, and she quickly flipped through it, looking for clues. What she found instead was history—in-depth history that she'd never seen before, about Amelie's birth, her death, her resurrection. Her parentage, both human and vampire. A list of all those she'd made vampire in the years after—a long list, but the intervals between making new ones got longer and longer in the most recent hundred years, until there was only Sam Glass, and then his grandson Michael.

In strangely loopy, antique handwriting, someone—probably Fallon—had left a note beneath Michael's name that said, *end of line.* That seemed ominous.

At the back of the file was a page, all handwritten, with Fallon's observations about Amelie—strengths and weaknesses. Claire scanned it quickly and felt a real chill crawl over her, because her own name was in it. Under *both* columns.

Under *strengths* she was listed as *Strong human advocate and ally.* That wasn't how Claire would have described her relationship with Amelie. But under *weaknesses,* he'd written *Amelie shows a great fondness for the girl, and threats to her may be successful in weakening A.'s resolve.*

Claire really doubted that, but she also thought it was a very bad thing for her that he might try it.

Michael was in there, too, under *weaknesses.* Fallon had written, *Threats to Michael Glass may prove effective, as he is the only relative of Samuel Glass left in Morganville, and her attachment to Samuel is well known.*

Definitely ominous.

Myrnin's folder would have been interesting reading, in the historical section, but she skipped it and went straight for the strengths and weaknesses section. She was in it again, but she'd expected that. Apparently Fallon thought threatening her would get Myrnin in line.

He was probably right on that. Probably.

She didn't even appear on Oliver's lists. The only one who did was Amelie . . . as a weakness. Under strengths there wasn't a person's name at all. Only one word.

Ruthless.

Michael's folder had a red stamp on the front page that said CURE.

Claire stared at it, frowning. The stamp had the Daylighters symbol beneath it, and she didn't entirely understand what it meant, but it didn't look good, she thought.

She wanted to take all of the folders, but there were too many, and they were too heavy. She just ripped out Fallon's notes on each person and made a sheaf of paper that she stuck into Eve's coffin purse. Then she slammed the drawer shut and started to get up.

Something caught her eye as she did . . . another folder, lying in the tray on top of the desk. This one also had a CURE stamp on the outside. She pulled it over and found that it belonged to a vampire she knew a little: Mr. Ransom. Ransom was an old, ghostly man who ran the local funeral home.

There were, she realized, little boxes under the CURE stamp. She hadn't noticed them before. One said VOLUNTARY. The other said INVOLUNTARY.

The INVOLUNTARY box was checked on Ransom's.

She opened it, and found the history again, and the strengths and weaknesses analysis page . . . in Ransom's case, not very informative. He was too much of a loner, hardly interacting with even other vampires, much less humans.

But there was another page, a new one. There was a photo of Mr. Ransom.

He looked . . . *dead.*

It was a very clinical kind of picture, taken from above; Ransom's body was lying on a steel table mostly covered by a thin white sheet. No wounds. He looked old and withered and pathetic, and she couldn't imagine anything that would have kept a vampire lying there like that, being photographed, except a stake in the heart . . . but there was no stake in Ransom's heart. No wound at all.

He just looked dead.

She flipped the page. It was a medical report, tersely worded.

Subject Ransom received the Cure in the appropriately measured dose as established in Protocol H, as determined by age, height, and weight. After a brief period of lucidity, his mental state rapidly declined, and he lapsed into a comatose state. He roused from this upon three occasions and indicated significant pain and distress. Recordings were made of his vocalizations, but the language was not familiar to any of the observers.

After the third period of partial lucidity, Subject Ransom experienced a rapid mental and physical decline, as has been previously documented in the trials; this decline fell within the boundaries of the approximately 73% failure rate. He evidenced a brief period of reversion to True Human before experiencing a fatal ischemic event. Time of death: 1348 hours.

May God have mercy on his soul.

Mr. Ransom was *dead*. Because of their so-called cure.

It couldn't be called a cure if there was a seventy-three percent failure rate, could it?

She opened the drawer and checked Michael's file again. The box was marked for an involuntary cure.

What had happened to Mr. Ransom— they meant to do it to Michael, too.

Claire ripped the information out of Ransom's folder and added it to her stash, then quickly made her way back to the storage closet and out through the window. No sign of Fallon and Eve, but she saw a car's taillights disappearing around the corner.

Claire ran for Eve's hearse, digging the keys out of the purse.

She'd rarely driven the thing, but it couldn't be much tougher than Shane's beast of a muscle car; this was more of an ocean liner, with all the problems of maneuvering it around corners. Claire started the engine and did a super-wide turn in the nearly empty parking lot, heading for the street. She was just pausing to check directions when a voice *way* too close to her ear said, "So where are we going, then?"

Myrnin. She got a grip on herself after the first, uncontrollable flail of shock, and turned to glare at him. He was leaning over her seat, cheek almost pressing hers, and his eyes reflected red in the dashboard lights.

"Would you please sit back?" she said, once she had control of her voice again—though it stayed up in the higher registers. "You just scared ten years off of me."

"Only ten? I'm losing my touch."

"What are you doing in here?"

"Hiding," he said. "You might have noticed that Fallon's got his very own vampire-hunting pack of human hounds. Unfortunately, they had my scent for a while. I think I've thrown them off, but I thought it wise to go to ground for a while. You know that I'm clever as a fox."

"Crazy like one, too," she said. "Where's Jenna?"

"Gone home," he said. "She took me to my laboratory, but I found it in less than salutary condition. I got what I need, however." He patted lumps under his shirt absently. "I do hope you're going my way."

"I'm following Fallon. I think he's taking Eve to the mall."

"Ah. Perfect, then. That will be fine. Proceed." He sat back, as if she were his private limo driver, which made her grit her teeth, but she concentrated on driving for a minute, until she had Fallon's taillights in sight again. He was, indeed, heading for Bitter Creek Mall, it seemed.

She said, "Fallon thinks he has some kind of a cure for vampirism. Did you know?"

"Oh, yes," he said. "I know all about Fallon and his misguided quest to become our once and future savior. It's never worked. It's never *going* to work."

"Do you have a plan?"

"Yes. I plan to kill Fallon and destroy everything he's built."

"I think Shane would say that's a goal, not an actual plan. How exactly are you going to do that?"

"Fangs in his throat," Myrnin said. "To be specific. I am going to take a great deal of pleasure in draining that man to the very last drop. Again."

"Again?" Claire hit the brakes and held them, staring at Myrnin in the rearview mirror. "What are you talking about?"

Myrnin clambered over the seat and dropped into the front next to her. He fussed with his clothes—still mismatched, of course—and finally said, "Fallon, of course. I killed him once. I brought him over as a vampire some, oh, two hundred years ago or more—it's difficult to be exact about these things. I didn't much care for him even then. He was a bit of a morose and morbid sort, but—well, circumstances were different. Let's just leave it there."

"He's *not* a vampire!"

"Well, not now, obviously. But he most certainly was once. Didn't love the life I'd given him, Fallon. Thought he was so much better than the rest who did." Myrnin shrugged. "He might have been right about that, of course. But the point is that he devoted all the time I'd given him to finding a way to reverse the process and make himself human again."

"He found one," Claire said. "He cured himself. That's what this cure is he wants to give Michael . . . the same one."

"I wouldn't call it a cure," Myrnin said. "He's simply no longer dependent on blood."

"What is he dependent on, then?"

"What are any of you? Air, water, food, the kindness of random strangers." Myrnin shuddered, and it looked genuine. "I'd much rather be dependent on blood. Much simpler and easier to obtain in times of chaos. Never rationed, blood. And very often freely donated."

"But he's—he's human."

"Well, yes. Heartbeat and all."

"Is he still immortal?"

"No one is immortal." Myrnin sounded quite serious when he said that, and he looked away, out the window. "Certainly no vampire. We are as vulnerable as humans to the right forces. Only gods and demons are immortal, and we are neither of those things, though we've been called one or the other."

"I mean—does he age now?"

"Yes. The instant he gave up his vampire nature, he began the slow march to death again. I expect after all that time with his heart stilled in him, he thinks of each beat as a tick off his mortal clock. I certainly would."

"How did he do it?"

"I don't know," Myrnin said. He sounded sober and thoughtful, and rested his head on one hand as he continued to stare out at the night. "I really have no earthly idea. He was desperate to find some kind of cure when I lost track of him. He'd employed physicians, scientists, even sorcerers, to try to break what he saw as his curse. Until I saw him again here, I'd have sworn that such a thing was completely impossible. There is still much to learn in the world, as it turns out. The problem is that some lessons are very, very unpleasant, Claire. I hope this isn't one of them, but I very much fear it will be."

She thought of the stamp on Michael's folder. INVOLUNTARY.

"Mr. Ransom is dead," she said. "According to the notes in the file in Fallon's desk, this cure of his—it's only about twenty-five percent successful."

"Unsurprising. The Daylight Foundation—which Fallon created, of course—has from the very beginning been intent on stopping vampires, eradicating them through whatever means necessary. He'd see a cure as a humane way to do it, wouldn't he? Even if three-quarters of those were put through such agony that they perished of it." He let out a sigh. "A humane process, after the word *human*. But in my experience, humans are capable of such spectacularly awful things."

She didn't like the sound of that, not at all, nor the thought of Fallon, with his calm, gentle manner and his fanatic's eyes, having control of Eve, and Michael, and all of the vampires imprisoned back at the mall. "How did he get Amelie to surrender?" she asked. Myrnin didn't answer. "He threatened someone, didn't he?"

"He threatened the people she least wanted to lose," he replied. "One of them was Michael, of course, but before our little party arrived back in town, Fallon had Oliver, and he used him against her."

"He used you, too, didn't he?" Nothing. She took that as confirmation. "Myrnin, he's got Eve now. And from what I saw written on Michael's file, Fallon's going to use her to make Michael take his cure or something."

"Well, that would be a problem," he said. "I quite like the boy. And Fallon's cure is certainly horrifyingly painful, even if one survives it, and as you know, the odds are against it. I've no idea what kind of damage it might leave in its wake on a vampire as young as Michael. Nor does Fallon, I suspect. Not that it would stop him."

Claire could see the mall ahead, its bulk lit up outside with harsh industrial lamps that made it look ever more like a prison, if prisons had abundant parking. "We have to do something."

"Oh, I fully intend to, and I will need you to make it happen. You are my assistant, after all. I pay you."

"*Amelie* pays me. I don't think you have the slightest idea of how to work a bank account."

"True," he said cheerfully. "It was much easier in the days when you could pay someone in food and a roof over his head, and the richness of knowledge. All this moneygrubbing is simply annoying. Do you still use gold? I think I have some of that."

"Let's not get off track," Claire said, although she was thinking, *You've got gold? Where do you keep it?* "What exactly do you want me to do?"

"I need a second pair of hands—human hands, as it turns out, and quite clever ones—to help me sabotage those damnable collars. Dr. Anderson is no fool, and although I've worked out how to do it, it does require nerve and someone with a pulse; two vampires simply can't manage it. Speaking of our dear, traitorous Irene, she'll be working around the clock to mass-produce your anti-vampire weapons, and once that happens, they will have absolutely everything they need to control, corral, and herd us to our destruction. We can't allow that to happen, Claire. So I need you to go into the prison with me and help me disable the collars."

"I'm not sure—"

"They're killing us when we fight back," Myrnin said. "They already know how to do it, of course. Very effectively, I might add, and quite painfully. The methods they use last long enough to be a very instructive lesson to others, and I might admire their ruthlessness if it didn't come at the cost of my old friends. This is a situation that cannot hold for long, and we must, absolutely *must*, free the vampires before it's too late." He eyed her sideways, then said, "I don't think you'll be in too much danger. Oliver and Lady Grey and I can ensure your safety. Almost certainly."

That didn't sound quite as positive as Claire would have preferred, really, but she couldn't expect much better. "How do we get inside?"

"Same way I got out," Myrnin said. "Through the waste chute. Come on, then. Park this ridiculous thing and let's make all haste. I do hope those aren't your best clothes."

She should have known it would be something horrible.

Getting in by the waste chute was even worse than Claire had expected. When the mall had been abandoned, the chute—leading from the second floor through a claustrophobic metal tube that angled down at a ridiculous slope straight into a long-neglected, rusted-out trash bin—the chute had apparently never been cleaned. The layers of ancestral rotten food, decay, and generally horrible filth were enough to make her seriously reconsider going at all, but Eve was inside, and she needed help. "I can't," Claire said. She wasn't talking about the slime, though. "I'm only human, Myrnin. I can't climb up that!"

"You won't need to," he said, and offered her a cool, strong hand. "Up you go. I'll push."

He shoved her up into the tiny, tinny opening without giving her time to get ready, and she felt a moment of utter panic and nausea that almost made her scream—and then his palm landed solidly on her butt as she started to slide backward. "Hey!" she whispered shakily, but he was already pushing her steadily forward, up the angle. One thing about all the awful slime, it did make her progress faster. She tried not to think about what she might be sliding through. Really, really tried. The smell was indescribable. "Watch the hands!"

"It's entirely propulsional," he whispered back. "Quiet, now. Sound carries." She had no idea how he was managing to climb, or to push her ahead of him, but she thought that he sank his nails deep into the ooze and anchored them in the metal to do it—like climbing spikes. Each push drove her steadily on. She gave up futilely trying to feel for handholds and instead focused on keeping her hands outstretched ahead, to shove utterly unknown and very disturbing blockages out of the way before she met them face-first. It was both the shortest and longest minute of her life, and she had to hang on tight to all of her self-control to keep herself from caving in under the stress and giving away their position with helpless, girlie shrieks of revulsion.

And then it was over, and she slid at an angle out of the metal pipe, and a pair of strong, pale hands grabbed her flailing wrists to pull her up and onto her feet. Claire blinked and in the dim light made out the glossy red hair and razor-sharp smile of her friend from Cambridge, Jesse. Lady Grey, as Myrnin called her. She'd been a bartender when Claire had met her, but that was before Claire had realized she was a vampire. She'd probably been a lot of things during her long, long life, and nearly all of them interesting.

"Well," Jesse said, raising her eyebrows to a skeptical height. "I admit I didn't really expect this." She let Claire go, and turned toward the pipe again to offer a helping hand to Myrnin, who was clambering out under his own power. Claire was sorry to lose the support, because her legs were still shaking, and she grabbed for a handy plastic chair to collapse into. *What did I just crawl through?* She supposed it really was better that she didn't know, but she desperately needed a shower, a scrub brush, and some bleach. And new clothes, because no matter how hard she washed these, she would never, ever wear them again.

Jesse was talking as Myrnin came sliding the rest of the way out of the pipe. "You brought *her* here? I have to ask, did you just crave a snack, or do you have some clever plan to save her life? Because you know the mood in here."

"I do," he agreed. "I also know her life wasn't worth a dried fig out there in Morganville. Better here where her allies might be able to protect her than out there, dodging enemies all alone."

"As if she doesn't have any enemies here?"

He shrugged. "None that matter. Oliver is not unfond of the girl, and there are many who have some graceful experience of her. She might have a few who'd be happy to feast, but not so many we can't stop them."

"We?" Jesse crossed her arms and stared at him, her head cocked. "Assuming a lot, aren't we, dear madman?"

"A fair amount," he admitted. "But needs must, from time to time, assume things. And I believe that I can count on you, my lady." He gave her a very elegant bow that was only a little spoiled by the slime that covered him. Jesse, for her part, didn't laugh. Much. She responded with a curtsy only a little spoiled by the fact that she was wearing blue jeans and a tight T-shirt instead of fancy court clothes.

"Fine," she said. "I'll play along and help keep fangs out of our little friend. Bad news: Fallon's here. He blew in like a bad wind a few moments ago. I think he's discovered that Amelie made it out alive."

"Then he's not pleased."

"Oh, no," Jesse said, with a broad, tight smile. "We've all been summoned to the bottom floor for questioning. You'll need to clean yourself off before they discover how it is you're getting out, though I think you've ruined all the extra clothes by now."

He shrugged that off with magnificent indifference. "I'll find something."

"I'm quite sure you will," she agreed. "Let me scrounge something for you. I might do a better job of matching colors, at least."

He gave her a wry slice of a smile, and between one blink and the next, Jesse was just . . . gone. It was her and Myrnin, alone in a room that was, Claire realized, sort of a bedroom. There were two camp beds in it, at least, each with a neatly folded thin blanket on it. Nothing else in the room, though—no personal effects of any kind. It could have been anybody's room, or no one's.

"Jesse will be back in a moment," Myrnin said. "She's right. If they've ordered us below, then I need to clean up quickly. If anyone comes to bite you while I'm gone—well, try not to attract attention. Die quietly."

"I *can* defend myself, you know."

"With your bare hands, against hungry, bored, angry vampires? Claire. You know I think well of you, but that is really not your best problem-solving work." He shook his head as if very disappointed with her lack of vision. "At least the offal you're covered in will disguise the scent of your blood for now. Just stay quiet and still, and you ought to be fine. Besides, I doubt anyone's hungry enough to bite you while you're quite so . . . filthy."

She was pretty sure there was something insulting in there, but it was also comforting.

Myrnin disappeared, just as Jesse had, and Claire was left standing alone in the dim, quiet room. She hadn't seen him do it, but Myrnin had replaced the grate over the pipe they'd used to enter; she went over and tested it, but it didn't budge, and she realized that he'd bent it into place. Nobody would realize it was anything but solid, not even on close inspection. It would take vampire strength to even begin to pry it loose.

Was that how Amelie had gotten out? Through the slime? Somehow Claire couldn't imagine Her Immaculateness sliding through the ooze on her way out, or making her way across Morganville looking like a refugee from the Nickelodeon Awards. One thing vampires were big on was dignity.

She was deep in contemplation of the vent and its implications when she realized that she had a visitor. It wasn't Myrnin. It wasn't even Jesse.

It was Michael.

She flinched, because he was just *right there*, no warning, no sound. He wasn't usually like that, so . . . vampiric. In the house, Michael always took special care to make sure they heard him coming, and she'd never bothered to wonder before if that took a lot of extra effort for him—if he felt as if he was forced to be embarrassingly clumsy around them, just to avoid scaring the crap out of them in the kitchen or the hallway.

Then in the next split second she realized that he certainly hadn't bothered this time, and there was something in the way he was watching her—the utter stillness of his body and face—that made her feel deeply uneasy.

"Michael?" She almost blurted out *you scared me*, but that was blindingly obvious from the way she'd jumped and from the no doubt deafening sound of her racing heartbeat. Her pulse should have been slowing down after the first instant of alarm/recognition, but instead it continued drumming right on, as if her body knew something her mind didn't.

She didn't move. That took a lot of effort, actually, because those same instincts insisting to her that she was scared were also wanting her to take at least a couple of steps back. Large steps, at that.

Michael said, "I lied to Eve."

As totally confusing openings went, that was a new one—both unexpected and ominous. "Um . . . okay. About what?"

"I said they were feeding us, but they like us weak. The weaker, the better. They do give us blood, but it's soured, somehow. Drugged. It doesn't really help," Michael said. His soft, measured voice sounded oddly soothing to her, and she felt her heartbeat slowing down, finally. He was her friend, after all. One of her very best and sweetest friends. "I heard your voice. I knew you were here."

"It's good to see you," she said. Her own voice sounded strange now, oddly calm and flat. "Are you okay?"

"No," he said. "He brought Eve. He's going to use her against me. I'm very hungry. And you shouldn't be here, Claire. I don't want you to be here, because . . ." A twitch of a smile, like a spasm of pain, came across his lips and then was immediately gone again. "You smell terrible, you know."

"Sorry. It's the slime."

"But I still want you."

She opened her mouth and realized she had nothing to say to that. Nothing at all. Because it was shocking and wrong and *so very wrong* and this was Michael saying it, and despite the fact that everything seemed weirdly okay, as if she was soaking in a soothing bath and everything was a dream . . . she understood two things: he didn't mean it as sexually as it sounded, and also, it was *so not okay.*

He was closer to her now, and she didn't see him move. He was just . . . closer. Watching her. She didn't like that. Inside the calm cocoon, something in her twisted and pushed and tried to break free of the sticky, syrupy layers of calm she'd become wrapped in.

Please don't do this.

He was too close now. She could have reached out and put her hand on his chest, and what was her hand doing rising like that, as if she had no real control over it, and why were his eyes turning so *red* . . .

"*Michael.*"

The voice was low and cold, and Claire felt the tone stab straight through that cocoon that wrapped her so tightly and rip it open. The air suddenly felt heavy on her skin, and too thick, and she couldn't get her breath. Her pulse kick-started faster again, and she stumbled backward until her shoulders touched a wall.

Jesse was in the doorway. She looked wild and dangerous and angry, and when Michael took another step in Claire's direction Jesse came at him, wrapped a fist in the fabric of his T-shirt, and threw the younger vampire ten feet toward the exit. When he tried to lunge for Claire again, Jesse caught him, steadied him, and held on when he tried to pull free. "Nope," she said, and patted his shoulder. "You're going to thank me later when you have a chance to think about it. Not your fault, kid. Believe me. But you'd take it hard if this went badly."

"I wouldn't hurt her," he growled, and Claire saw his fangs then, down and sharp and glittering. "She's my friend. I know what I'm doing. I'd only take a *little*."

"Just a sip. Yeah, I know. But it doesn't work. At times like these, the only thing to do is just say no."

He didn't like it, but he let Jesse turn him around and lead him away. She shut the door behind him as she pushed him.

Jesse looked frustrated and angry, and there was a flash of red in her eyes, like distant lightning on the edge of a storm. She began stalking the room with long, restless strides. As she walked, she gathered up her long red hair and twisted it into a rope at the back of her head, then ripped a piece of her shirt off to tie it in place. It wasn't in the best repair, her shirt. Claire wondered how many times she'd cannibalized it for hair ties already.

"They're dosing our blood," Jesse told her. "I'm not certain what they're using, but it seems to cut the effectiveness of our meals to almost nothing. We eat, but it doesn't nourish, and the hunger . . . the hunger won't stop. I'm not sure why they're doing it, and it worries me. Why would they want ravenous vampires?"

It was a very good—and scary—question. "I don't know."

"Why in the world did you decide to throw yourself in the middle of all this?"

"Well," Claire said, and tried a smile, "it was this or jail."

"Were they actively trying to eat you in jail?"

"Myrnin has a job for me, and he seemed to think you could keep me safe," she said. "Can you?"

Jesse let out an entirely humorless dry chuckle. "Depends on the circumstances," she said. "But against most of my fellow vampires I have a better than average chance, yes. The only ones able to shut me down would be Amelie and Oliver, and neither one of them seem likely to come against me. Amelie's vanished, and Oliver . . ."

"Fallon's got him," Claire guessed. "Downstairs. What is he doing to him?"

"Nothing Oliver can't endure," Jesse said. "He's been through worse—I can almost guarantee it."

"What about Eve? Fallon has Eve. He brought her—"

"I saw her through the door," Jesse said. "Outside, still locked in his car. She seems . . . impaired?"

"Drugged," Claire shot back, angry on Eve's behalf. "She's okay?"

"So far." Jesse was grasping her hands behind her back as if she felt the need to be restrained, and Claire wondered just how hungry she actually was. Probably quite very hungry. Myrnin would have fed outside, but Jesse hadn't had a chance, and that meant she was just as hungry as Michael—maybe even more. Oliver wouldn't have fed, either—even if he'd had the chance, he'd have made sure others went first, because he was the ruler, even if a temporary one, of this very sad little kingdom. "It's lucky that you have so little blood in you to go around, you know. That helps make you less . . . attractive."

Finally, a use for being smaller than normal. "I thought you needed me. Myrnin said he needed human hands to help him disable your shock collars."

"He's dreaming," Jesse said, and shook her head. "They're fitted with sensors from those monitors modern courts force felons to wear under house arrest, but significantly modified. If you so much as try to open the case, it'll stun a vampire into submission—and probably flash-fry a human brain."

"Myrnin said he could handle the shocks."

That made Jesse smile, but it was a sad sort of expression. "That's because he's mad as a hatter."

"I never understood that. Hatters, I mean."

"In the old days, people who made hats used mercury to produce felt," Jesse said. "They often went mad. And Myrnin's just as crazy if he thinks you can help us get these things off. At best, he'd electrocute you. At worst, he'd blow his head and your hands right off." She came closer as she circled the room, and an expression of disgust twisted her face as she retreated. "Right, we need to get you washed off. You smell like what a sewer would vomit up as too disgusting."

That was a tremendously colorful image, and Claire was glad her nose had gone too numb to notice anything. "Myrnin told me to wait here," she said.

"Myrnin did indeed, and you obeyed," Myrnin told her, just as he walked through the doorway. He was wearing some kind of threadbare floral silk robe held together by a leather belt—with studs—along with an untied pair of oversized rain boots. But he was clean. Just . . . ridiculous. "Go on, then, girl. She's right about the stench. Jesse will stand guard for you. You'll come to no harm. Shoo." He let out an exasperated sigh when she hesitated, then took her firmly by the shoulders and steered her to the door, where Jesse waited with her arms crossed. "Out," he said.

"Myrnin," Jesse said, "that wasn't too bright, was it? Now you've got slime all over your hands again."

"Oh," Myrnin said, staring crestfallen at his palms. "Damn."

Jesse grinned, but it looked more feral than friendly right at this moment. "Come on, Claire, before he tries to wipe it on me and I have to remove his limbs."

Outside the little room—which turned out to be what must have been some kind of staff room for a store, Claire guessed— there were more cots. Some were messy, some were neat, and a few were occupied . . . but the vampires lying there didn't so much as stir as they passed. Jesse was, Claire noticed, keeping an eye on them anyway. Maybe, she was afraid that they, like Michael, could smell the fresh blood under the stench of slime and decay.

What am I going to do when I'm clean? she wondered, and it was a valid question, but the truth was she wanted to be clean so badly that it really didn't matter what came after. She just had to trust that somehow Myrnin and Jesse could protect her.

And what about Oliver? What is Fallon doing to him?

The washroom was just that—a toilet with multiple sinks and stalls, not showers. There were stacks of faded old towels in the corner, all colors and sizes as if they'd come from some Goodwill bag, and she grabbed a couple and began to strip off the sticky layers of her clothing. Jesse held out a plastic bag at arm's length as Claire put in shirt, pants, and then underwear, face turned away as if she couldn't even stand the sight of the mess, much less the smell. "Well," Jesse said, "I feel like I hardly know you, Claire, but would you like me to pick you out some clothes while you wash?"

"Thanks," Claire said. She felt icy cold now, and incredibly vulnerable. She watched Jesse tie the plastic bag, and move away to a bin where—evidently—old clothes were kept. Claire took a ragged washcloth and wet it in the water—cold, of course—then scraped it over the old soap in the dish until it was brimming with suds. Cleaning off the slime wasn't so bad, but washing her hair was awful; it meant bending over the sink naked and scrubbing soap through it, all the while terrified that a vampire, *any* vampire, might be silently drifting up behind her to take a bite.

None did, though. Claire finished wringing out her hair, flipped it back with a wet slap against her neck, and grabbed a towel to dry herself off.

Jesse was sitting in a folding camp chair, blocking the doorway in case anyone else tried to intrude. "Clothes are on the second sink," Jesse said. "Sorry, the choices weren't great." They really weren't. The panties were too big, the bra threadbare and stretched, and the shirt looked like something even a grandmother might have thought too boring. At least the pants fit, even if they were several inches too long; Claire pegged the hems, shoved her feet into old, frayed, once-blue Keds that lacked any kind of laces, and said, "I guess I'm done."

Jesse put aside the book she was reading and looked over her shoulder. Her eyebrows rose just enough to make Claire think she was struggling not to laugh. "Good look for you, kid. Kind of a homeless hipster thing going on."

"Are you really some kind of—lady?" Claire asked her. "Because no offense, but you don't sound like one."

"I was once. I was a queen, too," Jesse said. "Don't take that too seriously; it didn't last long. But I spent my entire life talking as everyone thought I should, dressing to everyone else's standards, never having an opinion or a thought of my own. It was exhausting, being everyone's dress-up doll, and once I got the chance to be my own person, I never looked back. Myrnin likes the thought that I used to be a lady, but don't let it fool you. I'm not one. Not anymore. And in truth, I think that's what he likes about me the most—the change."

Probably, Claire thought. He'd been in love with a vampire named Ada who—according to everyone who'd known her in life—had lived to defy the expectations of those around her, even while looking prim and proper. *And I might fit that definition, too,* she thought. From time to time, Myrnin had looked at her with something that might actually be longing . . . but he'd been pretty definite from the beginning that his fascination was with her mind, not her body.

And Myrnin did take loving a girl for her brain a little too literally. Look what had happened to Ada: he'd saved her by putting her brain in a jar, plugging her into a computer that ran on blood, and pretending it was some kind of genuine life.

She couldn't imagine Jesse letting him do anything like that. And maybe that was just what he needed: someone to set limits for him. Limits that Claire, as a human, couldn't set and keep.

"Jesse—Michael looked bad. Is he going to be all right?"

Jesse cocked her head, and the heavy braid of red hair slid over one shoulder. "I think so. We're latecomers, so we're lucky; most of the poor bastards in here have been on the Daylighters formula for more than two weeks, which means that they're hungry enough to drink cockroach juice and pretend it's B positive. Michael's just not as used to being deprived."

"Why would the Daylight Foundation do a thing like that? Make vampires *more* hungry? Doesn't it put their own people in danger?"

"Of course it does," Jesse replied. "And the most effective way to demonize your enemy is to make them monsters. Most wars just do it through propaganda, but the Daylighters seem to feel it's more effective if they actually reduce us to fangs and rage. It doesn't take much to convince the average citizen of Morganville that we're parasites that need killing. We've certainly acted that part often enough." She looked sad and a little angry as she said it. "It's why I left this place. Because Amelie was too much in the past, too steeped in tradition, and convinced of the superiority of the vampire. I warned her that things needed to change, but it's never comfortable between us; we've both been rulers, once upon a time, and trust me, two queens can't ever really be friends. It may be harsh, but in some ways, she's reaping what she sowed."

Jesse had left Morganville long before Claire had arrived, and Claire could well imagine that Jesse wouldn't have been shy about her opinions. Amelie could be open-minded, but she didn't like direct challenges... and probably especially not from a vampire who'd been a queen once, even for a brief time.

"So they plan to let vampires out on a rampage? Then catch them and prove once and for all the vamps are a threat that has to be eliminated? Why not just do it without all the bloodshed? It's not like there's anybody much objecting that I can tell."

"Because Fallon doesn't like to be the villain," Jesse said. "He never has, as far as I can tell, and I think he needs the justification. In his eyes, he's on the side of right, and there are few out there who'd dispute it, but to be a hero, he needs villains." The weight of Jesse's gaze felt oddly intense now, and Claire wondered what she was thinking... and if she was being judged for some shortcoming as simple as breathing and having a heartbeat. "I have a question, Claire."

"What?"

"What makes you so well disposed toward vampires? I've lived here; I know what a pack of hyenas we can be, with very little warning. There's little about us that ought to compel your pity, not to mention your loyalty."

"You don't think much of your own people, do you?"

"Not much," Jesse agreed with an offhand shrug. "We're a sad lot, in general, clinging to the past and to our own survival, no matter the cost to the lives of others. If I was in your shoes, I'm not sure I'd stand in the way of our more or less inevitable ugly fate. My question stands: why do *you*?"

Claire opened her mouth to tell her why and then... couldn't, at least not at first. All the logical arguments she would have made seemed fake and cheap as old tinsel. She took a breath and composed her words more carefully. "Because no matter what any of you have done, you haven't *all* done it. Because it's not right to judge a class of people by the actions of one, or a few. That's not justice. It's prejudice, and I don't like it. Justice means judging each person individually."

Jesse's lips slowly curled into a smile, and her eyes warmed as well. "High-minded," she said. "I'm not sure you'll find a lot of people living up to your standard."

Claire shrugged. "Doesn't matter if they do or not. It's my opinion; I'm not trying to make anybody else agree. But I don't want them forcing their opinions on me."

"And thus begins the war," said Lady Grey, who'd once been queen. It sounded as though she knew exactly what she was talking about.

The certainty in her voice, and the sadness, made Claire shiver.

EIGHT

"We need to be doing something," Claire said, pacing the floor. They were back in the room where Myrnin had waited—she still didn't know if it was his bedroom, or someone else's, or even if the vamps cared where they slept at all. If they bothered. "If Fallon's got Oliver, and we should be doing something!"

"Fallon's quite busy trying to find out what Oliver knows about Amelie's escape," Myrnin said. He was sitting on the bed perusing a decades-old water-wrinkled magazine that apparently featured Princess Diana's wedding on the cover. Probably the only reading material left at the Bitter Creek Mall, Claire guessed. "And what Oliver knows is absolutely nothing. He didn't even know she'd escaped. So there's nothing Fallon will learn from him."

"He could kill him!"

"She's right," Jesse said from where she leaned against the wall, arms folded. "He could."

"He won't. He needs Oliver, especially if Amelie's nowhere to be found. Oliver is the only authority he has left that everyone respects. He's afraid enough of us now; if there's no one we all follow, then it's that much harder to keep us in line." Myrnin shrugged. "And as long as we can hear him screaming, then he's all right."

Claire flinched, and looked from him to Jesse, who nodded soberly. "Best you can't hear it," she said.

"Help him!"

Myrnin moved, with that eerie vampire speed and grace, and before she could finish saying the two words, he was kneeling next to her, chin raised. "Then help *me*," he said, and pointed to the collar. "Help me take this off!"

"No," Jesse said, coming off the wall to stand next to Claire. "Myrnin, you'll get her killed, and yourself along with her. You've seen how deadly these things can be if you tamper with them."

"Wait," Claire said. Her thoughts were racing, and she couldn't understand what she was trying to think of until an image resolved in her mind, vivid and bloody and sharp. Amelie.

Amelie hadn't been wearing a collar.

"I'm waiting," Myrnin said, looking just barely patient.

"How did Amelie take hers off?"

"She didn't," he said. "I staked her dead so that she would not feel the burns as they activated the shock collar automatically when we went beyond the border. I only woke her up once we were well beyond the effective range, and then I set her loose. But I had no way to take it off without setting off the explosive."

"She did," Claire said. "She wasn't wearing it when I saw her at the Glass House."

"The Glass—" Myrnin looked utterly astounded. "She was supposed to go straight for the border, leave this town. Why in the world was she at the Glass House?"

"I think the more urgent question is how did she get the collar off by herself?" Jesse asked.

Myrnin nodded. "Claire, take a look at mine. See if there's something we've missed."

"Okay," Claire said. He went to one knee, chin upraised and head tilted, and Claire bent over to study the latch. There wasn't much to study, really. It was featureless, almost seamless, and there was a keyhole lock. The casing of the collar was hard black plastic. "I . . . don't see anything that can help. Hold on . . . Do you mind if I . . . ?"

"Not at all," he said, and rolled his eyes. "Which should be obvious to you after all this time, Claire."

She hesitantly reached out and felt around the collar, looking for any hidden switches, catches, or other weird features that might have given her a clue. It felt smooth and regular, until she found a slightly rougher patch toward the back of the circle. She pressed harder, and felt it give.

A section of the collar's plastic casing snapped out, exposing wiring and a green circuit board. Claire sucked in her breath and carefully, carefully turned the collar around to expose the rest.

She saw a blinking red light and a gray string of rubbery material that ran through the middle. She stared hard at it, and realized that the gray stuff was probably the explosive that the Daylighters had built into the collars. The stuff designed to remove a vampire's head. Being this close to the compound was bad, and the smell of ozone and the faintly oily stench of it made her feel even worse, but she pushed that aside. *Focus!* The circuitry looked pretty straightforward at least, but as she reached in toward it, she saw the red light blink faster. Some kind of proximity alert, maybe a motion detector . . . She forced herself to freeze but not draw her hand back, then take in deep, even breaths as she watched the light.

It slowed down. Motion detector. Move too quickly, and it would activate. She didn't know whether it would administer a shock—which, as Myrnin had said, would probably fry her brain—or whether it would just blow up, taking her hand with it. Either way, not an outcome she wanted.

It seemed to take forever, but she moved very slowly, pushing her fingertip forward a quarter inch at a time, waiting for the light to slow down, until her fingertip brushed the bottom of the circuit board. She traced the line of the motion detector's wire to the processor, and spent another few seconds staring at the rest of the configuration to be certain she hadn't missed anything. It looked like there was only one connection going to the explosive.

"I'm going to try something," she told Myrnin. "It could go wrong."

"More wrong than it already has?" he asked. "Do what you must. I won't know if it explodes."

That was a grim thought, but she took a breath, held it, and slowly, slowly inched her finger toward the wire. Then she edged it underneath, and gave it a quick, sharp tug to sever the connection.

The blinking light went off.

Claire sighed and pulled back. Just a heartbeat after she did, the stun activated, a sharp blue hissing spark that zapped between the contacts underneath the collar and into Myrnin's skin, and he fell, convulsing. She smelled burned flesh and leaned forward toward him, but Jesse stopped her with both hands on her shoulders.

"No," she said sharply. "Wait. Just wait."

It took a few seconds, but the charge stopped, and Myrnin relaxed, eyes open and blank for a moment before he blinked, reached up, and fumbled the compartment shut. "Well," he said, "I think that's enough experimentation for today. By the way, Oliver's stopped screaming."

Jesse let go of Claire, after a reassuring squeeze not quite strong enough to hurt. "Fallon must have decided Oliver didn't know anything," she said. "That might be good news."

"It so rarely is," Myrnin said. "I've told you, we need to destroy the human guards. Rip them to pieces. I can take down at least a few now that they can no longer explode me like a piñata, and I assume you—"

"No," Jesse said, and reached a hand down to him. He took it and got to his feet. "They can still take you down. Besides, you don't want to die in a bathrobe, do you? So undignified."

"Has dignity ever been my outstanding characteristic, do you think?" he asked, as he flipped his still-damp, curling hair out of his face. "I'm talking about freeing the rest of us. I can act. You can act, to a point. We *must* do something. Claire's proven that given enough time we might be able to deactivate these collars—"

"I didn't prove that," she protested. "I just proved I could pull one wire—and even that shocked you senseless. What if I'd move too fast and set off the explosive?"

"You'd need another bath," he said. "And I fear this bathrobe would never be the same."

"Myrnin—"

He held up a hand and turned toward the door. So did Jesse.

Claire heard a quiet knock a few seconds later, and it opened to show the pale, silent face of a vampire woman, who nodded and stepped away.

"We're summoned," Myrnin said. "Claire, I should put you back down that pipe. Do you think you can make your own way out to—"

"I'm not going," she said.

"You can't *stay*."

"I'm not going until I find out what he's doing with Eve!"

"Claire, you can't—"

She locked eyes with him and said it again, quietly, fiercely. "I'm. Not. *Going*. Eve's in danger. If Fallon's willing to hurt Oliver like that, what do you think he'll do to Michael? To *her*?"

They were going to argue with her—she could see it—but then an odd stillness came over them, and Jesse broke out of it to say, "There's no time. We have to take her with us."

They took her downstairs, walking between them down the wide, curling staircase to the atrium. On the ground floor, ringing that open center of tile, was a solid wall of vampires, standing shoulder to shoulder. They surrounded the open space where she'd first entered this place with her friends. On the surface, it looked like some kind of vampire town hall meeting.

Oliver was lying crumpled on the tile a few feet from Fallon. He looked dead, until he moved just a little, trying to rise. He couldn't manage it.

Myrnin's hand pulled her to a stop and held her there, hidden by the crowd. "Silence," he warned her, and bent down to stare directly into her eyes. "On your life, *silence*."

A petite little vampire lady glanced over at them and fixed a hungry gaze on Claire's neck, but then moved aside as Jesse pushed in to guard her. She stood with Myrnin and Jesse on either side, totally surrounded by unbreathing bodies.

And she felt that every single one of them wanted to take a bite out of her . . . but not a single one of them dared to try.

The outer door opened, and two cops half dragged Eve in. She'd recovered a bit, because she was fighting—not effectively, but it took them some muscle to subdue her enough to move her to the center of the tiled atrium beside the dry fountain, where Fallon stood. They weren't alone—apparently even Fallon wasn't *that* sure of his prison. A full dozen armed Daylighters stood ranged around them, looking as tense and vigilant as Secret Service agents in a shooting gallery.

Eve stopped flailing and settled for glaring. She knew what kind of danger she was in, but she also kept studying the ranks of vampires, looking for Michael.

Who didn't seem to be present.

"Oliver has assured me that he had nothing to do with Amelie's disappearance, but someone here knows. Someone here helped." Fallon's voice, calm and confident, rang off the tiles and distant spaces. "And I can promise you that in the coming days, each one of you will be questioned, at length, about your involvement, so you may look forward to your turn, unless you want to confess it now. Anyone?"

Dead—pun intended—silence. Claire glanced around, but nobody moved. Not even a twitch.

"Then let me assure you that the offer I made you last night still holds today. Whatever you have done in your past, whatever atrocities, from this moment on, I can make you whole. I can make you clean. You can be forgiven and your crimes forgotten. You all know me; you know what I was. I made a new start in my life, and each of you can as well—all you need do is take a step. Just one single step."

Oliver was still lying on the floor, too weak to get up, but when he spoke, it sounded as if he somehow towered a dozen feet over Fallon and his people. "You'll get no volunteers here," he said. "Be off with you, and take the girl away. She's meat for the dogs if she stays here, and you know it. You've not forgotten what it feels like to starve, Fallon, and you're not so saintly as you pretend."

"Neither are you, for all you pretend to be a leader."

"I'm no leader," Oliver said, with a short, bitter bark of a laugh. "And you're no kind of holy man."

"I've never claimed that."

"You claim to offer salvation."

"Your salvation is your own affair. What I offer is a chance at *redemption*, pure and simple, and you'll never get such an offer again. You know that to be true." Fallon seemed to be almost pleading. "I know you think your cause is true, Oliver. Has there ever been a time you didn't? But even you must remember that the faith we share holds that vampires are damned. Cut off from heaven, doomed to walk the earth and drain the living of their hope and their eternal rewards because of their own sin of pride. You are not immortal. You are *lost*. And I am showing you the way home." He meant every word; Claire could see that. There were even tears shimmering in his eyes. He really did believe he was their savior.

"You're showing me to the grave," Oliver said. "A cold homecoming, indeed. The answer is no. You'll get no volunteers here."

"Not even Michael Glass? Not even when that would reunite

him with his lovely girl, who's been so brave in pleading for his release?"

"Wife," Eve said. Her voice sounded husky and wrong somehow—dazed, drugged, and deeply afraid. But she was still standing. Still fighting. "I'm his wife."

"You're his bait," Oliver said, and rolled painfully to his feet. Guards tensed, and Fallon hovered his thumb over the control on the box he held. "Michael won't be biting, Fallon, so take her out of here before something unfortunate happens."

"To her?"

"To you," Oliver said, and there was a deep, dark purr in his voice that made Claire's skin crawl with a strange mix of dread and anticipation. "No more games, you pathetic shell of a man. You haven't been saved—you've been hollowed out, emptied, made into a shadow of what you were. You're walking dead, and you know it. Go shamble toward the grave alone. You'll find no followers among Amelie's people."

Amelie's people, as Claire well knew, had never been unanimous about anything, but in this, at least, they kept their differences to themselves. It was just an unmoving, silent block of eerily posed statues, all eyes aimed at Fallon, Eve, and the guards.

Fallon looked defeated, Claire thought . . . but then he said, "Michael, I know you're here. Oliver's restrained you somehow, but I know you're listening to me. Watching. I know you can see Eve, hear her heartbeat, feel her anguish. She loves you, and even I can feel it. Don't pretend to be indifferent."

More silence. Fallon didn't seem surprised; he only paused for effect, Claire thought, before he dropped his bombshell. "She says she is your wife, but she isn't, you know. There can be no marriage between the living and the dead, neither in the eyes of God nor the eyes of the state. Morganville's mayor has passed a new law today, one that invalidates any marriages between vampires and humans. Your marriage has been officially dissolved."

"What?" Eve turned on him, her mouth open, and in the next second, fury splashed color over her cheeks and she slapped him. Hard. All her fuzziness was gone. "You *son of a bitch!* You lied to me!"

"Yes," he said. The mark of her handprint was red on his skin, but he hadn't moved an inch. "It was necessary. Now, you get to choose. Michael's made his choice; he could have stepped forward to take the cure, and join you again as your husband, but he's rejected it, and he's rejected you along with it. I'll offer you now the opposite: reject *him.* Take off that ring and throw it away. Tell them all that you are proudly human and will stay human, and in return you'll find a welcome home here in Morganville, with us."

"Go to hell," Eve said. Claire hadn't expected to hear anything else, but the ring of loneliness under the anger surprised her. But of course Eve felt alone; she would. The humans of Morganville had turned against her completely after she'd married Michael, and none of the residents of the Glass House had ever been accepted, not really accepted, because they hadn't fit into the framework in the first place.

The ground kept shifting around them, around their little island of misfits, and Claire couldn't help but feel this terrible sense, again, that what she was doing in helping the vampires . . . might all be wrong. But what was right? Fallon? The Daylighters? She couldn't believe that. She wouldn't.

Fallon was shaking his head. "Refuse to accept the facts, cling to this fantasy of loving a creature that cannot love you in return. . . . Well, then you'll end up in a cell, and we'll have to treat you for this mental illness you suffer from until you're cured of it."

"Listen to yourself. You're going to put me in an asylum?" Eve said. "For loving someone?"

"You don't love Michael. Michael died. You love a thing that once was him, and loving a corpse has always been a thing of horror to anyone with a shred of decency in them. So, yes. Call it an asylum if you wish, but that's what faces you if you won't renounce him. I'm not unkind; I'm giving you a chance to avoid that fate. Take off the ring and throw it away. Show them that you stand with me. With humanity. Become a Daylighter, Eve."

Eve took a step forward, right into his face, and looked him straight in the eyes to say, "Screw you, Fallon. If you want my wedding ring, I'll mash it into your face deep enough to leave a permanent tattoo."

Fallon didn't flinch. He just . . . smiled.

"Take her," he said, and one of the Daylighters grabbed Eve by the shoulder.

She spun into it, moving with limber grace, and slammed the heel of her right hand into his nose, jammed her shoulder into his chest, and knocked him right off his feet into a sprawl on the dirty tile. She still looked dazed and vulnerable, and she might have wavered a little on her feet, but Claire's heart swelled to about twice its normal size, because in that moment she was so *proud* of Eve she wanted to let out a war cry. "Who's next?" Eve yelled it for her, and pointed at another of the Daylighter guards. "You. Come on, sunshine, let's do it!"

At Fallon's nod, that guard stepped forward—but he wasn't caught by surprise, and he was more than a match for Eve, who landed a couple of punches but ended up off balance, which was all the man needed to sweep her feet out from under her and send her crashing to the floor, facedown. In the next second he had his knee in the small of her back and was twisting her hands behind her.

Eve was screaming, but not in pain. That was pure rage boiling out of her, and now Claire tried to move forward to help—but Myrnin put a heavy, strong hand on her shoulder to keep her in place, and she couldn't twist free.

"Get her ring off," Fallon said to the guard, and the man nodded, wrenched Eve's left hand up, and slid her wedding band off to hold it up for Fallon's inspection. "Now throw it away."

"No!" Eve screamed, but it was too late. The man pitched it through the air, and for a second it caught the diffused light from above and a red glint shone from the ruby in its center, and then it was heading for the shadows.

A pale hand caught it.

Michael Glass stepped out of the crowd and into the open space.

"No, you fool." It was just a soft, angry whisper from Oliver, but Claire felt Myrnin's fingers close tight on her skin, and she knew things had just shifted in a way she couldn't really define.

Michael stood there, staring at Fallon with the ring in his hand, and said, "Let her go. It isn't her you want. It's me."

"Amelie's child," Fallon agreed. "Yes. It's you I need, Michael, because you're a symbol. You're Amelie's weakness. And I know you need this girl just as much as she needs you. I can give her back to you—and you to her, in ways that neither of you have ever imagined possible. All you need do is agree to take the cure."

The cure. Of course. Fallon's salvation hadn't been some religious allegory; he'd been offering the vampires humanity. A change back to a regular, breathing, mortal life. *And isn't that a good thing? Shouldn't it be?*

He'd needed a volunteer, and here was Michael, standing in front of him with Eve's wedding ring clutched in his fist, looking at his wife with so much love and desperation that Claire felt a little faint from it. There was a kind of restless whisper that moved through the vampires . . . something beneath her hearing, beneath even her vision, but a sensation like nothing she'd ever felt before.

"No," Oliver whispered again. There was anger in that word, and there was also fear. If there was ever a moment when events were turning, when something monumental was happening, this was it. She could feel it, and so could they.

From the look on Fallon's face, he knew it, too. He was waiting for his triumph.

"I never wanted to be a vampire," Michael said. "You know that, Eve. I never asked for it."

The guard had let her get up to her knees now, but he held one wrist behind her back tight enough that it must have been painful. She didn't make a sound. Her gaze was locked on Michael's, breathlessly waiting.

"I love you," he said. "I always did, even when I was an idiot too stupid to admit it. By the time I could, it was too late, and I was . . . something else. I never had the chance to be with you when I was human. And I'm sorry for that. You deserve better."

"Don't be sorry," Eve said. Her voice was shaking, but she managed to smile. "It's not like I'm Jane Normal in the first place. Love you, too, Mike. Always and forever, no matter what you are."

Michael nodded to her, just a little, and his smile was heartbreakingly lovely. Something personal and private, just between the two of them. Then he turned to look directly at Fallon. Un-afraid.

He opened his hand and let Eve's ring fall from his fingers.

It tumbled through the air, wobbling and spinning, and hit the tile with a sound like breaking hearts. It rolled to a stop at Fallon's feet.

"Do what you want," Michael said. "But with or without the ring, with or without the law, Eve's my wife, and there's nothing you or anybody else can do about it. I'm not volunteering. If you want to give me your cure, you'll have to force me, just like the vampire who ripped my throat out in the first place."

"That's a grave mistake," Fallon said. "It will greatly diminish your chances of survival if you fight the therapy. Take it willingly. Please."

"You heard my wife. Go fuck yourself."

Fallon's face . . . changed. It went from a mask of calm friendli-ness to something so twisted with rage that it was very nearly de-monic, and Claire felt terror bolt through her—not for herself but for her friends, so alone and vulnerable and brave.

Fallon rounded on the guard holding Eve. "Take this deviant to the hospital. Tell Dr. Anderson that I want her given a complete course of aversion therapy until she loathes the very sight of vam-pires. Don't be gentle about it."

Michael lunged, but Fallon was faster—he had the remote control to the collars, and it must have been turned up to bone-splitting levels of pain because it knocked Michael out of the air in a graceless heap, his back arched as he convulsed against the cur-rent.

And not just him. *All of them.* The vampires dropped like bags of cement, and Claire realized in that single clear instant that if she didn't go with them, she'd be as obvious as a bug on a wedding cake—the only one left standing in the middle of the captives. Luckily, Myrnin helped with that, even if it was unintentional; his hand crushed down on her, shoving her toward the floor, and she let herself drop. His weight fell on top of her, hiding her almost completely from sight. She managed to squirm just a little and gain some air, and a sightline toward Fallon.

He turned down the intensity of the collars, but Claire could still feel the current running through Myrnin's body—enough to make his whole body twitch uncontrollably in pain. She was lucky that it wasn't transmitting through to her, except as a slight tingle.

Fallon obviously wanted his audience to see, but he also wanted them quiet.

Compliant.

Eve was pulled to her feet and hustled toward the door, screaming Michael's name. Fallon put a toe of his shoe under Michael's body and rolled him over on his back, then leaned down to stare at him. That horrible smile was still firmly in place.

"I did warn you. You'll be cured, whether you want it or not. I'll have you changed or I'll have you dead. As for your girl's unfortunately painful future, you brought that on her, Michael. I want you to remember that when the cure is coursing through your veins and everything you are is stripped away, never to return. I want you to remember who remade you in their image this time. Not Amelie. *Me*."

There was nothing Claire could do. Nothing but watch, concealed by Myrnin's body, as Michael was hauled away. But she had only one thought, one burning and utterly clear thought: *We're going to take you down.* Not just because what he was doing was wrong, but because he'd just made it personal. She might be wrong in helping the vampires over the humans; she might be wrong in thinking that Fallon had no right to shove his cure down their throats. But that didn't matter now.

This was about her friends.

Fallon was talking to the cop standing next to him. With a shock, Claire recognized the straight carriage, the blond hair. Officer Halling. "Valerie, pick twenty of them for the cure, please, and make sure Michael is among them. Have them shipped directly to the hospital and tell Dr. Anderson to start the treatment immediately."

"Yes, sir."

"One more thing," Fallon said. "We'll have to move up our timetable, since Amelie's evaded us. I can't take the risk that she'll be able to form some kind of resistance. Find the hungriest, most amoral sons of bitches in this building, pick ten, and let them loose tonight."

Even Halling seemed disturbed by that order. "Let them . . . loose? You mean free? We're not supposed to shock them, or—"

"I want you to disable their collars before you let them out to hunt."

"Sir, I don't mean disrespect, but why—"

"Morganville's forgotten its fear of the dark," he said. "They need a reminder just why vampires need to be cured, or put down. Too many in town have started questioning me, complaining about the imprisonment of the vampires. We need to demonstrate there's only one proper way to handle such wretched creatures: *our* way."

Halling didn't look happy, but she nodded and stepped back. She made sure Michael was securely bound and had him dragged out, and then she began counting off, pointing at bodies until she'd reached twenty. "Right, take those to the hospital," she said.

"These lucky bastards are getting the cure. They might be moving into their own homes in Morganville tomorrow, safe and sound."

But Claire knew—maybe they all knew—that the odds of that were pretty slim. Four to one.

The chosen twenty—including Michael—were dragged still twitching from the room. Claire held her breath and stayed very still as one of them walked near her; Myrnin's weight felt like bricks on top of her, and the pain in her arm was growing sharper and sharper with every second. She shut her eyes, concentrating on not reacting or moving, and the guard nudged Myrnin with his foot. His body rolled off of Claire and thumped limply to the tile floor.

"What the hell is up with this one?" the guard asked. "He's wearing some kind of women's bathrobe."

Fallon glanced over, and then focused in on Myrnin. He took several steps toward them. "I'd been wondering where the old spider had been hiding. Careful—he's dangerous even when he's sane, and from the looks of him, this isn't his best period of mental health." The cop backed away, and Fallon closed in and leaned down. He smoothed dark hair away from Myrnin's face. "Can you hear me, Spider?"

"Yes," Myrnin whispered. "I hear you."

"I'm not doing this for you," Fallon said. "Despite what you did to me, killing me, dragging me through hell to make me a blood-drinking demon. I'm not doing this to hurt you, Myrnin. I'm doing it to *help*." Maybe he believed it, but Claire could see his face through the gap, and what she saw in him was cruel. It was angry. And it was *personal*. "I'm saving you for last, dear blood-father. I'm going to make you the last living vampire in all the world, before I unmake you."

"I saved you," Myrnin said. "You know I did. You were dying."

"I was in God's arms, and you ripped me out of heaven. Did you think I'd ever forget? Or forgive?" Fallon pushed Myrnin, and next to him, Jesse tried to stir. He grabbed her red braid and forced her head up at a painful angle. "Who's this? A friend of yours?"

"Leave her," Myrnin said, and clumsily slapped toward Fallon. He fell short. "Please—"

"This one," Fallon said, and dragged Jesse out onto the tile. "Take her for the cure."

"No!" It was just a whisper from Myrnin, but it was full of anguish and horror, and Claire tried to think what she could do to stop it. *Maybe she'll make it,* Claire thought. *Maybe Jesse could be*—What? Saved? Jesse liked who she was. She was a good person. She used her strength to help others.

She didn't need saving.

I have to do something.

She didn't get the chance, because Oliver lurched to his feet and said raggedly, "Take me."

Fallon turned slowly to look at him. "Excuse me?"

"I. Volunteer. To take. Your cure." Oliver said it with precision, biting the words off in clean, sharp, cutting edges. "You need a volunteer. A symbol. Who better than me?"

"It's not like you, Oliver, all this self-sacrifice," Fallon said, but he shrugged. "You'd be useful, if you survive. You likely won't, you know."

"Then you'll have your way, and I won't have to look upon you again. We both win."

Fallon gestured, and the cops handcuffed him and took him away. Claire found herself wondering how they deactivated the collars. They must have, since they didn't remove it before removing *him* . . . but she also knew that problem was just a way for her brain to throw up an emotional shield to keep her panic at bay.

They were taking Michael, and Eve, and Oliver, and she couldn't do anything to stop it. The enormity of it crashed in on her then, and panic pressed down. Her lungs were burning, and she risked taking in a single, quick, trembling breath.

Fallon saw the movement.

His eyes widened, and he gestured at one of his black-jacketed Daylighter guards, who crossed the atrium, bent, and grabbed her by the arm.

Claire was ready.

She came straight up, launching herself at him with all the fury that had been building up inside her since she saw how Fallon treated Eve and Michael, and the top of her skull collided so hard with his nose that she saw stars. He let go of her and reeled back, and she charged forward, suddenly and icily calm, sliding into that empty space Shane had taught her to occupy when her life was on the line. She went low, dodging the man's wild one-fisted swing as he held his gushing nose with the other hand, and whirled like a dancer to come up inside his defense and smash another elbow right into the damage she'd already done. He screamed—a high-pitched scream that sounded as much surprised as pained—and went down hard on his back. He writhed to get to what looked like some kind of Taser, but Claire got to it first, yanked it free, and found the switch to turn it on. She shocked him, and left him bleeding and shaking on the floor as she went after Fallon.

He was holding a gun. Claire skidded to a halt, eyes widening, and took her finger off the trigger for the Taser. The menacing, comforting crackling sound stopped.

"Put that down," Fallon said. He sounded calm, and gently

amused. "You Glass House children are vicious when roused, aren't you? And for what, defense of vampires? Little girl, you really don't have the slightest idea what you're protecting, do you? What they are? What they do?"

"I know what you are," she said. "I've seen what you do. That's enough."

"When you fight your enemies, you must become them, or become worse. It's how wars are won, little girl, though I wouldn't expect you to understand that at your age." He'd seemed so careful and correct before, but now all she could see was the arrogance underneath all that—the pure, nauseating fanaticism. "You can't fight evil with peace and love."

"I thought you were a religious man," she shot back. "I'm pretty sure that's exactly what Jesus said to do."

"Jesus was crucified, and I don't intend to suffer the same." He gestured with the gun. "I won't warn you again. Drop that toy."

"Or what? You'll shoot me? I thought you were all about protecting humans."

"You're only technically human if you collaborate with the enemy."

She found she was smiling. No idea why, really; it wasn't a moment for smiling, but then again, it wasn't happiness driving the expression on her face. It probably wasn't a very nice look for her. "And thus begins the war," she said softly. She understood now what Jesse had meant by that. "You're willing to kill innocent people to save them. Sounds like a real crusade now, doesn't it?"

"Quiet," he said. He sounded gratifyingly angry. "Down on your knees. Do it. Hands behind your head."

She did it, because she didn't see how getting herself killed would make anything better, but she kept smiling because it seemed to upset him.

She kept smiling even as they grabbed her wrists and handcuffed her—for the second time in a day—and dragged her to her feet.

"You're going to lose," she told him.

"Take her out of here," he said, and this time he forced a smile, too. It didn't look convincing. "For her own protection, of course."

"Take her where?" She could barely understand the guard's voice; he sounded angry and muffled and bloody, and his nose was probably hurting him badly. She almost felt a bolt of guilt for it. Almost.

"The same place you took her friend," Fallon said. "Tell Dr. Anderson this one needs reeducation, too. And Claire? I'm going to raze your Founder House to the ground. You'll have no place to go back to. Call it a brand-new start."

He was going to do it anyway, Claire told herself, just to keep herself from lunging right at him. *It doesn't matter. We'll find a way to stop him. We have to find a way.*

"It's just a house," she said, and kept smiling. "And we're never letting you win."

But she knew that the first half of that was a lie. The Glass House was never just a house.

Not to them.

NINE

The guard brought along a friend to drive, since his eyes were swelling shut and his face was a gory mess of blood. His nose, Claire thought, looked like something a monster makeup artist might have rejected as "too weird." It was amazing how much damage she'd done to him, and she felt increasingly guilty about it. That was the difference between her and Shane in the end, she thought; she couldn't take any pride in her violence. But it was still good to know she could defend herself when it was necessary.

The guards didn't say anything to her on the way. She thought they were too angry to try to be civil, and truthfully, she didn't want to talk to them anyway. She was busy searching the dusty crack between the seat and the backrest, trying to see if anyone had dropped something useful. She found a rolled tube that felt like a cigarette but was probably something less legal, and left it there. Just when she was about to give it up as a lost cause, her fingers brushed across something that felt metallic. She grabbed for it, and realized it was a paper clip, one of the larger, sturdier ones. She teased it out slowly from between the fabric, then tried to think how to hide it. She settled for sliding it into a frayed opening in the jeans she was wearing, and clipping it to the thin white strings so that it dangled inside. It might fall off, but it was all she could do in case they searched her.

Not a long ride in the police car—Hannah was evidently allowing use of official equipment for private security guards, which seemed like a bad idea to Claire—before they pulled up at the front of the iron gates of an old, brooding place that looked as if it had been built to be some kind of fortress. Narrow, barred windows, and forbidding Gothic doors. The sign above the door read MORGANVILLE MENTAL HEALTH FACILITY. That didn't seem promising.

The guards turned to look at her as they pulled the car to a halt inside the gates, next to the front door. "Don't give us any more trouble," said the one whose nose she hadn't busted. "I don't like whaling on skinny little girls, but if you pull a stunt like that again, I promise you, I won't hesitate to put you on the ground."

The other one mumbled something that sounded like approval, but between his congested nose and his bad mood, Claire couldn't be sure of anything. She sat quietly as the uninjured man opened her door and then let him help her out, since having her wrists bound behind her back made everything about ten times harder (which was probably the point). The stony gray mass of the building—the *asylum*—loomed over her like it was planning to collapse and bury her, and she felt a small tremor of fear, looking at her future. *No, we're getting out of here*, she thought. *Me and Eve, we're blowing this place and saving the Glass House and Michael and Oliver and Myrnin and making it all right again.*

But Fallon had managed to plant one deep, sprouting seed of doubt. Because what did "all right" really mean, in the end? Status quo? Vampires continuing to oppress and disadvantage humans for their own wealth and benefit? Humans hating vampires and trying to kill them? Constant tension and bloodshed, on both sides? Was she on the right side—or was there a right side at all? There had to be, on balance. *You have to be on the side of the ones being hunted and imprisoned, don't you?*

Still. The gnawing sense that in this moral gray area she was walking on the wrong side of the line was really starting to scare her.

Or it did until the old Gothic doors swung open, and Dr. Irene Anderson stepped out to greet them.

She looked much the same as she had back in Cambridge, when Claire had liked her so much as a mentor; she looked calm and competent and quirky, not at all like an agent of evil and chaos. The white coat she was wearing gave her even more of an air of legitimacy. But the look she gave Claire was both pleased and chilling. "So glad to see you again, Claire," she said. "Please, come in. I'm sure you'll be just as happy as I am that we get to work together again for the common good."

"If that means not at all, then yes," Claire said. She had a real reluctance to take the two steps up to the doorway where Anderson waited, but there didn't seem to be much choice. The two wannabe cops behind her would push her in if she didn't go on her own, and Anderson would get a lot of pleasure out of that. Out of her fear.

Claire held eye contact and walked up to join Dr. Anderson, who put a friendly hand on her shoulder. "So nice to see you again," she said, and it was a lie, and the look in her eyes was unreadable. "Don't be afraid. We're going to help you get past these feelings of loyalty you have to the vampires. It's not your fault. More of a Stockholm syndrome hostage reaction, seeking to please those with power over you so you can survive. Nothing to be ashamed of, just something to be fixed."

"Thanks. Can you take these off, please?" Claire rattled her handcuffs. Anderson's smile deepened and turned just a touch mean.

"Maybe later," she said. "It looks to me like you've taken on some very bad habits, Claire. I want to be sure I can trust you first."

"You can trust me," Claire said.

"To do what? Act out? Yes, I'm certain I can trust you to be as much of a handful as possible . . . like your friend Eve."

Claire couldn't help but ask. "Is she all right?"

"Fine," Anderson said. "You'll see her soon."

The doors boomed shut and locked behind them as they passed into the shadows, and Claire fought back a feeling that she'd just made a really terrible mistake.

The asylum (okay, it wasn't called that, but Claire couldn't help but think of it that way) was surprisingly quiet, and once her eyes had adjusted to the lower light levels, it was also surprisingly lush. New, springy carpet cushioned her feet, and she smelled the sharp tang of new paint on the walls. Here, as in the rest of Morganville, there'd been a makeover.

But the doors—heavy metal doors, with sliding windows inset in them—still locked.

"Cheery," Claire said. "Where's Eve?"

"Beginning her course of treatment," Anderson said. "Don't worry, you'll see her, but not immediately. This is more of an immersive therapy."

"I figured you'd need my help making more copies of VLAD." That was the name she'd given—maybe a little whimsically—to the device she'd created in Myrnin's lab that worked as a kind of super-Taser on vampires, only it acted by attacking them mentally, not physically. It was effective. Way too effective, in fact.

"You sabotaged the last one I handed you, and are responsible for all the deaths that happened after, because of your actions," her former mentor said. She couldn't quite keep the resentment from her voice. "I don't think I can count on you to see reason anymore, Claire. It's too bad. You're a very bright young woman, and you could have done great things."

"Still can," Claire said. "But probably not with you, because you're insane."

"You should know all about that, given your . . . intimacy with Myrnin." There was something in Anderson's voice that made Claire give her a startled, then angry glare. "Does he know, your boyfriend? About your affair with the vampire?"

"I'm not having any kind of affair!"

"What is it people your age call it, then? A hookup?"

"Ugh," Claire said. "Just shut up. You're embarrassing yourself. I think it's you who wanted a hookup with Myrnin back in the day, and you never got it." She said it, and meant it, and even felt a little flare of pleasure when Dr. Anderson flinched. She'd learned dirty fighting from Shane, but she'd learned how to go for someone's weak spot from Monica Morrell. Funny, you could learn something from even your worst enemies. "Besides, I thought you were all about slimy Dr. Davis back in Cambridge. Did he tell you he talked my housemate into bed, too? Or maybe you're just hot for Fallon these days. Doesn't matter. They're both loser choices, and they say a whole lot about you as a person."

Hard to tell from Anderson's furious blush which guess was on target, but it didn't really matter; Claire had hit the mark squarely. Anderson opened a creaking metal door, shoved Claire off balance into it, and before Claire could hop enough to get her feet under her again, she heard the hollow boom of her only escape being cut off . . . and then, the key turning.

The room wasn't much—simple, plain as any cell, with a small twin bed, a pillow, a blanket, and a small wooden chest of drawers that Claire imagined would hold standard-issue pajamas and underwear for the patients. A mirror was bolted to the wall over the sink—not actual glass, of course. Plastic. At least the toilet/shower combination was in a separate little alcove.

It smelled like Lysol and desperation.

The window slid aside, and Anderson stared at her for a long moment. "Don't get comfortable," she said. "Your treatments will start soon."

"How about unlocking these handcuffs?"

"No." The window slid shut with a final click, and Claire heard that lock in place, too.

There was an odd sound just at the edge of her hearing. At first she thought it might be a siren . . . and then she knew it wasn't.

It was screaming.

Treatments.

Claire felt her knees go weak. She sank down on the bed, wincing at the shrill squeak of the springs, and took a deep breath. *I have to get out of here.*

She felt around the back of her pants to where she'd stashed the paper clip.

It was still there, tangled up in thin acid-washed threads. It took time and patience and cramping fingers to work the paper clip free; after she'd finally succeeded, she took a break, working her sore, still-pinned hands and trying to get some feeling back into them. The guards who'd taken her in had, not unexpectedly, put the cuffs on too tightly, and she had throbbing pain around her wrists. Her hands felt bloated and tingly, and for lack of anything better to do at the moment, she stretched out prone on the bed and held her hands up at a painful angle to reduce the blood flow. The tingling faded in a couple of minutes, and the fingers felt better. Still clumsy, but better.

She sat up again, took a deep breath, and started working with the paper clip. It took a *long* time to pick the lock on the handcuffs. Myrnin had drilled her, at one time, in the finer points of the art; he'd felt it was a necessary skill to have, in Morganville, and it turned out he was almost certainly right. Still, she was rusty, and it took too long to bend the tough, thick clip into the right shapes, and to maneuver it into position. Then she had to fight her own burning, cramping muscles to delicately trip all the little triggers inside the lock, but finally she felt the first of the cuffs slip free. The second took only about a third as much time, now that she had the right angle on the problem.

Freed, she took a few seconds to breathe and silently celebrate. Then she checked the drawers of her little room. As expected, there were ugly cotton undies, in a variety of sizes, and some equally ugly sports bras (though she quickly switched out what

she'd been given back at the Vampire Mall, since even this stuff
was an upgrade). Then she pulled on the drawer and found it slid
smoothly, in and out.

Good news.

Claire padded the area beneath the drawer with the pillow
from the bed, emptied out what was inside, and yanked hard on
the mechanism. It caught firmly, refusing to slide out. She worked
it up and down, side to side, until one of the small wheels inside
slipped free of the guides, and then the left side popped free. From
there it was simple enough to wrench it loose from the right, but
the drawer was heavy and awkward, and she was glad she'd put the
pillow in place to catch it as it fell or the noise would have echoed
down that hall—quiet, now that the screaming had faded away.

Once the drawer was out, she saw the metal guides screwed
into its sides. *Perfect.*

Claire worked on her paper clip until it was twisted into a
makeshift screwdriver that slotted into the heads of the screws.
Working with it took muscle power, sweat, patience, and more
strained muscles, but she managed to loosen two out of three fas-
teners on one side, and the third didn't matter; she torqued the
metal until it ripped loose.

She'd started handcuffed, armed with a paper clip. Now she
had a ten-inch strip of metal with sharp edges, handcuffs, *and* a paper clip. Her odds were improving all the time.

There wouldn't be time to fashion the metal properly, but she
found that using the heavy edges of the wooden drawer, she could
press on the metal and fold it into a sharp point. An extra pair of
undies wrapped nicely around the other end, to provide a decent
grip.

Instant knife.

She worked on the other guide and got it free, and bent it into a springy U-shape. With the carefully wrapped addition of a sports bra, she had a passable slingshot. The screws she'd loosened provided ammunition. So did pieces she managed to tease out of the bed's frame.

The drawer went back in, filled with the clothing, and the pillow back on the bed. At first glance, everything looked perfectly normal.

Claire made a sheath for her knife out of cardboard (they'd left some with crayons, for drawing, in a drawer) and fastened it with a loop of torn elastic to the belt loop of her jeans. Then she put the sheath down the side of her leg, inside the jeans, and slid the knife in. It did show, but not as much as it would have if the jeans had been tighter. Good enough.

The ammunition for the makeshift slingshot went into her pockets. On impulse, she broke up the crayons and added those, too. And the button off her blue jeans.

She was contemplating what to do with the handcuffs when the door rattled, and after a second's thought, she jammed the slingshot down the small of her back, and put the cuffs back around her wrists, but just barely clicked on . . . loose enough that she could get her hands free with a brisk shake.

She was standing in the middle of the room looking crestfallen when Dr. Anderson swung the door open again. "Can you please take these off now?" she asked, and tried to sound chastened. "They hurt."

"In a while," Anderson said, which was exactly what Claire had expected her to say. She gestured for Claire to come out, and she did. The metal slingshot jammed against her back felt raw and awkward, and she knew it would be visible from behind, poking out against her thin shirt, but Anderson didn't go behind her; she took her elbow and walked next to her quickly down the hallway toward the end. No one passed them, and when Claire risked a look behind, she didn't see anyone following, either.

"Not much of a staff," she said.

"We're just hiring," Anderson said. "You and your friend are our very first patients. I'm sure you're honored."

That wasn't how Claire would have put it, but she didn't have a chance to fire off a sarcastic rejoinder, either, because they turned the corner to the left and arrived at another metal door. This one had a sign that read: TREATMENT ROOM. NO ADMITTANCE WITHOUT PRIOR AUTHORIZATION. Anderson pulled a thick set of keys from her belt to open it up.

The screaming had started again—muffled, but clearly coming from the other side of this door.

It swung open, and Claire saw Eve. Her friend was strapped into a chair, completely locked down, and she was being *bitten by a vampire.* It wasn't Michael. It was some filthy, wild-eyed hobo with fangs, with his mouth on her throat. A tiny thread of blood dripped down her pale skin showed that he'd hit the vein.

"No!" Claire screamed, and lunged forward—into a plate-glass window that stood between them. "Stop it! Leave her alone!"

"She's the one who chose this," Anderson said. "She chose to degrade herself like this, offering herself to the vampires."

"No, she *didn't!* She and Michael—"

"Michael's a vampire."

"Stop this!"

"I want you both to see just what they are, these vampires. They're predators. Parasites. They don't care about you, except as food, and they never will. Look at him, Claire. *Look.*"

Anderson forced her to stay still for a torturously long few seconds, and then reached past her to press a button set into the wall next to her. "That's enough," she said to someone at the other end of the speaker. "It's time for the next phase."

Eve was barely conscious now; she'd stopped screaming, and her skin had an awful bluish cast to it. Two white-coated staffers came into the room through another door behind Eve; one had a Taser, and the other had a silver-coated collar on the end of a long pole. The Taser shocked the feeding vampire away from Eve, and as he snarled and showed bloodied fangs, the second attendant slipped the metal collar over his head and pulled it tight with a trigger mechanism on the side. The vampire choked and tried to pull free, but the attendant pushed it out the door and into a cage beyond.

Claire didn't pay any attention to the vampire after that; she was too concerned about Eve, who was breathing too fast, too shallowly, and stirring weakly in her chair. Her throat was still bleeding.

Another white-coated staffer came into the room and quickly, efficiently, bandaged up the bite. Then she brought out a syringe and shot it into Eve's arm.

Eve's eyes opened very, very wide, and she suddenly looked horribly alert, even though she still seemed weak. The attendant rolled a portable IV rack into the room and hung some bags on it—dark red ones. The woman must have had a lot of experience, because she hit Eve's vein in the bend of her arm expertly on the first try, and hooked up the IVs to drain.

"What are you giving her?" Claire asked. Her voice felt raw in her throat. She wanted to act, but she knew this wasn't the moment; there was no way to get to Eve from where she was, and she needed to help her friend, not just escape. "What is that stuff?"

"Blood, obviously," Dr. Anderson said. "Your friend has lost at least two pints, and she's dangerously low. Any more, and she might have suffered cardiac distress."

"So that's your aversion therapy? You let a vamp bite her, then you save her?"

"No," Anderson said. "That's part of it, of course, the loss of control and fear. But the most important part is what is *in* the blood she's receiving. It contains a compound I've developed that reacts intensely to the presence of a vampire. She'll feel terrible pain when she's around one, and after we repeat this process a few more times, she won't even need the transfusion to feel it. The human brain is funny that way; it will anticipate pain, and save itself from it. It will take a few weeks of this, but in the end, she'll be unable to tolerate the very sight of vampires—any vampires. Even Michael Glass. She'll be overcome by the conditioned fear and the revulsion."

"Can she see me?" Claire asked. She was trying not to let her anger get the better of her before she was sure it would be useful, but it was so hard, watching Eve shiver and twitch like that.

"No. It's one-way glass so we can observe the patient," Anderson said with a smile. "Don't worry. Her treatment will be over in another half hour, and then it'll be your turn. I thought it might be helpful for you to know what was coming."

It was absolutely all Claire could do not to shake off the cuffs right then and punch Anderson in the face, but she clung to one thing: *I'm going to punch you in the face. Just not now. When the time is right.* Because Anderson so utterly deserved it.

"You know that you're evil, right?" Claire asked. "I mean, genuinely, deep-down evil. You understand that what you're doing is wrong."

"Evil is being a Renfield, like you," Anderson said. "As in Dracula's minion in Stoker's novel. An apologist for the vampires. A collaborator. A traitor to humanity. And I think that before long, we're going to show you the error of your ways, Claire, and then you can help us find better, faster ways to get rid of the monsters. Finally, you'll be useful."

Claire bit the inside of her lip until it bled, and watched in silence as the blood bags emptied into her friend's arm. Eve seemed steadier, and her color was better, by the time the second bag had drained in, and that, at least, was a good thing.

As the attendant in the room took the empty bags from the stand, Anderson steered Claire back out the door they'd entered and to another one on the right-hand side. It was locked, but Anderson had a thick ring of keys on her belt, and she opened it and pulled Claire through it with her, then firmly shut the door behind them.

And they were in the room where Eve was being unstrapped from the "treatment chair."

"Claire?" Eve's voice sounded weak, and it trembled with tears, and Claire couldn't take it anymore. She couldn't stand to wait even one more second.

She gave her hands a sharp shake, and the cuffs slid off. She caught them in her right hand, slipped them over the back of her hand, and punched Dr. Anderson in the face. Shane had taught her how to do that, too, all the power coming straight from her shoulder, her body weight leaning into it, and the move caught Anderson completely by surprise. She stumbled, hit the wall behind her, and went down. Claire bent and ripped the keys from her belt, then realized that there were *two* attendants in the room, not just the one she'd expected.

No time to worry about it.

As the attendants were just starting to be aware of the violence, she dropped the handcuffs and took out her slingshot. She loaded it with a handful of screws and pieces of crayon and let fly as the two started toward her.

She hit them both in the face. They stumbled back, startled, and she reloaded and hit them again, moving the whole time. The male attendant had a Taser club in his belt loop, and she grabbed it, thumbed it on, and slammed it into his chest to trigger the charge. He went down. Seconds later, so did his colleague.

Eve shook her head, as if she was still woozy. "Claire? What the hell are you doing here?"

Claire was already unbuckling the rest of the straps that held her friend down. "Being a menace to society, I guess."

"Thank God!" Eve came up off the table and enveloped Claire in a hug that left her breathless and actually picked her up off the floor. "Sorry you had to rescue me, but thank you. They—they were—"

"I know," Claire said, and hugged her back, hard. "I saw." She wanted to cry, but this wasn't the time, and it certainly wasn't the place. "We've got to get the hell out of here, right now."

Dr. Anderson was down, but she wasn't out—not yet; she was trying to get up, in fact. Claire let go of Eve, grabbed the Taser from where she'd put it on the bed, and held it out, crackling, in front of the doctor's widened eyes. "Don't," she warned her. "I don't want to hurt you more than I already have."

"Then you're a fool," Anderson said. It sounded ragged and pained, and she spat out some blood. That, Claire thought with some surprise, had been one *hell* of a punch. Shane would have been so proud. "Because after this, there won't be any delicate little adjustments to your psyche. You're not going to be fixed—you're just going to be put down. I've said that would be necessary ever since I got here, but Fallon wasn't listening. Now he will know I was right."

Claire bent, picked up the handcuffs from the floor, and quickly clicked them over Anderson's wrists to pin them behind her. "Stay down," she said. "Eve?"

"We are *so* leaving," Eve said. She looked down at herself and shuddered, and Claire realized for the first time that she was wearing shapeless hospital pajamas—pale pink. "Okay, we are so leaving as soon as I find out what these fashion murderers did with my clothes, because, seriously, I would not be caught dead in this." She was trying to be her old self, but Claire could see the fragility in her, the fear, the horror.

"I don't think we have time to shop," Claire said, because the big orderly in the white coat was slowly getting his muscle control back and looking at them with murder in his bloodshot eyes. She darted over and collected his keys, and then the other woman's. "Flee now. Fashion later."

"There's always time for fashion!" Eve protested, but when Claire grabbed her hand and towed her toward the door, she followed. Claire slammed the door as they left, and locked it with Dr. Anderson's keys. No point in leaving her enemies behind her without at least trying to slow them down, she thought.

They ran down the hall toward the front, but Claire caught sight of figures heading toward them—three at least, all wearing white coats. "Not that way," she said, and they backpedaled and turned the other way. That hall ended in another locked door, but Claire had the keys from Dr. Anderson, and she rifled through the choices until she found one that fit. One quick twist and they were inside. The key lock was in place on this side, too, so Claire turned the key and heard the bolts slam home. "Done," she said to Eve, but Eve wasn't listening.

Eve was staring at the room they were in, and after the first blink, Claire was, too.

Because it was a room full of corpses.

Vampire corpses.

"Mr. Ransom," Claire said. She walked to the table that held his partially covered body. It looked exactly the same now as it had in the photo she'd seen in Fallon's office, and it also looked . . . sad. Alone and lost. She tugged the sheet up over his still face. "That one, that's Amelie's assistant. And that one used to be one of her guards." She covered each of them as she passed. She didn't know some of them, and some she didn't like, but that didn't matter now. They were victims now. There was no mistaking that they were dead—she couldn't explain how she knew, but it was the color of them, the fallen-in *emptiness.*

"What the hell happened to them?" Eve asked. She already knew the answer, Claire thought. There was dread in her voice, real dread.

"Fallon gave them his so-called cure," she said. "These are the ones who didn't make it."

"But—but he's giving it to Michael!"

"I know," Claire said. She took a deep breath and turned away from the dead. "And Oliver, and a bunch more of them. I heard Fallon; he was putting Anderson in charge of the cure, and if she's here that has to mean that Michael and the others are here, too. Maybe behind those locked doors in the hallway. We'll find them, Eve."

"You've got a Taser," Eve said. "I feel militantly underdressed."

She looked around the room, then pulled out the drawers. There were knives in them. Saws. All kinds of things that made Claire feel a little bit faint, seeing them.

Eve hesitated, then reached in and took out a thick, wicked-looking knife. Claire snapped the elastic holding her makeshift homemade weapons and traded out for a scalpel that fit inside the cardboard sheath. Then she looked at the shelves, and the ranks of bottles.

"Wait," she said, and began pulling things down.

"We can't wait. They're going to give that poison to Michael!"

"I know. Just *wait.*"

Eve didn't want to, but Claire had all the keys. "What the hell are you looking for?"

"Trichloroethylene," she said. "Hydrogen fluoride and bromine. I'm making anesthetic gas. Halothane."

"Is that *safe?*"

"No," Claire said. "But it's safer than using knives on people, and we might need to knock out a bunch of people all at once."

Eve kept her objections silent, at least, though Claire was pretty sure she was screaming them inside. Claire didn't let it affect her concentration, because doing this wrong would be a *very* bad idea. Halothane was volatile, and this wasn't the best-equipped setting in which to be making a gas. She found some breathing masks and put one on, then handed one to Eve, who only complained a little.

"They'll be getting here soon," Eve reminded her. "One of them is bound to have keys."

"I know," Claire said. "Here. Go jam this in the lock." She handed her the paper clip, bent into an almost unrecognizable shape now from all the uses she'd already put it to. Eve raced off to do it, and Claire began carefully measuring out beakers of fluids.

She had the bare minimum equipment necessary to capture the gas once it started to react: tubing and a container. She worked fast, with all her attention on the problem at hand. Her mind was clear, at least, and the picture of the chemical compound seemed so real she could have reached out to touch it. She prepped the burners. The last part would be the problem, because the bromine reaction needed a very high temperature, but she'd just have to do the best she could.

The synthesis of the trichloroethylene and hydrogen fluoride went easily enough; once the temperature reached 130 degrees, the gas progressed to the second stage. She added the bromide and cranked the heat as high as she could. The mixture boiled off into gas, precipitated into the tubing and the container, and Claire quickly stuck a cork in the tube and left it attached to the bottle.

"Are they outside?" she asked Eve, who turned toward her. Eve didn't need to answer, because Claire could hear the metallic clicking in the lock, followed by a loud bang on the metal door.

"Open up!" someone called. He sounded angry. "Open up *now!*"

Claire hurried forward and crouched down to uncork the tube. She crimped it in the middle, and then slid the flexible rubber under the door's bottom edge. "Talk to them!" she said to Eve. "Get them close!"

Eve began spouting something that sounded half crazy about the dead coming back to life and zombies lurching up off the tables, and if Claire hadn't known it was a lie she might have bought it, too, especially when Eve ended it with "Oh, God, help us, help . . ." and trailed off into a gurgle that sounded especially gruesome.

There was silence on the other side of the door.

"Do you think—," Eve whispered, but she didn't need to finish the sentence, because Claire heard a falling body hit the door and slide down. Then another, and another, farther away.

Claire yanked the tube away and rolled the bottle across the room, then pulled off her mask. Eve took hers off as well. "Hold your breath," Claire warned. She yanked the bent paper clip from the lock and used her key. As she pulled the door open, a man fell in with it—a heavyset older man, mouth loose and open and eyes rolled back in his head. She checked for a pulse and found one, slow but steady. The other two who'd been with him were also down, though one was mumbling sleepily.

Claire grabbed Eve's hand and pulled her over the bodies at a run, heading down the hall.

"They'll be okay," Claire assured her. "The fresh air will wake them up soon."

"Like I care," Eve said. "We need to find Michael!"

"Take that side of the hall. Slide the windows open and see if you spot anybody."

Eve wasted no time, but it didn't yield any victories. They opened every window on the hall, on both sides, but there were no vampires in the cells. Nobody at all, in fact. Eve sent Claire a despairing, panicked look that didn't need words to be understood, and they raced through the open reception area to the other side of the building.

There were no cells on this hall, only a single locked door. Claire fumbled with the keys. Her hands were shaking from the adrenaline, and a clock was running in her head. The three they'd left sleeping were going to wake up soon; they'd be groggy and unsteady, and probably have killer hangover headaches, but time was definitely running out on their window to find Michael and the others.

It was, of course, the second to last key Claire tried that turned the lock. She pushed the door open, stepped through, and had to grab the heavy metal slab on the backswing, because it was on some automatic pneumatic pressure to seal shut. Eve was only halfway through. Thick as it was, the steel could have broken her bones if it had hit her squarely.

Eve squeezed through, and Claire let go; the door hissed shut and locks automatically engaged. They were in a small antechamber, and there was another door. Another lock. "Hurry," Eve said. She looked around at the blank walls, and then up at the small glass semicircle set above them. Her face set hard. "They could be watching us."

"Shit," Claire whispered. She sorted keys again, nearly frantic now, and found one that slotted neatly in. It turned.

The door opened in front of her, on a room that was the mirror opposite of the one where they'd found the dead, discarded vampires—the ones who'd failed their conversion back to human. That had been a hastily assembled morgue.

This was a bright, clean, well-equipped lab, complete with glass-fronted cabinets and counters, stations for preparation of compounds, refrigerators . . . and it held about the same number of tables, and on them lay vampires.

The difference was that these vampires still survived, at least for now.

Claire's gaze swept down the line and fixed on tousled blond hair. "There!" she yelled to Eve, and they both raced forward . . . and then had to stop, because two guards stepped out into their path. These were police officers, wearing Morganville blues, with the Daylighter pins gleaming on their collars. Claire recognized one of them—Officer Halling, the woman who'd found the dead body at the Glass House.

Officer Halling unsnapped her holster and put her hand on the butt of her gun.

Eve didn't hesitate; she lunged forward with the Taser, but unfortunately for her, Halling's partner was fast, and he grabbed Eve by the arm and wrenched it hard, forcing the Taser out of her hand to drop and roll on the floor. Halling dismissed Eve, and focused her cold gaze on Claire.

Claire pulled the scalpel from the cardboard sheath, but she didn't attack. Instead, she ran in the opposite direction, to the last bed on the end. She'd seen a familiar face there, too.

Oliver.

He was strapped down with some kind of silver-coated webbing on his arms and legs, and there was an IV needle in his arm, buried in a thick, ropy, blue vein. His skin looked chalky, but beneath that his arms looked wiry and strong, and his chest thick with muscle.

His eyes were open. He lifted his head to stare at her, and his eyes were a ferocious, unnerving shade of red. He didn't speak.

Claire ripped the IV out of his arm, and took a scalpel to the webbing that held him down. It was tough and dulled the edge pretty quickly, but she managed to get one hand free.

Oliver did the rest. He rolled onto his side and ripped at the silver web until it was shredded, even though it burned and cut his fingers, and then sat up to tear at the stuff holding his ankles.

A shot shattered glass on a counter past Claire, and she looked up to see Halling taking aim again. This time she wouldn't be firing a warning shot.

"Stop!" Halling yelled. "Drop the knife!"

Claire did, and it hit the tile floor with a musical *clang*, but Halling was pointing at the wrong target. Maybe she'd thought it would take Oliver longer to get free, or to recover, but she was wrong.

Dead wrong.

Oliver came off the table in a blur and stopped with her gun arm in one hand and her throat in the other. Claire shut her eyes, because she didn't want to see, but she heard the snap of bones breaking... and when she was able to look again, Halling was down on the floor. *Not* dead, surprisingly, but her arm was at an entirely wrong angle, held close to her chest. She looked disoriented with shock.

Without much of a pause, Oliver turned toward the other policeman, who was holding Eve down. He turned sideways, an elegant and weirdly old-fashioned motion, held Halling's confiscated pistol at his side, and said, "I don't offer second chances. This is your first and only warning. Drop your weapon now and let the girl go." It was almost as if he was ... dueling. He even put his left arm behind his back, crooked at the elbow.

And then he *was* dueling, because the cop dropped Eve, stood straight, and pulled his own sidearm. It was a fast draw, as fast as anything Claire had ever seen outside of an old Western movie ... but it was miles too slow, even then.

Oliver didn't try hard, but before the man's gun was halfway up, Oliver brought his own weapon up, leveled, aimed, and fired.

The other man went down.

Oliver held the pose for a long second, watching the man to be sure he wouldn't get up, and then the tension released and he stumbled sideways. He crashed into another vampire's bed and grabbed for support, but couldn't hold himself upright. He slipped to his knees, tangled in sheets, and as Claire watched in horror, he began to convulse.

"Oliver!" She dropped down next to him in a crouch, not sure what to do, whether she *could* do anything. "Oliver, can you hear me? *Oliver!*"

It went on a long time, but he finally went limp. "I hear you," he said. His voice sounded raw and strange, and it sounded . . . afraid. He opened his eyes then, and they weren't vampire-red anymore. They were a plain, unremarkable brown. His skin had taken on an odd shimmer, as if it was shifting colors. "You must stop them, Claire. Don't let them destroy everything we—" He stopped and let out a cry of pain, real pain, and flung out his hand. She didn't think twice, even given what she'd just seen him do. She grabbed his fingers and held them, felt him shaking as if he were flying apart. His hand closed over hers with crushing strength, but it was only human strength now, not vampire strength.

His skin was *glowing* underneath, as if something was burning inside him. Or, as if something was being burned *out* of him. Whatever was happening to him, it was painful. The breaths he was pulling in sounded tortured and strangled, and his pulse . . .

His pulse? Breaths?

Claire's eyes widened.

Oliver was, before her eyes, turning human. And she knew, somehow, that this was the very last thing he would want.

"No," he said, and it burst up out of him like a growl, a primal and furious snarl. His convulsions jerked his back into a tight bow, and Claire gasped and had to pull her hand free as his grip grew tighter and tighter around hers. "No! I *will not!*"

It was almost a chant, or a prayer, but she couldn't imagine God listening to anything that savage, that angry. The rage that fueled it seemed totally beyond the capacity of any human body to create, much less contain.

And suddenly, the glow inside him died, leaving his skin that chalky, translucent white again, as if he was made of milky, empty glass.

He let out a sigh, and his muscles went limp. The brown, suffering eyes drifted shut.

She was terrified to touch him, but she put her fingers on his wrist. Silent. No pulse. No rise and fall of his chest.

But he didn't look quite as dead as the corpses in the morgue on the other side of the building. Not yet, anyway. He looked—comatose. Suspended between life and death, vampire and human.

She supposed he would have to fall in one direction or the other.

Claire dragged him to a more comfortable position—more for herself than him, really—and raced to the other side of the lab. There were manuals there, chemicals, ranks of IV bags, checklists and protocols.

She grabbed the protocol manual and feverishly slid her finger down the table of contents. *Outcomes.*

The section was a dry, clinical table of results. Seventy-three percent average deaths, which Claire already knew. But, strangely, only a flat twenty percent human conversion score.

Which left seven percent . . . REV? The code didn't mean anything to her, and she scanned the rows of legends until she found it. REV meant *reverted.*

Seven percent of those treated with the cure reverted to vampire. The line was marked with a footnote symbol, and she scanned down to read it.

Immediate resolution of all REV subjects using Protocol D.

Protocol D, Claire discovered, had an illustration of one of the Daylighters' special liquid-silver-filled stakes being plunged into a vampire's chest, then removed to release the liquid.

In other words, they euthanized any vampires who survived their cure and stayed vampire.

Claire let out a slow, shaking breath. She felt numbed, reading it; if she'd wondered before whether she was on the right side, she didn't now. If Amelie was the devil she knew, Fallon was far, far worse.

As she was closing the book, a word caught her eye, and she flipped back to it.

The last section was labeled *Counteragent*.

There was a whole chapter, and she skimmed it as fast as possible, raking her gaze down the thick columns of dryly written explanations.

The counteragent was designed to halt the process of the cure. They'd originally developed it so that they could study the effects while in process—part of their live experiments, and Claire really didn't want to think too hard about that. She found a handwritten notation to the side.

COMB 733118.

It was a combination, so there had to be a safe. Somewhere, there had to be a safe . . .

She spotted it, finally, half hidden beneath the counter—a small gray thing, digital keypad. She crashed to her knees in front of it and jammed in the numbers. *733118.*

The pad beeped, and the door clicked open.

But there was nothing inside it. Nothing at all.

"No!" She screamed it out loud and smashed her palm into it with all the anguish inside her. She could hear the cries coming from the vampires on the other beds now, and she could hear Eve calling her name with frantic desperation.

If the counteragent still existed, they'd moved it. There was nothing here. Nothing to reverse the effects of Fallon's cure. He'd taken it somewhere she couldn't find it.

Not in time.

For a moment, Claire thought she just couldn't do it . . . just couldn't get up. Couldn't rise to meet another challenge, face more pain. She just wanted to lie down, curl up, put her hands over her ears, and *hide*, just this once. She'd faced it all, as directly as she could. She'd fought and planned and tried.

But that open safe, that was the end of all her plans. All her hopes.

And now there was nothing left but to hold on to Eve, and Michael, while everything fell apart.

I need you, she thought. *Shane, please, I need you, please be here, please . . .*

But she knew in her heart that he couldn't be here. Not this time.

When she turned to focus on Eve and Michael, she realized that Eve hadn't gone to Michael's side. She was standing with her back pressed against the far wall . . . watching the vampires with frantic, horrified eyes. Gagging. Doubling over.

She tried to get closer, but she faltered, and backed up again, covering her face.

"Take it out!" Eve yelled to Claire. "Help him!" She pointed to the IV needle, and Claire yanked it free—but she knew, from the chalky glow of his skin, that it was already too late. His eyes were closed, and he wasn't responding.

Eve was weeping now, and she slammed her palm into the wall hard, over and over. She tried again to come toward him, but whatever they'd loaded into her blood made her sick, physically sick, the closer she got. "Come on, you're the brain, you're the smart one, you can fix everything, *do something!*" The horror and anguish in her friend threatened to knock down Claire's shocked numbness, and she squeezed her eyes shut to block it out. "Do something, Claire!"

And then Michael screamed. It was a sound that sliced through Claire's blanket of shock and stabbed her right in the heart, and her eyes flew open of their own accord to fix on his tense, suffering face, his *glowing* face, on the shimmering, flickering light gliding beneath his skin, tracing veins and arteries, centering in his heart...

And regardless of her pain, of the drug, of all that they'd done to make her loathe and fear the sight of a vampire, Eve shoved herself bodily off the wall and lunged forward to grab his hand in hers. She was gagging and shaking, but she grimly held on, even though every fiber of her body was trying to make her run away.

Michael was breathing in deep, agonizing gulps, and Claire could see his pulse pounding hard in the vein at his throat. His eyes were wide open, so blue, blue as the Texas sky, and he was staring mutely at Eve, shaking and trembling and *staring*...

"Live," Claire said. She whispered it under her breath, a chant, a prayer, a desperate plea. "Live, live, *live!*"

And then the light in him went out, and Michael went completely, utterly still.

TEN

*H*e's dead, Claire thought numbly. *I killed him.* It was an incoherent thought, and it had a sound to it like ashes falling, a taste like bitter acid at the back of her throat. *I killed him.* She hadn't, but it felt that way. She should have been faster. Better. Stronger.

She should have stopped all this from happening. But she hadn't, and now Michael was dead.

Eve was staring at him as if she hadn't realized the truth, as if somehow it would all still come out okay. "Michael?" she asked. His eyes were still open. "Michael?" The horror weighed her voice down, dragged it to a low, uneven whisper. "Please look at me. I love you, please look at me, please . . ."

Claire's eyes were filling with tears now, and her view of his face became a wash of color—palest possible pink for skin, blue for his eyes, gold for his hair. She blinked, and the tears glided hot down her face, hot as blood. She put her hand on his arm.

It shouldn't feel like that, she thought, so close to her own skin temperature. So much like he was still alive.

And then her fingertips felt a small whisper of a pulse.

No, I imagined that. I couldn't have . . . it couldn't . . .

Another beat. Then another. It wasn't her pulse.

It was his.

"Michael, you have to look at me," Eve was saying between tears. She looked pale and sick, facing what was, for her, the end of the world. "You can't leave me, you can't, you *promised me . . .*"

He took a breath.

Eve let out a muffled cry, and fell across his chest to kiss him. It was, Claire thought, maybe a little premature for that, because he seemed too dazed to understand what was happening . . . and then all that changed, and he was kissing her back, really kissing her, and his skin was taking on a skin tone that wasn't too much darker than before but somehow much more *alive*. He was gasping for breath when they parted, but smiling, and there was color in his cheeks and lips.

It struck Claire that she'd never seen him alive before. Not really one hundred percent alive, anyway. He looked as he had when she'd first met him, but this time . . . this time, he was simply and only human.

It was . . . She didn't want to call it a miracle, but that's what it was. A miracle.

It came to her slowly that he was still strapped to the table, and he was straining to break free. Claire wiped her tears, got hold of herself, and quickly sawed through the webbing on his left wrist, and then his left ankle. By the time she'd reached his right hand, she had to gently but firmly force Eve to back up as she freed him completely . . . and then *she* was the one getting shoved out of the way as Michael lunged for Eve and enveloped her in a hug so complete that it was as if he'd never really hugged her before.

Which, Claire supposed, he hadn't. Not like this.

"Can you feel it?" he asked Eve. He was crying. *Michael* was crying, tears flooding his face. He wiped at them, but he couldn't seem to stem the tide. "My heart. It's beating."

"I feel it," Eve said, and pressed her hand against his chest. "Oh, God, Michael, I—I should probably say something snarky right now, but I—"

He grabbed her hand, lifted it to his lips, and kissed it. Then he kissed her again, a long and deep kiss that said more than words ever could about how he felt. How they both felt.

Miracle, Fallon had called it. And in Michael's case he'd been right, because Michael Glass, who'd been various shades of dead ever since Claire had known him, was now himself again. Human. Vital. Alive.

And, Claire thought with a sudden chill, *vulnerable.*

She turned away from them, and it hit her with breathtaking horror that most of the vampires struggling against their bonds right now around her, glowing from within as Fallon's medicine did its work . . . most of them wouldn't make it.

And there was nothing she could do about it.

Claire channeled her anxious, sick frustration into action. She hustled Michael and Eve out of their own private world and put them to work tying up the lab workers, who were starting to rouse. She dragged the two police officers off to the side and covered up the dead one that Oliver had shot. Halling was spitting with fury, but Claire didn't listen to what she was saying. It would only make her angry, and she was feeling bad enough.

When there was nothing left to do, she crouched down next to the lab attendant who was waking the fastest, and helped her along by rubbing knuckles across her breastbone. That hurt, Claire remembered. And it roused the woman fast.

It didn't take the woman long to adapt to the new situation. She realized that she was tied up, and that Claire and Eve and Michael were the only ones standing. Not a stupid woman, either— fear flickered across her face before she concealed it beneath a mask of professional distance. "Untie me," she ordered.

"Bite me, Miss Mengele," Eve said. "Not that stupid."

The woman's eyes fixed on Michael, and she looked . . . elated. "You made it," she said. "I knew you would, Michael."

"You know me?" Michael asked. He wasn't smiling.

"Of course I do! I'm a big fan of your music. I'm Amanda. I work at the hospital."

He blinked. "But you stuck poison in my arm."

"To save you!"

He opened his mouth, then looked confused and weirdly embarrassed, and Claire realized he was trying to show fangs he no longer had. Well, that was awkward. "What about them?" He pointed to the others. Some had gone still. Some were still struggling.

Her eyes flickered toward them, then came back quickly to focus on him. "Better they die than live on in that hell," she said. "We're saving people. *People.* Not monsters."

"The counteragent," Claire said. "Tell me where it is."

"I don't know what you're talking about," Amanda said, but her round face wasn't made for lying. "What counteragent?"

"The one that used to be locked in the safe and isn't there any-more," Claire said. "Where is it now?"

"No idea."

"Don't play poker, Mandy," Eve said, "because you suck at it. Who has it?"

Amanda set her mouth into a flat, stubborn line and glared back. Oh, she didn't like Eve at all. Which was sharply contrasted with the worshipful way she looked at Michael.

Claire stood up and grabbed her friends. She dragged them off a bit and lowered her voice. "She's got a crush on you, Michael. Eve, she's jealous of you. So back off and let Michael charm the info out of her."

Michael looked a little bit ill. "Do I have to?"

"People are dying. Do you?"

He winced, nodded, and said, "Go do something else. I don't need you guys staring at me. I feel bad enough already." Claire knew he was thinking of the fact that he'd survived the process and so many . . . so many weren't going to. Or maybe he was hating the slimy necessity of charming someone who didn't see anything wrong with killing to cure.

But she took Eve's arm and said, "Check Oliver."

Eve's eyes went wide. "Claire—I—I can't. I can't even go near him."

"You just went to Michael—"

"That's different. And—he was changing."

"So was Oliver," Claire shot back. "Just *go!*"

Claire went to check the others. Half were already gone, their light extinguished, their skin left chalky pale and bizarrely hard to the touch, as if it had turned to ash. Those were, unquestionably, dead.

Two others besides Michael had made the transition back to human and were gulping in convulsive breaths, looking panicked and wild, as if they were drowning in a sea of air. One was weeping, and it looked like tears of joy. The other two, though . . . they looked lost and horrified. Claire supposed that after so many years—hundreds, maybe—of existence as a vampire, being plunged back into mortality must have felt a lot more like a punishment than a salvation.

One woman had settled into the state that Oliver had been in—more of a coma than either a recovery or a decline. Her skin had turned chalky, but it was still pliable to the touch, and she didn't have the fallen-in look of those who'd failed the process completely. *The REVs,* Claire thought. The ones Miss Amanda would have been happy to euthanize, for their own good. The thought made her ill, thinking of Oliver and this unnamed woman lying there helpless, trapped, unable to defend themselves.

Eve came back to her, looking flushed and scared. "He's not breathing, but he's not dead, either," she said. "I can't get too close, Claire, it makes me—" She swallowed hard. "I'm hoping this is just the doped blood they gave me, right? It's not—not permanent?"

"I don't think so," Claire said. "Anderson said the treatment needed to be repeated a bunch of times, so I think you'll be okay." She hugged Eve, impulsively, and Eve took in a shuddering breath

"Thank you," she whispered. "I don't know what would have happened if you hadn't—"

"None of that. We save each other, right? It's what we do."

"It's what we do." Eve stepped back and offered a fist bump, which they exploded and brought back, just because.

The moment of peace faded, though, as Claire looked again at the still, silent woman lying on the slab. "I don't know her, do you?"

"Ayesha," Eve said. "She's okay. I think she was a lawyer. I used to make a lot of bloodsucking attorney jokes. Not so funny now, I guess."

The woman was very small—maybe five feet tall—and had a rounded figure perfectly proportioned for her height. Pretty, too, under the unhealthy color of her skin; in human life she must have been of African descent, and she wore her hair in an abundant Afro cut held back with a colorful band. *A real person*, Claire thought. A real person, caught between life and death. They were all real people. That was what Fallon and his crew couldn't seem to grasp . . . the *cost* of what they were doing. The history they were destroying.

Claire held the woman's hand for a moment. It felt cool and unresponsive.

Michael was back a few minutes later, and when she looked up she was thrown off balance by the color in his skin, and the flush in his cheeks and on his lips. He looked like a young man who'd been locked away from the sun for too long, but he was definitely, unmistakably human.

It still seemed impossible.

"She doesn't know where the antidote is," he said.

"You're sure?"

"Positive." He didn't say how he knew, which was probably for the best for everyone. "How is Ayesha?"

"I don't know. Not dead, I guess. Like Oliver. But not alive, like you."

He nodded slowly, watching the vampire woman with a slight

frown between his brows. "We should get them out of here," he said. "Her and Oliver, anyway."

"What about the other ones who, you know, made it back to human?" Eve pointed vaguely at the other three survivors, who were still trying to get used to breathing for a living. "Shouldn't we take them, too?"

"Fallon won't hurt them. They're his success stories." Michael shook his head, still frowning. "I suppose I'm grateful to him for what he did, in a way. I wanted to get back to human, but I was afraid it wouldn't work for me. I was afraid I'd lose you, Eve, and I couldn't stand that."

"You'll never lose me," Eve said. She sounded totally confident of that. "Just make sure I don't lose *you*."

"Promise," he said, and kissed her again.

"Guys?" Claire hated to pop their private bubble, but she pointed to the silent form of Ayesha lying on the table. "If we're taking them, we'd better get going."

"The tables have wheels," Eve said. "They unlock." She stepped on a metal lever and pushed, and the table slid smoothly out a few inches before she stopped it with her hand. "We'll need transportation once we get them outside, though. Even in Morganville, rolling gurneys with half-dead vamps through the streets might seem a little out of the ordinary."

"Especially in the new, improved Morganville," Claire agreed. "Michael, go scout ahead, see if there is some kind of car we can grab. No, wait." She spotted a coatrack near the door. On it dangled a couple of purses. She sprinted over and dug inside, searching for keys. She came up with a set. There was a photo key ring on it, and it looked like Amanda really *was* a big fan of Michael's, because the photo was one of the promotional ones he used for gigs. Black-and-white, very moody.

She tossed him the keys, then almost laughed at his puzzled expression when he spotted the photo. "Get used to it, rock star. Wait until you're famous outside of town," she said. "Hurry. We'll be right behind you."

He kissed the back of Eve's hand, which was sweet, and then he took off out the door. Claire hoped he wouldn't run into any trouble, because she was afraid his human instincts for survival hadn't quite kicked in yet. He was still thinking of himself as a vampire. It would take time—and probably one or two wounds—for him to develop the caution that came with being mortal again.

Eve sighed. "Do you know how much I hate it that this turned out well for the two of us? Because now—now how am I supposed to feel about it?"

"Think about Oliver," Claire said. "And Ayesha. And all of these people lying on the tables who didn't make it. Fallon's perfectly okay with killing three-quarters or more of the people he experiments on. That's just not okay, even if Michael was in the lucky bracket."

"I know," Eve said. She took a deep breath, leaned over, and quickly pulled the IV tube from Ayesha's arm—it immediately sealed, which was interesting—and nodded to Claire. "You grab Oliver. Meet you up front."

"You can do this? You're sure? Even though she's—" Claire used the universal finger-fangs-in-neck symbol for vampire, and Eve gave her a pale, broken smile.

"As long as I don't have to do anything but push the gurney," she said.

Claire took her at her word, and moved on to do her part. Getting the limp body of Oliver up and onto the bed was a lot more trouble than she had reckoned. She finally got him in a fireman's carry over her shoulder and staggered the few steps to flop him crookedly onto the gurney. Not a neat job, but it would do to roll him down the hall, as long as she didn't encounter too many bumps along the way.

Eve was already rolling Ayesha toward the door.

As she left the lab, though, things went wrong. She'd just managed to prop the second door open for the gurney when alarms started shrieking—deafening alarms, designed to paralyze and panic, and it definitely had the second effect on her, if not the first. Her heart was pounding as she steered Oliver's gurney out. She heard the lock snapping shut behind her. *Lockdown.* She hoped Eve had kept the front door open.

She had. She'd jammed an empty gurney into it, and as Claire arrived, breathless, she saw that Michael had carried Ayesha down the steps and was putting her in the backseat of the car they'd liberated from lab rat Amanda. "Help me," Claire panted as she grabbed Oliver's shoulders. "We don't have much time!"

Eve just shook her head and stepped away, trying to control nausea with both hands over her mouth. Claire wondered how she was going to feel once it came down to getting into the car with a couple of vampires.

Probably wouldn't be pleasant.

Michael came running back. She nodded toward him. "Grab Oliver's legs," she said. He did, and the sheet around Oliver slipped, revealing way too much pale, ashy skin.

"Uh . . . have you noticed he's not wearing much?" Michael

asked. "At least I got to keep my pants." He'd thrown a lab coat on over his bare chest, but it didn't fit very well.

Claire hadn't noticed, actually, until that very moment, and while it was more than a little distracting, she just ignored all of it as they carried Oliver's heavy, limp form to the car and jammed it in next to Ayesha. There was a shout from the door, and Claire looked up to see one of the men from Eve's treatment room—if you could call it that—standing in the doorway, trying to force his way past the jammed empty gurneys. "Get in!" she yelled. She saw the furious face of Dr. Anderson behind the orderly. "We have to go!"

Michael started the car as Eve piled into the front next to him, which left Claire no choice but to climb into the backseat with two half-naked comatose vampires. She tried not to think about that, about the cool, dead-feeling bodies pressed against her.

Eve was gagging again, which was miserable for her, and potentially miserable for everybody else.

Michael jammed the car in reverse just as one of the orderlies—who must have scavenged a gun from one of the fallen guards—took a shot at them. It smashed the windshield into blinding cracks, with a neat hole high in the center, and it took a second for the delayed reaction to kick in. Claire checked herself for leaks, but the bullet had gone through the back without hitting anyone.

"I can't see!" Michael yelled. Eve, with barely a pause to flinch, braced herself and began to kick the front windshield. Somewhere in the confusion she'd switched out her paper house shoes for a too-large pair of men's boots, and they came in handy now as she smashed the whole shattered mess out, leaving them with a make-shift convertible. "Claire, get the back!"

That was a lot harder, because she had no leverage and no

room. Claire felt around on the floor and found a kid's baseball bat rolling under her feet; Amanda must have had a son or daughter in Little League.

She smashed at the back window until it broke out into a heap on the trunk. Not clean, but good enough to allow Michael visibility.

Claire lost her hold on the bat as he accelerated backward, and it rolled off, thumped down the slope of the metal, and clattered to the parking lot as Michael swerved, shifted gears again, and roared out at the top speed Amanda's car could manage.

The cool breeze felt good, and it wiped some of the blank shock from Claire's mind. There were no more shots from the building behind them, which was lucky. "Where are we going?" Claire asked. Unfortunately, Michael asked it at the same time, which meant none of them had any good ideas . . . and behind them, not more than a couple of blocks back, police lights began strobing. "They're on us!"

"I see them," Michael said tightly. "I—*holy shit!*"

He hit the brakes so hard that Claire—not belted in, for obvious reasons—had to grab his seat back in a death grip to keep from being catapulted through the front open window. The two limp vampires in the back with her slammed forward like crash dummies as the car skidded, tires smoking, and came to a shuddering halt.

Shane was standing in the road.

He looked violent and savage and crazy, and his eyes were that terrifying shade of gold. He was missing a shirt, his pants were ripped and bloody, and underneath it Claire could see that he'd been hurt—cuts and bruises.

But he was mostly human.

As the car stopped just inches from his thighs, he wavered, lost his balance, and slapped both palms on the hood for support as his knees went out from under him.

"Shane!"

"Claire, don't—," Michael yelled, but it was too late, she was already out of the car and racing toward him. *He won't hurt me,* she thought. *He didn't hurt me before and he won't hurt me now.*

And he didn't.

Shane's hands were back to normal human hands, though they looked bloody and bruised, and when he raised his head to meet her gaze, the hot golden color was fading out of his eyes. "Claire?" He sounded lost and scared. "I was looking for you. For Amelie— I smelled her blood . . ."

Michael had opened the driver's-side door and stepped out, watching them. Ready, Claire thought, to come to her defense if necessary . . . or to Shane's, if he needed it, too. Now he came up and put his weight under Shane's other arm as her boyfriend threatened to drop completely.

"Hey, bro, you found me instead," Michael said. "You been fighting without me?"

"You're—you're not a— Mikey, what the *hell* . . . ?" Shane was just beginning to realize the magnitude of what had happened, but nobody had much time to explain it. The sirens were wailing behind them. Granted, those cop cars would be making straight for the asylum, but they would definitely have the description of Amanda's car in minutes, and then it would be almost impossible to make it out of town.

"Got to go," Claire said, and on Shane's other side, Michael nodded.

"Let's get you in the car. We'll talk on the way."

"On the way to where?" Shane asked. "Can't go home. *They're* in the house."

Claire wanted to ask about that, badly, but they were out of time. Instead, she helped Michael drag Shane around to Eve's side of the car. Eve squished over, and Shane got his customary shotgun seat.

The door just barely squeezed shut.

Michael and Claire dove back in, and Michael hit the gas hard, peeling out with a screech that probably would have drawn attention if it hadn't been for the unholy racket of sirens a few streets over.

Sunset was painting the skies a bloody mess of red and orange.

"Um . . . are you okay? Is she okay?" Shane asked, looking at Eve, who was trembling and looking green around the edges.

"She'll be okay. Where are we going?" Claire asked, holding on to Michael's seat for dear life.

"We're getting the hell out of Morganville," he said. "We're going to Blacke."

Blacke, Texas, was a little town (small even by Morganville standards) about two hours away as the crows flew . . . but crows didn't build roads, and the road builders had no reason to want to go to Blacke. Most people didn't. Morganville was practically a tourist trap by comparison.

But the little place had the distinction—the secret distinction—of being the only other town where vampires lived in peace with humans. That wasn't because of the unselfishness of the vampires who'd moved there; the leader of that ragged band, Morley, didn't have even a hint of altruism in him. What he did have was a burning desire to run his own life and to not live by Morganville's rules . . . and a healthy fear/respect for Mrs. Grant, the town's librarian. Blacke had been overrun by a vampire plague brought on by a visit from another, much nastier predator who didn't care about the consequences, and Mrs. Grant had organized the town's survivors into an armed camp. Morley had intended to come to Blacke as a conqueror, but instead he'd become its protector and savior.

He seemed to find that oddly thrilling. Or maybe he'd just found Mrs. Grant thrilling. He'd had a hot-for-teacher thing going on when last they'd seen him. Their partnership running the town—and protecting the citizens of Blacke who'd been unwillingly turned into vampires—seemed to work better than anyone expected.

Or so Claire had heard. She hadn't visited since she'd left the town behind to return to Morganville.

"You're sure?" she asked Michael.

"Do you think we've got a choice?" They were heading fast for Morganville's town limits; she could see the silhouette of the billboard ahead. "If we don't get the hell out of here, then Fallon will have me, and he'll have Oliver. If Amelie's still free, he'll have what he needs to bring her back in. Plus, whatever else happens, he is *never* going to touch Eve again." Wow. Michael was usually a calm guy, but Fallon's attack on Eve had put him on the edge, for sure.

"That's sweet," Eve said. She was pressed up against him, a situation Claire was sure she didn't mind, and now she let her head rest lightly on his shoulder. "Sweetie, I'm sorry I lost my ring."

"Didn't lose me."

"I know." She gave a happy sigh and wiggled closer. "Is it weird to say this is nice?"

"Yeah," Shane said, but he was smiling. He looked . . . more himself, Claire thought. "Pretty weird, weirdo."

Eve turned her head toward him, considering him carefully. "Speaking of. What the hell happened to you? I mean, your eyes . . . they're okay now, but I'm pretty sure you didn't have a night-light feature before. Unless you swallowed your phone, your eyes really shouldn't do that."

He shrugged. "Dog bite, remember?"

"So now you're what, a hellhound?"

"Would it be too much if I said, *Bitch, please*?"

"Probably."

"Consider my manly silence an answer, then."

The banter sounded normal, but underneath there was fear—fear from both of them. For each other, and maybe even about each other. After a second or two of silence, Shane said, "Hey, Mikey?"

"Yeah, man."

"So you're not a vampire."

"I'd have let you know ahead of time, but it happened pretty fast."

"I think that just saved your life," Shane said, and leaned his head back against the seat. "They sent me to hunt Amelie down, but you've got her blood in you—*had* her blood in you. I can still kind of smell it, but it's faded now."

"You'd have killed me?"

"I'd have tried really hard not to, if that's any help." He closed his eyes and swallowed hard. He looked tired, Claire thought, and her heart ached for him. "Can't swear I wouldn't have, though. It was hard enough holding off to let Claire go, and let Amelie escape."

"She got out?" Claire leaned forward and put her hand against

his face. He still felt feverishly hot. "I know that was hard for you.
I saw how much it hurt you to let me go when I—"

"Yeah, about that . . . Next time you decide to take a bath in
the Founder's blood when you *know* there are hellhounds like me
out to track her—"

"Wait, what?" Eve interrupted, and twisted, as much as she
could, to look at Claire. "What did you do?"

"It worked, didn't it?" Claire asked, and smiled, just a little. "It
gave her a chance to get away."

And Shane smiled back. "Yes. Yes, it did."

The car flashed by the billboard. Claire didn't know how fast
they were going, but she was willing to bet it was approaching the
speed of sound from the wind buffeting they were taking. She'd
had no idea Amanda's beater of a vehicle could go this fast, and she
was fairly sure it had never tried it before, because it was shimmy-
ing something awful.

She didn't even see the police cruiser parked in the shadows beneath the sign until it came careening out onto the road behind
them, trailing an airborne plume of dust. The flashers popped on,
and the howl of a siren split the night.

"Hold on!" Michael said, and the car seemed to go even faster.
It hardly mattered, though; the police cruiser was built for inter-
cepts, and it was gaining on them. It was another two miles to the
next intersection, but all of the roads out here were straight and
boring, with nowhere to hide, no traffic to use for cover.

"You're going to blow the engine on this thing!" Shane yelled
over the roar of the wind. Claire felt like her hair was lashing her
face raw. "Mike, you can't outrun him!"

"Can't outgun him, either!" Michael shot back. "And I'm not
bulletproof anymore. Are you?"

"No, but they are," Shane said, and pointed behind him at the unresponsive forms of Oliver and Ayesha. "Wake them up."

"How?" Claire yelled back.

"Have you tried blood?"

Crap. She hadn't even thought about that, but it made sense. They would be hungry, and maybe, just maybe, they needed a blood catalyst to fight their way out of their comas.

And maybe when they woke up, they wouldn't stop at just a taste, either. It was risky, but they needed an advantage, fast, and it was the only thing Claire could think of at the moment. "Glove compartment," she said. "I need something sharp."

Shane was way ahead of her, pulling a knife from his belt. She hadn't even known it was there, but of course he was armed. Wasn't he always? "Be careful," he said. "Don't trust them, and use that knife if you have to."

It was, of course, edged in silver plate. "What about you? Will you be okay? I mean, they're vampires and you're . . ."

"A friggin' werewolf vampire hunter? Yeah, I know. I'm still primed to go after Amelie, not specifically targeted on these two right now, so it should be relatively okay. If it isn't, I'll deal with it. Eve has permission to whack me over the head or something."

"Goody," Eve said. "Always wanted your permission for that."

She was not, Claire noticed, looking as bad as she had been, and the nausea seemed to be subsiding. Maybe whatever they'd spiked the blood with was finally starting to dissipate.

They were chattering because they were scared, and Claire knew it because she was scared, too. She was sweating, her heart was hammering, her mouth felt dry, and her tongue scraped like leather. The wind whipping into her face made it hard to focus, and she wished she had glasses to protect her eyes from the blowing, ever-present dust.

Just do it already.

She put the knife to the meaty part of the palm of her hand, below the thumb, and sliced. Fresh blood spurted out, and she gasped at the hot bite of pain, then turned to Oliver and pried his mouth open. Inside, it was dry and pale.

She squeezed blood into his mouth.

Nothing happened.

Dammit. "Come on," she said under her breath, her words lost in the roar of the wind hammering through the car. "Come on, swallow, just swallow . . ." She milked more blood from the wound until there was a shallow pool of it in his mouth, then closed his jaw and tilted his head back.

She felt a muscle move beneath his skin, just a twitch . . . and then she saw his Adam's apple jerk as he swallowed.

Oliver's eyes opened. He looked confused and disoriented, and then the red flecks began to swirl in his eyes. He blinked and held up a hand to shield himself from the wind.

His gaze fell on Claire, slipped down and focused on her bleeding hand. Without permission, without hesitation, he grabbed it and put it to his mouth. She let out a muffled sound of protest, but he didn't seem wild or out of control. It was a subtle difference, but one she'd learned to distinguish, with vamps.

And he let go after he'd sucked out two or three more swallows.

Oliver licked his lips clean, cleared his throat, and half whispered, "Thank you." She couldn't hear him over the road noise, but she understood anyway.

"Welcome," she shouted back. "Need your help!"

"Of course you do." He looked deeply cranky, which wasn't at all strange for him, but he raised his voice so she could hear him. Barely. "It might have escaped your notice, but I very nearly died!"

"That could still happen," she shot back. "We need to stop the police car behind us. I think they've probably got orders to shoot us on sight—and take you back to Fallon so he can finish what he started!"

Oliver still looked cranky, but now he also looked stronger, and resolved. "Tell Michael to slow down."

"But—"

"Do it!"

She turned to Michael and screamed the instruction in his ear. He didn't ask any questions; he just hit the brakes, and the sedan decelerated, fast.

Oliver slithered through the broken back window, got to his feet on the trunk lid, and launched himself onto the hood of the onrushing squad car with hardly a pause—but Claire could tell, from the way he moved, that he was weak, and hurting. His lithe grace was gone, leaving a kind of brutally clumsy strength.

He smashed a fist through the windshield and grabbed the driver, and the police car swerved violently, veered off the road into the desert, and was lost in a plume of erupting sand.

Michael stood on the brakes and brought the car to a complete, tire-smoking halt. He and Shane were out in seconds, heading for where the other vehicle had disappeared, and Claire bailed as well, joining Eve at a dead run to catch up. Eve tripped over her too-large men's boots and almost went down, but Claire caught her arm and kept her upright and moving. She choked and coughed on the drifting sand, and as it cleared she saw Oliver sliding down from the hood of the cruiser. He was scratched and cut from the broken windshield, but he looked otherwise unharmed. Just . . . really, uncomfortably nearly naked, and Claire wished that she could unsee that.

Shane opened the cruiser's front driver's-side door. He crouched and checked the man inside. "He's alive," he said. "I'm surprised."

"I haven't had time to feed," Oliver snapped. "Get me something to wear."

Shane popped the car's trunk, pulled out a blanket, and tossed it to Oliver without moving any closer. *Fighting his instincts,* Claire thought. He dived back into the police car and grabbed the keys, which he used to unlock the shotgun behind the seat from its rack; he tossed it to Eve, who caught it with perfect ease. He confiscated the man's handgun, too. By this time the cop was starting to come around, moaning and shifting in his seat, so Shane took the handcuffs from his belt and locked the man's right hand to the steering wheel, then patted him on the head. "Cheer up, buddy," he said. "The good news is, you aren't dead."

"You will be," the cop mumbled. "They'll hunt you down. Kill you."

"Then we'll be going," Michael said. "Everybody, come on. In the car."

Claire and Eve started back, and so did Shane and Michael. Oliver, on the other hand, didn't.

"Hey!" Michael said, without stopping. "You're losing your ride, Oliver, I don't think you want to be out here by yourself."

"A moment," Oliver replied, and stepped over to the cruiser.

Claire turned and ran back as the vampire leaned in, fangs out and gleaming. "Wait!" she shouted. Oliver turned on her, but she'd had plenty of experience with his particular brand of intimidation. "Please, Oliver. Don't kill him."

"Would you rather I take it from you?"

"I didn't say you couldn't bite him, just—be careful."

"Afraid of more blood on your hands?" His fangs were still down, and they made his grin particularly terrifying. "Unhand me, woman, or I'll unhand *you*. I'll decide how much I need."

"Kill him and you're walking," she said.

He stared at her for a long moment, and his anger turned to something oddly like . . . interest. "You know, you are not the mousy little thing I met that morning in Common Grounds," he said. "You've become something else entirely. It's to your credit, but it's also extremely inconvenient."

He raised the policeman's free arm, ripped the sleeve loose, and pressed the man's wrist to his mouth. Claire winced at the shriek the cop let out, but it was more surprise than pain. He shut up after that, except for moans of fear, and Oliver ignored him as he continued to draw blood and swallow.

Just when Claire was starting to really worry, he let go of the cop's arm and stepped back, fastening the blanket around his body. It was one of those soft jersey things, so it looked almost like a toga. She could imagine him back in ancient Rome, presiding over some bloodbath in the Colosseum.

Somehow he made it look like being merciful was his own idea.

"After you, Miss Danvers."

ELEVEN

The drive to Blacke wasn't comfortable, but it was less crowded in the backseat, since Oliver had settled himself in and put the limp, still form of Ayesha in his lap. He sat very straight, eyes closed against the rushing wind.

"Eve," Michael finally said, "why do you have a bandage on your neck? Did someone bite—"

"Can we talk about it later?" she asked.

"What happened to you?"

Eve didn't seem willing to say, but Claire was still simmering over it, and she thought Michael needed to know. "They started her—what did Fallon call it?—aversion therapy. Which involved a vampire."

"It's fine, it's nothing." Eve took Michael's hand in hers. "Look, I don't even feel sick anymore. It's just a bite. I'll live."

He put the back of her hand to his cheek. He didn't say anything, but his gaze sought out Claire's in the rearview mirror, and she knew he would have some questions later. She didn't blame him. She knew Eve wouldn't feel like talking about it, and he'd need to know.

Night had fallen, and the air coming in was cold enough to chill Claire to the bone. Michael had rustled up a discarded jacket from the trunk of the car, but by common agreement they'd given it to Eve, who was freezing and shivering in her light hospital clothes. Not that Michael had on much more.

"Mike," Shane said, and pointed. "Pull in up there." *Up there* turned out to be a light shimmering in the distance, off the small farm-to-market road they were following—a single square house out in the middle of nowhere with a porch light glowing yellow, security lights on a barn out back, and the homey glow of lamps behind curtains.

"We're not going to do anything to those people," Claire said. "We're not."

"Of course we're not," Shane said. "Trust me, okay?" He bailed out when Michael stopped the car, and then—inexplicably—took off his jeans. "Keep the lights off. I'll be right back."

They all watched him jog away in his Joe Boxers. Claire felt a little dizzy, actually.

"I don't like this," Eve said. "What the hell is he doing? What if they just, you know, shoot on sight?"

"He said to trust him," Claire said. "I do."

And she was right to do it, because after about ten minutes, he came back with a whole plastic bag full of clothes. "Here," he said, and began digging out baggy sweatpants, hoodies, jackets, and shirts. "Sorry, ladies, they're all men's sizes, but I'm sure you'll still look awesome."

"How?" Michael asked. He grabbed a pair of the sweats and ducked out of the car to pull them on, then added a zip-up hoodie. The logo on the faded cotton was—ironically—that of Texas Prairie University. Morganville's school. Claire's alma mater, sort of. "How the hell did you get these?"

"Well, I said I was pledging a frat at TPU with a car full of other guys, and we got driven out here and left naked by the side of the road, and the old bastard cackled and thought it was funny as hell. Then he gave me clothes." Shane put on a hoodie from the bag—another TPU legacy—and snagged his blue jeans from the floor. "Here, put on another layer." He handed Eve more clothes, and she bundled up gratefully. Claire was doing the same, taking both a T-shirt and a hoodie to add to what she was wearing, and for the first time, she felt something like warm again. "Oliver?" Shane held out something to the vampire, and got a dismissive stare in return. "No? Sticking with the toga look? Well, I always said you were an ice-cold killer."

That almost woke a smile from Oliver. Almost.

Once they'd donned all the donated layers, they headed out again. "You know, we probably should have jacked that cop car," Eve said. "At least it had more windshield."

"Except for where Oliver punched through it, and we couldn't see to drive?"

"Oh, right. Except for that."

They passed a deserted, falling-down old diner that had served its last crappy sandwich at least twenty years back, and right on cue, Claire's stomach rumbled. Loudly.

"Are you hungry?" Michael asked. "Because I'm starving." He

laughed then, as pure and free a sound as Claire had ever heard from him when he wasn't singing. He sounded ... whole. "You know, as a vampire I was never really hungry for solid food, even though I could eat it. I didn't know how much I missed that. I could really kill for a burger right now. And fries. With salt."

"Stop it, man, you're killing me," Shane groaned. "Maybe they've got an all-night diner in Blacke."

Mention of the town—of their destination—brought them back to reality with a crash. This wasn't some larky road trip. It was a mission.

"You should know something," Claire said, and swallowed hard when they all turned to look at her. Even Oliver. "I heard Fallon give an order to release some of the vampires tonight from the mall. The hungriest and meanest ones."

"Of course," Oliver said. "Fallon does so need his righteous justifications. Once he whips the people of Morganville into a frenzy of fear, he'll be free to do whatever he likes with us, and no one will stand in his way. He can burn us all on pyres in Founder's Square if he likes. And he might find that a just punishment."

"As somebody *you* once sentenced to that kind of execution, maybe the shoe fits," Shane said.

"Shane!" Claire said.

He shrugged. "Sorry, but there are plenty of regular people who've been hurt in Morganville. Who've lost family. That flapping sound? It's the chickens coming home to roost."

"He's right," Oliver said, which was a little unexpected—even to Shane, as evidenced by the startled look he threw back toward Claire. "The problem with ruling by fear is that eventually, when the fear fades, fury replaces it. That's a lesson I should have learned in my breathing years, perhaps."

"Damn straight," Shane said, but his outrage had lost its force. "So . . . is there anything we can do to stop Fallon tonight? If it's not too late already?"

"No," Oliver said. He had turned his head, and was staring out at the desert whipping by beyond the window. "But it's possible, just possible, that Fallon's plan might backfire. Most of us older vampires have vast experience in managing our hunger; the poison he put in our blood supplies made us restless and peckish, to be sure, but not uncontrollably so. It's the younger fledglings who have . . . difficulty. He might have lost enough touch with his vampire roots to think he can drive us so easily into marauding."

"I thought you were all just waiting for the chance," Shane said.

"Did you?" Oliver shrugged. "I'm not saying a hunt isn't something we crave, but to a man, we hate to be manipulated. And this is our town, as much as any human's. Our home, and our neighbors and perhaps even our friends. You fall into the trap of thinking as Fallon does, that there are only heroes and villains, monsters and victims, and nothing between. We all stand in that space, crossing the line to one side, then the other. Even you."

That was unusually chatty for Oliver, and strangely lyrical, too. They all sat in silence for a while, until Michael cleared his throat and said, "I'm making the turn up ahead. Should take us straight to Blacke."

"Hope that diner's open," Shane said. "Because now you made me think about French fries."

Claire's stomach rumbled again, right on cue, but she was watching Oliver. Watching the calm strength with which he cradled Ayesha, still locked in her coma. He hadn't asked for blood for her, or more for himself, though she could see from the color of his skin and the shine in his eyes that he needed it.

He was teaching them all something about vampires, simply by being who he was. Maybe bad things, maybe good. But that had been his point.

That nothing, absolutely nothing, was all that straightforward.

Blacke kept its town purposefully dark; it didn't want casual travelers looking for gas stations, or all-night diners. In fact, if Claire hadn't known that the town had a population of at least five hundred, she'd have been fooled into thinking it was a ghost town. Only a few cars in sight; and the lights were off inside businesses locked up tight for the evening. It was a tiny little one-stoplight place anyway.

The hulking courthouse was just as Claire remembered it, though the damage to the iron fence had been fixed and the statue of Mr. Blacke, the town's most eminent (or at least richest dead) citizen, had been restored, except it still leaned a little bit. They'd knocked him down with the school bus, hadn't they? It seemed like such a long time ago. She swore that Morganville years were worse than dog years. The people of Blacke had boarded up the courthouse windows, though, and a faded red CONDEMNED sign creaked in the night wind. The only light in the place came from the glow from the clock tower, permanently frozen at three a.m. Claire checked her watch to be sure, but her instincts were right; the time was just past midnight.

The witching hour.

"We're being watched," Oliver said as Michael eased the car to a halt. "Although I expect it is thoroughly unnecessary to say it. Even a breather ought to be able to feel it."

"Is that some bigoted term you guys use for us?" Shane asked.

"In the same way you use *bloodsucker, leech, parasite?* Yes. Although considerably more flattering."

"He's right," Eve said, and Claire saw her shoulders bunch together as she shivered, even though she was warmly wrapped up now. "They're watching us."

Oliver stepped out and raised his voice. "Enough of this, Morley. You've had your gawk. There is serious work ahead."

"Is there?"

Claire heard the lazy voice drifting down from far above. From the clock tower. She tilted her head back and spotted the shadow then, standing just under the glare of the light on the dials of the clock. Morley himself. He walked to the roof's edge and stepped off, as if the four-story drop were nothing—and it might have been, for vampires. He hardly even flexed his knees on landing, and as he rose, Claire saw he'd managed to find clothes that suited him in Blacke—a dramatic full-length leather duster in faded brown, a long red scarf that trailed in the wind, a flat-brimmed hat. His eyes gleamed crimson in the darkness.

"Do tell me all about your crisis, Oliver. You built yourself a kingdom of cats and now the rats have gotten the upper hand—is that right? They've put all you sleek little mousers in a cage and fed you on scraps. Soon they'll put you down and celebrate and then it will be the kingdom of the rats. Rats and cats, cheese and please may I have a bite." Morley paused, leaned an elbow on the hood of the car, and gave Oliver a long scan from head to toe. "I knew you were old, dear boy, but really, the Romans?"

"It's been a long day. I'm not in the mood for your idiocy."

"And yet you're in the mood for my assistance. Interesting. Well, then, come along. Mrs. Grant is waiting."

Morley didn't wait for any of them to agree; he simply set off down the street. The snap of his coat in the wind was the only sound he made as he walked down the deserted road and took the sidewalk to the right.

They all exchanged a look. Oliver shook his head in disgust, reached in, and picked up the limp body of Ayesha. He held her as easily as a pillow. "Well?" he barked. "Morley may be a theatrical posturer, but he's a decent grasp of tactics. And I might point out that we're standing targets here for his followers. They have a kill shot on each of us."

Eve blinked. "Um . . . how do you know that?"

"Tactics," Oliver said, and walked away down the road in the direction Morley had gone.

Claire shrugged when Shane raised his eyebrows at her. "Right," he said. "Guess we're going, then."

Michael looked up at the silent, dark windows around them and yelled, "You can keep the car!"

Then he linked his arm with Eve's and led the way in Oliver's wake.

"Oh, no, not the old library," Shane said, in a pretty good approximation of Oliver's voice and phrasing. "How very tiresome of him to take us there."

Claire elbowed him. "You must be feeling better."

"Seems like it, doesn't it?"

That, she thought with a sudden rush of disquiet, was not an answer. It was an evasion. "*Are* you feeling better?"

"If by better you mean much more aware than I ought to be of the fact that there are freaking vampires all over the place, then yes, much better. But I'm dealing with it."

"If you can't, will you let me know?"

"Sure thing. I'll let out a howl."

"Not funny."

"Well, in my defense, it wasn't really meant to be. I mean, I might literally howl."

"Shane." She pulled him to a stop, and when their eyes met, he dropped some of his smart-ass shield. "We're going to get through this. I promise you that."

He leaned forward and kissed her on the lips—warm, sweet, gentle, all the things she loved about him. All the things she knew were inside him, buried sometimes by the tough-guy attitude and smack talk. "I think you can get through anything," he said. "Hey, I'm happy sticking with you. As long as you don't cover yourself in Queen Vampire blood again—I may be a freak, but there are limits."

"Be serious."

"I'm trying. It's not what I do best."

He was making her laugh, and that wasn't what she wanted right now. Not what she needed. "Shane, when we get out of this—and we *will* get out of it—I want you to know that I'm . . . I'm ready."

He raised his eyebrows, and jumped to the wrong conclusion. Of course. "That's good, because I'm a guy, Claire. I'm pretty much always—"

She put a hand over his mouth. "You asked me to marry you. Were you serious?"

She took her hand away. He didn't say anything. His lips formed what would have been the start of a word, maybe a sentence, but he didn't actually speak.

She'd scared the words right out of him.

"Uh . . . that came out of nowhere," he said.

"Is that a no? Were you just saying it before because you thought you had to say it?"

"No! I mean, not no to the original question, obviously, no to that last—" He took a deep breath. "Let me start over. Claire . . . look, you just startled me, that's all." He took her hands, both hands, and twined their fingers together. Then he leaned forward and rested his forehead against hers. "Of course I mean it. I always meant it. I will always mean it. I just thought . . . I thought you wanted to wait."

"I did," she said. "But if these past years in Morganville have taught me anything, it's that sometimes you have to just . . . jump. It's not safe. It's never safe. But sometimes you have to live danger-ously."

He laughed a little. "You're talking my language now."

"You said *I* wanted to wait. You didn't?"

"We should probably go back to that earlier thing about me being a guy, right?"

"I got that part." She kissed him, just a tingling brush of lips, their foreheads still touching. "You waited anyway."

"Well, yeah. Because you're worth waiting for." He said it as if it was simple and self-evident, but it made her shiver. It was such a strong, sexy thing to say, and she knew he meant it. He would al-ways mean it. "If you want to get married now, tonight, then let's find whoever passes for a justice of the peace in Blacke."

"Wouldn't *that* be a story to tell the kids," she said, and then she held her breath, because she'd said it without really thinking, and she was waiting for him to get weird about it, to pull back, to say something like *whoa, girl, hit the brakes.*

But instead he just smiled and said, "I'm pretty sure we'll have lots of stories to tell the kids. Almost none of them are going to be appropriate."

"Good."

"Excellent."

"So. Justice of the peace?"

"No," she said. "How about we do it in Morganville, once this is over? Do it right. For real."

"You mean, gown and tuxedo? Because I was getting used to the idea of saying *I do* in sweatpants I borrowed from some toothless old country coot. It's different."

"It's different in an utterly bad way."

"Would that be the eighties definition of *bad*, as in *great*, or . . ."

"Shouldn't we catch up?" she asked. Because the others had disappeared inside the darkened library building ahead, and she had that feeling again, of people watching from the shadows. Vamps, most likely. She supposed they were listening, too.

"In a second," he said, and pulled her close, body to body, fitting in all the right places to start a breathtaking fire inside her. "You know they're watching us, right?"

She nodded.

"Let's give them something to watch."

And then he kissed her, all passion and intensity and heat and dark chocolate sweetness melting on her tongue, but not just sweet because there was spice in it, too, bursts of searing pepper, and he made her hungry, so incredibly hungry to feel his skin on hers that it almost drove her crazy.

Almost.

"Good effort at making me want to rip your clothes off," she said when he let her breathe again.

"Didn't work?"

"Oh, it worked. I'm just better without an audience."

He kissed her gently on the nose. "I'll hold you to that later."

When they opened the door of the library, they found themselves catapulted back into the past. The windows had been blacked out to hide the lights, but apart from the fact that the electricity was on, the Blacke Public Library hadn't changed very much. The same battered wooden tables, the same sturdy chairs, the same scarred linoleum floors and doubtful carpet. It was neater, though. And it wasn't full of Blacke citizens standing around with weapons.

Instead, people were standing around in groups of two and three, whispering, and not displaying visible armament. They were mostly watching Morley, who had leaped up onto one of the study tables and was pacing around, hands behind his back, with the duster swirling around him. Claire half expected him to have jingling spurs. He certainly had the cowboy boots, and they looked old enough to have survived the Civil War and been on the march ever since.

Shane must have been thinking the same thing, because he said to Morley, "Nice outfit. Whose smelly old corpse did you steal it off of?"

It was hard to read Morley's expression, since he wore his hair long and wild and it concealed his face pretty well. "I could ask the same about your ill-fitting rags, boy. Though I doubt you killed anyone. Perhaps mugged. I doubt you have the stomach for it."

"Oh," Shane said, with a grin that was at least half wolf, "you might be surprised."

"Do tell," Morley invited. "By all means. Oliver, where do you pick up these . . . feral children?"

"You remember Shane," Oliver said. He'd stripped off his blanket toga, and Claire quickly turned her back as she saw the white flash of skin. With no hesitation at all, he was stripping and putting on clothes that had been laid out for him. She heard cloth rustling and zippers fastening, and finally risked a look over her shoulder. Yes, he was dressed, in a pair of jeans that actually fit him and a plain dark shirt that he somehow made look edgy. "And Claire. And, of course, Michael and Eve."

"Charmed yet again, I'm sure," Morley said. He didn't sound charmed; he sounded utterly impatient. "Weren't some of you vampires before? Oh, never mind. Boring. To the point, then. You brought Ayesha to us, and I thank you for that, but I notice you've not rescued anyone else. Thoughts?"

"Several. None that don't involve you screaming."

"Don't be so limiting, I'm sure you can imagine several that involve me begging as well. Did you run away, Oliver? Leave your pride of caged cats behind?"

"Fallon's got them," Oliver said.

"Ah."

Silence fell. Morley jumped down from the table and leaned against it, eye to eye with Oliver for a change. He pulled off his hat and dropped it on the table and ran both hands through his wildly messy hair. "Well?" he finally said. "He was never my problem, nor yours, nor even Amelie's or even her dead father's. He was your madman's doing."

"Myrnin," Oliver said. "Yes."

"Wait," Claire said. "What do you mean, it's Myrnin's problem? He had nothing to do with it!"

"Oh, he did, girl, he most certainly did," Morley said. He sat down on the table and gave her an amused stare. "He's never told you the story? Ah, well, probably because it isn't to his credit, I imagine. So poor, sad, unstable Myrnin was all alone after his vampire maker was killed. And he became friends with a clergy-man, a very learned one, who was also a secret student of alchemy."

"That was Fallon," Oliver said. "In case you might miss the obvious."

"Quiet, it's my story. Yes, it was our dear friend Fallon, who most earnestly wanted to cure Myrnin of his madness . . . and his curse. He found, most horribly, that he only made things worse, and next thing you know, Myrnin's drained Fallon like a cask of wine. As ever, he immediately regretted it, and decided to resurrect him, within the doors of Fallon's own church, no less. A thing Fal-lon most assuredly did not want to do, resurrect—at least not as a vampire. But our dear madman dragged him kicking and shriek-ing back to life. Broke him most sincerely, I'm afraid . . . and then left him to fend for himself."

Claire wasn't sure what was worse, hearing that Myrnin had killed a priest, or that he'd made him a vampire against his will, or that he'd abandoned him like some unwanted pet.

"He was not himself then," Oliver said. "Myrnin isn't solely re-sponsible for Fallon's . . . excesses. Or his equally excessive self-loathing, which led to his crusade against us."

"Nonsense. In short," Morley said, "all this is Myrnin's fault, and it's his mess, and why I should have to sweep it up is not at all clear."

"I agree that Myrnin should be the one to eliminate Fallon for us," Oliver said. "Sadly, he seems more curious than outraged at the moment. Something about the progress that Fallon's made on his *cure*. You know how the fool can get when you dangle a shiny bit of science in front of him."

"I heard a rumor," Morley said. "Scarcely credited it, frankly. Is it true Fallon thinks he can cure us back to human?"

"It's true he thinks it. It's also true he can do it, at least in a few cases." Oliver pointed a finger to where Michael and Eve sat at one of the study tables together. "You mentioned it earlier. Remember the boy?"

Morley gave Michael a long look, and his eyes slowly narrowed. "Ah. Well, that seems a pity," he said. "Hardly had time to get the taste for it, did he? And now he's dumped back on the long human road to dust. Still. Not much of a loss to the rest of us, it would seem."

"You miss my point, mummer. Fallon *can* do as he says. Not all the time, not with any great certainty, but he has a cure. How many do you think would reach for it if the prize was before them?"

Fallon shrugged. "Not so many as all that. You watch enough friends march to their graves, you lose the taste for ashes. Blood has a flavor so much more compelling."

"You and I share a faith, if not the particular details of it. What if he can restore us to a state of grace?"

"I knew that in the end it would come down to religion for you," Morley said, and rolled his eyes. "Do you feel damned and outcast from God's love, poor dove? I don't. I feel quite blessed to be able to wake every day knowing that I'll see yet another, free of weakness and sickness and pain."

Michael stood up. His chair screeched loudly on the floor, and both of the vampires looked toward him with identical frowning expressions. "We're not here to debate how many angels are on the head of a pin, or whatever it is you're about to get into. Fallon intends to turn vampires loose on humans in Morganville, then use the killing to justify giving them his cure until there's nobody left.

And when he's done with Morganville, he'll come here, Morley. He'll come for you. All of you. He has to."

A quiet, slender, middle-aged lady sitting nearby in an armchair said, "He's right. We knew this couldn't last if Morganville fell. The draug almost took everything, and now this Fallon's coming to finish the job. I'm not letting him finish *us*. We've fought too hard."

That was Mrs. Grant, the librarian—and, along with Morley, the one who ran the town of Blacke. She might look sweet and friendly, but Claire had seen her fighting off vampires and knew that she was nobody to mess with. Even Morley knew that.

He bowed his head slightly in her direction. "We can always run. I only ended up in this hick-town Eden through the misfortune that has always dogged my steps. What if we load our vampires into a light-proof truck and simply drive away?"

"Those vampires have family here. They're our sons, daughters, fathers, mothers. They didn't ask for any of this, and you can't just make them leave. Most of them will want this cure you're talking about, you know."

"'Tis exactly what worries me," he said. "You heard dear Oliver. Most won't survive. And we have no real surety that those who do won't have their lives cut short by his potion, do we? What if his humanity cure lets you live only a few days, or weeks, or a year? What value does it have then?"

Claire hadn't thought of that—hadn't even considered it. And now it struck her with terrible force. Fallon wasn't really concerned with making sure his "cured" vamps lived long and productive lives, was he? He just wanted them not to be vampires anymore. He'd probably consider a week of life without drinking blood worth the trade-off.

What if Michael had survived only to get sick and die? It would break Eve. It would just break her in half.

"We're not running," Mrs. Grant said.

"But dearie——," Morley began.

"Don't you 'dearie' me, you wretch. I'm not your wife and I'm not your mother. I'm the head of the human part of this town and you *will* pay attention to me. Agreed?"

"Yes," Morley said. There was a little smile on his lips and a crinkle of amusement around his eyes. "Of course. Very well, then, how do you think we should proceed in our grand quest to liberate Morganville? Descend upon them in a furious horde of fangs? It has a certain theatrical appeal, but——"

"They'd be ready," Oliver said. "They were ready before they came here. They ignored the vampires at first; they brought good works to the human community, won their trust, fanned the flames of anger. And Amelie was slow to act when there was no threat in sight. If she'd known what we who'd met them before did, she would have taken steps. But she hesitated. If I'd been here, by her side . . ."

"But you weren't," Morley said. "Because you had already failed her."

Oliver's body went tense, and his head lowered with unmistakable menace.

"Luckily," Morley continued with that strange trace of a smile, "I did not, and neither did your human companions. She's escaped from Fallon. What, did no one tell you? That chit of a girl with you, the one who looks so inoffensive——she covered herself in Amelie's blood to distract the hellhounds from her. And that boy, the one who looks so incapable of self-control——despite Fallon's infection in his blood, he held off from killing both his lady and *yours*."

Oliver's face twisted into a frown, and he cast a sharp look at Claire and Shane, but before he could ask anything at all, a woman dressed in blue jeans and a buttoned shirt stepped out from between the bookshelves. Her white-blond hair fell in a wavy rush across her shoulders and halfway down her back, and her ice gray eyes looked weary. "It's true," Amelie said. "Morley exaggerates, but he rarely lies outright. If not for these children, I'd be in Fallon's hands now, and this . . . this would be over for the vampires of Morganville."

Shane's hand crushed Claire's, a sudden and convulsive reaction that made her wince and look at him in alarm. He'd turned pale, and his whole body had gone tense, as if he were fighting an internal battle of epic proportions.

A battle he lost, as it happened.

His eyes took on an eerie golden shine, and he let go of her hand to lunge forward. There was a table in the way, but he vaulted it, heading straight for Amelie, and Claire saw bloody claws pushing out of his fingers.

"No!" she screamed. "Shane, *no!*"

Michael got in his way. Maybe, in that moment, he was thinking that he was still a vampire, capable of speed and strength; it must have been hard to shake that off after years of being used to it. But he didn't have those things, and Shane hit him like a freight train, slamming him backward.

Michael raised his left arm to protect his throat as Shane lunged for it, and Shane's teeth bit into his flesh in a violent blur.

Oliver was already in motion. He took a standing leap from halfway across the room, landed on the table, and launched himself like an arrow straight for Shane. He ripped him away from

Michael, spun him, and slammed him down. Then he held him there, flat on the floor, as Shane shredded the linoleum with his claws.

"As ever," Oliver said, "I am at your service, Founder."

"I know." There was a shadow of a smile in Amelie's eyes, and no trace of fear. "Michael?"

"I'm okay," he said, but it was just an automatic response, not true at all. His arm was bloody, and Eve was already beside him and helping to brace him as he staggered. She grabbed a chair and got him safely into it, and quickly stripped off her hoodie to wrap it around his bitten arm.

On the floor a few feet away, Shane was still changing, triggered by Amelie's presence. "He'll need to be locked away," Amelie said.

"No, you can't—," Claire blurted, and even as she said it she knew Amelie was right. Still, it felt wrong. Sick. Horrible. But Shane was dangerous, obviously; he'd hurt Michael, and Michael wasn't a vampire anymore; he'd just been in the way. He'd have done the same to anyone.

"I don't think you'd want me to reconsider," Amelie said, "since the alternative would be to put the boy down, and neither of us wants that."

"Speak for yourself," Oliver grumbled, and had to put a quelling hand flat on Shane's shoulder blades to keep him from pushing up. He was, Claire realized, still changing, his body contorting into a new, horrific shape. "Down, boy. Stay down."

"Don't hurt him!"

"Then I need something to tame him," Oliver said, ignoring her completely. "Quickly, please. He's strong."

Mrs. Grant was walking toward them, unsnapping an old-fashioned doctor's bag—Theo Goldman's, Claire was surprised to see. She remembered that bag. It even had the vampire doctor's initials on it in faded gold. "Wait, what are you doing?" Claire said. She didn't remember moving, but she was clutching the edge of a table now. "Shane, don't fight! Please!" Mrs. Grant set the bag down and took out an ancient-looking syringe with a hideously long needle.

She caught her breath as Mrs. Grant, with a decisive thrust, stuck the needle into Shane's back. He let out a howl—an actual howl, pure and shivery—and Amelie herself bent a knee to help hold Shane down as Mrs. Grant depressed the plunger, emptying the contents of the syringe into him.

"Get back," Oliver snapped. The librarian capped the syringe and put it in Theo's bag before she retreated, leaving the two vampires to handle Shane as he continued to thrash and struggle for freedom. He was growling now, a low and vicious sound that made Claire feel short of breath.

And then his growling turned to a pained, puzzled whimper, and faded into panting.

Claire gasped and lunged to where Amelie and Oliver were still holding Shane—what Shane had *become*—down. He didn't look human at all now. He looked more like a black dog, massive and terrifying, with those eerie inhuman eyes staring blearily up at her.

"Muscle relaxer," Mrs. Grant said. "It should hold him for a bit, but in my experience, with vampires at least, it doesn't last long. So we'd better find out what we're dealing with. From the looks of him, there's no place we can lock him up here that he won't break through."

"Oh, I've seen something like this before," Morley said. He was still sitting on the edge of a table, looking mildly surprised but not alarmed. "Ages ago. An alchemist turned someone into a wolf, one of those elaborate demonstrations so popular back in the day."

"Did he turn him back?" Claire asked.

"Wolves weren't terribly popular back then. He didn't have the chance." He stared at Shane thoughtfully for a moment, then moved his gaze to Michael as Mrs. Grant moved toward him with the doctor bag and unwrapped his wounded arm. She had him wiggle his fingers, and seemed satisfied when he was able to do so without much pain. "But it would seem to me that it's a similar thing to what's happened to *him*."

Claire had no idea what he meant, and she couldn't take it all in; it was too much, too fast, from the warm, romantic moment outside to . . . *this.* "Michael was healed. Whatever this is—it isn't being healed!"

"Well, it's an essential change of state. Vampire to human is just as great a change as what's happened to your dog boy; perhaps whatever cure Fallon forced down young Michael's throat might work just as well to change your hound back to his proper form, yes?"

That was . . . crazy. Unscientific. It was the kind of thing Myrnin would think of—but what Claire couldn't shake was how often Myrnin was right in these situations. "But we don't have any of the cure," she said. "And even if we did—it kills most of those who get it."

"Didn't kill *him*," Morley said, nodding toward Michael. "His blood still smells rank with whatever he was dosed with. And young Shane has just consumed a mouthful of it."

It struck Claire, finally, what he was saying, just as it also struck

Michael, who met her gaze, looking horrified. "No," he said. "It can't work that way."

"Tell that to him," Morley said, and pointed at Shane . . . who was changing.

It didn't happen as quickly as the shift he'd experienced in Amelie's presence, and Claire recognized, with a sick horror, the silvery glow that played on his skin underneath the matted coat of fur. She'd seen that before, in the vampires who'd been given the cure.

She'd seen it *kill them.*

"Get off him!" she screamed to Oliver, and when he didn't immediately move, she shoved at him. It was about as effective as shoving at a building, but after an eyebrows-raised glance at Amelie, he rose and let her kneel next to Shane's quivering body.

She wasn't afraid of Shane, even though she supposed she ought to be; he wasn't himself—the fact that he'd attacked Michael was proof enough of that. But she couldn't think about that, couldn't worry about that.

She was so afraid *for* him.

Within another minute his body had begun to warp back toward human shape. She watched the claws that had pushed out of his fingers turn glassy and brittle, then break off. The fur that had covered him grayed and fell away, leaving silvery, pulsing skin.

He was whimpering under his breath. She shifted him into her lap. He felt hot and clammy, and she could feel his bones moving and shifting under his skin at utterly wrong, sickening angles . . . until they were right again.

He opened his eyes, took in a slow, deep breath, and said, in a rough but recognizable voice, "Claire?" His eyes were brown again.

Human. "Sorry." He swallowed hard, and she saw that the silvery glow was fading from his skin. "Sorry." His eyes drifted shut again, as if he was too tired to keep them open.

"No," she said, and shook him. "No, stay awake! Shane, *stay awake!*"

His eyes opened again, and he blinked and focused on her face. "Tired," he said. "Hey, did somebody drug me? I feel drugged." He sounded out of it, too, but peaceful. She checked his pulse. It was slow and steady. His skin had taken on its more usual color, an even, smooth tan. "Did I hurt somebody?"

She involuntarily looked to where Michael was having his arm looked at by Mrs. Grant; he was pale, but he gave her a thumbs-up. "No," she lied. "No, everything's okay. You're okay."

"Did I turn into a hellhound again? Damn. That's embarrassing."

"Just rest." She kissed his forehead gently. "Rest." She was afraid to see his eyes close, but he was too high on muscle relaxers to stay awake. His temperature felt . . . normal. And his pulse strong.

"What the hell was in that shot?" He sounded blurred and sleepy now. "Wow. Party drugs. Got any more? Ow." He raised his arm and looked at it; the bite mark was almost gone, reduced to twisted scar tissue. "That still hurts. Feels like I burned it. You're pretty, did you know that?" He gave Claire a sweet, sloppy smile.

"What *was* in that shot?" Eve asked. "Because you are high as the space shuttle, dude." She crouched down next to Shane on the other side and helped Claire get him up to his feet. He felt . . . boneless. "Okay, he's going to be pretty much useless for a while."

"We've got a place you can all rest for the night," Mrs. Grant said.

"Any idea how long—this—will last?" Claire waved helplessly at Shane, who was staring at his fingers and wiggling them. He looked fascinated.

"A few hours, most likely. Let me get the keys to the guest-house," Mrs. Grant said, and disappeared into an office.

"I have to ask," Michael said. "Did my blood just . . . cure him?"

"Looks like it," Claire said. "Morley said he could smell the medicine in you. Maybe it counteracted whatever Shane's infection was."

"Let's be clear about this," Eve said. "My ex-vampire husband just cured your boyfriend of werewolfism with his blood."

"Seems about right," Claire said, and almost laughed. "Typical Morganville, right?"

Eve offered her an upraised fist. "Typical Morganville." They bumped.

Across the room, Oliver ignored them. He sank to one knee and bent his head to Amelie, the same way some ancient nobleman might have bowed to his queen. She silently offered her hand, and he pressed it to his forehead, then his lips. All weirdly formal.

"I've twice failed you," he said.

"You just stopped the boy."

"That's not what I meant."

"I know what you meant, Oliver. You count too many things as failures when they are merely setbacks." She beckoned him up, and he stood, still intimately close to her. She didn't seem bothered. "I feel safer with my old enemy beside me."

"Then you have a plan?"

"*We* have one," she said, and cut her gaze toward Morley, who gave a theatrical, fussy little bow that was somehow even more antique than the one Oliver had pulled out. "I trust you'll help."

"In any way you deem necessary."

She nodded, stepped even closer, and put her pale hand on his cheek. "Then eat, and rest until morning," she said. "In the morning, we are taking back our town."

TWELVE

Mrs. Grant opened up Blacke's little bed-and-breakfast for them. Basically, it was a four-bedroom house with doors that locked and a self-serve kitchen, located just about a block from the library. Claire's exhaustion was starting to make the world seem too bright, and when she found herself standing in the kitchen of a strange house, sipping spiced hot chocolate, it seemed a heavenly, strangely unreal experience. Which, she thought as she leaned against the counter, somehow seemed appropriate.

Eve raised her eyebrows as she drained the last of her cocoa. "What?"

"I'm just thinking," Claire said. "Thinking that maybe Shane—"

"Might relapse or something? Oh, honey, don't borrow trouble.

We've got enough here and the interest rates will kill you. Shane's tough. He'll be fine."

"Right," Claire said softly. "Eve, about what Morley said back there, about the cure . . ."

Eve turned away and rinsed her cup in the sink, but it was more about avoiding eye contact than anything else. "You think there could be side effects? I don't believe that. I can't. I got him back, and that's all I can think about right now, Claire. I've got Michael back, the real one, the one I crushed on from the time I was fourteen, the one I fell in love with so hard when I was eighteen. Anything else . . . anything else is something for tomorrow."

Claire nodded. She understood that, the need to just block everything out and be *still*. Feel as if there was still hope in the world, and love, and a future.

"Go on," she said, and finished her own drink. The cocoa was having its usual effect, and on top of the general exhaustion she felt almost as warm and fuzzy as if she'd had a shot of Shane's happy juice. "I know you're dying to tell him that."

Eve's smile lit up the room. The world. "Oh, he knows, if he's got a brain in his head," she said. "But I'm definitely looking forward to saying it, anyway." She grabbed Claire into a hard, firm hug. "Love you, Claire Bear. See you in a few hours."

"Love you, too," Claire said. It felt so good, being together again. "Go on. Michael's waiting."

Eve's smile was still warmer than the sun, and the warmth lingered even after she'd left the room.

Claire rinsed her own mug and put it in the dishwasher, then went to the small central bathroom. There were guest soaps and disposable toothbrushes, and she cleaned up as best she could, then took a deep breath and walked down the hall to the room where they'd put Shane.

She was afraid that he'd be worse somehow, but instead, he was lying curled on his side in the center of the king-sized bed, with blankets piled on top, and he was sound asleep. She pulled off her shoes, pants, and hoodie and climbed into bed next to him. He was warm, but not feverishly hot, and as she snuggled close to him he made a pleased noise in the back of his throat and put his arms around her. He didn't quite wake up, which was good; she was so tired that she wanted to weep, and the feeling of him, the dreamy gentle warmth—that meant more to her just now than anything else in the world.

She curled against him, pulled up the covers, and was asleep in under a minute.

Claire woke up slowly—not in a panic, for a change, not convinced that there were monsters lunging for her from the shadows. Shane had kept all that at bay. The light creeping through the lace curtains wasn't yet exactly announcing morning, but it was enough to start her lazy climb up toward it. She was still in the same position in which she'd fallen asleep, she realized, except that Shane's warmth wasn't next to her anymore.

She rolled over, and saw that the bed was empty.

That drove the lazy good morning feelings away. She sat up, fast. "Shane?"

The door to the room opened, and Shane came in carrying two coffee mugs. He looked pale and tired, but he definitely wasn't flying high anymore. He sat on the bed cross-legged next to her and passed her a cup—steady enough to not spill a drop of it.

He'd remembered how she liked it, too. "You're up early," she said. "How do you feel?"

"Hungover," he said, and took a deep swallow of his coffee. His eyes shut in pleasure. "Oh, thank God. I was about a million percent caffeine-deficient. Did I say anything embarrassing?"

"You went all hellhound and attacked Amelie in the library."

"No, really, did I say anything embarrassing?"

"You said I was pretty," she said, and smiled.

"Well, you are, even with your hair sticking up funny." He put his cup down and reached over to smooth it down. She looked at his forearm. The bite was now a faded scar, not red at all. "Yeah, I know what happened. I remember biting Mikey. He's okay, right?"

"He's okay."

"It felt—it felt like I was burning up inside. That was his blood, right?"

"The best I can tell, the cure was still in his bloodstream, and it attacked what Fallon had put into you to make you—change. So they kind of canceled each other out."

"For now," he said. He picked at a loose thread on the blanket.

"Shane, you're okay. Really."

"Sorry. You're right. Not enough coffee." He reached for his cup again and took a long gulp, then set it on the bedside table. "How's yours?"

"The coffee? It's great." She kissed him lightly. "Thank you for bringing it."

"You're welcome," he said, and kissed her back. Oh, that was nice. *Really* nice. Claire broke free long enough to put her cup down, before the coffee ended up all over her chest, and leaned into the kiss as if she'd never left it.

"Well," Shane murmured against her lips, and brushed hair

back from her face with warm, lingering touches, "this is nice. I could almost forget we're about to go to war. Again."

"Let's not think about it right now."

"Okay." He leaned forward, and she let herself fall back to the soft comfort of the pillows. "Let's think about something else, like . . . letting the coffee get cold."

"It's good coffee."

"I'll make more."

It was a lovely warm hour, sweet and slow and breathtaking, and Claire thought that maybe it was weird how they knew each other so well now, so that every touch was in the right place, the right pressure. It was exciting, but it was also comfortable in ways she could never have imagined, as comfortable as she could have ever been with anyone. No secrets. No shame. Nothing but complete, sweet trust.

Right up until the knock came at the bedroom door.

They were lying in each other's arms, pleasantly drowsy, but Claire's eyes flew open at the sound, and so did Shane's. They hesitated for only a second before they rolled in opposite directions to fish clothes off the floor and start dressing. "Just a sec!" Claire said, and yanked up her pants, then threw on the hoodie over her T-shirt. The TPU VIPERS logo on it seemed appropriate this morning. She jammed her feet into her shoes, but as fast as she was, Shane was even faster. He was sitting on the bed calmly sipping coffee when the door banged open.

"Good morning," he said to Morley, who looked full-on Vampire Western again in his duster, boots, scarf, and hat. "Kind of rude to come in when the lady asks you to wait, isn't it?"

"My sincere apology," Morley said, and did a straight-legged bow, whipping off his hat with a flourish. "But we're about to go retake the town of Morganville, and manners are not my greatest concern. Might you want to join us, or are you, ah, occupied?"

"Is that a choice? Because if so . . ."

"We're coming," Claire said. She downed the rest of her coffee—cold, now—and walked over to Morley. "Come on, Shane. Do you really intend to sit this one out?"

"You're right. There's a fight, and I'm not in it? That seems wrong." Shane made sure to finish his coffee. "Okay, let's do this thing. Wait, what exactly *are* we doing?"

"I have no idea what you're doing," Morley said, "but Mrs. Grant is killing Amelie."

Claire thought it was a flippant, weird thing to say until she saw Amelie lying on the table in the library, not moving, with a silver-coated stake in her heart.

"What are you *doing?*" she blurted, and pushed forward. Michael and Eve were already there, standing together. "What happened?"

"Don't touch her," Mrs. Grant warned. "Trust me, we've calculated this very carefully."

"Stabbing her? With *silver?*" Because even Amelie couldn't resist that poison for long, not in her heart. She had more of a resistance than most of the other vampires Claire had ever seen, but this . . . this was extreme. And extremely dangerous.

Then she saw the symbol on the side of the stake—an etched-in sunrise.

"You're a Daylighter," Claire said flatly, and looked around for a weapon. She didn't see one handy, so she grabbed a chair. It was heavy, but she raised it anyway. "Step away from her."

"Put that down," said Oliver, and took the chair from her with one hand. He placed it back at the table, handling it as easily as if it was made out of matchsticks. "It's an illusion. A carefully crafted one. The stake *is* silver, stolen from the Daylighters; their weapons come loaded with silver nitrate." She knew that, because she'd seen one buried in Michael's chest, back in Cambridge. They were designed to deliver a fatal dose of silver when anyone tried to remove them. "We've removed the nitrate from this one, and coated the stake with plastic. It's not toxic to her, but it's no doubt ridiculously painful. She's most convincing in her death."

Amelie opened her eyes. "I can hear you, you know."

"Yes, I'm well aware," he said, and however much he liked Amelie—which, Claire thought, was a lot—he also couldn't resist taking a little bit of pleasure in her discomfort. "Stay quiet. You're dead."

"We could always bury this stake in *your* chest, you wretch."

"I wouldn't look half so lovely wearing it."

Morley shook his head impatiently. "Can we please just get on with it? Mrs. Grant and our humans will take Amelie into town and convince Fallon that they will trade her for some righteous revenge upon the vampires he has penned up in that mall. He'll believe it; the story is more than convincing, considering the havoc Amelie's blood-father wreaked upon this town. In the wake of last night's vampire attacks, who better to swell the ranks of the true believers than the residents of a town already savaged by the monsters?" He looked *very* pleased with himself. Disgustingly so.

"I'm so glad you think so, Morley," Mrs. Grant said. "Because we had a discussion, and we decided to alter the plan a little bit. As an actor, you understand that we need to really sell the concept." She nodded, and from the shadows behind the bookcases, two men stepped out, both armed with crossbows.

Morley snarled and snapped to the side, and the bolt meant for his heart missed him. Oliver was slower—probably the result of all the terrible things heaped on him for the past few months—and the silver-tipped arrow sliced right into his chest and dropped him where he stood.

But Morley wasn't going down without a fight. He rounded on Mrs. Grant, roaring in fury, and she calmly brought up the small crossbow she'd held under the table. As he raced toward her, she sighted and fired.

Morley slumped against the table, eyes and mouth wide, and finally collapsed.

I was right, Claire thought with a jolt of real fear. *They are Daylighters.* But Amelie wasn't reacting, even though she could have; the fact that she'd been able to talk proved that well enough.

Which meant that it was Amelie's plan, and had been from the beginning. She just hadn't told Oliver and Morley how far it would go.

Shane, Eve, and Michael hadn't moved to protest, probably all for different reasons: Shane because he wasn't inclined to protest vampires getting shot *ever*, Eve because she was conflicted about Oliver and had never liked Morley, and Michael because . . . well, probably because he'd figured it out the way Claire had.

Mrs. Grant looked at the four of them. "Don't just stand there, get them on the tables," she said. She hadn't *liked* shooting Morley, Claire could see that. "They're old, but that wasn't a bug bite. We need to get the coated stakes into them quickly."

That was a more clinical process than Claire was strictly comfortable with; she helped pull the arrows out, but pushing the stakes in was a lot more quease-inducing, and she let Michael and

Shane handle that part. Not that they seemed to take much pleasure in it, either.

Eve just turned her back entirely. "Are we sure this is a good
plan?" she asked anxiously. "Because I'm starting to worry. It seems
scary."

"That's because it is," Mrs. Grant said. She walked over to the
four of them as Michael and Shane rejoined them. "I'll have to
keep an eye on my two gentlemen here to be sure they don't do
something silly like remove the stakes, but I expect this will appeal
to Morley's acting instincts, and Oliver can surely see the advantages. Now, as to the four of you: I'll need you to put on a show as
well."

"Wh-what kind of show?" Eve asked. She sounded even more
doubtful.

"Nothing too difficult, I promise," Mrs. Grant said. "You simply have to be our prisoners." She nodded, and more of her Blacke
townsfolk moved up, armed not with crossbows this time but with
zip ties. "Sorry about this, but we'll cut you loose when the time
comes. Fallon seems to want you all back—especially you, Michael.
He seems to think you're his new poster child for conversion."

"He's not wrong," Michael said. "Feels pretty good, having a
heartbeat again. I was resigned to being a vampire, but I'm not going to lie . . . it was a gift I'm not turning down."

"Me neither," Eve said. "You don't have to put us in cuffs. Really. We'll go along."

"Okay," Mrs. Grant said. "I'm going to trust the two of you.
Don't let me down."

But, Claire noticed, that didn't seem to include *her*, or Shane,
because the next thing she knew, her wrists were being pulled together and zip ties efficiently applied. She exchanged a glance with

Shane, but he shrugged. "Got to admit, Fallon wouldn't buy either one of us as having a change of heart, especially when he realizes I'm not on Team Hellhound anymore. Makes sense. We haven't exactly made ourselves potential allies of his, have we?"

"No," she admitted. "Not really. But—you're going to cut us loose?"

Mrs. Grant didn't waste words. She just passed a small set of nail clippers to Eve, who winked and stuck them in the pocket of her hoodie.

"Got you covered, girlfriend," said Eve. "And if I lose these and have to gnaw through the plastic to get you loose, I will. Virtual high five!" She raised her right shoulder. Claire raised hers. They bumped.

"That," Shane said, "is the nerdiest thing I've ever seen the two of you do, and that's saying something."

"This from a man who has *Blade* action figures."

"Hey, those are classic! And collectible."

Mrs. Grant sighed. "Let's get everyone loaded. Remember: Fallon may be in Morganville, but the Daylight Foundation has branches all over the world. They *will* come for us if we don't come for them first. We might not be able to take them out, but we can at least remove the man who turned a search for a cure into a crusade. Let's ensure he doesn't do any more damage."

As battle speeches went, it wasn't great, but obviously the folks from Blacke—mostly everyday folks, the kind of people you'd see in a bigger town at a Walmart or eating at the Dairy Queen—were already on board. Blacke wasn't Morganville; by the time Morley and the rest of his vampire refugees from Amelie's rule had arrived here, the town had already been ripped in half by an uncontrollable infection that had taken half the residents and reduced them to mindless, blood-craving monsters. Amelie's father, Bishop, had done that, and then moved on, probably amused by all the mayhem he'd left behind him. That was why Blacke wouldn't go with the Daylighters' agenda; it meant subjecting their own families to a cure that was bound to kill most of them. In Morganville, the lines between humans and vampires were generally pretty well drawn.

In Blacke, there were no lines. Only heartaches.

In a fine display of symmetry, the townspeople piled into the same battered bus that Morley had commandeered from Morganville; it still had most of the body damage, but it was at least running, and it was relatively light-proofed. Amelie, Oliver, and Morley were loaded in last, lying stretched across seats. Amelie maintained her calm illusion of death—maybe it was easier for her that way. But Morley complained bitterly, and Oliver seemed uncomfortable even though he didn't do more than glare at those around him.

"Hey, man, don't look at me," Shane told him. "I'm back in handcuffs. Do you have any idea how many times this makes?"

"Do you have a stake in your heart?" Oliver said. His voice sounded strained and faint, as if he was using all his willpower to suppress a scream. "At least if it was wooden, I'd be unconscious. This is hideous."

"I'm sure you can cope just fine," Mrs. Grant said. She didn't seem sympathetic. "Is everyone in?" She looked around at the rows of people—men and women, a few teens, even some elderly citizens. They all looked hard, tough, and ready for action. "Let's go, then."

The driver looked as if he might have actually once driven a school bus, back in the dark ages; he was ancient, and Claire was a little afraid that he was so old he might nod off at the wheel. But his arthritic old hands seemed competent enough as he steered them away from the curb and picked up speed. They made the turn and went past the shuttered courthouse. The smug statue of Hiram Blacke stared after them.

There were vampires in Blacke standing in the shadows, or in the windows, watching them go. This time Claire didn't feel so creeped out by that. It was more as if they were wishing them luck.

She really hoped it worked.

It was a long, bumpy ride, worse by far for the three staked vampires, but they bore it in relative silence—even Morley, after a while, when he realized nobody was going to respond to his outbursts. Claire decided not to complain about the chafing of the bands around her wrists. Seemed like the least she could do was bear it with the same stoic silence as the others.

When the bus finally started to slow down and the brakes engaged, Claire looked up through the front window to see that they were approaching the Morganville billboard. It brought a flood of emotions—relief that the ride was nearly over, and the very real fear that what they were doing would go wrong. Badly. But she didn't know what else they could do, except walk away . . . turn their backs on Morganville and just let it all happen without them. But how would that make them any different from the other Morganville residents who were willing to let horrible things happen to the vampires so long as it happened out of their particular view?

The feeling came back again, sick and dark. *I'm bringing trouble to Morganville. They've finally got their peace, what they always wanted, and I'm coming back to rip it apart.*

I'm the villain.

All she knew was that she couldn't run, not from this. She knew Shane wouldn't do that, or Michael, or Eve. They'd grown up here. They had roots. And she had to confess it: she did, too. Her parents might live somewhere else, might not remember anything about Morganville except a vague sense of unease, but if her family history came from here, she didn't think she could have run, either.

Face it, the sensible part of her said. *You can't run because you don't run. You're stubborn. That's always been your biggest problem. If you weren't so stubborn, you'd have run away from this town the day Monica Morrell and her Monickettes pushed you down the stairs at the dorm.*

And if she'd done the reasonable thing and run home to Mommy and Daddy, what would she have missed?

Everything. Including Shane.

Mrs. Grant stood up and stepped into the aisle, facing back toward the rest of the people in the bus. "All right," she said. "Remember: we're not fighting for Morganville, we're fighting for our own families. No matter what happens, you keep them in mind. Things are going to get ugly."

There were solemn nods from everyone from Blacke. From where he lay on the front seat, Morley said, "And if you lack for motivation, remember that you hate vampires for what they've done to you."

"Well," Mrs. Grant said, very reasonably, "we do, so that isn't much of a stretch, Morley."

"You wound me, sweet lady."

"You annoy me, troublemaker."

It had the well-worn feel of familiarity, and Claire wondered just how close Mrs. Grant (a widow, she remembered) and Morley had actually gotten. Not that it was any of her business, but it was more fun to speculate on that than on what Fallon was going to do next.

"Speak of the devil," Mrs. Grant said, turning to look out the windshield. The billboard of Morganville was looming, but so were the flashing lights of two police cars. There were also three solid black SUVs—new-looking SUVs (unusual for Morganville)—with the rising sun logo on the doors. At least ten armed men and women were braced for a fight out there.

"Showtime," Morley said.

"Shut up," she told him. "You're dead, remember?"

"Will you miss me when I'm gone?"

"No."

"Liar." Morley's dry chuckle faded into silence, and the driver of the bus brought them to a rolling stop several feet from the roadblock.

Claire heard an amplified voice—Hannah Moses's voice, she was sure—ring even through the closed windows of the bus. "Out of the bus," she said. "Do it slowly, hands raised, one at a time. When you come out, form a line and get down on your knees, hands on top of your head. You have ten seconds to comply."

Mrs. Grant nodded to the driver, who turned off the engine and opened the bus's doors. "One at a time," she told the rest of them. "The vampires and the prisoners stay in here. Michael, Eve, you're getting off with me." She was the first off the bus, and demonstrated the perfect technique of moving away, kneeling down, and putting her hands on top of her head.

Michael and Eve got up from the seat in front of Claire and Shane. Eve looked anguished. Michael was hiding it, but he was feeling terrible about it, too.

"Go." Shane nodded to them. "You're our aces in the hole. Don't let us down."

"Never," Eve said, and leaned over to give him a quick kiss on the cheek. Then she gave Claire one, too. "Love you guys."

"Love you, too," Claire said, and managed a smile. "Both of you. Be careful."

Michael nodded and ruffled Claire's hair, like a big brother, then led his wife off the bus.

The rest followed in a slow, methodical procession, disembarking and kneeling. Claire heard Mrs. Grant explaining things to Hannah. Hannah was no fool; she would probably get the subtexts. She knew the history of Blacke well, and she wasn't going to believe the story as much as newcomers to town like the Daylighters would.

Claire's instincts were that Hannah didn't *want* to help Fallon, but she was forced to, and they were proven right as Hannah heard Mrs. Grant out, and said, "You've done the right thing turning them over, and Mr. Fallon will thank you for that. But I have to ask, why did you bring so many with you?"

"These are the humans from Blacke," Mrs. Grant said. "I figure when you're done ridding Morganville of the vampires, you can take care of the nest in our town, too. Until then, it's safer for them here, with you. They're eager to learn about the Daylight Foundation. Bring a little light into our lives, too." Her tone turned dark. "And we deserve a chance to kick some vampire ass for a change. They destroyed us. Tore our town apart."

It sounded good, especially the angry way Mrs. Grant referred to the vampires. Claire had no doubt that she was being honest about that. Bishop's nasty, gratuitous feeding in that town had brought disaster down on it, divided families and killed friends.

Of course she hated the vampires, on some level, even if none of that was their own fault. Who wouldn't?

What if this is all just a scam to get us to go along with it? What if those Daylighter silver stakes are loaded with liquid silver? She got them to agree *to be staked. How* genius *would that be?* It was just plausible enough that Claire caught her breath in real alarm, but it was too late, way too late, and Hannah Moses was now mounting the steps into the bus and surveying the situation. It wasn't much of one, by this point. Just her and Shane, zip-tied, and the three staked vampires.

Hannah knew that it was some kind of trick; Claire read that in the way she looked over the bodies. But instead of raising the alarm, she nodded slightly and stepped aside as Fallon's Daylighters moved in behind her. "Take them all to Fallon," she said. "He'll want to see this."

She meant Fallon would want to enjoy it . . . enjoy the sight of Amelie dead at his feet.

Claire sincerely hoped that Mrs. Grant hadn't brilliantly played them all.

Morganville was having some kind of celebration today; there were new, bright red-white-and-blue banners hung across the streets that flapped in the wind, and Daylight Foundation flags on the lawns of most of the houses, and in the windows of the shops and businesses.

The banners read, WELCOME TO THE *NEW* MORGANVILLE! YOU'LL NEVER *NEED* TO LEAVE!

Right sentiment, wrong reasons. Claire shuddered, because it was a play on the town's original motto: *You'll never want to leave.*

And it was a lie. She knew Fallon now. He might have started out with good intentions a long time ago; he might have sincerely wanted to protect humans from vampires and save the vampires from themselves. But he'd gone wrong somewhere, probably when he'd decided it was okay to kill a lot to save a few. What was the old saying her mom used to love? *The road to hell is paved with good intentions.*

Now, all these years later, Fallon saw anybody who didn't agree with him as a traitor to humanity, worthy of punishment and death. And she knew that she and Shane, by their actions, had definitely earned that label. They'd helped vampires over humans. He wouldn't forget, or forgive.

"What do we do with them?" one of the men asked Hannah, and nodded toward Claire and Shane as the three silent, limp vampires were carried out. The self-control required for them to look that dead was beyond Claire's comprehension, but none of them— not even Morley—so much as flickered an eyelid at the jostling, even when they were carelessly knocked against metal rails or bounced off of steps.

Hannah raised her eyebrows for a second, considering, and then said, "I think they go with the vampires. They've obviously thrown in their lot with Amelie. They should stay with her. Fallon will want to show everyone they've been caught and the situation is under control."

"How many people died last night when he let the vampires out, Hannah?" Claire asked. She kept her voice quiet, but she knew the question would cut. "How many?"

"Two," Hannah replied. "And six vampires. The rest were recaptured and confined. They're awaiting trial."

"You know he engineered that attack. He *wanted* it to happen. He's probably disappointed that his body count was so low."

"Shut up," the Daylighter next to her said, and he sounded angry. "You don't know anything about Mr. Fallon. He *saved* this town, and everybody in it. We don't have to live in fear anymore. Not now that we're getting rid of the vampires."

Shane raised his head for the first time. "Getting rid of, how?"

"The only way to be sure. We've tried to be kind and give them a place to live in peace. They couldn't follow the rules. They never could. You should know that, Collins. The rules of Morganville, the rules they made up to control us . . . they never applied to *them*." The man wasn't actually all that old, Claire realized; maybe the age of Monica's deceased brother, Richard Morrell, mid- to late twenties. He knew Shane, clearly.

Just as clearly, Shane knew him. "You've always been a cowardly little whiner, Sully. I didn't see you or your family stepping up to defend people. You just kept your heads down like good little citizens. Hell, you didn't even have the guts to stand up with Captain Obvious when you had the chance."

He'd struck gold with that one, Claire saw from the red flush that spread across Sully's broad face. "Collaborator," Sully spat back. "Traitor. You'll get what's coming to you, and I'm going to enjoy seeing it." He literally spat the words out; Claire got flecks of saliva on her face. Ugh. She felt filthier than ever, which was saying something, considering she was wearing someone else's underwear.

"Sully," Hannah said, with the snap of command in her voice. "As long as you're working with me, you'll treat my prisoners with respect and keep quiet. Shane's no danger to you, and all he can do is needle you. Don't let him score points."

"Did I?" Shane asked, and smiled the most casually bitter smile Claire had ever seen on his face. "Score points?"

"Quiet," Hannah said, but Claire caught a quick gleam of humor in her expression before she locked it down to her professional mask again. "Time's wasting. Get them out of here."

Sully took personal charge of Shane, which was weirdly comforting; Claire knew Shane could get to him, and that was a kind of control that they both needed just now. Her own guard was one of Hannah's cops—a familiar one. "Officer Kentworth," she said. He was one of the two who'd searched their house with Halling: the polite one. He touched his fingers to his cap.

"Miss," he said. "Let's be businesslike about this, okay? No funny business."

"You know you're taking us to be killed, right?"

He flinched, but controlled that quickly, and gave her a flinty stare. "You're just being transported, miss. Let's not make this any more complicated," he said.

Shane was led to yet another car by Sully, and Claire could almost imagine how much fun *that* ride was going to be. She hoped Shane didn't push him so far that Sully really snapped. With his hands pinned, Shane couldn't fight back very well . . . and Eve was the one who still had the nail clippers to snip their zip-tied bonds. Eve and Michael, she noticed, were also being separated out from the folks from Blacke and loaded into a car.

Claire hoped they would all end up in the same place, because she had the feeling they'd really need those nail clippers before too long, regardless of what kind of positive spin Officer Kentworth tried to put on things.

Claire expected to be driven to the Daylight Foundation's building, but instead, the little parade—complete with flashing lights, though no sirens—wound its way through Morganville's main streets toward Founder's Square. That seemed odd. Founder's Square was vampire territory; it was where they'd lived and worked and had their own late-night businesses. It was where Amelie had her offices, and where they kept the records of their long, long lives.

It was also where they'd executed people, from time to time, for infractions of the Morganville rules. Where they'd threatened to execute Shane, when Amelie had thought him guilty of a vampire's murder.

It was, Claire thought with a sinking feeling, exactly where Fallon would choose to make his new headquarters.

The parade turned and took the ramp underground, into the parking garage Claire remembered so well. It was full of cars, mostly black-tinted vampmobiles that had probably been confiscated when their owners had gone into "protective custody" at the mall. What had Fallon called it? *The enclave*, like it was some fancy, exclusive members-only apartment complex instead of an eighties nightmare of a building stripped down to dust and concrete.

And now Fallon lived in Amelie's palace.

The other cars parked in the lot alongside her own transportation, and one by one, they were brought out—Shane, still sniping at red-faced Officer Sully, and then Michael and Eve, not in handcuffs but obviously being escorted along by their own guards.

She, Shane, Eve, and Michael, plus their minders, all crowded into one elevator for the trip upstairs. They were taken to the first floor, the entry level. It looked just like Claire remembered it— lush carpets, expensive chandeliers, the faint, oppressive smell of roses, and gloomy, brooding paintings hanging on the walls. Anything that displayed someone who was recognizably a vampire had been taken down, and there was a stack of canvases in the corner of the central atrium.

"This way," said Hannah, meeting them in that space. Claire

didn't know how she'd arrived before they did, but somehow, she had. Maybe she'd been at the front of the parade. She led them down the hall and out to the big fancy entryway, with its vast, vaulted ceiling . . . and then out onto the porch, where the morning sun was dazzling the marble.

Once her eyes adjusted to the glare, Claire saw that Founder's Square had been kept looking perfect—the hedges and lawns were neatly trimmed, the flower beds exploded with fresh, live color. It all looked as clean and graceful as anything you could find in a picture of Paris, complete with the marble-columned buildings ringing the park.

Except for the banners, which were red, white, and blue, snapping and lifting in the breeze that swirled through the courtyard.

A Morganville-sized crowd, maybe three hundred people strong, had gathered on the lawn. They were conducting some kind of ceremony in connection with the sunrise. Claire spotted a raised stage at the other end, where the vampires had once kept a cage where those who broke their laws were displayed . . . and sometimes held executions, too. The cage was gone, and that was a good thing, but she had a sudden nasty flashback to a photograph she'd seen in history class—a fancy square with dignified grand buildings, long red banners, a stage. A passionate, fiery speaker delivering his speech to a sea of rapt people.

History, repeating.

Fallon must have been delighted, thinking his timing couldn't have been better. The bodies of Morley, Oliver, and Amelie were being carried through the aisle in the center of the crowd, and there was total silence until the procession was halfway to the stage . . . and then someone started to clap.

Then it was an avalanche of applause, and cheering.

They were cheering *dead bodies.*

Claire looked over at Shane, and saw that he was watching with a stony expression on his face. He was probably thinking how he might have been in that crowd, cheering, at some point in his life. Maybe he'd have even been the first to clap.

"Makes you proud to be human, doesn't it?" he said to no one in particular.

Eve moved up beside them. "So proud," she said. "They'll probably open a souvenir shop later. Vampire-bones keychains and stake earrings. Maybe they'll even put the town name on them."

Claire felt something cool and metallic brush her fingers, and flinched, but then she realized that it was the nail clippers, and it was Eve's hand pressing them into her palm. She clenched her fist around them.

"Time to go," Hannah said, and walked their group down the steps toward the ceremony. The cheering had mostly died down by the time they got there, and the three vampires were being laid on the stage, in the sun. They'd be burning—slowly, because they were so old, but still. Definitely painful.

Michael paused on the steps, and Eve stopped with him and anxiously asked, "Honey? What's wrong?" His eyes were shut, and he looked very strange. "Are you feeling okay?"

When he opened his eyes, Claire saw tears break free and run down his cheeks. "It's the sun," he said. "Eve, I'm standing in the sun. It's so *warm.*"

She understood, and she hugged him. Claire didn't get it for a second, until she realized how long it would have been since Michael had felt the touch of sunshine without the horrible scorching and scarring that came with it as a new vampire. It must have really hit him in that moment that he was genuinely human again.

Genuinely cured.

He hugged Eve close and said, "I hate that he's the one who gave me back my life. You know that, right?"

"I know," she said, and rubbed his back. "Doesn't matter. You're here, and that's what counts."

They held hands on the way down the steps, the sun gilding Michael's golden hair into blazing glory. He looked even more like his grandfather Sam now, Claire thought; Sam had been frozen at an age not too much older than Michael when he'd been made a vampire. Apart from the fact that Sam's hair had been more red than blond, they'd been very similar.

That thought made Claire wonder how Amelie really felt about Michael's conversion back to human. Glad, or sad? She'd loved Sam so intensely that she'd shown public grief for him when he died; maybe she'd want to keep Michael preserved forever at the age where he resembled his grandfather.

Or maybe she'd be happy to let him go and live his life. It was never easy to tell with Amelie.

It made it all the more difficult, though, because Michael was now Fallon's symbolic victory.

Hannah led them through the crowd to the stage, then went up the steps to whisper to Fallon. He nodded, and beckoned; Eve and Michael were brought onstage.

Shane and Claire were kept where they were, at the edge of the steps.

Everybody's attention was on Fallon, and Eve, and Michael, so Claire risked flipping the blade on the nail clippers and working the tiny jaws up until they were gripping the plastic of the zip tie around her wrists. She'd have to cut it in stages; the ties were broad and thick, but when she squeezed the clippers, she felt them slice cleanly through the restraints. She adjusted it another quarter of an inch and pressed again. It was harder this time; the angle was more acute, and she couldn't get leverage as easily. But it yielded.

The third and last time, though, as she tried to slide the clippers into position, her sweaty fingers slipped, and she dropped them.

Claire shifted position backward gradually until she could see the metallic shine of them on the grass. She tested the restraints. She'd cut through two-thirds of the band, but what was left was still pretty thick, and she didn't have the strength necessary to rip the cuffs apart. *I need to work out more,* she thought, but that wasn't going to help her much right now.

She needed to get the clippers.

She took a step, and faked stumbling and falling to one knee, then toppling over in a graceless loss of balance. That put her hands within grasping distance of the clippers, and she raked frantically at the grass until she touched them and pulled them into her fist.

Officer Sully grabbed her elbow and yanked her to her feet. "What the hell's wrong with you?" he asked, frowning.

"*You* try keeping these things on for hours," she said. "It throws off your balance, okay?"

"Don't try anything."

"I won't," she said, and it was the truth. She wasn't going to *try.*

Up on the stage, Fallon stepped to the microphone, and the whole crowd quieted. "Friends," he said, "fellow residents, thank you for coming here to celebrate the dawn of a new day in Morganville, a day without fear of violence or suppression. As of today, you're no longer slaves to monsters who murder to stay alive, who take your blood and your money and use it to fund their own endless, selfish existence. As of today, you don't have to fear the dark. Your children can grow up knowing that they're safe from harm. That's the new Morganville. That's Morganville in the *daylight*."

He paused, and applause erupted. He held up his hands to quiet it. "As proof of this new day, I'm delighted to introduce to you one of our greatest successes . . . someone you all know and recognize, someone from one of the thirteen founding families of Morganville. He was the victim of the vampires twice over—once by Oliver, and then by Amelie, who made him one of her own. But now he stands with me in the light, alive and free of his curse. Michael Glass!"

Michael didn't like it; Claire could see that. He didn't want to step forward, but Fallon whispered something to him, and he complied, standing rigid and expressionless as the crowd erupted into cheers. They were cheering for him becoming human, but it still had a raw edge of bigotry to it. Some of those cheering right now would have been happy to stake him through the heart a day before, and he knew it. Of all of them, he knew what it meant to be labeled as less than human.

"Wow, this is a boring, bullshit propaganda show," Shane said as Claire maneuvered the clippers into position and pressed hard, gritting her teeth as pain streaked up her arms from the stress and angle. "Hey, Sully, are you serving doughnuts and coffee, at least? Because I hear the KKK runs a great craft table."

Claire's bonds snapped, and the pressure on her shoulders eased from a red-hot burn to just a tingle. She caught Shane's eye as Sully moved toward them, and gave him a sharp upward jerk of her head.

"You," Sully said between gritted teeth. "Come here, you little asshole."

"Hey, I'm not little," Shane said. "So tell me, is your white sheet in the laundry, or did you just forget to pack it?"

Sully grabbed Shane's arm and dragged him off balance and away from the stage. There was a backdrop set up, and he yanked Shane behind it.

Hannah sighed, shook her head, and pointed at Kentworth to go see what was happening. That left just her and Claire standing together.

Claire took a long step back toward where Shane had disappeared, careful to make her wrists seem like they were still pinned behind her.

Hannah was watching her.

Claire kept moving until she could put the barrier between her and anyone in the crowd who might be watching. Hannah followed.

As Hannah stepped into the shadow, Claire pulled her freed hands out from behind her back and grabbed for Hannah's gun.

She wasn't fast enough.

Hannah's hand clamped down hard on the butt of the automatic pistol, holding it in the holster, and Claire realized with a sinking sense of bitter disappointment that she should have known a former Marine wouldn't be taken that easily. Not by some inexperienced, untrained girl half her size.

"Nice work on the cuffs," Hannah said. "Now take your hand off my gun, Claire."

She did so, slowly, and stepped back. Shane was having a full-on bar brawl, still cuffed, with Sully. Kentworth was standing back, Taser in his hand, looking for an opening. He didn't look especially happy about the whole thing.

Shane slammed his forehead into Sully's face and grinned with bloodied teeth. "Amateur," Shane said, as Sully cried out and went down hard, holding his gushing nose and whimpering. "That's called an Irish handshake. Somebody named Sullivan ought to know that."

Kentworth moved in with the Taser, and Shane arched his back and sidestepped the lunge, like a matador with a bull. But he wasn't going to be able to get away, not with his hands still pinned behind him.

Claire looked wide-eyed at Hannah. *Now or never,* she silently thought. She couldn't take the gun, not against Hannah's well-trained reflexes.

But Hannah could give it up voluntarily.

Chief Moses nodded slightly and moved her hand away from the holster.

Claire lunged forward and grabbed the weapon; she checked the safety, which had been ingrained in her by weapons training with Shane, and clicked it off. "Call him off," she said. She didn't aim the gun at Hannah. She didn't think she had to.

Hannah said, "Kentworth. Back off. Now."

He stepped away, leaving Shane wobbling a little, bloodied but still standing. He had a red bruise forming on his forehead, and he spat blood from a cut lip, but she'd seen him worse. A lot worse.

Sullivan was still on the ground, cradling his nose. He yelled something, but it was incomprehensible.

"Knife," she said to Hannah. Hannah unsnapped a holster on her other side and pulled out a military-style blade with a black grip, which she handed over. Claire took it and backed toward Shane. She kept the weapon raised this time, and focused on Kentworth, who was casting doubtful looks at Hannah, clearly not sure what he was supposed to do about this.

She sawed carefully through one side of Shane's flex cuffs, and as his hand came loose, she pressed the handle into his palm.

"You give me the best presents," he said, then freed his other wrist with a practiced slice. The flex cuffs dropped to the grass. "We're going now. Keys."

"What?" Kentworth asked.

"Car keys. Toss 'em."

Kentworth was clearly considering going for his weapon, not his keys; whatever doubts he had about the Daylight Foundation— if he had any at all—were back-burnered by the fact that two of his prisoners had somehow managed to escape their restraints and gain weapons. When he twitched slightly, though, Hannah said flatly, "Give them the keys. That's an order."

"I can take her, ma'am."

"And you'll have to wake up tomorrow knowing you shot a teenage girl dead when you didn't need to," Hannah said. "Toss the keys, Charlie. They're not going anywhere."

Kentworth looked doubtful, but Hannah's firm, calm tone made the difference. He unclipped the keys from his belt loop and tossed them at Shane's feet. "It's a long way to the car, son," he said. "You might want to think about the danger you're putting your girlfriend in out there."

Shane twirled the keys around his finger for a second, then tossed them. Claire thought for a second that his aim was off, but it wasn't, because he wasn't throwing them toward her at all.

He was throwing them toward Hannah, who effortlessly fielded them. "Sorry about this," she told Kentworth, and before Claire could really understand what exactly had just happened, Hannah walked past Kentworth to Sullivan. She rolled the protesting man over and used her handcuffs to pin his hands behind his back. When Sully gave a gargling yell of protest, she leaned an elbow into his back. "Sully, I could do a hell of a lot worse to you than just handcuff you. If I have to gag you, you'll choke on your blood from that broken nose. So stay quiet, or I'll make you quiet."

Sully shut up. He took Hannah seriously, no question about that. She stood up and looked at Kentworth, who slowly raised both hands in the air. He reached up, took the Daylighter pin from his collar, and dropped it on the ground.

"Happy to help, ma'am," he said. "Never really liked any of this from the beginning. I only joined them because you did."

"That was my mistake," Hannah said. She looked at Claire and Shane. "Amelie's not really dead, is she?"

"Nope," Shane said, and held out his hand to her. She shook it and nodded gravely. "Nice to have you back, Hannah."

"Nice to stop pretending that I'm a true believer," she said. "Fair warning—I'm not sure I can stay on your side for long, if Fallon sets me to hunting vampires. Can't control that much at all."

"The good news is that Fallon's vampire cure seems to work for whatever we are, too. But word of advice—try biting somebody who survived it. Not Michael, though. He's been through enough."

For the first time in a long time, Hannah actually smiled. "I'll keep that in mind. Tactical question—what's Amelie waiting for? Why isn't she taking Fallon down right now?"

"Well, I'm pretty sure she'd love to, but she wants to be sure that her people are free before she does it. No more hostages. That's how he got her in the first place—hostages and threats, right?"

"No," Hannah said. "Not threats. His task force took ten vampires hostage, all right, but his first act when he got Amelie to show up to rescue them was to stake half of them with those booby-trapped stakes. They died when she tried to help them. She gave herself up to stop him from killing the rest the same way." She hesitated, then continued, "They were all her bloodline. Siblings, and vampires she created. Family, as vampires count these things."

Amelie had never seemed all that easy to manipulate, but Claire knew how she felt about her people—she'd created Morganville specifically to protect them against all the threats that surrounded them. She would fight and die for them. And when it came to *actual* family . . . "That's horrible."

"Yes," Hannah said. "But I don't think Fallon recognizes it anymore."

Shane exchanged a look with Claire and said, "We need to get Michael and Eve out of the middle of this. Michael isn't used to being human. He's going to make a mistake, get himself killed trying to react like a vampire."

"We can't," Claire said. "They're on the stage. We have to leave them there for now." She saw the expression that crossed his face, and she sympathized; she didn't like it, either. But he knew she was right.

"Then we have to hurry," Hannah said. "Kentworth, you're in charge of Sully. Keep him quiet."

"Yes, ma'am," he said. "Be careful."

"Always."

Turned out there was no easier way to leave Founder's Square than in the custody of the Morganville chief of police.

THIRTEEN

Mrs. Grant hadn't backstabbed them after all. By the time they arrived at the Bitter Creek Mall, the bus from Blacke was idling on the north side of the parking lot, out of sight of the front doors, where the guards were stationed. Claire spotted it from the road, and pointed it out to Hannah, who nodded and turned into the street that looped around the mall. The asphalt was cracked and split, so she took it slow, avoiding the occasional bush that had pushed its way up from the darkness.

Mrs. Grant stepped off the bus as the police car pulled to a halt. She was holding a shotgun, which she pointed at the driver's-side window.

"No!" Claire yelled, and fumbled at the passenger-side door.

She exited fast and waved her arms frantically. "No! She's on our side!"

The older woman hesitated for only a moment, then nodded and returned the shotgun to a resting position on her shoulder. "Just rock salt, anyway," she said. "Don't want to be killing any innocent people, even the ones the Daylighters have got their hooks into. We're visitors here. Wouldn't be polite, would it?"

Hannah got out of the cruiser and gave Mrs. Grant a professional threat assessment, then stepped forward to offer her hand. "Chief Hannah Moses," she said. "You must be Mrs. Grant."

"Heard of me?"

"You left an impression. You may be the first combat librarian I've ever met."

That earned an almost-full smile from the other woman. "I think most librarians are combat qualified," she said. "It's not as peaceful a job as it looks. We were about to go in without you. What about the others?" She meant Amelie, Oliver, and Morley.

"Fallon's making them a spectacle," Hannah said. "Good for us, because that means the attention won't be here. If you want to save these vampires, you'd better do it now. He plans to start his conversion therapy on all of them today. Odds are, three-quarters of them won't survive."

"They won't just let him do it to them. I know vampires. They're not very biddable."

"If they resist, he'll kill them," Hannah said flatly, "and call it a riot and a necessary defensive measure. He'll firebomb the place. If there are any survivors, he'll give them his cure. One thing about Fallon, he's not squeamish. He's already got most of his Daylighter guards and my own people in there, armed with things lethal to vampires and ready to use them."

"And he's got the vampires wearing shock collars," Claire added. "So he can stun them first. No matter what, they can't win without our help."

"Is there any other way in except the front?" Mrs. Grant asked.

Claire shuddered, thinking of the horrible garbage chute. "None that humans could do on their own, or would want to."

"Frontal assault it is, then."

"Maybe not," Hannah said. "I can even the odds a little." She went back to the cruiser and picked up the radio mike, adjusted the frequency, and squeezed the button on the side. "Bitter Creek team, come in. Moses here."

The response came within seconds. "Salazar here, boss."

"Situation?"

"Same as ever. Bunch of freaking statues staring at us. Nobody's doing nothing. They're hungry, though. When is the next blood shipment coming?"

"A few hours," Hannah responded. "Listen, I'm going to need you to send four more men out to Founder's Square for crowd control."

"Boss? That just leaves me here."

"You've got Fallon's Daylighters, right?"

"Yeah, but—"

"That's an order, Salazar."

He hesitated just a few seconds before his voice came back over the radio. "Yes, ma'am. Sending the rest to Founder's Square. ETA about ten minutes."

"Ten-four." Hannah hung up the mike and nodded to Mrs. Grant. "That takes most of my guys out of harm's way for now. Salazar's a good man. I'll go in first and have him turn over the collar control box to me. Look, you're not going to like it, but we have to wait for the others to leave, and I need Shane and Claire to run a little errand for me."

"What?" Claire asked.

"Blood," Hannah said. "If you don't want those vampires in there snacking on us as soon as I release their collars, we're going to need a lot of blood. Blood bank's still got a stockpile. Go get it."

"Are they just going to give it to us?"

"I've got a contact inside," she said. "I'll call ahead. You pull around to the back vampire entrance, and they'll bring it out to you. Hurry."

She stepped out of the way, and Claire got in on the driver's side, racked the seat forward, and started the car.

It was only then, when she looked in the rearview mirror, that she saw Shane still sitting in the backseat, looking annoyed. "Oh," she said, and covered her mouth with her hand, mostly to hide a smile. "Sorry. We should have let you out."

"You think?"

"Sorry. We're going—"

"—to the blood bank. I heard. Awesome. Always wanted to be the plasma delivery service for a bunch of cranky vamps with a grudge. Wait, that pretty much describes daily life around here, doesn't it?"

She let him have the last word as she pulled the car out to the uneven street, heading for the blood bank.

It was actually a smooth exchange, though Claire had expected something to go really wrong. As she pulled the police car to a stop, the alley door opened, and a man in a white lab coat wheeled out a large cart, like something hotels would fill with laundry.

Only this was filled with blood bags.

"Trunk," he told her through the rolled-down window, and she searched for a bit to find the release for it. Then she got out, remembering to open Shane's door along the way, and ran to help the doctor—Was he a doctor? She didn't ask—fling the bags into the trunk of the police car. Shane joined her, and with the three of them working it took only a couple of minutes to pack the space available. There were a few bags left, and Shane stacked them on the car's floorboards in the back.

"Tell Hannah it's the pure supply; I destroyed the stuff they contaminated," the man said, and rolled the cart back inside.

Claire slammed the trunk shut and jumped in the driver's seat while Shane climbed in the passenger seat this time. She drove carefully, trying to avoid being spotted by anyone she recognized or by any other patrol car. So far, there were no alerts. She hoped Kentworth still had Sully under control.

As she parked next to the bus once more, she saw that Hannah was organizing the Blacke residents into teams of four—enough to cover each other's backs if necessary. Claire gave her a thumbs-up as she rolled down the window, and Hannah replied with a crisp nod and turned to address everyone.

"Right," she said. "We've got the blood. Here's how this will work. I go in and recover the controller for the collars. I shock the vampires down—for their safety as well as ours. Your job is to take down the Daylighter guards—but be careful. They won't hesitate to fight back. While you're taking them down, the kids and I will be piling all the blood in the center square of the atrium. By preference, most of the vamps will go for it when I free them, but I warn you: some will come for you or the Daylighters. Be prepared to defend yourselves there, too, and get out of the building while they feed."

It sounded like a solid plan, and Claire swallowed hard as Hannah ordered her into the backseat. Hannah drove slowly to the edge of the building, and watched as Mrs. Grant's people followed on foot, keeping to the edge of the wall.

Hannah turned the corner. "Both of you, get down and stay down until I come out," she said. "I don't want them seeing you or this could all go bad."

They followed instructions. Claire had a clear view of the blood bags stacked on the floor beside her, the thick dark-red liquid shifting inside the bags as Hannah got out of the car and walked away, toward the entrance. The morning heat was starting to make itself felt, and Claire felt sweat forming on her back, where the sun shone brightly. Without the AC running in the car, it would get uncomfortable quickly.

But it wasn't long before the radio in the car crackled to life, and Hannah's voice said, "Give the signal to Mrs. Grant."

Claire wasn't sure what the signal was, but Shane rose up from behind the dashboard and gave Mrs. Grant, staring into the windshield from a few feet away, a big thumbs-up.

The people from Blacke—thirty strong, at least—rushed into the building.

No need to hide now, Claire thought, and she sat up to try to see what was going on. Which was useless, since there wasn't much of a view inside. But after a few long minutes of silence, Hannah's voice came over the radio again. "Pop the trunk. Bring it in."

Shane opened her door on the way to the back of the car, and they grabbed full armloads of the squishy bags and ran for the entrance. Hannah opened the door for them. In her right hand, she was holding the controller box for the shock collars, and Claire saw that there were vampires down on the floor, still convulsing. She was holding them that way.

The Daylighters were mostly down, too, being tied up by the folks from Blacke, but not all of them had fallen into the trap. In fact, one was leaning over the second-floor balcony, aiming a hand-gun at them. Claire would have missed him, except that she heard Myrnin shout, "Claire, get down!" and she obeyed without question, dragging Shane with her.

The gun went off, and the bullet went over their heads to shatter one side of the entry doors into an explosion of glass shards.

Then Myrnin rose up pale behind the shooter, and sank his fangs into the man's neck.

Claire watched, horrified, because in that moment her gentle, sweet, goofy boss became Vampire, with a capital V. She remembered moments like this, when all his humanity stripped away, but this time it seemed even more frightening—mainly because he was *angry*. Really, really angry.

He drained the man dry, and snapped his neck when he was done, simply out of sheer fury . . . and then he tossed him over the railing, to smack like a rag doll onto the tile floor.

That made everyone stop what they were doing for an instant—even the other Daylighters who were still fighting.

Myrnin, Claire realized, was still getting shocks from the collar. He was just . . . ignoring them. Hannah realized it, too, and she didn't like it; she unsnapped the fastener on her sidearm as Myrnin leaped over the balcony's edge and landed catlike beside the body of his victim.

"You can stop that now," he said to Hannah. His voice was uneven and ragged, and his eyes were burning red, but she still shook her head.

"I can't," she said. "The others are starving. If I release them, they'll rip us apart. We've got blood. We're bringing it in. Myrnin, back off. Don't make me have to hurt you."

He laughed, in a tense and wildly crazy way that made Claire get a very bad feeling in her stomach. "*Hurt* me?" he asked. "How would you do that? By taking away everything I love? Everything I honor? You're too late, Hannah. Far too late. Fallon already did that."

Claire's terrible feeling suddenly condensed into a heavy, sickening weight. "He took Jesse," she said. "Fallon took Jesse."

"Because he knew it would hurt me," Myrnin said. "Fallon likes to pretend his crusade is to save us, but in the end it's about *me*. He wants to see me suffer, for turning him vampire so long ago. For abandoning him once I did. It is my fault, you know. All my fault. But Lady Grey shouldn't pay the price."

"We have to save her," Claire said, and turned to Hannah. "We have to."

"Never thought I'd say that, but, yeah, she's our friend, too," Shane agreed. He dumped the armload of blood bags on the floor next to the fountain, and Claire added her own to the pile.

"Then the faster we get the blood in, the faster you can go find her," Hannah said. "Help move it."

Myrnin, despite the shock collar still crackling around his neck, despite the intense sunlight outside, helped them carry the rest of the blood into the atrium, running back and forth, until the pile of bags was waist-high, and the trunk and backseat of the cruiser were empty.

Claire remembered, despite the frantic pace, that they still had a problem—a big one. "The hellhounds," she said. "Fallon could activate them at any time. If Hannah turns against us—"

"I've been working on adapting Fallon's filthy cure to the purpose," Myrnin said. "During my time outside this prison. I have a small supply made up in my lab. It's hidden in the back by my armchair, behind a pile of books. Enough for three more doses, if you're careful. Oh, and while you're there, do feed Bob. He's been hunting on his own lately, but he does enjoy being shown a little kindness."

And that, Claire thought, was Myrnin in a nutshell. He was capable of wild mood swings that went from murder to concern for a spider in under five minutes. In the end, loving Myrnin, *really* loving him, would be like living with an unexploded bomb—sooner or later it was bound to go off, and for someone fragile and human, it would be fatal.

It didn't make her love him any less, but she knew better than to think that she could fix him . . . or survive him, if she let him get too close.

"Mrs. Grant," Hannah said, "get your folks out of here. Take the prisoners with you. I'm going to release them."

Mrs. Grant nodded and gave quick instructions. Each team of four took one of the guards and escorted them out. Most looked relieved to be going, honestly.

"We're going to wait the rest of this out in Blacke," Mrs. Grant said. "Morganville's your town, not ours. We said we'd help free the vampires, and we have. Now it's up to you." She looked at Claire and Shane, and for a moment she looked as if she was going to reverse that, or at least regret it. She came to Shane and gave him a hug, then embraced Claire. "You two, you take care. I've gotten fond of you."

"Thanks, Mrs. Grant," Shane said. "You've done enough. You're right. This is Morganville business now."

Then they were headed out, back to their bus. Knowing Mrs. Grant and Morley, Claire was pretty sure that Blacke would already be prepared for an all-out war with the Daylighters, just in case. Armed to the teeth.

She and Shane looked at Hannah, who nodded and backed up toward the doorway. "You two, get in the car," she said. "Once I hit the releases for their collars, they'll be shaking it off and getting up fast."

Myrnin didn't follow them. He stood where he was, staring blindly at the pile of blood bags. Claire didn't think he was really seeing them, though. "Find her," he said. "Find Jesse. I'll lead the rest of them once they're fed. Leave Fallon to me."

"Myrnin—Fallon's a zealot. He played on people's fears. He made them believe that killing all of you was the only way to stay safe. Don't prove him right," Claire said. "Please. *Don't prove him right.*"

She didn't know if he heard her, or understood; he didn't give even the slightest indication. But there wasn't time. Hannah was hustling them out the door, and Claire saw her thumb come off the button. "In the car," she ordered, and practically shoved them inside.

They were already driving away when the first vampires, collars off their necks and drained blood bags in their hands, appeared in the doorway of the Bitter Creek Mall.

Myrnin's lab was located in a cul-de-sac at the end of a small, run-down neighborhood. It was next door to a Founder House—the Day House, built along the same plan as the Glass House.

Only the Day House wasn't there anymore. There was a pile of old timbers, and some construction equipment.

Fallon was making good on his threat to destroy the Founder Houses.

Claire swallowed hard. "What happened to them? Gramma Day?"

"Moved," Hannah said. "She was grateful to be going, in the end. The Day family never were too comfortable with that house, though they stayed in it for the better part of a hundred years. But she's fine. Got a brand-new place over on the other side of town, where the new development is going in."

"And Lisa—did she join the Daylighters?" Claire wouldn't have been at all surprised by that from the Day granddaughter, who'd been totally anti-vamp for as long as she'd known her . . . but Gramma Day, ancient as she was, had a broader view of things.

"Lisa did. Gramma declined," Hannah said. "Gramma said it reminded her of all those speeches out of Germany in the war. I don't think she was so far off."

Claire didn't, either. The image of those banners around Founder's Square still gave her a chill.

She led the way to the entrance to Myrnin's lab. It was locked up by an iron grate and a shiny new padlock, but Hannah had the keys. "Fallon had it secured," she explained. "I have no idea how Myrnin would have gotten into it."

Myrnin always had his ways, but Claire didn't explain that; she didn't think Hannah needed any more nightmares. As they descended the steps, the lights came up, responding to motion, revealing . . . a wreck. Well, even more of a wreck than it normally was. The equipment was mostly shattered, the books ripped apart, the furniture broken. Either Myrnin had thrown an epic tantrum—which frankly wasn't all that unlikely—or Fallon's goons had been in here making damn sure nothing useful would be coming out of the lab again.

Claire climbed over the piles of rubble, careful of the broken glass, and made her way to the back of the lab. Myrnin's armchair had been broken, but the remains of it were more or less where they'd originally been. Bob the Spider's tank had been turned on its side, but not broken. There was no sign of him in the webs, but he certainly wasn't starving; plenty of unfortunate insects had been cocooned into his pantry.

Claire combed through the wreckage, and under a pile of books that included a battered first edition of *Alice in Wonderland* and two sketchy-looking volumes written longhand in a language she didn't even recognize, she found a box. It didn't look like much—old, battered, not very clean. She flipped the lid off, and inside, packed carefully in old newspapers, was an old-style syringe full of brownish liquid.

"Got it!" she called back to Hannah and Shane, and scrambled over the piles to them. Hannah was already unbuttoning her uniform shirt.

"Hurry," she said. "Something's happening." Something was. Hannah's eyes looked different, lighter, and between blinks Claire saw them quickly shifting to yellow.

"Crap," Shane said. He took hold of Hannah's arm and held it steady. "He's activated her. Do it fast."

"In the bite?" Because Hannah's bite was raised and inflamed and prominent, just as Shane's had been.

"Yes! Go!" Shane yelled, just as Hannah let out a vicious snarl.

Claire jammed the needle home, and depressed the plunger—

but only about a third of the way. She hoped Myrnin was right about the dosage; if she undermedicated Hannah, that might be worse than not doing it at all.

Hannah's snarl turned to a startled yip, and then she was collapsing to her knees, trembling, mouth open in a silent scream. Her eyes were wild and yellow, but only for a moment. Then her skin took on a muted silvery glow as the cure took hold.

Claire held her breath. Myrnin had adapted this from Fallon's cure, but what if it had the same shortcomings? What if it only worked *part* of the time?

It seemed to take forever. Hannah never quite collapsed completely, but she trembled, clearly very ill, and as the silvery glow finally faded under her skin, she looked up at Claire. Her eyes, after one last acidic pulse of yellow, settled back to their normal human brown color.

Hannah pulled in a few hard, quick breaths, and nodded. Shane let go of her. She made a face. "Tastes funny," she said. Her voice sounded hoarse. "Aches, too."

"It'll pass," he said, and helped her up. "You took it a lot better than I did." He wasn't looking at her face, though, he was examining her arm. The bite was looking a little better. "I think I screamed like a baby."

"Give me a minute and I might just get there," Hannah said, and attempted a smile. It wasn't quite right, but it was brave. "Let's get out of here."

Claire would have, but as they turned for the stairs, she caught sight of a fuzzy black spider about the size of her palm sitting on top of a book, watching her with eight bright, beady eyes. He looked almost cute.

"Hey, Bob," she said. She reached down, and he climbed up on her hand. "Let's get you back in your tank, okay?"

He didn't seem unhappy with that. She carried him back over the rubble, and he clung to her hand easily, riding all the uneven progress without much concern. She righted his tank and held out her hand, and he scuttled off and settled into the gauzy webs, looking perfectly comfortable.

She resisted the urge to pat him on the head. Thorax. Whatever. "Good boy, Bob. I'll be back soon."

He hopped up and down a little in the webs, then turned his attention to one of his stored insects.

She was happy to skip that part, actually.

As she came back to them, Hannah already seemed much better, and Shane looked relieved. "Swear to God, I don't get you and that spider," he said. "But if you're done playing Dr. Dolittle . . ."

"I know where they'll have Jesse," Claire said. "Let's go."

But she was wrong.

The asylum—mental hospital—whatever the current politically correct term might be—was closed and locked. Nobody there. Claire went around back to check windows, but she didn't find anything. Just to be thorough, Hannah broke in (though according to her it was an emergency entry), but she came back shaking her head. She looked disturbed, though. "Bodies," she said. "Quite a few. He's been processing vampires through his conversion faster than I thought. But Jesse's not in there."

"Then where?" Shane asked.

Claire thought frantically. It could be anywhere, absolutely anywhere in Morganville, but Fallon seemed to be a man who enjoyed sticking the knife in and twisting it just a little bit more. That meant if he'd moved Jesse, he'd moved her for a reason.

"I think he's got her with him," Claire said. "At Founder's Square. Don't you?"

"Well," Hannah said, "we have to go there anyway. Hop in."

The ride back to Founder's Square wasn't as easy as leaving, mainly because the alerts about Hannah had gone out; they heard it on the police radio in the car when the news dropped. *Chief Hannah Moses to be arrested on sight. Armed and dangerous.*

"That," Hannah said, "is code for *Killing her would be just fine.* Most of my folks won't feel that way. I hire good people, mostly, though some of them got forced on me, like Sullivan. But Fallon's Daylighters will be out for blood, and they won't hesitate."

Not good news, Claire thought. They needed Hannah by their side. "So how are we going to get there?"

"On foot," Hannah said. She stopped the car and parked it in front of the City Lights Washateria, where only a couple of people sat inside, looking depressed and watching the dryers spin. "Give me two minutes."

She went in, had a short exchange with the woman sitting there, opened the dryer, and pulled out some clothes.

"Um . . . ," Claire said, and poked Shane in the ribs. "Is she changing clothes?"

"Yep," he said. "Normally, if we weren't in mortal danger, I would really find this fascinating."

It was actually less than two minutes before Hannah was back, carrying a bundle with her uniform and gun belt. She'd found a slightly large pair of dress pants that weren't really long enough (but flood pants were in, Claire remembered) and a too-frilly pink shirt that was also a little big, but surprisingly cute. The only things that seemed far out of place were her shoes, which were typical police issue, but at a glance she could pass easily as a civilian.

She'd also taken the Daylighters pin from her uniform collar and was wearing it on the shirt.

"Camouflage," she said, when Claire pointed at it. She opened the doors. "We'll be walking from here on in. Shane, you're familiar with this." She tossed him the shotgun from the rack in front. "Claire—take the Taser."

"What about you?"

Hannah slipped her sidearm into a pancake holster at the small of her back, and flipped the shirt down over it.

"Unless it's take-your-shotgun-to-work day, I'm going to get noticed," Shane said. "Not that it isn't a great late birthday present, though."

Hannah looked around the other stores on the block, and grinned. "I can fix that."

And she did.

"I hate this," Shane complained, and sneezed. Turned out he was allergic to roses. And he was carrying a thick bundle of them to conceal the shotgun. It was kind of bizarrely clever, because nobody thought a guy carrying roses was dangerous in the least, did they? Especially one who was sneezing.

Claire could tell from how hard he was gritting his teeth that he really *did* hate it. A lot.

They walked quickly but calmly the short distance to Founder's Square. Hannah must have thought ahead, because they went to one of the side entrances; it was guarded by a police officer, but as Hannah got closer, she locked stares with the woman and said, "Get on the right side, Gretchen. Semper Fi."

Gretchen—a trim woman with thick white-blond hair—nodded, gave them all a quick glance, and swung the gate open. "I never saw you, boss," she told Hannah.

"Affirmative."

And then they were in, approaching from the side. There was a school choir onstage, singing something that it took Claire a moment to realize was "Here Comes the Sun." They weren't very good.

"That's a little on the nose," Shane said. "I think maybe 'Black Hole Sun' might be more appropriate."

He was right, of course. The audience Fallon had gathered, though, seemed entranced; they were swaying to the music, holding hands, looking for all the world like they were having a religious experience.

Amelie, Oliver, and Morley were still motionless on the stage, blistering and steaming in the sun. It must have been agonizing, waiting for their chance. Claire wondered why they hadn't done it already, but then she realized they were waiting for word that the vampires in the mall had been rescued.

It was up to her, and Shane, to let them know.

She spotted Eve and Michael. They were sitting in chairs onstage next to Fallon, pretty much held there by the two Daylighter guards standing behind them. Maybe that was another reason why Amelie hadn't moved; Eve and Michael would be the first in danger if she did.

The choir was still singing when the vampires began to arrive at Founder's Square.

Some were covered by blankets, coats, whatever they'd been able to scavenge along the way from the mall. Some, the older ones, had made do with a hat or some kind of cap. They came over the walls in a silent stream, landing quietly in the bushes and moving forward to gather at the edges of the crowd. It was done very calmly. Nobody threatened. Nobody attacked.

Then someone in the crowd must have noticed that a vampire was standing *right beside him*. He yelled, and a flurry of confusion erupted. People began drawing back, flinching from the sudden appearance of the bogeymen all around them . . . and as their false sense of security shattered into chaos, and the crowd began to stampede in all directions.

Faith in the sunlight wasn't enough in the face of real danger, apparently.

The choir was still singing, but it was falling apart, too, and Fallon shoved through them to get to the microphone. "Don't run!" he shouted, and his voice rang out over the square, echoing back from the buildings with their fluttering banners. "Don't run from them! Stand up to them! Fight for your town. You have the advantage—they are few, and they are weak. Take Morganville *back!*"

"Go," Hannah said. "Get Michael and Eve out of there! I need to make sure nobody does anything stupid." She was already gone, running flat out for two of her own cops, one of whom was drawing his sidearm but not quite sure where to aim it.

Shane grabbed Claire's arm and towed her quickly toward the stage. That wasn't easy, because a lot of the crowd was running in that direction, as if Fallon's presence was somehow going to protect them from about vampires gathering on the other side of the folding chairs. Fallon was right—the humans outnumbered them.

But the fear of vampires was so ingrained that it didn't seem to be making a difference.

Myrnin was in front of the rank of vampires, Claire saw, but he didn't move forward. He held up his hand, and the others stayed behind him, ready to move. She'd seen them in army mode before, fighting the draug, but it was still eerie and terrifying, knowing how much hell they could unleash.

"Myrnin," Fallon said. His voice held so much, just in saying the name—so much anger, and so much pain. "Come to mourn your fallen?"

"This doesn't have to end this way," Myrnin said. "I have no quarrel with you, Rhys. I never have."

"You *destroyed my life*, spider. You preyed upon me and blackened my soul, and it took me hundreds of years to claw my way back to the light. Well, I've done it. And now I'm going to drag *you* into the light, too."

"I'm standing in the light now," Myrnin said. "Lest it escaped your notice. Not even a hat on my head. What makes you think I fear it?"

Fallon pointed at the sizzling bodies of Amelie, Morley, and Oliver. "Ask them," he said. "They're proof of your damnation. Proof that the sun itself hates and rejects your kind." He shifted his gaze away from Myrnin to the people crowding around the stage. "We *will* stand in the sunlight and they *will* be defeated! The sun makes us strong. Stand together!"

"Come on, we need to get Eve and Michael out of there," Shane said. He shoved through the crowd, heading for the stairs that led up to the stage. As they took the steps, they were crowded to the edge by the fleeing choir, but he practically body-slammed his way through, heedless of their yells and cries, and he somehow kept hold of Claire and made enough space for her to follow.

Then they were at the top, and Michael spotted them.

It was what he'd been waiting for, apparently, because he turned and threw a sharp elbow right into the jaw of the man behind him and Eve. Eve let out a war yell, threw her chair aside, and kicked the man solidly in the chest as he tried to throw a punch in return. It threw him backward and tangled him in the curtains, and they were ripped loose as he toppled off the stage to the rear.

Eve turned back, color burning in her cheeks, and grabbed Claire's hand. She didn't speak, but the pressure of her grip was enough. Michael and Shane exchanged quick nods. "What now?" Michael asked.

"We get the hell out of the way, because hell's coming," Shane said. "Come on, man."

But they didn't make it. The man Eve had kicked off the stage came scrambling back up, and his companion came back from the other side, dragging the limp body of a red-haired woman that Claire recognized a heartbeat later as Jesse.

He dumped her on the stage beside Fallon's podium, and even from this far away Claire saw the tremor that went through Myrnin.

She saw his eyes turn bloody crimson.

But if Fallon expected him to attack, he was disappointed. Myrnin said, "You're a fool, Rhys. You achieved your own mortality. Congratulations. Let your anger go. Let *her* go."

"After I send your friends to hell, where they belong," Fallon said. He crossed to Amelie, reached down, and yanked sharply up on the stake.

He expected it to release silver nitrate and destroy her, of course, and it must have come as an awful shock to him when she opened her eyes, sat up, and said, in a calm, clear voice, "Thank you. That was unpleasant."

He stumbled backward as Amelie climbed to her feet. She was burned and weak, but moving, and the sight of her sent a ripple through the crowd of vampires that were standing so still. She crossed to Oliver and yanked the stake from his chest, too, then helped him rise. Then Morley.

That's when Fallon stumbled back to the podium and pulled out a copy of Claire's VLAD device—the clumsy, bulky gun that she had made and Myrnin had steampunked out. This one looked sleeker, and deadlier, and Fallon aimed it at Amelie.

Of course. Claire had been told that Dr. Anderson had been working on making new models. This was a prototype, something he'd brought today to show the true believers. A real weapon they could use to protect themselves from the vampires.

Claire could tell that it had been pushed to its highest setting. It might not kill Amelie, but it would disable her so badly she'd be utterly helpless. *My fault,* Claire thought in a sickening rush. *My invention. I'm the villain after all.*

She watched helplessly as Fallon pressed the trigger.

Oliver threw himself in the way of the blast. He must have known what it would cost him; he'd been hit with it before, twice, and he understood the pain he was in for. But he didn't hesitate. Claire saw the beam hit him, and saw him fall to the stage floor. He writhed in agony and then curled into a helpless ball, shaking with fear and horror.

That gave Morley an opportunity. He grabbed Fallon, ripped the gun out of his hands, and shattered it over his knee as easily as if it had been made out of balsa wood. Fluids sprayed, sparks flew, but just like that, he'd reduced Fallon's ultimate weapon to junk and recycling.

It cost him his life.

The Daylighter who'd dragged Jesse up to the stage pulled out a silver stake and lunged forward to drive it into Morley's chest. Morley might have survived that, at least for a while, but the man quickly pulled it back out . . . which triggered the release of the liquid silver solution inside.

It flooded into Morley's chest cavity, and he began to burn, screaming.

Claire clapped hands over her mouth and looked away in horror, knowing there was nothing they could do for him; it was fast, and it was deadly. It was also an awful way to die. She heard him fall, and smelled the bitter stench of ashes.

Amelie ignored Fallon, who was backing away now. She moved in a blur to the man who'd staked Morley, and she threw him off the stage—as far as the wall, into the bushes—and dropped down next to her fallen ally. She took his hand as he trembled, staring into her face as the silver bubbled and hissed in his chest cavity.

"I'm here," she said. "Morley, I'm here. Thank you, my old friend. May God grant you rest."

He couldn't speak, but he held her gaze until he was gone, his chest eaten away to a smoking hole filled with ash.

Then Amelie rose, and looked at Fallon with those calm, ice gray eyes, and Claire knew he was finished, one way or the other. He backed away from her, and it came to Claire that what he feared most in the world was being made into a vampire again. Amelie might find that a fitting punishment. Might even find some satisfaction in it.

But Claire really thought she would kill him.

She didn't do either of those things. Instead, she reached to the podium and took up the wireless microphone and spoke into it.

"People of Morganville," she said. "Please be calm. No harm is going to come to any of you."

"Liar!" Fallon said, but he didn't have the mike anymore. And Amelie turned her back on him to address the crowd. She was blistering in the sun, and starting to smoke; she was weak, and still recovering from the wound in her chest. But even with all that, even in stained clothes and with her hair long and wild, she looked like what she was, and always had been.

A queen.

"You've gone to great lengths to make us the monsters, Fallon," she said. "You talk of how we cannot control our bestial impulses, our appetites. About how those different from you must be eliminated, for safety, or converted to a form you find acceptable. But here we stand, different. We could stop every beating heart in this place. In this town. We could rampage across the *world*, creating more and more of our own kind. *But we do not.* Do you know why?" Her calm, calming voice was having an effect on the crowd of panicked Daylighters. They were standing now, listening, not pushing or fleeing. If Amelie was worried about the other guards who were closing in on her—Fallon's fanatical loyalists—she didn't betray it by so much as a twitch. "Because we are *not monsters*. We are you, given a curse that most of us never sought but came to accept. Would we return to our human state if given the chance? Some would. Some would not. But forcing us, with the knowledge that you will destroy so many in the process . . . That's not mercy, Fallon, no matter what you pretend. It's murder."

The Daylighter guards were closing in now, silver stakes out.

Amelie sank gracefully to her knees, still holding the microphone. "By all means, murder us in the sunlight you love so much. Murder us in front of witnesses. Show them just how *merciful* you are, because I know you, Rhys Fallon. I know the callow heart in you, and the selfish rage, and the bitterness. I know that you pursued your humanity with ruthless purpose, and once you had it back . . . you loathed it. You've created this to destroy all that reminds you of what you've lost."

It was a powerful image—the most deadly vampire in the world, on her knees, voluntarily. The Daylighters ringing her with their weapons.

But she wasn't striking out, she wasn't killing, she wasn't even threatening.

And the guards didn't know what to do with that.

Some people in the crowd looked confused now, and some seemed uncomfortable. As if the truth was starting to dawn.

"We've been harsh masters here," Amelie continued. The strength of will it took to ignore her impending death in those silver stakes the Daylighters held, having seen how it had destroyed Morley, was staggering. Claire couldn't imagine how she was doing it. "Vampires are slow to learn, and slow to change, but we *have* changed. We know we *must* change. Before Fallon arrived, we were building a new Morganville, an equal Morganville, one where we might all live in peace together. Don't let him take that from you—because if you build your new town on the bones of victims, it will never bring you peace. Watch what he does to us now, and remember."

Fallon knew he was finished, then. He must have. The fact that the vampires hadn't attacked, that his side had been seen to shoot Oliver and kill Morley, and was now threatening to kill a woman who kneeled, weaponless . . . it was a PR disaster for him. Morgan-ville resented the vampires, yes, but Claire realized that the crowd here in the square wasn't as big as it could have been. A lot of the town *wasn't* here. *Wasn't* singing about the sun and celebrating the de-feat of the vampires. Maybe that other half still resented the vamps, but if they weren't here, that meant that they'd had a reason not to show up. It meant that some of them, a lot of them, didn't agree.

And Amelie knew that.

Fallon could have made a graceful retreat, kept his cool, preached his anti-vampire screed. Amelie would have let him, most likely.

But he wasn't content with that. He didn't want to lose.

"Kill her!" he told his men, and snatched up Jesse's limp body from where she'd fallen to the ground. He took a silver stake from his coat pocket. Sweat was pouring down his face, and his skin was flushing an unhealthy red from the strength of his fury.

Shane dropped the roses he'd been holding and racked the shotgun, then aimed it at the group of men standing around Ame-lie. "Hey, guys? Don't," he said. "This won't hurt her so much, but it'll definitely hurt you."

They froze. All but one dropped their stakes, which tumbled to the stage and rolled to the edge.

One decided to go for it. He stabbed down, hoping Shane would hesitate to fire . . . as he did.

Amelie reached up and effortlessly caught his arm as it de-scended toward her chest. She turned and looked at him. "No," she said. "Not today." She plucked the stake from his hand and plunged it into the wooden floor of the stage next to her.

Then she let him go. He backed away, clearly not sure what to do with a vampire who *didn't* want to hurt him.

It should have been over, but Fallon still had Jesse, and a stake of his own, and although he should have been making his escape, he was moving *forward* . . . to the edge of the stage, where he grabbed Jesse's limp body and stood with her clasped against his chest.

"Myrnin!" Even without the microphone, his shout was loud enough to be easily heard over the crowd. "You need to live in the same hell you left me to rot in—and that means you will rot alone." He raised the stake.

Myrnin was too far away. Too far away to save her.

But Claire wasn't.

She fired the Taser into Fallon's back.

He convulsed, slumped, and fell with a heavy thud, still shaking.

Myrnin arrived just a second later, traveling at blurred vampire speed, and vaulted up onto the stage to gather Jesse in his arms. "Dear lady, dear lady, what's he done to you . . ." He took her wrist and nipped at it, drawing just a little blood, which he licked. It must have told him what he needed to know. "He's given her a sleeping drug. It'll pass soon. She's all right. Claire, she's all right." He looked up, and there were tears in his eyes as he smiled at her.

She smiled back. Her heart was breaking a little bit, because she felt something changing in Myrnin, and she knew that she would no longer be the center of his gravity. He'd always be there for her, and he'd always be her friend, but there was something in the way he held Jesse, stroked her hair, whispered to her in a way that Claire couldn't ever see him doing with her.

Shane's warm weight settled in behind her, and his arms went around her. He'd passed the shotgun over to Eve, who was holding it on the Daylighter guards. Beyond him, Amelie had finally risen to her feet. She looked at the vampires still standing in the sun—a sign of their loyalty to her, Claire thought—and raised the microphone.

"Get under cover, friends," she told them. "Thank you. Today you've shown me, and all of Morganville, what we truly can be. It will always be a struggle for us, but we can learn, and we will. Go."

As soon as they started moving, heading for the shadows on the porches of the buildings, Amelie turned to Oliver, who was still lying on the ground, shaking. She knelt gracefully next to him and took his hand.

"I'm here," she said. It was what she'd said to Morley, but where that had been compassion, this was something far stronger.

"Fool," he managed to whisper. "Never trust a human's good intentions."

"Perhaps we'll both learn to do better," she said, and bent to place a kiss on his lips. "Over time."

"Perhaps you shouldn't trust *my* intentions."

"I never do," she said, and raised her brows just slightly. "Rest. You can bedevil me later."

"I will," he said. "Perhaps you might get me into the shade?"

She laughed and picked him up in her arms—a very odd sight, and one Claire was pretty sure Oliver wouldn't remember fondly—and carried him away out of the sun.

Michael still guarded Fallon. He stood there with one of the silver stakes, turning it restlessly in his fingers. Fallon was starting to shake off the shock.

The look in his eyes was pure, cold hatred.

"Yo, Mikey," Shane said. "He ain't a vampire anymore. If you do that, it's murder."

"I know," Michael said. "I won't do anything he doesn't make me do. Please don't give me an excuse, Fallon. I do owe you for giving me back my life."

Fallon had recovered enough to say something, but it was faint, and Claire almost missed it. "You were a means to an end, boy," he whispered. "To hurt *her*."

Michael shrugged. "Then I won't invite you to my wedding."

"What wedding?" Eve called from where she was standing.

"They annulled our marriage, remember? You don't think I'd let you walk away, do you?"

She blew him a kiss. "Never ever, rock star. Leave him. Let's go home."

Fallon smirked as Hannah Moses put handcuffs on him. "You think you have a home to return to?"

They all stopped and stared at him—at the hot, bitter triumph in his smile.

"Michael," Shane said, "wouldn't we know . . ."

"We were out of town," Michael said, and looked at Claire for confirmation. "We wouldn't, would we?"

She searched inside herself for that connection to the Glass House, that little thread of feeling that she'd come to recognize.

It was still there . . . but it was weak. Very weak.

"We have to go," she said. "Right now."

FOURTEEN

They commandeered a police car from Hannah, and Shane hit the lights and sirens while Michael drove, ignoring stoplights and weaving around other cars as if he'd plunged into a real-life video game. Claire and Eve, on the other hand, just clung to their seats in the back. It didn't take long to spot their house.

And the massive bulldozer that was heading relentlessly for it.

"Oh, God," Eve said. As they made the turn, the treads of the giant yellow monster mowed down and crushed their mailbox, hit the white picket fence, splintered it, and crushed it into the nice, neat grass. It wasn't neat for long. The treads chewed the yard into muck as the bulldozer moved forward, raising its bucket. It was aimed right at the corner of the house, and as Michael brought the car to a screeching halt at the curb Claire saw Miranda's face at the window, eyes wide in terror, staring at the thing that was coming to destroy their home.

And her.

There were no plans made for this contingency, and Claire knew there was no time for any; Shane and Michael bailed out the front, and Shane remembered—barely—to yank open Claire's door in the back before he dashed after Michael, too.

"Get the driver!" Michael yelled, but it wasn't going to be that easy, because the driver wasn't alone—he had a couple of other burly construction-hardened guys with him. Shane veered off and made a running leap for the cab of the bulldozer. It was brand-new, barely dirty yet, and it had an enclosed, probably air-conditioned cab . . . with a locking door.

And the driver, of course, had it locked.

Shane yanked on the door, but that was useless; he tried driving his elbow into the glass, but it was thick, designed to resist flying debris. And then the bulldozer, which had slowed down as the operator assessed the threat Shane represented, sped up again, and the lurch threw him off to roll on the grass.

There wasn't time for anything too fancy, but Claire stopped, ran back to the police car, and frantically searched around the seats . . . and found an expandable, flexible baton. She raced past Shane, who was rising to head for the bulldozer again.

"Help Michael!" she yelled. He and Eve were in the middle of a scrum with the two other construction men, and Michael still hadn't realized the limitations of his all-too-human body yet. "I've got this!"

He gave her a quick, worried look, but he didn't argue. Besides, he loved a good fistfight, and this was shaping up to be one he'd remember fondly.

Claire took a deep breath, a running jump, and landed on the rubber-coated step next to the cab. The driver gave her an irritated, smug look; he sneered and didn't bother to put the machine in idle this time.

At least, not until she drew back and smashed the heavy baton into the window glass, cracking it into frost. A second blow rained chunks of safety glass all over him, and he let out a yelp and took his hand off the throttle—which automatically shut the bulldozer down to an idle again, five feet from the corner of the house. He swore at her, loudly, and shoved the door open, which pushed her off and onto the grass, where she hit and rolled to her feet, breathing hard.

She'd been hoping he'd jump out and come after her, but he'd done what he intended to do by brushing her off, and now he slammed the door again and jammed the throttle forward.

"No!" Claire screamed, and leaped back on. She collided with the metal door. He hadn't locked it properly this time, and she stepped back and yanked it open, holding on for dear life. She'd dropped the baton somewhere, but she didn't have room to wield it inside the cab anyway.

"Are you crazy? Get the hell out! Don't make me hurt you!" the man said, and shoved at her. She clung on, so he let off the throttle to get a better grip on her with both hands . . . and she let him. He had hard, strong hands, and she knew it was going to leave bruises, but that was okay right now. Bruises were fine.

Because she was able to lean over across him and grab the key from the ignition before he threw her out of the cab and off the machine.

The bulldozer coughed and died, locked in its muddy tracks, and Claire shook off the fall and got to her feet, grinning. He didn't get what had happened for a moment. He kept jamming his thumb on the button to start the engine, but then he must have spotted what was missing, because he leveled a black, furious look at Claire and jumped down from the cab to come after her.

She ran for the messy brawl that was spilling all over the lawn—Michael and Eve were tag-teaming one of the construction guys, who looked furious and frustrated, not to mention a little worried. His fellow neon-vested buddy was throwing punches at Shane, which Shane was easily dancing around while snapping hard, accurate blows to the man's midsection, and—as Claire dashed past them—a stunning right hook that spun the guy halfway around to spiral limply to the ground.

"Hey, Claire!" Shane called to her, and then spotted the furious bulldozer operator, hard in pursuit. He stepped in the way.

That was a mistake, because the bulldozer guy had evidently paused to pick up Claire's fallen baton, which he whipped out to its full length and smacked into Shane's leg. Shane yelled and went down to his other knee, and his grab for the man's foot failed to slow the guy down.

Claire ran up the steps to the house. The door opened ahead of her, because Miranda had been waiting, and the instant Claire was clear, the door tried to slam shut.

The tip of the riot baton got in the way, and the front door sprang back open, banging hard into the hallway wall.

The construction guy stepped into the Glass House, flexed his wrist, and lifted the baton as he bared his teeth at Claire and Miranda.

That was when all hell broke loose.

Miranda must have had some warning, because she grabbed Claire and pulled her down to the hardwood floor an instant before the battered little table they used as a backpack/purse/key depository lifted up off the floor and smashed hard into the intruder's chest. He yelled in surprise, but it didn't do much damage; he grabbed it and flung it off to the side, into the parlor, then came after the two of them with murder in his eyes.

Claire felt the equally furious surge of energy rising up—out of the floor beneath her, swirling in from the walls, down from the ceiling, a thick but invisible cloud of power that raised goose bumps and tingles all over her body.

And then the coffee table from the parlor upended itself and body-slammed him into the wall, hard enough to leave cracks in the plaster. He dropped the baton and staggered.

An old, weirdly shaped vase in a particularly unpleasant shade of brown flew off a shelf and smashed into bits against his head.

And then he was *down*, sagging down the wall. Groaning.

The house seemed satisfied with that—Claire felt the surge of triumph and knew it hadn't come from her or Miranda. She scrambled up, moved the coffee table out of the way (it was heavier than she remembered), and kicked the sharp pieces of the vase aside as she picked up the riot baton.

The construction worker looked up at her woozily through bloodshot eyes. She stuck the bulldozer keys in her pants pocket and said, "Are you okay?"

He mumbled something that sounded rude, so she just assumed he was, and looked outside. Jenna's car was screeching to a crooked halt at the curb ahead of their police cruiser; she must have sensed the house's distress, or Miranda's. The fight on the lawn was still going, but it was just about over, and as Jenna got out of her car and strode over to help Shane to his feet, the remaining construction worker raised his hands to signal surrender. "Okay, okay," he yelled, as Michael and Eve paused, fists raised. "Enough already. They don't pay us enough for this!"

"Surprise," Jenna said crisply. "They aren't paying you at all for this. If you think the Daylight Foundation is writing you a check, you're in for a surprise. They just shut their doors for good."

He must have been the foreman, Claire thought, because he just looked disgusted. "Well, crap," he said. "I ain't paying for that broken fence, lady. I had my orders."

"Let's call it even," Eve said. "I never did like that fence, anyway. What do you think, Michael? Something Gothic, like wrought iron? With spikes?"

"Spikes are good," he said, and grabbed her to look her over. He ran a thumb over her chin. "You're going to have a bruise."

"Jeez, I hope so. Didn't do my part if I don't."

He kissed her, looped an arm around her shoulders, and walked her toward the house.

Shane was limping, but when he got to the door with Jenna, he gave Claire a reassuring grin. "It's a bruise; I'll shake it off," he said. "You might have to kiss it better later."

She rolled her eyes. "Dream on," she said, but she reached up to push back the sweaty, thick hair from his face. "Look at that. Still handsome."

"Damn straight." Shane nudged the bulldozer guy with his foot. "Hey. Want to get the hell out of our house, fool? Don't make me tell you that you're not welcome. Bad things happen."

No kidding, Claire thought. The house was practically vibrating, it was so upset. She shook her head, helped the guy up (seemed like the least she could do, really), and pushed him out the door into his foreman's arms. "I think you'd better call it a day," she told him.

He nodded. "You got it, kid. It's beer o'clock."

Claire dug the keys out of her pocket and tossed them to him. "Then get that thing off our lawn." She hesitated, holding his stare. "You understand that if you even *think* about putting it in gear the wrong direction..."

"Oh, I get it," he said. "Trust me. Far as I'm concerned, this damn house can stay standing until the whole town falls down around it."

That seemed like an acceptable way to look at it, but Claire checked her friends to be sure. Miranda nodded gravely, and hugged Jenna tight. Michael raised his eyebrows at Eve, who polled Shane, and then spoke for all of them when she said, "Sounds good. Oh, and I'd get your friends checked out at the hospital just in case."

"Them? What about me?" He rubbed his jaw. "You kick like a mule, Mrs. Glass."

He retreated with his two weaving, staggering buddies.

Eve smiled and relaxed against Michael, who wrapped his arms around her. "We're home. I like the sound of that," she said, and looked up at him. "Wait, weren't we talking about a wedding before all this?"

"We were," he said. "Let's go discuss it. In private." He grabbed Eve's hand and towed her off down the hall. Eve waved back toward the rest of them, and all the Goth makeup in the world couldn't have concealed the blush in her cheeks.

"We should go," Miranda said to Jenna, in a very businesslike tone. "Because they get weird about me being here when they're, you know."

"I've been thinking that maybe we should make you a bedroom at my house," Jenna said. "I've got a spare room. You'll have to visit here to keep your connection, but you're welcome anytime."

Miranda's eyes widened, and she looked so bright and hopeful that it almost hurt Claire to look at her. After all the kid's misery, maybe things were starting to finally, finally look up. "Yeah, that sounds okay," she finally said, and managed to make it sound teen-indifferent, even though she definitely wasn't. "Can I bring my posters?"

"Of course. I love posters." Jenna smiled at her with genuine warmth and walked her toward the door. "You going to be okay until we get home? Not feeling too weak?"

"No," Miranda's voice drifted back, as they picked their way across the destroyed lawn. "The house is happy. I feel strong."

Shane put his arms around Claire from behind, and kissed her in a place just behind her ear, a place he knew made her shiver. "Hmmm, so there's going to be a wedding. What do you think?" he asked her.

"You mean Michael and Eve's wedding?"

"Yes. And no."

She turned in his arms and looked up into his eyes. Felt as if she was falling, and falling, and falling, but it wasn't frightening, not at all. It transformed into a feeling of flying. Of freedom. Of possibilities.

She took a deep breath and said, "Yes."

None of it happened instantly. Couldn't, because even though Fallon had been taken into custody and the vampires released from

the prison, there were . . . issues. Of course. Morganville was never
without them.

"I frigging hate politicians," Eve sighed as she dumped her coffin purse on the kitchen table and dropped into a chair next to
Claire, who was surfing the Web on her laptop.

"How was the mayor?"

Eve gave her a *look*. Then an eye roll. "Mayor Ramos is resign-
ing. She says she can't serve in a council with vampires. Guess we
should have seen that coming, right? I waited for two hours for her
to show up, and then she told me she couldn't help straighten out
the mess with our marriage license. I mean, how hard can it be to
get married, involuntarily divorced, and remarried? Don't they
want me to be happy? Don't answer that."

Claire didn't. The old, bitter lines of Morganville would never
completely go away; with the vampires back, if not back in charge
exactly, some people blamed Eve (and the rest of them) for screwing things up just when they were going right. If by *right* they meant
horribly wrong, then Claire supposed they were correct. She found
that she didn't mind being thought of as a villain quite so much,
after the fact, because the people who were blaming her for the
generally crap state of their lives had a lot to answer for in general.

"So, no date yet?"

For answer, Eve slapped a piece of paper down in front of her,
onto the keyboard. Claire looked up, then down at the document.
It looked official, all right. "I didn't say *that*," Eve said, and smiled
in slow delight. "I got an Amelie-class override. Plus, Ramos is
cleaning out her desk, and the incoming mayor said he'd stamp it
the second he took over the office."

"Charlie Kentworth? Really?" There had been a very hasty
two-day campaign and election for the suddenly open mayoral

chair, and Officer Kentworth had been the fairly obvious choice. Especially since his sole opponent, recycling her campaign materials from her last failed attempt, had been Monica Morrell. She'd gathered about five percent of the vote, mainly from the irony demographic, but she was still determined to find *something* to be in charge of. She'd talked about buying the old Daylight Foundation building—locked up tight now—and making it into a dog boarding facility. Shane had found that weirdly, hilariously appropriate.

"He's a pretty decent guy when he's not finding dead bodies in your house," Eve said. "Speaking of that, I'm not going into the basement anymore."

"The laundry room's in the basement."

"Then you are on laundry duty."

"Hey!" Claire poked at her, and Eve poked back. "So . . . the date?"

"We were thinking next Saturday. You busy?"

"I might be," Claire said. She kept her poker face well enough that Eve looked momentarily crushed, and then she reached into her backpack to pull out another piece of paper, which she slid across to Eve.

Who unfolded it, read it, squealed in ranges that only dolphins could hear, and practically knocked Claire's laptop off the table in her haste to hug her.

"Wait, am I late to the orgy?" Shane asked as he came through the kitchen doorway carrying two Cokes. "I didn't get the Evite. Man, I hate slow Internet."

"Shut up," Eve said. She wiped her eyes, carefully because of her extremely expert makeup, and hugged him, too, before he even had the chance to set down the glasses. "Why didn't you tell me?"

"Uh . . . did I mention slow Internet? Wait, what?"

Eve brandished the marriage license in his face, and he gave Claire a quick glance before he said, "Because you were all knee-deep in the paperwork swamp. It took us about an hour. I didn't want to rub it in, because you get all blotchy when you angry-cry."

"Idiot," Eve said, and kissed his cheek. Then she kissed Claire's. "Now I'm all blotchy."

"Can't even tell," he said, and finally set down the Cokes. "What with all the layers of spackle on your face."

"It's nice to know that being on the verge of losing your freedom hasn't made you any less juvenile."

"Excuse me, you're dressing like a Living Dead Doll, and who exactly is—"

"Hey," Claire said, and held out both hands to stop the comebacks. "I love you both."

"Let the orgy begin," Shane said. "Who brought tacos?"

"Michael."

"And he left them unattended? What a fool." Shane grabbed two from the bag, along with a paper plate, and dumped them on it. "More for me."

As he was taking his first bite, Michael came down the steps, guitar case in hand, and set his instrument down on his armchair before he said, without even looking, "Those better not be my tacos, bro."

"They're not yours anymore," Shane mumbled around a mouthful. "Chill. You have a bagful."

Michael gave Eve a quick kiss on his way to the table, sorted out tacos onto three more plates, and took his seat. "I heard squealing. What did I miss?"

"Matching licenses," Eve said, and displayed them. When he

reached for them, she smacked his hand. "Oh, no, you don't. Your hands are greasy."

"You're actually going to marry this taco thief?" Michael said, and shook his head. "Disappointed."

"Hey, man," Shane protested. He took the hot sauce when Michael reached for it, and then tossed it in his direction. Michael fielded it with almost as much grace as he'd had as a vampire. "So when's the do-over?"

"Do-over?"

"What do you call it when you get second-time-fake-married?"

"Excuse me—that's *real* married," Eve said, smacking his hand when he tried to take another taco off her plate. He took it anyway. "When's yours?"

"Um . . ." He chewed, swallowed, and shrugged. "Actually, I was going to talk to you about that. About maybe . . ."

"Doing it together?"

"Are we back to the orgy talk? Because I'm—"

"God, be serious a second," Eve said, and rolled her eyes. "Claire?"

"I'd love it if we could have our weddings together," she said. "If you're okay with it."

"As long as Shane gives me the taco he just straight up snaked off my plate."

Shane solemnly put it back. They all looked at each other, and then Michael took Eve's hand, and then Shane's, and Shane took Claire's, and Claire took Eve's . . .

. . . and it was a little like a prayer, and a little like a hug, and a lot like home.

"So," Shane said after the silence went on just a beat too long. "Tacos, or orgy?"

"Tacos," the rest of them said, all together.

"I knew you were going to say that."

Somehow Claire hadn't expected to be quite so *scared.*

She'd faced down humans, vampires, and draug. She'd regularly done things that most people would go a lifetime without ever having to deal with even once. And yes, she'd been scared, even terrified from time to time. . . .

But not like this.

"Breathe," Eve advised her, and tugged slightly at her dress. It felt heavy and close around her, and in the warm air of the church's dressing room, Claire was afraid she might pass out if she tried to move. The person in the mirror was someone else entirely—someone dressed in a long white gown of satin, with a high-waisted beaded bodice that managed to make her look tall and regal and still gave her curves. A long fall of sheer fabric cascaded from the back, almost touching the floor. Along with the fancy necklace and sparkly bracelet (both lent from Amelie's no doubt vast collection), and with her hair worn up and fixed with glittering pins, she felt like a princess.

She felt like a woman, and somehow she'd never thought of herself that way before. She'd never stopped being a girl, had she? Well, she had, but gradually, so gradually that she hadn't even noticed.

Her mother was sitting in the corner of the room, and now she came forward to put her arms around Claire and rock her slowly, side to side. "You look amazing, honey," she said. "I could not be happier for you."

"Really?" Claire turned to look at her, trying to remember not to cry. Eve had been very strict about that rule, because of the makeup. "I didn't think you totally approved of Shane. You or Dad."

"He's . . . changed," her mother said. "And you love him. And I think your dad's smart enough to know that you're the second most stubborn person in the world, and he'd be wise not to cross you."

"Only the second?"

"Well, you did get it from me. Someday, when you're older, I'll tell you all about how I convinced your father to marry me," her mom said. She picked up the bouquet from the table—red roses wrapped with white ribbons. Eve's bouquet, of white roses wrapped with red ribbons, beautifully complemented her totally nontraditional red dress. Of course, it looked awesome on her and even showed off her tattoos well. "If you're ready, dear, I just heard the knock on the door."

"Mom—" Claire didn't know what to say, or what to do, so she just lunged forward and hugged her mother. Hard. Tears pricked at her eyes, but she forced them away. Because, mascara. "I love you."

"Love you, too, sweetie," her mother said, and kissed her cheek, then rubbed the lipstick away in an absent gesture so familiar it melted Claire's heart. "I'm so proud of you. Always."

She opened the door, and Claire almost couldn't take the step, except that her dad was standing right there, looking tall and trim and—for the first time in a long time—healthy, despite his heart condition. Maybe it was the suit he was wearing, or just the pleasure of the day, but she'd take it—she'd take every day she had with her parents gladly.

Her dad gave her the biggest, most amazing smile she'd ever seen, and then offered her his arm.

It wasn't so much like walking as gliding through a dream . . .

Eve was walking ahead of her, vivid in her dramatic red dress with its train. And she had a vampire giving her away, remarkably enough: Oliver. He was wearing some extremely old-fashioned tuxedo thing with a gold sash over it, and he looked feral and handsome and slightly bored, but when he left her at the altar next to Michael, he kissed her hand, and that looked honestly nice. He took his place to the side, next to Amelie. Out of deference to the brides, she'd forgone the white suit she normally wore and instead had chosen a tailored teal blue that still looked like it cost more than the jewels heavy around Claire's neck.

The church was packed with people. Regular humans and vampires. And one hundred percent Morganville.

She hardly felt the steps down the aisle, though she did feel the weight of all the eyes on her as she walked. It was over in what seemed far too little time, and then her dad handed her off to Shane, and her heart almost stopped as his eyes met hers.

She hadn't seen Shane all morning, and sometime since she'd seen him last, he'd gotten his hair cut—not short, but shorter. It suited him, brought out the strong lines of his face and made him look fierce and amazing. He'd never, ever looked so good, she thought; he probably hated the tuxedo, but he utterly rocked it, even down to the ruby pin in the lapel.

Then he winked at her, and she knew that he was still Shane, and the tension in her eased. She had to fight the sudden, dizzying urge to giggle.

The service passed in a blur of words she wasn't sure she got out right, and then the cool touch of the ring sliding onto her finger, and then the warm pressure of Shane's lips on hers, and the sudden dizzy rush as he bent her backward, because, of *course*, and the laughter from the audience.

She didn't completely get her breath or her sanity back until they were in the reception hall, and Myrnin, resplendent in an utterly (for a change) appropriate suit and tie, pressed a cup of punch into her hands and said, "Nonalcoholic. Also not containing actual blood. You seem to need it."

"Oh," she said, and looked down blankly at the red liquid. She sipped; he was right. It was just fruit juice with a sizzle kick of ginger ale. "Thank you."

"You're most welcome," he said, and leaned against the wall beside her. "So. Happy?" He crossed his arms, staring out at the people milling about the buffet and taking seats at round tables. "Truly?"

She thought about it for a few seconds, and then said, very quietly, "Yes." She resisted the urge to apologize for it, and he nodded.

"Good," he said. "Clearly, that's good." He was watching someone, she realized, and after searching for a second Claire spotted Lady Grey—Jesse—talking with Amelie; two queens, chatting together like friends, although there was just a little stiffness between them if you knew what to look for. Jesse had on a black leather dress, probably just to be sure that she thoroughly contrasted; her red hair was loose around her shoulders, like a coat of fire.

Claire sipped her punch again. "She looks pretty today."

"Doesn't she?" he said, and sighed. "Terrifyingly so."

Up on the raised stage, Michael finished tuning his guitar and pulled the mike close to say, "So, welcome to the afterparty," which made quite a few people laugh. "This is a song I wrote for my wife. Feel free to get out there and dance."

He started playing, and it was an aching, amazing song that poured out of him, and Claire was so intent on the music, the passion of it, that she was surprised when Myrnin took the cup out of her hands, put it aside, and pulled her out onto the dance floor. He twirled her around in a rush, and then settled into an easy, effortless glide.

Myrnin could *dance*. Who could have predicted that?

Claire caught her breath on a laugh, and fell into the rhythm.

"I'll miss you," she said. She didn't know where it came from, but this close to him, it needed to be said.

"No, you won't," Myrnin said, and smiled at her. "Since I shall expect you at your table in the laboratory at ten a.m. sharp next Monday. Oh, and I'm to tell you that you will need to repeat some credit hours at the university. Apparently, some problem with your transcripts."

"What?"

He shrugged. "Oh, don't pretend you don't love class, Claire. We both know better."

Shane tapped Myrnin on the shoulder, and just for a second the two of them stared at each other . . . and then Myrnin gracefully, flamboyantly, bowed himself out. "Let me just say this once," Shane said, as he slipped into place to whirl Claire away on the dance floor. "No more flirting with the crazy."

She kissed him, and even though they stopped dancing, even though the world spun around them on its axis, even though things would never be exactly right, and vampires would fall short of their promises, and humans would be mean and spiteful and murderous . . . even with real life looming all around them, for that moment . . .

Everything was perfect.

"Mrs. Collins," Shane whispered in her ear. "Let's blow this party and go home while we can have it to ourselves." He was right. Jenna was here, and Miranda was alongside her, looking sweet and pretty in a pink dress and getting invitations to dance from high school boys. She'd never looked so happy. Or so alive. Michael was onstage playing, while Oliver whirled Eve around the dance floor in an impressive show of grace.

Her heart pounded hard against her chest, and the beautiful white wedding dress felt too tight to hold her. Too tight to hold all the emotions that rioted inside her.

"Yes," she said. "Let's go home."

EPILOGUE

"Founder."

Amelie looked up as Oliver slid yet another dreary file folder in front of her on her desk. She frowned at it peevishly. "And what's this one?"

"For your signature," he said, and settled with insolent ease into a chair on the other side. He'd gone back to his customary black, which—she was sure he was aware—looked quite intimidating on him. "Reports on the ongoing prosecutions. Rhys Fallon is pleading not guilty, along with Anderson and some of the other key members of the Daylight Foundation. I assume you will sign the orders to terminate them once the verdict is in." He was watching her carefully, probing for weakness. As always.

She handed the folder back. "No. My original decision still stands."

"You really must disabuse yourself of the notion that mercy will heal all wounds. Some diseases need surgery."

"Fallon thought he had such a surgical cure," she said. "I am not so foolish. If they're found guilty, they will serve prison sentences, Oliver, and I shall hear no more of it. Chief Moses and I are in perfect agreement on this matter."

"Chief Moses is just as much of a sentimental fool as you are."

"Careful," Amelie said in a low, even tone that nevertheless was edged in ice. "I have ceded control of most things to the humans, but within our ranks I still rule. You know that."

"I do," he said. "But you'd be terribly disappointed in me if I didn't test you from time to time."

He was, unfortunately, right. All rulers needed gadflies to keep them alert, keep them questioning. And for better or worse, for eternity, he was hers.

And she could not deny that it suited them both, very well.

"Anything else? The night is growing short."

"The university is reporting a few incidents," he said. "It would appear not all vampires are behaving themselves quite as well as you require. I assume you'd like me to look into it."

"Send Jason Rosser," she said. "Since you're grooming the psychotic little beast to act as your second-in-command, best give him the responsibility for keeping others in line. He will hopefully learn some restraint himself in the process, with your oversight. No deaths involved, I assume?"

"No," he said. "I suppose the three vampires you locked up for murder did get the message across effectively."

"Then I suppose we are . . ."

"At peace?" Oliver stood up and offered her his hand. She took it, and he escorted her to the door of her office, which he held open as he saw her out. "There are still humans who hate the sight of us, and you've given them power and trust. Myrnin is still running about unattended in that lab of his, concocting God knows what new nightmare. There is an emissary from the new Pope coming to *review our status*, which may be unpleasant. A blogger in Kansas wrote an incoherent piece about vampires hiding in Texas. A number of vampires have requested Fallon's cure, despite the slender odds of survival. And I believe that Monica Morrell is demanding your presence as a judge at a dog show. Peace, dear Founder, might be a bridge too far."

"Ah," she said, and gave him a cool, calm smile as they walked the hallway toward Founder's Square and the night. "Then I suppose we must settle for controlled chaos."

"As ever, Amelie," he said.

"One might think you far too familiar," she said.

As they stepped out into the moonlight, he bent and raised her hand to his lips. "I am not familiar enough, dear Founder. Yet."

"Good," she said, and controlled a shiver. "Very good."

It was, when all was said and done, now a human town, with human values.

But in the dark . . . Morganville was still hers.

Always.

TRACK LIST

It's bittersweet to say good-bye to Morganville, and I needed a sound track that said everything about these characters and this special place in my heart. So listen, enjoy, and support the musicians who create this great music. They need your ears, but they need your financial love, too.

"Can't Play Dead (Radio Edit)"	The Heavy
"Put the Gun Down"	ZZ Ward
"Man Like That"	Gin Wigmore
"Afterlife"	Switchfoot
"Bring It"	Trapt
"My Sorry Cinderella"	Kev Bayliss

"My Songs Know What You Did
in the Dark (Light Em Up)" Fall Out Boy

"Alright" Kinnie Starr

"Too Close (Acoustic Version)" Trapt

"Be Tomorrow" Madlife

"Move Like U Stole It" ZZ Ward

"Back to Life" Lansdowne

"Daylight" Maroon 5

"Seasick" Silversun Pickups

"Virgin" Manchester Orchestra

"Going Under" Trapt

"Blue Eyes Blind" ZZ Ward

"Spiritus Khayyam" Globus

"Living in the Eye of the Storm
(Acoustic Version)" Trapt

"Surrender" Digital Daggers

"Justified" Rhino Bucket

"Secret Things" Ken Andrews

"Love Hate Relationship
(Acoustic Version)" Trapt

"Wicked" Greg Dulli

"Holy Doom" Jason Edwards

"Boy (Hostage Remix)" Nina Nesbitt

"Sacrilege" Yeah Yeah Yeahs

"Home" ZZ Ward

"Sinister Kid" The Black Keys

"Stand My Ground" Within Temptation

"All Waters" Perfume Genius

"What Makes a Good Man?
(Original Version)" The Heavy

People often ask if I pick a particular song to represent a character, and I think I did, in this particular book. So here are some specific thoughts:

The Town of Morganville: "Can't Play Dead" by The Heavy really captured the feeling of this post-takeover Morganville for me . . . eerie, menacing, edgy, and cool. And "Leave This Town" by Kev Bayliss really plays us out nicely.

Claire: Definitely, it's "Stand My Ground" by Within Temptation . . . there's a kind of ultimate bravery about a song that says that even if you go down, someone else will stand your ground for you. Sounds like Claire to me!

Shane: Trapt's "Going Under" lyrics really sound like him to me, and there's this feeling of determination and strength that matches Claire exactly. Or, you could take a listen to "What Makes a Good Man?" by The Heavy. Funky and kick-ass. It also asks a lot of the questions Shane asks about himself.

Michael: Just close your eyes and imagine Michael singing ZZ Ward's "Blue Eyes Blind" to Eve. Groovy and sexy. True love at its finest.

Eve: Likewise, ZZ Ward's "Home" sounds just like everything Eve feels about Michael. Beautiful and brave. (And appropriate that the same artist sings both sides of their relationship, I think.)

Myrnin: I just thought "Be Tomorrow" by Madlife (how perfect!) was Myrnin to the bone. It even sounds like the way he thinks. Which is nothing like you'd think he would.

Oliver: Try "Wicked" by Greg Dulli . . . there's a lot about that song that speaks to Oliver's character and state of mind. Or, you could also say that "Love Hate Relationship" by Trapt might be appropriate, too.

Amelie: "Virgin" by Manchester Orchestra had this amazing feeling of ancient strength, determination, and ruthlessness to it. Which sums her up completely.

Monica: Kev Bayliss's "My Sorry Cinderella" had a Monica feel to it, lyrically—and a kind of broken doll, broken person vibe with a creepy edge. Although musically it also would be something Eve would love, I think. Weird to think they might bond over musical tastes!

And I think Morganville's future is summed up by Imagine Dragons's amazing song "Radioactive"—because it's a song that makes me feel like the story's really just beginning for this brand-new Morganville.

Welcome to the future of Morganville. Now, *you* get to continue the adventure in your imagination and dreams and passion and fighting for those you love. GO! Adventure awaits.

Photo © 2011 Robert Hart Studio

Rachel Caine is the *New York Times* bestselling author of more than thirty novels, including the Weather Warden series, the Outcast Season series, the Revivalist series, and the Morganville Vampires series. She was born at White Sands Missile Range, which people who know her say explains a lot. She has been an accountant, a professional musician, and an insurance investigator, and, until recently, still carried on a secret identity in the corporate world. She and her husband, fantasy artist R. Cat Conrad, live in Texas with their iguana, Popeye.

Read on for a stunning excerpt from Rachel Caine's
new retelling of the star-crossed tale of Romeo and Juliet,

Prince of Shadows

Available now in hardcover from New American Library

I stood in the dark corner of my enemy's house, and thought of murder.

In his bed, Tybalt Capulet snored and drooled like a toothless old woman. I marveled as I thought of how the women of Verona—from dewy-eyed maids to dignified ladies—fell swooning in his wake. If they could see him like this (a drunken, undignified mess in sodden linen), they'd run shrieking to the arms of their fathers and husbands.

It would make a good, vivid story to retell, but only among my closest and dearest.

I turned a dagger restlessly in my gloved hand, feeling that murderous tingle working its way through my veins, but I was no assassin. I was not here to kill. I'd come stealthily into his house, into his rooms, for a purpose.

Tybalt, the heir of Capulet, swaggered the streets of Verona and used wit like weapons; that was nothing new among our class of young cocks. He was never above offering insults, to low or high, when opportunity came. Today he'd offended my house. House Montague.

The victim was a serving girl. Insults to servants didn't call for open challenges from those of my station, but still, it pricked me, seeing the self-satisfied grin on Tybalt's face as he emerged from that rank little alcove where he'd reduced her to tears; I'd seen her run from him red faced, holding the tattered rags of her clothes together. He'd injured the girl only to prove his contempt for my house, and that required an answer.

It required revenge, and that was something that I, Benvolio Montague, would serve him—not in the streets, in open war, but here, in the dark. Tonight I was clad head to toe in disguise, and there was nothing about me to indicate my station, or my house. To-night I was a thief—the best thief in Verona. They called me the Prince of Shadows. For three years I had stolen from my peers with-out being caught, and tonight . . . tonight would be no different.

Except that it *was* different. My hands felt hot and restless. So easy to drag a dagger across that hated throat, but murder spawned murder, and I didn't want to kill Tybalt. There had been enough of that between our two houses; the streets ran slick with spilled blood. No . . . I wanted to humiliate him. I wanted to knock him from his perch as the man of the hour.

I had the will, and the access. All that remained now was to choose how to hurt him best. Tybalt was the God-crowned heir of Capulet; he was rich, indulged, and careless. I needed to wound him where it counted—in the eyes of his family, and preferably in the eyes of all Verona.

Ah. I spotted a gleam as something caught the light on the floor. I crossed to the corner, where he'd dumped a tangle of clothing, and found the jeweled emblem pinned to his doublet—a gaudy piece in Capulet colors, one that would feed even a well-done-by merchant family for a year. No doubt he'd underpaid for it, as well; Tybalt was more likely to terrify honest men into bargains than to pay fairly. I added the prize to my purse, and then drew Tybalt's rapier from its sheath, slowly and carefully. It came free with a soft, singing ring of steel, and I turned it in the moonlight, assessing the quality. Very fine, and engraved with his name and crest. A lovely weapon. A *personal* weapon.

He did not deserve such a beautiful thing.

I sheathed it and belted it on, opposite my own rapier. As the heir of Capulet snored, drunken and oblivious, I pulled off my black cap and bowed with perfect form, just the way I would have been honor bound to greet him if we'd had the mischance to meet on the street. Under the breath-moistened black silk of my mask, I was smiling, but it felt more like a grimace.

"Good night, sweet prince, thou poxy son of a dog," I whispered. Tybalt smacked his lips, mumbled drunkenly, and rolled over. In seconds he was snoring again, loud as a grinding wheel against a knife.

I slipped out of the door of his apartments, past his equally dozy servant, and considered my exit from the Capulet palace. The obvious way was to return as I'd entered, but I'd come in during the height of the busy afternoon, carrying a box of supplies from a provisioner's wagon. I'd spent the day admiring the brickwork of the Capulet cellars. Going out the same way was unlikely; the kitchen door was almost certainly locked and guarded now.

Out through the narrow gardens, then. Once I was beyond the wall's high stone barrier, I would be just another bravo on the moonlit streets, making for my bed.

I went up the stairs, taking them two at a time; my soft leather shoes made no sound on the polished marble. I'd worn gray to blend into the ever-present stone and brick of Verona; in the shadows, there was nothing better in which to disappear. Even here, inside the quiet house, it was a reasonably good disguise. I ghosted past murky squares of paintings upon the walls, and a candelabrum with two still-burning tapers (a true sign of family wealth); the tapestry at the top of the stairs was rich and very tempting to steal, but too heavy, and I had enough trophies already.

Upstairs was women's country. Lady Capulet would have the largest and most lavish quarters, to the right—the grand palace was almost a mirror of my own family's, in many ways. That meant the girls would have the smaller apartments to the left— the oldest, Rosaline, said to be studious and bookish, was probably well asleep by now. She'd have the far rooms, since she was only a cousin, not the lady's own daughter. She was Tybalt's sister, arrived in Verona only a few months before, and kept shut up hard in the palace. I'd heard a rumor she was nothing like her loathsome brother, at least; that was to her credit.

There was no servant on duty at her door, and when I tried it, I found it unlocked. A trusting lot, these Capulets, at least within their own walls. I slipped the latch and stepped quietly inside, only to find that the room wasn't as dark as I'd hoped. There was a low-burning fire crackling on the hearth, and a candle flickering on the table. It scarcely mattered if the girl had left lights burning, as the bed curtains were pulled. She'd hear and see nothing through the thick coverings. I took reasonable care not to allow the floor to creak as I crossed it, and I was almost to the window when I realized that I had erred.

Badly.

Rosaline Capulet was not in bed. She was, instead, perched in a chair on the far side of the table, reading a slim book.

I saw her before she saw me. Candlelight dusted her skin with gold, and flickered in her large, dark eyes; her neck was swan-graceful, and her slender hands cupped the spine of the volume with care. She wore a simple lawn nightgown. I could make out the shadowed curves of her body beneath the white fabric. She had put her midnight dark hair into a long braid for the night, and was thoughtfully twirling one end of it as she read.

No one had warned me she was beautiful.

She saw me in that next second, and shot to her bare feet in alarm. The book thumped down on the table, and I expected her to scream the house down around our ears; it was the usual response from a maiden surprised in her chamber by a masked stranger.

Instead, she took in a deep breath, then let it slowly out.

"What do you mean here? Who are you?" she asked. I was surprised by the steadiness of her voice. Her fists were clenched tightly, and I could see she trembled, but her gaze was clear and her chin firm. Not fearless, but brave. Very brave.

I put my finger to my masked lips in a request for a lower volume. She didn't respond, so I said softly, "You may call me the Prince of Shadows, lady."

That sparked interest in her expression, and a new light in her eyes. "I've heard rumors. You exist!"

"Thus far."

"I dismissed the tales of you as drunkard's gossip. I've heard such an array of deeds I hardly know what it is you do."

"Thieving," I said. "That is what I do."

"Why?" It might have sounded like a foolish question, but

there was a sharp intelligence behind it, and I waited for the rest of it. "You're no starving beggar. Your clothes are too fine. Your mask is silk. You've no need of stolen gold."

She was not only brave, but unnaturally self-possessed. Mine was the upper hand, but I was beginning to wonder whether that might last only a moment. "I enjoy taking from those who have too much," I said. "Those who deserve to lose for their arrogance."

She stood very still, watching me, and then slowly inclined her head. "Then it follows you stole from someone in this house. Whom did you make your victim this night?"

It was a test, I realized. She had her standards, and her favorites. But I refused to lie, damn any consequences. "Tybalt," I said. "He's a bully and a fool. Few deserve a comedown more; don't you agree?"

The tension in her relaxed. She didn't smile, but there was a slight lift at the corners of her mouth, as if she felt tempted. "Tybalt is my brother, and a dangerous man," Rosaline said. "You should take to your legs before he steals something more precious from you than you have from him."

"I take your meaning, and it has wisdom," I said, and gave her a bow cut even deeper than I'd given her brother, and a great deal more sincere. "You have a kind and generous spirit."

"Never kind, and no kin of yours, sir," she said. She sat down at her table again, and picked up her book, and pretended to ignore me. It was a good act, but I saw the tension crinkling the corners of her eyes. "Go quickly. I've already forgotten you."

I gave her another bow, and opened the shutters to her window. Beyond was a balcony overlooking the small walled garden; it was a startlingly lush Eden set in the heart of heavy stone. A fountain played in the center, sprinkling gentle music over the night. No bravos strolled in sight, though I knew the Capulets employed many. Tybalt hadn't been in his cups alone this murky evening.

I climbed over the balustrade, clung for a moment to the edge, and then dropped the long distance to a soft flower bed below. Luridly flowering irises snapped and pulped under my feet, and the thick, sweet aroma clung to me as I raced forward. In a heartbeat I scaled the wall, dropped into the street, shook off the dirt and manure, and began what I hoped was a calm and untroubled walk toward the Piazza delle Erbe.

I'd only just removed my mask and folded it into my purse when I heard the smack of boots on stone, and two of the city watch turned the corner ahead, dressed in the livery of the ruler of Verona, Prince Escalus. Both bore heavy arms, as they should in the dark streets, lest their wives wake to find themselves widows. The men cut a course in my direction. When the moonlight caught my face, they slowed, and bowed.

"Sir Montague," the taller one said. "You stand in danger here. You're in Capulet territory, and walking alone. Unwise, sir. Very unwise."

I stumbled to a halt, as unsteady as if I'd been into Tybalt's wine cellar instead of his apartments. "So it would be, good fellows, save I'm not alone. Montague never walks alone."

"Faith, he's most certainly not," said a new voice, and I heard footsteps approaching behind me. I turned to see the familiar form of my best friend, Mercutio, who doubtless *had* been imbibing, and heavily. He slung an arm around my neck for support. "Benvolio Montague is never alone in a fight while I draw breath! What now, you rogues, do you need a thrashing to teach you manners?"

"Sirs," the guard said, with just a shade less patience. "We are the city's men. A quarrel with us is a quarrel with the prince of Verona. Best you turn your steps to more congenial streets. Besides, the hour is very late."

I let out a laugh that might well have been fueled by raw wine. "Did you hear that, Mercutio? The hour's late!" It was the first line of a popular—not very polite—drinking song, and he instantly joined in for a rousing chorus. Neither of us was musical. It provided great theater as the two of us staggered in the direction of the Montague palace, drawing angry and sleepy curses from windows we passed.

The watchmen let us go with rueful shakes of their heads, well glad to be rid of us.

Mercutio dropped the song after we'd passed the piazza's beautiful statue, the *Madonna Verona*, as armed soldiers stationed in front of the overblown Palazzo Maffei watched us pass. He didn't take his arm from my neck, so he truly was drunk enough to need the support, but he had the sense to keep his voice down. "So? How fared your venture?"

I dug the jeweled emblem of the Capulets from my purse and handed it over; he whistled sharply and turned it in the moonlight, admiring the faceted shine before slipping it into his purse. "I have more," I said, and drew Tybalt's rapier, which I tossed up in the air. Mercutio—even drunk—was a better swordsman than I, and he snatched it out of the sky with catlike grace. He examined the elegant blade with a delicate brush of his fingers.

"Sometimes I think your skills come from a lower place than heaven," he said very seriously, and patted my cheek. "The emblem we can sell, if we break it to gold and stones, but this . . ."

"It's not for sale," I said. "I want it."

"For what?"

I smiled, feeling fierce and free and wild in ways that no one would ever believe of the quiet, solid, responsible Benvolio Montague. At night I could be something else than what my city, my station, and my family required. "I don't know yet," I said. "But I promise you it will be the talk of the city."